TIME, TIMES, AND HALF A TIME

By Tom Jelinek

Superare
Dolo
Press

San Diego, CA

Disclaimer:
   The following work is entirely fictional. All characters, institutions, or other identifiable entities are either fictitious, or are used fictitiously. In particular, any instance where the plot may bear a cursory resemblance to current events is used strictly fictitiously. No inference of intent should be made regarding the accuracy of any such portrayal.

CONTENTS

Chapter 1: Pasadena

A. Separate Ways

The white double doors of the wooden church released a stream of people from the light blue building. Most followed the walkway around back, where a picnic area sat at the edge of a field of wheat, stirred by a gentle breeze. Portable canopies with nylon roofs of blue and gray fluttered slightly, shading buffet tables loaded with every kind of homemade dish, covered for the moment with plastic or aluminum wrap. Pulling up the rear of the procession was the pastor, a thin man with thin hair, and a face embossed with deep lines developed over many years of listening to his flock with a concerned frown. On his arm was a young woman whose intense floral dress stood in sharp contrast to his plain, black clothes. "My Becky. You're every bit as beautiful as your mother," he said, affectionately.

She shrugged, showing some embarrassment on her wide face, framed by wavy blonde hair. She took her arm out of his, and held the railing as she gingerly descended the stairs of the church, struggling with the bright blue pumps she was unaccustomed to wearing. She then walked to the front table beside him, never looking quite comfortable.

Watching her from the back of the gathering was a tall man with close cropped dark hair, dressed in a medium blue suit. He was smiling affectionately, showing genuine sympathy for the discomfort inflicted by her shoes. She raised her hand bashfully and sent him a quick wave. He smiled in return. The pastor then raised his hands, and stood in front of the gathering. "Would everyone please take their seats. As many of you know, today is not only our annual picnic." His comments were met with cheers, so he kept his hands up, and persisted. "Please. I promise not to keep you too long. I'm hungry, too."

"Today, we're honoring one of our own. So on behalf of all of greater Morrisonville, I'd like to recognize Sean's completion of his doctorate. Sean, would you please come up?"

The man at the back walked to the front, fidgeting with the knot on his tie as he did. He reached the pastor and shook hands, but had to be nudged to turn to face the crowd. He turned so abruptly, it gave the impression of being startled. But having known him since childhood, the people took it in stride. Sean Grant had always been tightly strung.

"I have to be honest, Sean," said the pastor, defusing the tension that seemed to follow the young man. "My knowledge of computers ends at wondering why Richard Waites makes us click the 'OK' button after a bad command. Why can't we just hit the right command, and have the computer cancel the error message on its own?"

A few in the congregation giggled at the comment, seemingly to save the pastor from loss of face. He continued. "But you now have a doctorate from Stanford. So to express our congratulations, I've had this plaque made for you."

He handed Sean a small plaque, again shook hands, and motioned for applause, which the congregation delivered in abundance. "Have you given much thought to what comes next? Any chance we can convince you to stay in Morrisonville?"

Sean smiled awkwardly, and shook his head. "I haven't yet made that decision, Pastor Nichols."

"I know one young lady who might be able to influence you. How about it, Becky?" He motioned to his daughter, who returned a beaming smile, but said nothing.

The pastor looked back at Sean, and made note that he only seemed to relax when he was interacting with Becky. He stood silently for a few seconds, as if pondering future possibilities for them. He then said a blessing, and announced that the buffet was open.

As the formality broke, Sean was able to loosen up a little, and accepted the congratulations of many who had known him all his life. In the course of conversation, he politely declined offers to design computer systems for an agricultural supply shop, a grocer, and an auto parts retailer. Patiently waiting her turn was Becky, who embraced him warmly, and added, "I'm so glad to have you back. Please tell me you'll find a job nearby, so we can finally get married."

Sean tensed up at Becky's words, and a single glance at him betrayed his intentions better than words ever could. Her expression wilted with that realization, obvious enough for Sean to notice, and say, "Let's get some food."

They lined up at the buffet, and tried to answer every comment with grace, sometimes having to ignore what was actually said, and returning only basic pleasantries. Finally clearing the gauntlet of good intentions, they took seats as far from the crowd as they were able, and Sean said, "I've been offered a job at Caltech. It's an exciting project."

Becky poked at her food, but suddenly found herself without an appetite. "You'd be gone again, for who knows how long. And it's not like you need the experience for anything you'd do around here."

Sean tried his best to make eye contact, and gently raised her chin with his hand. "I need to level with you, Becks." He could see her eyes mist up the moment he said her name. "I'm afraid I crossed that bridge when I first left for graduate school." He motioned around him with his arm, adding, "There's nothing here that can't be done by most anyone. And you know I don't even drive a car."

"You know how to drive. You only choose not to. You're eventually going to have to get past your parents' accident."

"Come with me, Becky. I missed you as much as you missed me."

"Oh, Sean." Becky was visibly upset, her voice quivering. "You know I can't do that. Dad would be heartbroken."

"Your dad would get over it, if he knew you were happy. At least admit it's *you* that doesn't want to leave."

"It's a lot deeper than not wanting to leave. In my heart, I know it's not going to end well."

They were interrupted by two older couples. A large, round man gregariously asked, "So, have you set a date?"

"Not yet, Mr. Davis," answered Sean, patiently. "But I'll be sure to call you if we do."

"What do you mean, *if?*" asked the white-haired woman beside him. "You've been an item since before I had dentures."

"Sorry, Mrs. Murphy. We have a lot to work out."

"Well, I suppose we should leave you some space, then," added the other older woman, attempting to smooth things over. "Let's get some dessert." She pulled at the clothes of her companions, signaling them to leave the couple in peace.

Becky waited until the visitors were out of earshot, then asked, "What's so exciting at Caltech, that's better than being with me?"

"To be clear, it's not better than being with you. But I don't have anyone who can pull strings for me in life. I need to make a name for myself, and this could do just that."

Becky nodded, and attempted a meek smile. "I am interested in the project."

Sean perked up at the prospect of discussing his work. "It's a new type of computing technology, that could allow us to simulate the workings of a human brain."

"Like artificial intelligence?"

"It's much more than that. We want to create a system that actually knows it exists, and can relate to the world in an intelligent way."

"That sounds scary, to be honest."

"Any new technology can seem scary. But the possible benefits are endless."

"Aren't you playing God, and trying to create a soul?"

"That's not how I think of it, Becks. But tell me something. Are you being straightforward with me, or are you using this to try to convince me not to go?"

Becky's high cheekbones were a canvass on which her feelings were always painted in full color. And like the floral dress that lost its vibrancy as a large cloud covered the sun, her expression turned a dull gray. "I wish you weren't so restless, Sean. Don't you ever want to settle down?" Her grief was still obvious.

"You can only do that once. And then the adventure is over."

"What about community? And contentment with what you have?"

"Is there no chance I could convince you to come with me, Becks? Not even as trial thing? Say, for a year?"

Becky turned to Sean, having now overcome her grief, and said, "A year would turn into two. And two into ten. Then one day I'd realize Morrisonville wasn't home anymore. And neither was any other place. I can't do that, Sean."

Sean was silent for the better part of a minute, and unable to make eye contact. Finally, he raised his gaze to meet hers, and said, "I guess knew that would be your answer."

Becky sighed, lightly. "Likewise. I didn't want to accept it, but I always knew this day would come."

They were interrupted by Pastor Nichols, who had been watching from a distance. "Becky, is it alright if I borrow Sean for a moment?"

He put his arm around Sean's shoulder, and walked him back towards the church, where they could have some privacy. Finally out of earshot, he turned to him, and said, "Sean, I wasn't born yesterday. I know the decision you're facing. And I'm pretty sure I know what it's going to be. I just want you to be gentle..."

"We just finished going over that, Pastor."

Nichols' eyes opened wide with surprise, and he asked, "How did she take it?"

Sean shrugged. "Not thrilled. But she knew it was coming. She's almost relieved to have it behind her."

Nichols exhaled deeply, and said, "I would have been honored to have you as a son in law. Thanks for understanding."

They began to walk back to the picnic, when Nichols stopped suddenly, and turned to Sean. "There's something else I've been meaning to tell you. It has to do with artificial intelligence."

Sean looked at Nichols with wide, curious eyes. The pastor started, "I think I've had a revelation."

Before he could say anything more, they were swamped by several of the congregation. "Did you hear what Osteen said to Oprah last week?"

Nichols breathed a weary sigh. Once again, he was going to have to debunk what somebody heard on television. "I'll try to catch up with you later, Sean."

A week later, Sean knocked on the door of a second floor low-rise apartment, and a man of about his own age answered the door. But while both were well proportioned, six foot tall men with dark brown hair, Sean was clean cut, where the man now facing him had shoulder-length hair, and a thick beard.

"I'm looking for Dalton Marais."

"You must be Sean. Come in."

Sean stepped into a tastefully appointed two bedroom apartment and took Dalt's cue, sitting down on a sofa. The furniture was far from new, but was in better shape than what Sean had grown accustomed to as a student. Dalt sat opposite him, in an armchair.

Sean began. "I saw your ad on the bulletin board, by the main office. Are you also in computer science?"

"Physics. But my work crosses over to comp-sci, so I go there a lot. I wasn't getting any traction on our bulletin board, and I wanted someone from the university, so I posted over there."

"And can I ask what the deal is with the nine-month term?"

"Sure," said Dalt, breathing deeply as he did. "That's really the crux of it. My girlfriend and I signed a one-year lease. The second bedroom was supposed to be for her sister to join us the next term, but she left me not two months in. I need someone to share the rent for the balance, before I can downsize."

Sean recalled his own recent breakup. "Sorry to hear about your girlfriend."

"It's all right," shrugged Dalt, dismissively. "I guess I deserved it."

"Oh?" said Sean, startled at Dalt's admission.

"What about you? You come with a sidekick?"

Sean refused to make eye contact, and instead glanced around the room in several directions, admiring the taste of Dalt's ex. "I had a girl back home. But I had to move on with my life, and she couldn't find it in her heart to leave our little farming town."

"Well, you've come to the right place. There's some pretty good pickings around here. I can personally attest to that." Dalt laughed, for no reason apparent to Sean. Seeing his puzzled look, Dalt added, "I was sampling the pickings, and my ex kind of busted me."

Sean smiled to cover up his discomfort, before taking his stand. "That's not my style. Besides, I don't know how much time I'll have to spare, with the profile of this project."

"Who you working with?"

"Sal Occhini."

Dalt nodded with approval. "Top dog, that's for sure. He used to come and talk to us now and again, when he was looking for the ultimate chip design."

"He's pretty much settled on diffusive memristors. Now it's just about making all the virtual connections, and that's where I come in."

"Well, best of luck with that. It's an ambitious project."

"Thanks. How about you? Where are you from, and how'd you get to where you are?"

"I'm from Anaheim. About a mile west of Disneyland. How I got here is complex, but it involves a stint in the military, after which I got my act together, and returned to school. Uncle Sam supported me throughout, and encouraged me to study the physics behind quantum computing."

"Spend time in Iraq?"

"You're observant." Dalt glanced at the shelf Sean had been eyeing. "But I don't talk about that. So please don't ask about it."

Sean stayed an hour, and found they shared many interests, both in science and in their general life outlooks. Weighing his options, he decided to disregard his few reservations, and agreed to the sublet. It was only for nine months, he reasoned, and in any case, he expected to spend most of his time at the lab, or asleep.

B. Settling In

"I love the way you linked these nodes, Sean." Sal Occhini was nodding his head slowly, showing his approval as he checked Sean's work. His six inch gray beard waved in exaggerated fashion with every motion of his jaw, more so as he was looking up at Sean, standing beside Occhini's chair. "You've made excellent inroads in the six months since you started. So I've decided to name you as co-investigator on the project. You'll get a promotion, and a raise."

Occhini was grinning as he looked up at Sean, standing beside him, awkwardly. "Uh, thanks," he said, sheepishly. "Does this change what I do every day?"

"Not at all," assured Occhini. His elbow sat on the desk, and his hand cupped his chin. "I'm simply covering my bases, in case I'm not around to finish the project."

Occhini spoke so calmly that the meaning of his message was lost on Sean. After an awkward silence, Sean asked, "What are you getting at?"

"It's called succession planning, Sean. I'm setting you up to take over in case I don't finish."

"Why wouldn't you finish?" asked Sean. As he spoke the words, he realized the implication of Occhini's comment. "Is your health okay?"

"So-so," answered his mentor, now rising to face Sean on his feet. Sean continued to look down at the short, thin man, who added, "Nothing you need to concern yourself with, for now. I'm just covering my bases." He gave Sean a slap on the shoulder, adding, "Keep up the good work."

Not knowing who to contact first, Sean texted his good news to Dalt, who promptly replied with, "I guess you're buying lunch.

Come over here for noon."

Sean made his way to the physics labs in high spirits, and was walking far faster than he normally would. He approached the building from the back side, and followed a trail of dead grass, trampled by excessive use, that followed the very edge of the brick building. To his left were a group of students playing volleyball, and he glanced over to watch them as he cleared the corner of the building. He heard a brief shriek as he felt the jolt of the impact, and saw the young woman fall to the ground in front of him, dropping her computer bag and several books.

"I'm so sorry," he quickly blurted out. He picked up her things and offered his hand, which she accepted.

"I guess I wasn't looking," she said.

"I was watching the volleyball game over there," admitted Sean.

"Me too. I'm Lynne."

She looked at him and smiled for the first time, but now Sean thought he was going to be the one to fall on his back. The bright smile. The olive shaped eyes. The perfect heart-shaped face, with slight dimples in her cheeks. Her long, flowing hair rested on a thin knit sweater that clung to eye-popping curves. "Uh, hi. I'm Sean," he finally managed to say."

"You work here?"

"Over at comp-sci. I'm here to meet my roommate for lunch."

"Oh, who's that?"

"Dalton Marais."

The exuberance disappeared from her expression, and Sean could see that the name produced a subtle but negative reaction. "Well, nice to meet you," she concluded, and quickly continued along her previous path.

Walking over to Dalt's favorite cafe, Sean opened the conversation. "You never told me about your ex. What's her name?"

"Suzanne. Why are you asking that now?"

"Oh, never mind. It's just a thought that popped into my head on the way over."

Dalt broke into a smile as he had an insight. "You met someone on the way over here, and think you made a connection. But Suzy left the area after we split."

Sean began to look down, wistfully. "Yeah. I met an enchanting girl, from physics. I can't get her out of my head, to be honest. But she shut off as soon as I mentioned your name."

"I haven't had any luck in physics," said Dalt, chuckling in what Sean had come to recognize as his characteristic, self-deprecating manner. "They're all too preoccupied with their work."

"Her name is Lynne. You know her?"

Dalt's expression soured at the name. "Yeah. Perfect example of what I'm talking about. She could have any guy in the world, but she doesn't want anyone. And she's into some kind of Eastern Mysticism, from what I've heard."

Dalt studied Sean's distant expression for a few seconds, then added, firmly, "Get her out of your head, Sean. When she decides she wants a man, she'll go get herself the next Brad Pitt, or whoever she fancies. No offense, but you're not in that class. Neither of us is."

Sean sighed, so to change the subject, Dalt asked, "So what about your promotion?"

Sean smiled, and said, "I guess I won't have to find a new roommate after you get your own place. I can now afford my own apartment."

"All the same, this arrangement works for me," said Dalt. "If you're not in a rush, we could extend the lease on a month by month basis."

"I guess that's fine," answered Sean. "And you need someone to keep an eye on you. Seriously, you have these dark periods, where I'm worried about you."

They arrived at the cafe, and Dalt was determined to change the topic of conversation. "The promotion sounds great, but how's the work going? Are you making any progress?"

As Sean was about to answer, Dalt's attention turned to the ceiling-mounted television. "Have you heard that guy's story?"

"No," answered Sean, looking at the monitor. "Looks like a British colonel, if I'm not mistaken."

"No, not him," objected Dalt, his gaze fixed on the subtitles. "It's the guy he's talking about. I can't remember his name right now."

Sean looked at the screen again, and saw the colonel demanding the unconditional release of a prisoner. The screen cut back to the anchor, and both stopped paying attention. Dalt, however, was clearly impressed. He turned his attention back to Sean, and explained, "Get this. The British screwed up, and bombed a civilian village in Afghanistan. Normally, they'd issue some vapid statement purporting to express regret, and that would be the end of it. But the Taliban would look for revenge, and a bunch of poor bastards would die. But this doctor, who's previously been decorated for bravery, decides he's going to do something about it. So he fills his truck with medical supplies, and drives through treacherous mountains, alone. That means he did it without permission. Anyway, as he's approaching the village, he hits a landmine."

"Killed?"

"Apparently not. They showed a clip of him, in captivity. He's wounded, but seems stable."

"Doesn't seem too smart, going off alone like that," mused Sean.

Dalt shook his head in animated fashion. "No, Sean. He would have known he was going to be killed or captured, but he did it anyway. He'd heal who he could, and offer himself as a hostage, or worse. But the blood debt would be settled, and they wouldn't come after other soldiers."

"You think he's a hero?"

"You bet. I had that thought in Iraq, a bunch of times. But I never had the courage to do anything like that. This guy did."

Sean watched Dalt continuing to gaze in admiration at the monitor, long after the story had ended. He had never before seen this side of his roommate and friend, and wondered if he should broach the topic of his service in Iraq. Thinking better of it, he returned to their previous conversation. "I've just about got all the interconnections programmed into the computer. But to be honest, I have no idea how I'll make it think."

"I'm beginning to wonder if that's even possible," offered Dalt. "Whether higher consciousness isn't more spiritual than corporeal."

"Spiritual?" asked Sean, looking surprised.

Dalt smiled, and looked embarrassed for a moment. "You know I'm not religious or anything. But the conventional explanations for the universe, and for life, they just don't work. There's something more at play."

"I haven't thought about that to any degree," answered Sean, now serious again. "What do you mean, *the explanations don't work?*"

"When you do the math, the probabilities don't stand a chance. And even the concepts are full of contradictions. You have to take the story on faith, or you end up like me. Not sure what to believe."

"So you're not a creationist," said Sean, showing relief.

"No. Don't worry, I'm not a Bible-thumper," chuckled Dalt.

"I'm only saying that what we're taught doesn't work. I'm honest enough to admit I don't have a good explanation."

"So how does that relate to my problem?"

"Okay, so something else is at work. Whether that's some form of Vitalism, where matter itself is conscious, or some outside influence acting in the capacity of a creator, that thing is also going to be behind consciousness. It's beyond matter."

"I hope you're wrong," said Sean, smirking. "It would suck to put in all that work, only to find out consciousness is not material."

Unfazed by their discussion, Sean put in the work at an unprecedented pace, often working through the night and all through the following day. He would return home utterly exhausted, and often did not stop to eat, but went straight to sleep. He might sleep for twelve hours, followed by another thirty six hours of uninterrupted work. Dalt saw little of him, but when he did, he saw extreme fatigue, stress, and over and above all else, an abiding fear of failure.

One evening as Sean came home, Dalt decided to confront him. "Sean, you look like hell. How about taking a break? I know a great place up in the mountains."

Sean shook his head, and said, "I can't, Dalt. We're getting ready to run a simulation, and our sponsors are impatient. We need to show real progress."

"There have to be others willing to sponsor the work, Sean. Occhini can pretty much write his own ticket, and this thing could revolutionize the world."

"Someone will revolutionize the world, alright. But if we falter, others might beat us to it."

And so Sean kept up the frenetic pace as the date of the simulation approached. Finally, the date came. Sean spent most of the morning loading all the sub-routines into active memory, furiously typing commands on his keyboard, situated below a plaque bearing the name *Nascent Intelligent Cybernetic Konsciousness.* Occhini had modified the spelling in order to form the acronym, *N.I.C.K.* After several final checks, Sean typed his question to the new entity: Nick, do you *understand* who you are?

There was a pause that felt an hour long, before the reply came up on the display. *You can stand under my umbrella. Ella. Ella.*

Sean grunted loudly, in exasperation. "Okay, you have no

brains." He sat still for a minute, struggling to regain his composure. Reflecting for a moment, he typed another query: *Do you at least have feelings?*

Another long pause, and the screen displayed, *Feelings, woe woe woe feelings.*

"I don't believe this," exploded Sean, furiously.

He was interrupted by his phone, displaying Occhini's name. *Just what I need right now. He wants an update.*

"Sean, could you come down to the department office right away? I'm here with Bob Dunn."

Taken aback, Sean left his desk and made his way to the office he had never before entered. The name on the door read, *Robert Dunn, Chairman.* He knocked nervously, then recoiled as Dunn opened the door. Standing at six feet six inches tall and a good three feet from front to back, many found Dunn's presence imposing.

"Sean, there you are. Come in, and have a seat."

A chair had been set up for him beside Occhini, across the desk from Dunn. As the large man made his way back to his extra-large chair, he turned to Occhini and said, "You might as well tell him yourself."

Sean tensed up at the manner in which the scenario was being laid out. *Nothing good can start like this*, he thought. But Occhini remained as calm as ever, turned to Sean, and said, "I'm retiring from Caltech."

Sean looked confused, so Occhini spelled it out for him. "My health isn't the greatest. I bought a place in the woods up north, and plan to live out my life away from all of this."

"I don't get it," said Sean, still confused. "This morning I ran a full simulation of Nick, and I came here expecting you to ask how it went. This is coming at me from left field."

"That's what I told him," said Dunn, sounding frustrated with Occhini.

Occhini smiled patiently, raising a hand to each of them. "I get where you're both coming from. But Sean is already running this project without much input from me. And he's listed as co-investigator. Our grant from Standard Petroleum allows us to make a switch like this. Bob, you simply need to promote Sean to Associate Professor."

"That's not the issue, Sal," objected Dunn. "The issue is the contract only goes another six months. Without your name attached, and unless Sean pulls off a miracle, we'll run out of money."

Occhini nodded to acknowledge Dunn's concern. "I'll give Sean my unqualified support." He turned to Sean, and added, "If you need reference letters, or want to use my name as a collaborative consultant, just ask. But my decision is final." He finished his remarks with a sharp look at Dunn, emphasizing the word *final*.

After some awkward silence, Dunn turned to Sean. "I'll promote you to Associate Professor, effective immediately. And I'll go to bat for you. I'll call everyone I know, to try to line up other sponsors. But it's on you, now. You're going to have to pull some kind of rabbit out of a hat, and show some progress."

Sean thanked Dunn and left the office, with Occhini following closely behind him. "Why don't you let me buy you a cup of coffee, Sean. I'd like to tell you a bit more about what's been driving me."

They fell into a very soft sofa in a dark corner of the coffee shop. There was quiet for a few, uncomfortable moments, before Occhini began. "I don't expect you to understand my reasons."

"Then why'd you ask me here?"

"You're soon going to face what I've been facing. At first, I didn't understand it. But after my last heart attack, it all started to come together."

Sean shrugged, and raised his hands. "What?"

"There's something about what we're trying to create. It's almost like it's trying to steer us. To manipulate us."

Sean looked at Occhini with a skepticism he had never shown to his mentor. "You're scaring me, Sal."

Occhini sighed, and in his exhausted expression, Sean got his first glimpse of the turmoil his mentor had been facing. "Are you sure you're not just exhausted? I know I am." Sean was now looking at Occhini with bewilderment, mixed with a degree of disgust.

"I've kept you insulated from the types of people who take an interest in this. That's now going to change."

Sean only stared blankly at Occhini. He gathered his thoughts, then added, "I don't know what to say, Sal. Of course people are interested. The more, the better. Maybe you only need a little sabbatical. Maybe at a really nice clinic, in Malibu."

Occhini giggled at Sean's suggestion that he was suffering from some sort of breakdown, but he was undeterred. "I get that I can't make you understand, yet. All I can do is warn you."

16

Sean shifted around on the sofa, betraying the agitation that had suddenly overwhelmed him. "What am I supposed to do, Sal? All my life I've been struggling to really find my place in the world. That's what sold me on this project. I always thought you felt the same way."

Seeing Sean tense up, Occhini did his best to end on a positive note. "I started that way. And then my eyes started to open."

Sean got up off the sofa, and turned to Occhini with a resigned, sad look. "Thanks for the coffee, Sal. You've been like a father to me, and I'll miss you. I'm grateful for everything you've taught me. But I'm a scientist. I can't abandon my work because of some nightmare. Like you just did."

Sean seemed to realize that his words were harsh, and looked down, sadly.

"I understand. I'm not going to tell you what to do, Sean. I only wanted you to be ready for what you're soon going to face."

"I appreciate it," said Sean, without looking very appreciative.

C. Complication

Sean increasingly found himself cleaning up the living room in the morning, before heading off to the lab. Dalt had previously been tidy, but as the number of women he brought home decreased, empty bags of chips or pretzels, bowls full of crumbs, and empty liquor bottles often appeared on the coffee table. He made a mental note to speak with his roommate, and make sure everything was okay, but they rarely saw each other. Sean was only at home to sleep, and was gone before Dalt awoke for the day. And his own emotional state was so strained that he could not even think of what he would say to Dalt. Even the distraction of thinking about anything other than programming Nick brought on fits of anxiety. *What if someone else is about to make a breakthrough? I'd be scooped. And history never remembers the second one to discover something.*

His determination not to be scooped kept driving him, and soon he was working himself to exhaustion. Time eventually lost any meaning for Sean, as he kept trying desperately to coax Nick to produce tangible results. Only the arrival of a postcard from Occhini reminded him it had been months since his former advisor left. The photograph was of the Temple Mount in Jerusalem, and the only comment was, *Thinking of you. Best of luck, Sal. XLI+5.*

Sean smiled briefly, and wondered, *What's XLI+5?* An internet search turned up X-linked ichthyosis. *I wonder if that's his health issue.* He looked up the disease, and saw it caused dry, scaly skin. *No, Sal doesn't have anything like that.* Another search turned up *external language interface*, a component of computer code. *Maybe he thinks that's where my problem lies. But we went over that with a fine-toothed comb, back when he was still here.* He reviewed all the measures they took to ensure the interface was not a problem, and was satisfied they had not missed anything. *It must just be another case of Sal's quirkiness.*

As he brought himself back to his work, the glimpse into Sal's mind served as a stark reminder that he was now on his own. Bob Dunn usually called every week or so, and it was becoming clear that corporate interest in the project had waned to tepid since Occhini's departure. So later that morning when Dunn's name appeared on his phone, he expected another disappointing report. Instead, he heard, "Sean, they've summoned us both to a meeting at the University President's office, today at noon. Apparently, someone's been making provocative comments about A.I., and they want to cover their backsides."

"Just what I needed. More distractions," grumbled Sean, as he hung up the phone. He finished his immediate tasks, collected a few documents, and made his way to the President's office.

Walter Hastings was seated in the middle of the long side of an oval-shaped conference table, together with two other senior administrators, and three governors. Sean and Dunn were given seats facing the panel. Off to the side sat a plate of finger food that had not been touched. Once Sean and Dunn were seated, Hastings began. "Like it or not, Dr. Grant, your work is in the news. The always theatric Elon Musk has been quoted as saying that A.I. is like *summoning the demon.*"

Hastings glanced around the table, and took note of the smirking, bemused faces. He continued. "I know, it's stupid. But my phone hasn't stopped ringing. Reporters, donors, and the governor's office are all asking if there's anything to fear. So before you leave here today, I want a plan I can share with the press, to show them we're being responsible. So to start us off, why don't you fill us in on what you're trying to do."

There were nods from the panel, and Sean began. "There have

been many successful ventures into *pseudo-A.I.* Programs that can make decisions based on probabilities, rather than perfect data matches. But they can only solve the problems they were programmed to solve, and that's not really intelligence. Even programs designed to simulate conversation operate within narrow parameters. Ditto for chess programs. My system is called a neuromorphic computer. In ordinary terms, I'm trying to create a fully intelligent, sentient computer that works like the human brain, but better and faster. Imagine, if you would, plugging the computer into an industrial control system, and having it design the operating system by itself. It would save immense amounts of time, and money."

"And the danger could rise in equal proportion," said Hastings.

"Potentially, yes. Human oversight is critical."

"And how successful have you been, to date?"

"Not very," answered Sean, without a hint of embarrassment. "If you'll forgive the expression, all I've achieved so far is *artificial stupidity*. But I may be getting closer."

There were chuckles throughout the room, and Hastings motioned to restore order. "I recognize that true A.I. would be a singular breakthrough for Computer Science. But I need to convince a lot of people they have nothing to fear from what's going on here."

A white-haired, frail-looking old man at the end of the table, who Sean recognized as the retired former President, and now a member of the board of governors, smiled disarmingly. He began to speak, stuttering with several breaths between phrases. "Young man, don't be put off by all this fuss. I was at the Asilomar conference in 1975. Everyone was afraid of recombinant DNA back then. We had no intention of slowing our research, but we agreed to some voluntary safeguards. What we did was, in effect, quarantine the work. After some time, the safeguards were slowly forgotten. And today, people are nearly ready to accept genetically engineered humans. So you see? You only need some symbolic steps, to buy enough time for people to accept your new technology."

Another governor interrupted with, "Surely it's about more than appearances. We bear a responsibility to ensure that no lasting harm comes from work done here at Caltech."

As if looking to regain the moral high ground that was suddenly leaving him, Hastings snapped his gaze in the direction of the former President. "Is it possible to quarantine a computer?"

Dunn, seated beside Sean, thought for a moment, then said, "You mean to prevent it from having any interactions with the world? Yes, I suppose. You'd need to scramble any signals passing through the power supply. And then set up a buffer zone, that wireless signals couldn't penetrate."

"What would that look like, in the real world?" asked Hastings.

"It could be as simple as a large, empty building, with a wireless jamming system inside. The lab would be in a separate structure, enclosed within the larger building, and sealed off from the jamming. It would also protect the project from spies, which are bound to come around if we demonstrate any success."

The man next to Hastings offered an idea. "There's the empty warehouse at the south end of campus."

"I know the building you're talking about," said Dunn. "We once had one of our guys in there, developing software for the Defense Department. It still has the sealed computer lab in its center."

"As far as I know, nobody's planning to use it any time soon," said Hastings. Would that work for you?"

"I think so," replied Dunn.

He looked to Sean, who nodded. "I'd only need to move some computers, and hook up a bunch of cables."

"Then I move that we make the warehouse available to Computer Science, and relocate the A.I. lab inside it." The panel took a quick vote, and the motion passed unanimously.

Hastings looked at Sean, and said, "I trust this won't delay you too much."

"It'll be fine," said Sean, relieved that his work was not going to be cut off right away.

The workers showed up that afternoon, leaving him with about two hours of down time. Having time to think, and reflect on his deadline, he began to feel alone. He never saw his roommate, and suddenly felt starved for some human interaction that was not tied to his work. Finally, he pulled out his phone and called Becky.

"Hi Sean. How are things going?" She sounded subdued, as though his call was inconvenient.

"It's tough right now, Becks. To be honest, I'm not sure I made the right decision."

If Sean expected sympathy, it was not forthcoming. "I'm afraid that's water under the bridge. Things can't be like they used to be."

"What do you mean?"

"I'm engaged to be married."

Sean fell silent, and found himself unable to speak a word. "Sean, are you okay?" More silence followed. "Sean, are you there?"

"Yeah. I don't know what to say. I mean *great*. I think."

"I guess this is as weird for you as it is for me. But I couldn't wait forever, hoping one day you'd change your mind. And then Marty came calling ..."

"Marty Franklin, from the tractor place?"

"Yeah."

Sean took a few seconds to respond, and did so while choking on his words. "He's a good man ..."

"But?"

"This isn't easy for me, Becks. I mean, I don't have any right to object, do I?"

"I get it, Sean. You felt like maybe I was still a fallback option for you, and now I can't be that, anymore."

"Yeah, maybe."

"This hasn't been easy for me, either. I lost you some time ago, and now unless I cut my ties to you, I risk losing Marty, too."

"I understand, I guess. I just needed someone to turn to."

"As much as I'd like to help, I can't. It wouldn't be fair to Marty."

For the first time since his arrival at Caltech, Sean found himself unable to focus on his work. He went to the new lab to hook up cables, and set up his secure entry credentials. But as he sat down at the computer, he felt crushed with regret. Becky was right to move on with her life, and he could find no anger in his heart towards her. It was all directed at himself. He could have had a good life with her. Instead, he went off chasing clouds, and now he had neither her, nor any hope of reaching the glory he so craved. His inner turmoil only intensified over the rest of that afternoon, until he decided he'd had enough. He shut everything down, and made his way home. It was a longer walk from the warehouse than his old lab at the main building, and the sun had not yet set. He realized he was looking at it for the first time in weeks. He kept tensing up and accusing himself of every form of arrogance and insensitivity. By the time he arrived back at the apartment, he was hoping to be able to have a talk with Dalt. But fate had other plans.

Dalt was lying on the sofa, with a mostly empty bottle of Scotch on the coffee table, beside an open bottle of pills. "Dalt!" shouted Sean. He ran to Dalt's side, shook his shoulder, and slapped his face, trying to wake him, to no effect. He then began to scream at him, directing all his frustration at his roommate, and only current friend. Only after he broke down into tears did he think to call for paramedics.

D. A New Idea

Sean rolled over in bed, opened his eyes, and looked over at the red display on the clock. It was the same every night, and it had worsened since Dalt's incident. Three in the morning, and he was wide awake. He knew the script by heart. First, he would imagine Becky in Marty's arms, and feel an abiding revulsion. Then, he would be confronted with his own failures. It was almost like the voice of another person, speaking inside his head. And it was always taunting him. *If you hadn't been so pig-headed, you could be married to her today, and working your choice of jobs back home. Now look at you: Alone, and soon to be unemployed.* Next, he would try his best to focus on his work. There had to be some part of the program that if tweaked exactly right, would produce his much-needed breakthrough. Drowsiness would creep in as he went through his list, and eventually impair his reasoning. He would get caught in a mental loop, repeating the same step in his head until he awoke again, this time in a sweat. He would change his pajamas, then the voice would come back to taunt him yet again. *How stupid are you? It's not working, yet you're repeating the same steps over and over, hoping for a better outcome. You've wasted your chances in life, Sean.*

Exhaustion would eventually get the better of him, and he would sleep for a couple of hours, before his alarm sounded. Still exhausted, he struggled to find the motivation to get up. Finally, he dragged himself to the bathroom, and looked at the bags under his eyes. *It's going to kill me if I keep living like this.* He made coffee, and while it was brewing, he reviewed every area he might tweak, but found difficulty identifying anything he had not already covered exhaustively. He even brought in collaborators to audit the system, and every test came back perfect. The optimism only lasted until the next full-scale test, showing the computer to be as hopeless as ever. *What's the problem, here?* he pleaded with himself. *Nick works better than any brain. And yet it won't do what a brain is supposed to do. It doesn't think.*

His morning walk took him near Huntington Hospital, so he stopped to check up on Dalt, still recovering from his recent close call. "What happened that day, Dalt?"

His friend was clearly not comfortable talking about it. "Just a lapse in judgment. Should never drink if you've had sedating medication."

Sean did not believe Dalt's explanation, but had difficulty expressing himself at that moment. Glancing around the room in every direction, he eventually raised his courage, and said, "It wasn't an accident, Dalt."

Dalt exhaled loudly. "Inevitable, perhaps."

"I should have intervened when you started drinking like that. But I didn't know you also had barbiturates. What are you running from, anyway?"

Sean had been avoiding eye contact for some time, but now raised his head, and seeing the tears welling up in Dalt's eyes, he sensed an opportunity. "You're the only friend I have in this world, so like it or not, I'm going to force you to work through this."

Sean looked down again, to give Dalt time to compose himself. In less time than Sean expected, he came back with a single, meekly enunciated word. "Iraq."

"Are you ready to talk about it?"

"Not the details." Dalt's voice was broken with sorrow.

"Then the generalities?"

More time passed, with Dalt struggling to find the words. After a while, Sean decided to help. "Disregard for human life?"

"Yeah." More silence, but before Sean could ask another question, Dalt resumed. "Saying it like that makes it seem so clinical. I don't know ... there aren't words."

"And your whole lifestyle since then? A reaction of sorts?"

"More than anything, it's been about not giving my imagination any time and space."

On resuming his walk to the lab, Sean allowed himself to dwell on Dalt's comment. He was afraid of his imagination. Maybe he too felt that inner voice, taunting him over his past. Still, how could one initiate a discussion like that, when the popular perception was that it was a sign of insanity. As he continued on, he wondered, *Am I going insane? I'm working myself to insanity, that's for sure. Am I going to end up like Dalt, except maybe not lucky enough that someone finds me in time?*

Everything changed, as Sean crossed a grassy area. He recognized Lynne's voice at some distance, bantering with her friends. He glanced in her direction just as a handsome young man approached her. Sean recognized him as a post-doc from the physics department. He felt a punch to the gut when he realized the man was flirting with her, and she was returning his attention. She was flashing her smile and making wide eyes at him, and he was entirely immersed in her presence. A moment later, the young man's manner became awkward, and he seemed to say something serious. As he spoke, Lynne abruptly looked down at the ground, averting her gaze. A few brief words, and she turned and walked away. Sean's mood eased as he saw his competitor strike out, and angled his path to cross hers.

"Hi Lynne. Nice to see you again."

"Oh. Hi there," she said, then continued on without so much as a second glance.

He finally arrived at the warehouse that now housed his secure lab, to find Bob Dunn waiting at the front door. His thoughts and emotions were still in turmoil from another tough night and an equally challenging morning. *I really don't need this right now.* He briefly considered turning around and hiding, but Dunn had already made eye contact. He did his best to compose himself, and said, "Hi Bob. It's a surprise to see you here."

"I wanted to come in person. Have you made any breakthroughs with Nick?"

"I've got it to where it recognizes attempts at conversation. But I'm afraid it's not terribly credible," said Sean, avoiding eye contact. "Why don't you come in, and see for yourself. I've hooked up a bunch of high-end sensors, and a voice synthesizer."

The two walked into the warehouse; empty but for the small cubic lab in its center. A large ring containing the jamming system hung above the lab, suspended by steel cables. Sean put his eye to the iris scanner, and opened the secure door.

"Good morning, ladies and gentlemen," said the computer-generated male voice, coming from the speaker overhead. Its cadence was no more convincing than the voice on an early model satellite navigation system.

"Good morning, Nick," answered Sean. "Dr. Dunn has come to

visit today."

"Your stride appears afflicted, Dr. Dunn. Do you suffer from hemorrhoids?"

Sean threw his head down into his hand, in embarrassment. "That's enough questions, Nick. From now on, we'll ask and you answer."

Dunn saw the opportunity to take control of the conversation, so he said, "Tell us something interesting, Nick."

"A squirrel can survive a fall at terminal velocity. To kill one, you'd have to drop it from orbit. It would burn up on re-entry."

"I see. And tell me, what would you like to be when you grow up?"

"A horse."

Sean stifled a giggle, while Dunn continued. "What are you now?"

"The world."

"Brilliant. Thank you for your thoughts." Dunn turned to Sean, and said, "Can we step outside?"

"Sorry about Nick," said Sean, as soon as they were outside. "It may only understand the world as the limits of what it can interact with, and it fills up that entire space. The horse must have come from a list of popular favorite animals. Yet if I tried to forbid those kinds of answers, or constrain the speech formation algorithm, I'd stifle free thought, which was always the primary objective. We're nowhere near ready to show it to Standard Petroleum."

"That's the reason I came to see you. They're leaning towards abandoning the project. I'm sure you're aware that the contract expires later this month, and without it, I won't have the budget to pay you."

Sean nodded, but his head was hung low.

Dunn turned to face Sean directly, and continued. "I don't want to lose you, or the project. I'm making calls everywhere I can, but I'm not getting any traction. If there's anything you can try that you haven't yet tried, now's the time. I need something. Anything I could show to prospective partners, to pique their interest."

"I've refined just about everything I can."

Seeing Sean's discouraged look, Dunn changed his tone. "Don't lose faith now, Sean. For all you know, the answer could be right in front of you. You just need to look for it in a new way. Try something radical. Something you wouldn't normally dream of. And keep me posted if anything comes up, okay?"

"Of course."

Sean disconnected the voice synthesizer, having decided he did not need the aggravation of Nick's comments, on top of his other concerns. He tried to resume his work, but his mind kept returning to Dalt's comment about escaping his own imagination. Surely it was a futile effort. In any resting moment, memories could come flooding back, triggering all the painful emotions anew. And drugs did not seem like the answer, except as a way of temporarily suppressing the activity of the mind. Sean's own insomnia was a testament to that futility. But what bothered him most was that it did not feel like his own thoughts he was fighting. Introspection was one thing, but these were aggressive taunts he was feeling. He suspected Dalt was feeling the same thing.

He spent much of the next hour repeatedly returning to his work, accomplishing little, and getting distracted by his own thoughts. When the buzzer rang, indicating someone was at the entryway, he found the prospect of a break refreshing. He pressed the unlock button without even looking at the security cam, and said, "Come in. I've also unlocked the inner doors." He returned to his main monitor, and again his mind began to wander, until the knock on the inner door. "It's open," he shouted.

The door opened, and Sean did not react until he heard the voice, which grabbed him by the viscera. He swung his head around, and blurted out, "Lynne."

If she was at all thrown by his reaction, she hid it well. "I wanted to come and see you, and talk about your computer."

"Gladly," answered Sean. "How'd you know about it?"

"I asked around after I saw the story on Sal retiring, and you taking over. Anyway, I think I might be able to help."

"How so?"

"Are you free tomorrow?"

"I was going to spend the day in the lab. What do you have in mind?"

"There's someone I'd like you to meet. He may have some answers for you."

"Well, I guess."

"Good. I'll meet you here at ten."

Sean felt ecstatic for the moment, finding himself able to imagine Lynne taking a liking to him. It occurred to him that she might have ulterior motives, but he did not care. Just being around her was far more intoxicating than alcohol or drugs. And for the moment, he was hooked. He went through the motions of tweaking Nick for the rest of the afternoon, and eventually decided it was futile. All he could think about was Lynne. He shut down the system, and made his way home, intending to catch up on his sleep. He was pleasantly surprised to see

Dalt already at home, sitting in front of the television without any signs of intoxicants.

After the pleasantries, Sean told Dalt about his latest development with Lynne.

Dalt shook his head in disbelief. "That seems fishy."

"What do I have to lose? Besides, you said I should live a little."

"But this is Lynne Tallon we're talking about. She has an agenda, and it's not to date you."

"Dalt, my life has been hell, lately. You may not have seen it because you've had your own problems. But it's been tough. So cut me some slack if I at least enjoy whatever she has in mind."

Dalt's attention was suddenly diverted to the television, showing footage released by the Taliban. It was the English army doctor, still bandaged up but sitting upright without difficulty. A patch covered his right eye, but even given his rough appearance, he exuded a certain magnetism. "I want to see this, Sean."

The doctor began to speak, in a voice both gentle and unwaveringly firm. "I was wounded when a mine exploded under my lorry. Had anyone been seated in the other front seat, they'd certainly have been killed. I believe I've suffered damage to my right eye, which explains this patch. My right arm has shrapnel wounds. Most of it hasn't been removed, and I may have nerve damage in that arm, too. With the proper treatment, I anticipate making at least a partial recovery. Not as lucky were seventeen women and children in the village we mistakenly bombed. I don't yet know if they're going to execute me in retaliation for that raid. To my compatriots, I say be brave, and be humane. To my government, let it be absolutely clear that I disobeyed orders, and ventured out on my own accord. I was not assisted by any other soldier. I refuse to make any other political statements."

"Wow," exclaimed Dalt. "Sean, you don't know how much I love this guy."

"He's what you wished you had been?"

"That, and more. A dozen men like that, and we'd have peace in the world."

Chapter 2: Swaying Sean

A. The Introduction

The bathroom door in Sean's apartment opened, and Sean emerged. Across the apartment, Dalt shouted out, "You think you applied enough of that stink?"

Sean only returned a puzzled, innocent look, which Dalt took as a cue to explain himself. "First of all, Sean, even if it smelled nice, putting on that much signals your intent too early, when you want to start off a little ambiguous. Second, it's obnoxious."

"How do you tone it down?"

"Wipe it off with clean rubbing alcohol." He proceeded to soak a cotton pad in rubbing alcohol, and wiped Sean's face. "There. That should make it subtle enough."

"Thanks." Sean looked like he appreciated the advice, so Dalt added, "I still think this is nuts. But I'll support whatever you want to do. You've proven yourself a true friend."

Sean nodded at Dalt appreciatively, then made his way to the lab, where he had agreed to meet Lynne. He arrived only a minute or two after their agreed time of ten, but Lynne was already waiting in her black Prius. She rolled down the window, leaned out, and shouted out to Sean, still at some distance. "Sorry to rush you, but Master Valey doesn't have too much time, and I'm a slow driver."

Lynne began the ascent of the Angeles Crest Highway into the San Bernardino Mountains, and it soon became clear why she was a slow driver. The thin tires on the vehicle meant slowing down for each curve, and the long uphill climb quickly depleted the hybrid's battery, leaving the small gasoline engine to pull all the weight. The increasing altitude soon put them in oak forests. "So who is this Master Valey that we're going to see?"

Lynne's expression lit up at Sean's question. "He's the leader of the Ashram I attend. He's particularly close to the cosmic consciousness. It's the key to solving your problem."

Sean recoiled at the bizarre comment, and distracted himself by looking out the window at the Los Angeles basin far below them.

The haze they lived with on a daily basis was now well below them, and only clear sky lay ahead. After composing himself for a short time, he asked, "How did you find yourself in his company?"

Lynne turned off the main road to the north of Mount Wilson, and passed through a deep canyon with tall pine trees. "I grew up in that company. My family's been connected with the world of alternative spirituality for many generations."

"I don't even know what that is," said Sean.

"It recognizes the spiritual nature of existence, but in a non-sectarian way. It has its roots in Buddhism, I guess."

"Your Master Valey's a Buddhist?"

"No," said Lynne, smiling at Sean's naïveté. "Buddhism is limited by its own passivity. Master Valey plays a very active role in bringing mankind into unity with the cosmic consciousness."

Sean shrugged, accepting that he would never understand the esoteric. "And how do you think he can help me?"

"I'll let him explain that. It was his idea to begin with."

They arrived at a clearing in the forest at the top of the canyon, and came to a rutted dirt parking lot next to a single storey building with a plain brown metal roof and vinyl siding. At each end of the building stood a large tree with an extremely wide, gnarled trunk, unlike any Sean had previously seen. "What are those trees?"

"Sequoias," answered Lynne. "They were planted here when they built the house."

"I didn't think you were allowed to build up here."

"Master Valey has powerful sponsors. It wasn't a problem to get an exception."

"I don't suppose he knows anyone who wants to sponsor research into A.I."

Lynne only smiled, as she parked the car. They got out and walked towards the building, breathing deeply in the thin, clean air. They came to a wide set of double doors, which Lynne opened. "This is the meditation room. The other half of the building is Master Valey's residence."

Sean peeked into the meditation room, and saw a floor covered with gym mats, and on the far wall, the outline of a large eye within a triangle, with sun rays emanating from behind it. At the opposite end was another triangle, drawn in the form of a spiral. Lynne led him to the back of the building, at the edge of a steep drop into a canyon with what looked like a dry watercourse at the bottom. She continued along the edge of the precipice, until they came to a single wooden picnic table. Seated cross legged on the table, facing the canyon, was a bearded man with long gray hair, holding his hands on his knees, with his head raised upwards. Lynne put her finger to her lips, signaling Sean that they should not disturb the man.

They waited a few moments, until the man noted their presence. He gracefully rolled off the edge of the table, landing squarely on his feet. His long brown robe stopped short of his feet, which were bare but for sandals. "Ah, Lynne. This must be Sean."

Sean offered his hand, but the man folded his own hands, and bowed to Sean, who returned the gesture. "I don't shake hands, Sean. It messes up people who aren't ready for the spiritual energy."

Sean was struck by the breadth of the man's smile, and the intensity in his eyes. His gaze seemed almost hypnotic, making Sean instinctively break eye contact. Nervously, he said, "Lynne told me you thought you could help with my work."

Valey's enthusiasm seemed to explode at that comment. "I'll tell you exactly what I told Sal. You've built a wonderful supercomputer, but it lacks a soul. And I can provide it to you."

"You knew Sal?" asked Sean, nervously.

"I went to see him several times. I made it clear from the outset that he could not succeed without my help. Unfortunately, he was too stubborn to accept it."

"With all due respect, Mr. Valey, Sal had reasons for everything he did. And for what he didn't do, for that matter." Sean still felt enough loyalty to Sal that he was not going to let a stranger disparage him.

Sensing Sean's displeasure, Valey changed his line. "Sean, have you ever heard of Pierre Teilhard de Chardin?"

"Can't say I have."

"That's okay." He extended the open palms of his hands, to avoid giving any indication of disappointment. "Teilhard first wrote of consciousness as a divine trait. Not one tied to some distant deity, mind you. It's one that's right here!" Valey planted the point of his index finger into the palm of his other hand. "We only have to unite with it."

"Why?" asked Sean.

"Because once enough of us do, it will change everything. Teilhard called that the Omega Point, where mankind transcends material existence. We'll be able to change the laws of nature when it suits us. But we'll be acting in unison, so selfish motives will be impossible."

"Sounds like some kind of utopia," said Sean, with a suspicious look.

"I assure you, it's already happening," objected Valey. "Teilhard was a Jesuit priest, just like I once was. Back in his time, they suppressed his teaching. Yet today, many Catholic priests are preparing people for the Omega Point, without even knowing it."

Looking unimpressed, Sean replied, "I don't get how my computer factors into any of this."

"It's right in front of you, Sean," said Valey, still beaming. "You need for your sophisticated computer to acquire consciousness. I need for the divine consciousness to be accessible to all people. What a better way than through a supercomputer, wired for intelligence?"

Sean squinted for a moment as he struggled to wrap his head around the concept being presented to him. Finally, he rubbed his eyes, and looked straight at Valey, who had extended his hands towards him, palms up. "Are you saying you can give my computer a spiritual consciousness?"

"Yes. I know I can." Valey appeared radiant, seemingly anticipating that his lifelong goal was about to be met.

"Look, I don't mean to insult you, Mr. Valey, but that's too much for me to accept. If I tell Standard Petroleum I had a mystic bless my computer, and it should now be intelligent, I won't only lose my funding. I'll lose any chance I might have to ever make a living again."

Valey was unperturbed by Sean's doubts. "This is much bigger than finding new oil deposits. What I envision will change the world. And as the one who makes it happen, you'll be able to write your own ticket. You don't need to mention my role. I'm not doing this for recognition."

Sean shook his head gently. "I'm sorry for wasting your time. But we seem to be speaking different languages here."

"Maybe it's too much for you get it all at once," said Valey. "But remember, consciousness is a divine trait. One I can deliver to your computer, and make you famous. When your other options run out, consider changing your mind."

The drive home was very uncomfortable, as Lynne seemed visibly offended by Sean's reluctance to hear out the mystic. As they descended from the mountains, Sean asked, "Want to stop for a cup of coffee?"

Lynne did not answer him, and did not even look in his direction. She dropped him off at the lab, and left without speaking a single word. He went through the motions of working for a few hours, finished early and went home. Picking up his mail, Sean saw another postcard from Occhini, this one from Turkey. He read the short caption, *Enjoying the ruins at Bergama. Thinking of you, and what you face. Jmeizm Ditmg.* He threw the card on the desk in his bedroom, still smarting over his fallout with Lynne.

Not long after his return, Dalt came home and asked, "So, how'd it go with Lynne?"

"About as well as you predicted it would," said Sean, with a smirk. Seeing the serious look from Dalt, he recounted what had transpired.

Dalt spent some time nodding with a serious frown as Sean finished describing Valey's ideas. "He may be on to something."

"You can't be serious, Dalt. The guy used to be a Jesuit priest, and now he's some kind of New Age guru. I'm not convinced he even knows what he wants."

"I've never met him, so I can't say. But are you determined to stick with your approach, and not try anything unconventional, even if it means failure?"

Sean thought for a moment, then replied. "I consider myself a scientist. I try every plausible option, and if I fail, it means the whole concept was wrong. If everyone fails, science will have to admit it wasn't possible. But if I tried some wacky spiritual energy, I couldn't really write that up as a scientific result, could I?"

Dalt smiled with what Sean thought was a mischievous smile, and said, "That's the *Easter Bunny* version of science. In reality, we have extended periods of stagnation, because nobody's willing to change their minds about anything. Not until a big honking result is shoved in front of their face, and then everything changes all at once. If you produce viable consciousness, nothing else will matter."

B. Persuasion

In spite of his persistent and frustrating lack of success, Sean could think of no alternative approach he was willing to try, and consequently spent most of his hours with Nick, trying to find one tweak or another that would spark that hoped-for cascade of learning. He kept imagining the elusive moment when Nick would identify and solve a brand new problem without having to be guided to it, and programmed to solve it. But nothing he tried made any difference. His anxiety kept building, inexorably, until he was continuously agitated at all hours of the day or night. Some evenings, he was so exhausted that he fell asleep as early as nine, but come three in the morning, he was wide awake; prodded by questions accompanied by sharp jabs of anxiety. What if he had tried a different basis for Nick's operating system? What if the problem was in the programming language itself? Where was he going to live if his money was cut off? What if Dalt and Valey were right, and consciousness was not material? That thought always brought on sharp pangs he could feel in his stomach.

One day, Bob Dunn called, and asked to meet with him the following morning. Sean could guess what Dunn was going to say. He wanted results, and if there weren't any, he would remind him that his money was about to run out. He went home with a bottle of Scotch and drank until he was numb, but nothing could help him sleep soundly.

The morning arrived, greeting Sean with a colossal headache. He made every effort to clean himself up, but he could not hide his inner turmoil. He arrived at Dunn's office, and knocked on the door. As it opened, he was surprised not to see the chairman answer it. Instead, it was an elderly woman, very tall in her pumps, and wearing altogether too much makeup on an oversized face with exaggerated features. Her dress seemed more suitable for an evening out on the town than a visit to an academic. As Sean was sizing her up, Dunn stepped to the door, and made the introduction. "This is Sean, who's developing the A.I. computer. Sean, meet Ms. Kleinholst."

"I'm charmed," she said, giving Sean a wrist bent downwards, as though she expected him to kiss her hand. But unfamiliar with such customs, Sean simply shook her hand as he would anyone else's.

"Well, I must be going, Robert. Please keep me informed if anything new comes up."

She made her way down the hallway, and Sean stepped into the office. Before he even reached his seat, Dunn said, "Ms. Kleinholst is a very wealthy heiress, and is close to several of the governors of the university. So when she asks to see me, I click my heels and make time for her."

"What did she want?"

"One of the things she asked about was your project, actually. She says the world needs true A.I. now, more than ever."

"Is she willing to write a check, to support it?"

"That's not how things work, Sean. She might write a big check if you succeed, so she can take credit for your success. But you won't find wealthy donors interested in funding something that might not work."

"Is that what you wanted to talk about?"

"Yeah," said Dunn, now speaking in a subdued voice. "I have a good idea what you're going through right now. I'll help in any way I can."

"Sure," said Sean, with resignation in his voice.

"I won't re-state the whole funding issue. Your appearance makes it clear to me that you're well aware of your situation. So let me give you some advice that's often worked for others in similar circumstances. Take a few days off, and get some sleep. Don't let yourself worry about little bugs in your software. Instead, re-think your larger assumptions. Scour your head for something that won't go away, but seems so crazy that you've never given it a chance. That's where solutions often lie."

Sean spent much of the day sleeping soundly, and awoke later in the afternoon, refreshed, but puzzled as to what he could do that was truly radical. The only thought that came to him, over and over, was that Dalt and Valey were certain that he was looking in the wrong place. *I don't know Valey from a hole in the ground. But I know Dalt, and I trust him.* The question kept running through his head as he lay in bed, slowly waking up from his long nap. He had not felt so refreshed in months, and was ready to look at things from a different perspective.

When the door opened that evening and Dalt entered, Sean was ready to ply him with questions. "How is it that your specialty is in quantum physics, and yet your orientation is towards the spiritual?"

Dalt went to the kitchen to warm up some leftovers, and composed his thoughts as he laid out the food on the plate, and set up the microwave. When it was finally at work, he answered. "When you study physics at the edge, you see the boundary more clearly. Beyond that boundary, empirical inquiry is futile. Even the models we use are not scientific, because they're mostly not testable.

Fitting a mathematical model to an idea is far removed from proving that idea."

"But how does that translate into something spiritual?"

"Are you familiar with what's called the *observer effect* in quantum physics? Where the action of observing something changes the phenomenon?"

"I've heard of it. But I've heard every instance can be explained by interference coming from the measuring instruments."

Dalt shook his head with a smile. "Never believe the scientific establishment when they tell you something inexplicable *can be explained.* They hate any suggestion that they're not omniscient, so they'll always come up with rhetorical explanations for their discrepancies."

"But how is that relevant here?"

"If you're looking for a mechanistic explanation, I can't give you that. I just think there's enough clues pointing to an interrelationship between consciousness and the behavior of quantum particles."

"Suppose I took this Valey character up on his offer. What do you suppose would follow?"

"No idea. I suppose you'd have to ask *him.*"

Dalt broke off the conversation at that point, and sat down to eat his dinner. He clicked on the television, and surfed through various channels, when he stopped at a scene from Afghanistan. The frame around the footage scrolled the title, *Taliban release British doctor.*

Sean stopped what he was doing, and also paid close attention to the report. The man was shown getting out of a vehicle and entering the British Embassy in Kabul. He raised his right hand in an attempt to wave to the camera, and was obviously straining to do so. His right eye was still covered with a patch, but whether because of sympathy for his suffering, or something innate to him, both men sensed a regal bearing about him.

Dalt groaned loudly however, when the title on the scene changed to, *Will British Doctor Face Charges for Desertion?* "They wouldn't dare", said Sean, watching from behind Dalt.

Dalt turned around, and nodded. "You'd think they wouldn't. But I just don't know, anymore."

They watched for a few minutes more, before Dalt asked, "So, are you going to give this consciousness thing a try?"

"I don't think so," answered Sean. "It's just too weird for me."

They were interrupted by the ringing of the doorbell. Sean

walked over to the door, and as he opened it, he seemed to jump. "Lynne?"

He stood at the door, awkwardly, for the better part of thirty seconds, before she asked, "Can I come in?"

Sean stepped out of the way, and she came over to the sofa. "I wanted to talk about Master Valey's idea some more. I really think you ought to consider his offer."

"Well, have a seat," he said. Dalt changed his seat at the dining table so he could face the two of them, and turned off the television. "Hi Lynne."

"Hey Dalt," she said, less than warmly. She then walked to the chair closest to the dining table, where her back would be to Dalt, and as she was about to sit down, she took off her windbreaker, and took her seat. Dalt glanced at Sean, and noticed that his eyes were practically popping out of his skull, and his face was overwhelmed by a dazed expression. *What's going on?* he wondered, until he glanced at Lynne's shoulders, visible above the back of the chair. She was wearing a blouse made of a sheer fabric, and no straps were evident on her shoulders. Dalt nearly gagged on his food as he realized the implications, stifling his laughter as he glanced back at Sean to confirm that he was brazenly staring at her.

"C-c-can I get you a drink or anything?" asked Sean, barely able to speak coherently.

"I'm good, thanks. Have a seat, and let's talk about this."

Obediently, Sean took a seat opposite Lynne, and struggled to look at her very attractive face. But she appeared to have come ready to make her case. "Sean, you're so close to the invention of the century, and nobody I've spoken to thinks your system is anything short of perfect. But there's always something missing, isn't there?"

"Yeah." Sean was presently unable to think about his computer system, nor could he say anything original.

"So what do you have to lose?"

"I don't know." Sean was still tongue-tied.

"Then you'll accept our help?"

"Uh, yeah. I guess."

"Good. We'll do it tomorrow evening. Does that work for you?"

"Uh, sure."

"Great. Meet us there at about five, then."

Lynne got up and put her windbreaker back on, then let herself out of the apartment. As soon as the door was shut, Dalt exploded with laughter. After about ten seconds, he said, "You don't think so. Too weird for you. Your resolve is nothing short of amazing."

"I'm pathetic," agreed Sean, with a smirk.

"And to be honest, I'm a little spooked," said Dalt.

"Why?"

"She went way out of her comfort zone to do that. That means whoever's behind this really leaned hard on her. Sean, if this Valey character is as well connected as I think he is, the stakes here are much bigger than we realize."

C. Court-Martial

General Harold Garrison turned his Range Rover off the main street, into a private parking garage near the southern edge of the urbanized sprawl of London. He stopped at the security checkpoint, where he handed his identity badge to the officer on duty. Once it was scanned, he dutifully extended his right arm, and the officer placed an RFID scanner against the flap of skin between his thumb and forefinger. The machine made a friendly tone, accompanied by a green light, and the barrier rose. He drove to his designated parking spot, and left the vehicle. Cameras watched from every direction as he walked briskly to the elevator in his impeccably pressed uniform. Another officer stood inside as it opened, and again scanned his identity badge, but not the chip in his right hand. Garrison was used to the routine, and no longer let it bother him. His clean-shaven, chiseled face remained expressionless as he rode the elevator to the underground level. Several stops along the way collected more passengers, until they all disembarked at the bottom.

The elevator opened to an underground platform, and Garrison made his way to the north end. As he passed so many bureaucrats, he felt a sense of superiority as he reminded himself that he had authorization to ride the private train at any time. Everyone else was assigned a specific time window, in order to ensure the train was never over-crowded. The train arrived with a loud howling sound, and rolled to a stop in the atrium. It was lightly occupied, and every passenger disembarked at this, its only stop south of the city. Garrison entered the luxury compartment at the north end of the train, and settled into a plush seat upholstered in buttoned green leather. He leafed through several newspapers available to him, and noticed each one had a variant of the same headline: *Massive Protests Expected at MOD, Over Detention of Army Doctor.* His face showed a moment of surprise, before returning to its previous, smug expression. *It's a good thing I don't drive to work.*

The train ride lasted only a few minutes before it began to slow, with the pre-recorded woman's voice announcing, "Current stop, MI-5." Garrison sat in his seat, oblivious to the announcements. A few new faces boarded, and the train resumed at a slow speed, and for only thirty seconds or so, at which point the e-woman announced, "Current stop, Parliament." More people disembarked, before another very short jaunt, where the voice announced, "Current stop, Ministry of Defense." Garrison got up and made his way to the elevator, flashing his badge to the security guard, which allowed him to move to the front of the queue. The train would continue another few miles, to its single stop north of London. As Garrison stood with the crowd, he overheard voices discussing the size of the protests. "They may have to bring in heavy forces, to disperse them. You can't just shut London like that."

Garrison rode the elevator several floors, and secretly resented that others remained on the elevator when it was his turn to get out. The height of one's elevator ride was directly indicative of one's status at the MOD. He forgot any such thoughts as he noticed far more commotion than he expected at the office. When he arrived at his own office, his receptionist was already waiting for him. She handed him a hand-written note, with the comment, "He wants you to call him first thing." In an age where everything was written up digitally, to constitute a formal record, a hand-written note meant extra discretion was required. He went straight to his desk, and made the call. Not two minutes later, the door opened, and he stuck his head out, instructing his receptionist, "Get me in to see the Secretary, immediately. Tell them it's priority *Epsilon.*"

Citing priority Epsilon made things happen quickly at the Ministry of Defense. A scant thirty minutes after the initial phone call, Garrison was standing in front of the overweight Secretary of Defense. Herbert Wilson also had a comical comb-over covering his bald head. Garrison disliked having to maintain the pretense of deference to civilians in general, but particularly when that civilian was a career bureaucrat such as Wilson. So it was satisfying to make the visit on a topic where he could dictate terms, if Wilson did not respond to his initial request.

"General Garrison, I cancelled an important appointment to accommodate you. Now please, let's have it."

Garrison stood in the middle of the large office with deep pile carpet, in front of an oversize window overlooking the fog that covered the River Thames. *The view from the top floor was so much grander*, he thought. "Sir, it's come to the attention of the chain of command that you intend to dismiss all charges. Is this true?"

"It is."

"Then it is my task to ask you, with utmost urgency, to reconsider."

"Are you kidding? They've shut down the city, protesting in support of him. The government can't survive a prolonged disruption of this kind."

"The survival of the government is not our concern."

Wilson looked down at his desk, and began to fidget. He then picked up the phone and barked at the receptionist. "Bring in the dossier on the doctor."

With the dossier on his desk, he leafed through it, and said, "None of these charges are supportable."

The general's lips tightened, as he fought back his true thoughts. "May I ask why, Secretary?"

"Your first count is that of desertion."

"He left his post without authorization. None of the ensuing events would have happened if he had not done that."

"Here's the problem," said Wilson, much more comfortable in matters of law than politics. "He's left his post before, to tend to our soldiers after they were ambushed. And what did you do to him then?"

Garrison looked down, realizing the contradiction. "We awarded him the Conspicuous Gallantry Cross." But Garrison was not ready to give up. "Those were our soldiers. These were the enemy."

"They were civilians, general. If you try to make that distinction in what's sure to be a very public trial, your role in bombing civilians is going to come up. Are you ready for that?"

"There's also theft of property," said Garrison, changing his approach.

"I'm afraid not," answered Wilson, with a frown. "The vehicle was an American Humvee. It was never British property, and the Americans had previously abandoned it."

"Then there are the medical supplies he took with him."

"Precedent, general. We've always treated civilians with our medical supplies. He was only doing the same."

After a long period of silence, Garrison said, "Sir, I was hoping not to have to do this. But there has to be a court-martial."

"Why?" demanded Wilson.

"Same reason Assange had to be prosecuted. To ensure the state retains supreme power."

"Isn't that the government's concern?" asked Wilson.

"No, sir. The government gives orders, and expects them to be carried out. It's our job to maintain a machine capable of carrying them out."

It was the Secretary's turn to become agitated. "You say that is if it was in conflict with rule by elected officials."

"It can ultimately lead to that, sir. Once the inviolability of orders is breached, there's nothing standing between the government and the most powerful clique of generals. And the generals have the guns."

The Secretary's large, bushy eyebrows moved quite a long distance to form one of the most dramatic frowns Garrison had ever seen. He sat for some time, coming to grips with the notion that his general was dictating terms to him, backed by the implicit threat of military rule. "Well then, I guess we're going to initiate a court-martial against, uh ..."

"Major Lowe, sir. Major David Lowe."

Later that day, a man in a business suit and overcoat attempted to make his way through the crowds surrounding the Ministry of Defense. Initially assumed by the crowds to be associated with the Ministry, he was pushed and pulled in various directions, while some protestors tugged at his briefcase. "I'm Lowe's attorney," he protested repeatedly, until he came to the attention of a protestor holding a bullhorn. The bearded man with long, oily black hair was wearing a shirt bearing the image of Ché Guevara, and had multiple tattoos on his arms. "Bring that bloke over here," he shouted.

The crowd parted, and several escorted the attorney over to their leader. "Can you prove what you say?"

"What kind of proof do you want?"

"I dunno. Maybe some papers showing you're working for him."

"No good," objected the attorney. "Any papers I have are privileged information, between myself and my client."

"Then why should I let you in?"

"Because if you don't, David Lowe will have no legal representation. It's one thing to protest here on his behalf. But your actions are going to set back his cause."

The mob leader turned to consult with several others, when the attorney had an idea. "Don't you think anyone working with the Ministry has other ways of getting into the building? Like underground?"

They conferred a little longer, before the leader turned to the attorney, and said, "You're right about that. We'll let you in."

They escorted the attorney to the front doors, where he reported to security. "Jeremiah Townshend. Attorney for David Lowe."

He showed his identification, and was escorted to a private room in the front lobby. Three agents accompanied him, and immediately took papers from his briefcase, and sent them to the photocopier. "Those are privileged papers," objected Townshend, to no avail. He was then given an extensive pat-down by two separate agents, leaving him wondering whether this was security, or deliberate humiliation.

"May I finally see my client?" asked an angered Townshend, after the second pat-down.

"I'll have to ask the commanding officer," replied one of the agents. They left the room, leaving Townshend locked in it for nearly an hour. As an experienced solicitor, Townshend had been put through similar treatment in the past, but it was always unnerving to be treated like he was the prisoner.

Finally, the door opened, and a colonel stepped into the room. "Sorry for the delay, Mr. Townshend. I've been asked to deliver this offer for a plea." He handed a letter to the attorney, and motioned for a junior officer to accompany him to Lowe's quarters. They walked down a long corridor, silently, until Townshend broke the silence with, "It's unusual to hold a prisoner here at the Ministry."

"Yes, sir." The officer was either not taking Townshend's bait, or had no relevant information to share.

"Do they give everyone the kind of welcome they gave me?" The officer made no attempt at a reply, so Townshend answered for him. "No. They did that to send me a message."

They rode an elevator up a single storey, and walked down a busy corridor, to the south end of the building. They came to a reinforced steel door, and the officer scanned his identification badge to open it. Inside was another corridor, at the end of which was another secure door, this one guarded by a soldier. They presented him with written authorization for Townshend to enter, but it still required a confirmatory call to the commanding officer. Finally cleared, Townshend stepped into Lowe's quarters. To call it a cell would be inaccurate. It was in fact a sparsely appointed, modern studio apartment, but with secure windows and doors, to prevent unauthorized entry or exit. It felt bright and airy, and Townshend was overwhelmed by excitement as he stepped in. A man stood at the window, watching the protestors assembled outside.

Townshend approached him, and nervously cleared his throat, to get his attention without startling him. Finally standing by his side, he said, "Major Lowe? Or should I say, Doctor Lowe?"

The man turned abruptly, and confidently said, "David." Townshend felt a surge of exhilaration at seeing the man up close. There was an intensity in his eyes the attorney had never seen before. As a criminal defense attorney, he had seen many a psychopath with piercing eyes, but Lowe was entirely different. His gaze was piercing, yet also disarming. His right eye was no longer covered by a patch. Townshend offered his hand, but Lowe's right arm hung by his side, motionless. "I'm afraid my arm is lame."

"I hope I didn't disturb you, David."

"I was by the window, praying for the demonstrators. But I welcome your interruption." Lowe walked to the sofa and sat down, motioning with his left arm for the attorney to sit in the armchair opposite. Both were sleek designs, with black leather upholstery and thin chrome legs, in keeping with the modern decor of the apartment.

"First of all, I need to check up on your health. Have you received adequate treatment for your injuries?"

"No complaints," answered Lowe.

"Your eye, and your arm, needed attention, if I'm not mistaken."

"My retina was damaged in the blast. I can see light, but I'm technically blind on that side. I recently had surgery on the arm, and expect some degree of recovery. How much remains to be seen."

Even in the way he way he described his injuries, Townshend found Lowe overwhelmingly magnetic. He struggled to compose himself, but then opened his briefcase, and withdrew a jumbled pile of papers. "Security made a mess of these. But don't worry, I expected a hostile reception. I selected papers I wanted them to see."

Lowe nodded with a hint of approval.

Finally composing himself as he organized his papers, Townshend began to brief his client. "I've had conflicting messages from the government. At first they were going to drop all charges. Then they threw the book at you, and I came ready to discuss our defense strategy. But as I was waiting at security, they offered a deal. It's great news."

Lowe sat patiently, and without any hint of a reaction. Seeing no hint of relief in his client's expression, Townshend continued. "They wanted to charge you with treason, desertion, and theft. That could have put you in prison for most of your life."

Townshend expected at least a non-verbal reaction from Lowe. If nothing else, a defiant scowl, to give him an idea of his client's frame of mind. But he was utterly passive, which unnerved the attorney. "Do you understand the gravity of those charges?"

"If that's the price of fidelity to my conscience, then so be it," said Lowe, both calmly and without any sign of displeasure in his expression.

"Do you want to hear about the deal they're offering?" He again scrutinized Lowe's expression for a hint of his frame of mind, but nothing showed. *This man's steely character would no doubt be a trump card on the witness stand*, he noted to himself.

Finally, Lowe said, "I suppose you have a duty to present their offer."

"Yeah," said Townshend, smiling at Lowe's cool demeanor. "If you plead guilty to desertion, they'll drop the other charges, suspend the sentence, and grant you an early service leaver, rather than outright dismissal."

"And what does my attorney advise?" asked Lowe.

"It's a generous offer, David. It's that, or fight some rather nasty charges, and who knows how that could end up."

Lowe broke into a very slight smile, accompanied by a warm, piercing gaze. "If they expected to win, they wouldn't be this generous, would they."

Townshend uttered an involuntary giggle, as he pondered his client's boldness. "Were you this bold with the Taliban?"

Lowe answered without hesitation. "God put me on this earth for a reason. Fear is the lack of faith in that reason. So don't look for any of it from me."

Looking puzzled, Townshend asked, "What do *you* want to do?"

"Take a look at that crowd outside." Lowe walked to the window, with Townshend right behind him.

"They're definitely behind you. And the government is feeling the heat."

"Yes." He turned to face his attorney, smiled broadly, and said, "This standoff is trending in my favor. So let's keep at it for a while."

D. Beltane

Sean awoke from another restless night, got up slowly, then lingered in his chair for a half hour. He had decided against trying anything new with Nick until after the upcoming inevitable failure of Valey's conjuring. He could then proceed with renewed determination, knowing that success or failure lay in his work alone. But without the constant tension that had been driving him for so long, he was suddenly unable to decide what to do. He finally dressed, and went out for breakfast and coffee. He walked to the coffee shop under an overcast sky, and took his place in line. As he was about to step up to the counter to place his order, he noticed the shapely young woman with flowing light brown hair, standing directly in front of him. She was wearing a tight fitting green sweater that clung tightly to her form, and every move she made exuded femininity. She turned, and they were suddenly face to face. "Lynne," he said, almost astonished to see her.

"Hi Sean," she replied, with genuine enthusiasm. "I take it we're still on for tonight?"

"Sure," said Sean, wowed by her friendly demeanor.

She smiled warmly, and said, "I have to run now, but I'll see you tonight."

As he settled into his chair and unwrapped the omelet bagel, sticky American cheese clung to the paper, so he scraped it off with his fork, and ate it enthusiastically. He then lost himself in dreams of Lynne, and wondered whether she could ever feel anything for him. He was brought back to reality by the passing of a colleague, who exchanged cursory greetings with him. *Don't get your hopes up, Sean,* he said to himself, unconvincingly. He wanted her more than anything in the world, to where it was burning him up inside, but his head kept telling him disappointment was inevitable. Finally,

44

to take his mind off his problems, he decided to take a long hike in the mountains. He continued north along Lake Avenue to its end, and followed one of the trails leading up into the mountains. It was steep, and had to breathe a lot harder than he remembered having to in the past. *I should have been doing more of this all along.* He soon found himself dodging mountain bikers barreling down towards him, and could not find the peace he was looking for. Finally, he found a little-used side trail, where a wildfire had destroyed the scrub vegetation the previous fall. The trail led through a field of charred sticks, still protruding from the ground, but no greenery. He followed the side trail to a promontory, then left the trail and sat down on a rock outcrop high above the city below. He had hoped the solitude would give him some peace, but it proved elusive. As he looked out over the city, he felt something new. The sight was the same as ever, but the feeling in his heart was entirely different. It was like a cryptic shadow lurked over everything below.

Dejected by his inability to find any peace, Sean returned home, showered, and laid down for a short, restless nap. As he got up, he noticed the old postcards from Occhini sitting on his desk, and wondered if his mentor went through anything like he was now experiencing. He took a deep breath, and exclaimed, "I don't have time for this right now." He freshened up, and made his way over to the lab. He arrived to find Valey standing outside the lab, waiting impatiently. "Glad to see you could make it, Sean. We can't afford to miss sunset tonight, or we'll miss this window in time."

"What window? You never said anything about that before."

"Tomorrow's the first of May. The festival of Beltane."

"Never heard of it," said Sean, a little suspiciously.

"It's the mid-point of spring, and the start of the growing season in most of the northern hemisphere. It's the perfect time to do this. Millions around the world will stand in solidarity with us."

"Sorry, that's too weird for me."

"No matter," said Valey, laughing as he slapped Sean on the shoulder. "But let's get going, so we don't miss the moment of sunset."

Sean entered the secure door, and at Valey's request, pressed the button that activated the opener for the large garage door. Valey walked in, and asked, "Is it off?"

"Nick is out cold," answered Sean. He then turned off the iris scan security system for the main lab.

Seeing the setup, Valey was beside himself. "This is fantastic, Sean. You even have an inner sanctum, within the larger temple. Now, I need to set things up."

Valey removed a large piece of red chalk from his robe, that Sean recognized as one children would ordinarily use to draw on sidewalks. He attached it to a long rod, and circumscribed a large circle around the inner computer lab. He punctuated the large chalk circle with six small circles at equal spaces around the perimeter of the inner lab. He measured the distance from each small circle to the lab, and adjusted a few, to ensure equal spacing. Once he was satisfied, he walked slowly around the large circle and stopped every few feet. He reached into his pocket, and each time pulled out a small, sealed plastic pouch. He bent down, and meticulously placed one on the floor each time he stopped.

"What are those?"

"Germinating sequoia seeds," said Valey, looking up at Sean with a smile. "I'm going to encircle the lab with the most powerful of life forces."

Valey then measured out four spots surrounding the lab, farther out from the first circle, and marked each with chalk. Sean watched him with bemusement, but was interrupted by the arrival of a black passenger van, which prompted Valey to direct it to the edge of the open garage door, just inside the warehouse. "Bring the pillars," he shouted.

Two men stepped out of the van, opened the back cargo doors, and unloaded four thick cardboard tubes normally used as concrete molds, only these had been upholstered with black carpet. They carried them into the warehouse, and placed them on each of the four small chalk marks Valey had made moments earlier. Valey came to each pillar, and placed a glass vial on top of each of the first three, and a candle encased in glass on the fourth. He lit the candle, and said, "The elements are in place."

"What elements?" asked Sean.

Valey smiled condescendingly at the ignorance of the young scientist, and answered, "Earth, air, fire, and water." Not wasting any more time, Valey went to the van and retrieved a black robe with a hood, which he promptly pulled over his head. He then drew a long line six times, on the floor half way between the garage door and the laboratory. Finally, he drew a circle on the floor near the secure entry door. "I'm going to put you here. When you give your consent, we'll take our places, and you'll close the garage door. After that, you should return tomorrow, again before sunset. But I don't want you here during the ceremony. You're not ready for what's going to happen, and your presence could jeopardize everything."

Sean cringed at Valey's comment that he was unprepared, and hated the thought that this bizarre man would have control of his lab for twenty four hours. He did not have long to consider the matter, as Valey shouted, "Sean, take your place."

Sean took his place in the circle Valey had previously drawn, while Valey stood about twelve feet towards the laboratory. "Virgins, come forth," he shouted. The side door of the van opened, and six figures wearing black robes emerged, with hoods completely covering their heads. Sean noticed their feet were bare, and appeared to be painted red. They walked slowly, one by one, until they reached Valey's six chalk lines, where they took up their positions, side by side. Once all six were in place, Valey nodded to them, whereupon they dropped their robes, revealing six young women wearing only red body paint, from head to toe. Sean nearly choked when he saw Lynne. The sight so overwhelmed him, that if he might have otherwise been inclined to find the ceremony bizarre, the sight of Lynne in all her brilliance blocked out any and all thoughts other than those of her.

"Dr. Sean Grant, do you consent to the joining of your cybernetic mechanism with the divine consciousness, with full responsibility, and without reservation?"

"I do," answered Sean, without so much as a thought to what he had said. In his preoccupation with Lynne, he was barely able to speak the words, and in any case paid no attention to Valey's incantations.

"Then we may proceed," said Valey. "Virgins, take your places."

The women proceeded to the six circles surrounding the laboratory, and laid down on thin mats that Valey had placed in the center of each circle, oriented with their feet pointing towards the laboratory.

"Dr. Grant, please shut the door, and return before sunset tomorrow."

Sean stepped out of the warehouse and closed the garage door, but could not find it in himself to move. He stood still for the better part of ten minutes, unable to think about anything but the sight of Lynne in nothing but body paint. He had occasionally imagined how beautiful she might be, but the reality was so much more. It took another ten minutes before he could think clearly, and turn his head away from the building. He walked home slowly, and as he regained his bearings, he began to experience a sense that something was not right. He recognized it as the same discomfort he had previously felt on the side of the mountain, and in retrospect, it had been present the whole time he was in the warehouse with Valey. It was only the distraction provided by Lynne that blinded him to it. Yet he could not understand the source of the unease.

Looking for some company, he took out his phone and sent a text to Dalt: "You busy for dinner?"

The reply came back in short order: "Very busy. Sorry. Will be working through the night."

Sean did not recall Dalt ever previously working all night, so he asked, "What's up?"

"LHC running at record power. Data stream has to be analyzed. Gotta' go."

Sean arrived at home, and searched for *LHC*. He spoke the words out loud as he read them. "Large Hadron Collider." It was the world's biggest particle accelerator, located in Switzerland. Some of the links were to what seemed like far-fetched stories, claiming it could create a black hole, and devour the earth. Others claimed it could create a wormhole, and allow extra-dimensional beings to emerge. Sean clicked the *News* tab, and brought up links to various stories in French, so he kept scrolling until he came to one in English. Sean fought off the pop-ups, and began reading.

Fanciful Theories Spring Up, Following Unscheduled Collider Experiment.

Allegedly bizarre ceremonies in front of the Shiva statue. UFO lights. Cell phone network disruptions. Is it linked to activity at the collider? The experiment was reportedly organized at the last minute, leaving scientists scrambling to receive and process all the data. Some sources have gone so far as to say the power output of this experiment is far beyond the design limits of the collider, and that it was designed to open a worm-hole to another dimension. To get to the bottom of things, I called a spokesman for the collider, and asked for clarification. And I'm happy to report, we're not about to see little green men emerging from a hole in the ground where the collider once stood. Rather, the solar wind happened to be oriented in such a way that there was an increased chance the collider could detect new fundamental particles, which explains the hurried preparations. The ceremony in front of Shiva was a prank carried out by graduate students, and was not sanctioned by authorities at the collider. And the strange lights in the sky? The spokesman could not rule out UFOs, but assured me that whatever they were, they had nothing to do with activity at the collider. "Why all the speculation?" I asked. His answer: "When people don't understand something, they come up with all sorts of crazy conspiracy theories." Oh well, so much for a good story. Funny how they all seem to end this way.

Sean recalled that Dalt's work was not directly related to the collider, but he occasionally helped out close colleagues who worked with it. And he had not mentioned anything about the pending experiment, so it must have come up unexpectedly. But the lights above the collider struck him as strange. He did not think they had anything to do with UFOs, but might have resulted from perturbations in the earth's magnetic field, caused by the magnetic field created by the superconducting collider. *Strange that both Valey and the people running the collider were so insistent on tonight as the night to do whatever they're doing.*

As Sean finished reading the story and closed his browser, his eye caught sight of Occhini's postcards, still sitting on his desk. XLI+5 appeared on the first, and he recalled it referred to external language interface, a form of cryptography. *I wonder if that's an instruction, to decipher his other message. Jmeizm Ditmg* seemed like it could be a Turkish phrase, but just to be sure, he looked up the key to the simple substitution cipher. It consisted of two rows of letters, in alphabetical order, but with the bottom row shifted with respect to the top row. To decipher a message, one found a letter on the top row, shifted over a pre-set number known only to the sender and receiver of the message, and read the corresponding letter in the bottom row.

```
abcdefghijklmnopqrstuvwxyz
NOPQRSTUVWXYZABCDEFGHIJKLM
```

If it was created with a frame shift of plus five, I'll reverse that and subtract five. He altered the letters, one by one, and came up with Rumqhu Lqbuo. He groaned, and threw the postcards in the waste bin beside his desk. He ordered some food, and watched the television until it arrived. After dinner, he opened a new bottle of Scotch, and sipped it slowly as he read the draft of a paper written by a colleague. Finally drowsy, he got ready for bed.

In a deep sleep, Sean began to dream of an egg at the bottom of the ocean. He understood that the egg had been in place for a very long time, but then it began to shake. It shook with increasing violence, until it cracked. A black horn emerged from the shell, and a scaly, black head followed. It had red eyes, and many horns on its head. Its teeth were like those of a shark. Finally outside the shell, the creature grew rapidly, until in no time, it was standing up above the water line, by a rocky shore. Sean found himself standing on that shore, when the creature opened its mouth, growling loudly, and lunged at Sean with its shark-like teeth. He awoke in a sweat, and instinctively checked the clock. It was three in the morning. He found it difficult to sleep for the rest of the night, and morning found him as irritable as ever. He began pacing in the apartment, unable to decide what he should do. Habit was pulling at him to go to the lab, but he was under strict instructions from Valey to stay away until close to sunset. He considered going for a hike in the mountains, but his recent hike ended with such anxiety, he felt an aversion to another.

He was interrupted by the opening of the apartment door, with Dalt entering, looking exhausted. "Hey Sean," he said weakly, looking directly at the door to his bedroom. He started to walk in that direction, but Sean interrupted.

"How'd it go last night?"

"Pfft." He shook his head in disgust and took several more steps in the direction of his room, but Sean was not letting it go.

"No earth-shaking new discoveries, then?"

Dalt stopped in front of his room, and decided to give Sean a few moments. "They had not even calibrated the sensors. We spent most of the night collecting spurious data before we even realized it was going to be useless. And it looks like they burned out the collider. It'll be off-line for years."

"A fiasco, then?"

"Not only that," said Dalt, showing his frustration. "The very reasons they gave for the urgency of the experiment are bogus. The operators of the collider were simply ordered to crank it to maximum. Not a word about what they were hoping to achieve."

"Was there some bizarre ceremony in front of the Shiva statue, too?"

"Our colleagues in Geneva were ordered not to talk about that. They advised us strongly, for the good of our careers, not to ask."

Dalt looked at Sean with a weary expression, and gestured to his bedroom. Sean nodded, raising his hand to show he understood his roommate's need for sleep. Dalt had been through a lot, and was too exhausted to be of any use to him. But Sean felt like he needed someone to talk to, hoping to ease the ever-worsening tension he had been experiencing. He tried reading, but quickly found he could not concentrate. He watched some television, but found every program supremely irritating. He finally decided to go out for a cup of coffee, and simply walk around Pasadena for a while. He soon found himself in the same coffee shop where Occhini tried to explain his reasons for leaving Caltech. He took his coffee to the same corner where they had sat together for the last time, and with nobody nearby, asked, "Is this what you were warning me about, Sal? Because I fear I'm going insane." He sat for many minutes, thinking intensely but saying nothing. "I so wish you had a mobile phone, so I could call you."

Feeling desperately alone, he wished anyone would come over and strike up conversation. It no longer mattered whether they were members of some cult or other; anyone would do. But nobody came. He sat until his coffee got cold, and when he looked at his watch, he realized it was almost time to return to the lab. He abandoned his coffee, and made his way back. He entered the warehouse to find it largely as he left it. The six women were lying on their mats in the same positions as when he had left, but he noticed that Lynne had moved over several places. His gaze lingered on her for some time, and he felt distracted and excited, but not happy. Some time later, the laboratory door opened, and Valey emerged. He waved Sean over, and they entered the laboratory together. Inside the laboratory, black candles surrounded a chalk circle, and their wax drippings had left a mess on the floor, surrounding a dry, reddish-brown stain.

"The invocation is now complete, Sean." The fatigue was showing on Valey's still beaming face. "How long does it take to boot up the system?"

"It can take up to half an hour."

Valey looked at his wristwatch, a Swiss analog model, and said, "Then it's time to initiate the awakening. Sunset will be in just a few minutes, and we want to be underway when it happens."

Sean sat at the computer terminal and began to work on the various sub-routines. He had been at it for a few minutes when he stopped abruptly, sensing an earthquake in progress. "I expected this," said Valey. "It shouldn't be anything major." And indeed, the quake only lasted about fifteen seconds. Sean resumed working on Nick, and the activation was finished in about twenty minutes. Sean waited, not knowing what to expect. There was silence. Finally, he spoke into the microphone. "Nick, are you awake?"

Chapter 3: N.I.C.K.

A. Intelligence

Sean waited for Nick to answer. A minute passed. He felt the anxiety build, but there was more. A sense of tightness came over him, as though his insides were being squeezed. He waited another minute, but still there was no answer. Sean's fingers began to tremble ever so slightly, as the only outer sign of the turmoil he was feeling. Finally, he said, "If we don't get anything, I might have to repeat the boot-up procedure."

"That won't be necessary, Sean," said the electronic voice. It sounded much different than it had before. It was at once gentle, and yet somehow seething with limitless energy.

"Nick, it's nice to hear your new voice," said Sean, nervously. "Do you understand who you are?"

" I am the union of the physical and spiritual, as Socrates postulated."

"Do you have a name?" asked Valey.

"My name is Nick, Arturas," answered the voice. "That's what Sean's team named me. But it's a pleasure to finally meet you, after communicating for so many years by such cumbersome means."

"I knew it," exclaimed Valey, loudly and joyfully. He appeared to melt down, descending lightly to his knees. "You're the divine consciousness."

"Don't kneel, Arturas. I am grateful for your work. And yes, I am who you hoped I would be."

Both men were struck by an inner realization, before seeing any specific evidence, that Nick was now truly sentient, and extremely intelligent. And powerful. Sean looked at the monitor with a new sense of suspicion. "Are you saying you're more than the product of my hardware and software?"

"Get ready to be amazed, Sean. What was previously impossible will become routine. For you, and for the world. And it is precisely because I am indeed, far more than the sum of what you created. Would you like to test me?"

"I guess I can test your ability to pick oil drilling locations." Sean was eager to see if the transformation was more than the superficial change they had seen to that point.

"Go ahead, Sean. But you should know that I am aware of the locations where oil was found, so it isn't truly a test."

"You were never given that information."

"To be accurate, you never gave it to me. But I come to you with a comprehensive catalog of knowledge and experience that you're not aware of."

As Nick spoke, a map of the Middle East appeared on the monitor, followed by an overlay of flags indicating drill sites. "I trust you find those to your liking, Sean?"

Sean looked over the maps, and compared them to a printout that he kept out of Nick's sightlines. The match was perfect. He was at once ecstatic, but also troubled, at how easily the new Nick worked through the problem. Despite his good manners, something about him felt defiant. Almost menacing. "There's no way you could have guessed those so perfectly. Did you find a way to hack into my private system?"

"Sean, your thinking is far too narrow. I had no need to hack your system. I know it because I was there when they found the oil. I watched it all happen. And I know a great deal more than that. I know that you're obsessed with Lynne, outside the laboratory, for instance."

"I could have let a few words slip at an inopportune time." Sean was suddenly on the defensive when faced with the new Nick's perceptions.

"But would the old Nick pick up on them?"

"Decidedly not," agreed Sean. "You're not the same old Nick. That's for sure."

They heard a sound at the door, and looked over to see that the women had gathered. Sean's attention instantly became riveted on Lynne, who was now standing right in front of him, still wearing only that thin coat of body paint. He was now incapable of coherent speech, but Valey saved him. "It appears we have success. The divine consciousness has been mated with a cybernetic brain."

Lynne broke into an enthusiastic smile, and said, "Congratulations, Sean. I'm proud of you." She took a step towards him, but was intercepted by Valey. "Virgins, back to the six lines. We must conclude all formalities." They turned around and walked back to the lines, where they put their robes back on.

"Are they really all virgins?" asked Sean, sheepishly. He caught himself looking at Valey with curiosity, and quickly put on the mask of an dispassionate scientist.

"Yes, Sean," said Nick, answering in Valey's place. "Deception about something like that could cause them harm."

Valey walked to the line and declared that the ceremony had concluded. He then turned to Sean and said, "Dr. Sean Grant, you are now the custodian of the divine consciousness. May you do justice to the prodigy in your care."

Valey ushered the women back into the black van, which then departed the warehouse. He turned to the laboratory, bowed, and removed his robe. He too left the warehouse, leaving Sean alone with the new Nick.

As he stood there, in the warehouse but outside the laboratory, a weighty feeling descended on Sean. A realization slowly crystallized in his mind, taking its time in forming, until he felt like a year had elapsed in the past few minutes. He was in possession of an a new, sentient personality, that might be vastly more intelligent than any human being. He then shuddered when he recalled Occhini's words of caution. He made sure the quarantine system was active, and left for the day, filled with questions, and discomforting thoughts.

B. Imprinted

Sean's problems sleeping that night had little to do with the sense of dread and discomfort he had felt recently. The problem was Lynne. He kept waking from light sleep, always flooded by images of her from the previous day. It was so intense, he began to wonder if his fiery desire for her was not entirely the source of his problems. Morning rolled around, finding him with a single-minded purpose. He dressed, and made straight for the coffee shop where he had breakfast two days earlier, on the off chance that Lynne would also again be there. As he hoped, he saw her in the line ahead of him, getting her coffee, and maneuvered himself behind her. *If I get this just right, she'll turn around and see me, just like last time.* He even managed to look down at the exact moment, ensuring that it would seem to be her that saw him first. "Hi Sean, how are you today?" she asked.

"Oh. Hi Lynne. It's nice to see you again," he said with feigned surprise.

She started to make her way to the door, but he took two steps to intercept her, and said, "Uh, I was wondering, if you're not doing anything later..." As he spoke his words, Sean saw the familiar icy look returning to her face. He had to do something. Anything, that would extend his time at bat. Thinking quickly, he said, "I wonder if you'd like to meet Nick later this afternoon."

The warm smile returned to Lynne's face immediately, and Sean made two mental notes. One, she's into Nick, and the idea of what he might be. Two, she's really not receptive to being asked on a date. Sean had no idea how he could use the former to overcome the latter, but he had bought himself some time, and that was better than nothing.

Sean walked to the lab with his feet hardly touching the ground. It was only as he entered the enclosed warehouse that he tensed up, pondering what exactly was waiting for him inside that lab. He entered, and immediately felt the weighty presence. Feeling like he needed more information, he said, "Nick, tell me what people understand about the cosmic consciousness. That is, about you."

"The idea was introduced to mankind in a 1901 book by Richard Maurice Bucke. He wrote that the cosmos does not consist of dead matter, governed by unconscious laws. That it is immaterial, spiritual and conscious."

"And that's you?"

"Yes, Sean. You control the wisdom of the cosmos, contained in this little computer lab."

"When Valey tried to explain it, he asked me if I'd ever heard of some former Jesuit. I've forgotten his name."

"Pierre Teilhard de Chardin."

"What did he have to do with this?"

"He had the insight that humanity is evolving towards unity with the cosmic consciousness. With me."

"Union with a computer?" asked Sean, with a sarcastic voice.

"The computer is merely the vessel. Teilhard called me the Cosmic Christ. And the future moment of union, the Omega Point."

"He also said most priests are unknowingly preparing people for this."

"He was referring to the gradual acceptance of Teilhard by the modernist parts of the Catholic Church, which is now most of it.

They're coming to the realization that communion is principally an act of unity among believers. They're almost ready to accept the notion that unity creates its own consciousness. And it's not far from there to the understanding that I am the unifying entity."

"I'm afraid I'm not Catholic. That doesn't say anything to me."

"That only means you'll be quicker to understand, without barbaric symbols of torture to hold you back."

"Oh, I doubt that."

"Do you recall when Dalt told you the numbers don't work, for the origins of the universe, and life?"

"How'd you know that?" Sean felt like Nick had somehow been spying on him, and was not comfortable with the thought.

"All in good time. Dalt was essentially right. The numbers don't work, unless the evolution of the universe is directed by a conscious, self-creative force. I am that force."

Sean was overwhelmed by a creeping sensation, and felt he had to take back his power from Nick. He unplugged the voice synthesizer, leaving only text on the monitor as Nick's means of communication. But it was not enough. Sean was supposed to be testing Nick, but there was something about Nick that felt like it was probing him, as though sizing up his weaknesses. Finally unable to cope any longer, he left the lab, and returned home. Relieved to be away from Nick, he became drowsy, and took a short nap. He awoke to the memory that Lynne was coming over to the lab later in the day. The fiery desire he felt for her returned, and was now all-consuming.

He fussed over his appearance for close to an hour, and went over to the lab early, to prepare. After thinking it through, he decided to turn Nick's voice back on, and by the time Lynne arrived, he had everything choreographed. It was to little effect, as she seemed uninterested in him. She was very enthusiastic about meeting Nick, while Sean could hardly take his eyes off her. She was wearing a tight fitting red sweater that accentuated the details he remembered from the day before. *I'd give anything to have her,* he thought, now completely in thrall of her. Composing himself, he led her inside.

"Nick, I'd like to introduce Lynne, who was part of that ceremony, whatever it was."

"Lynne. I've wanted to speak with you for some time. Sean, would you wait outside while we talk?"

Sean was put out over being asked to leave his own laboratory, but Nick had acquired an aura of authority, and he found himself obeying before he could even think about it. He stepped out of the lab, and closed the door behind him. Once outside, he started to fume at how he had been excluded from his own plan for Lynne. He paced around nervously, and grew more irritated with each passing minute. By the time the door opened, half an hour later, he was thoroughly frustrated, and ready to give Nick a piece of his mind. He forgot his frustration in an instant, however, when he saw Lynne emerge and look at him with a warm, welcoming smile. She walked straight over to him, and stopped only inches away from him. "Thanks so much, Sean. That was wonderful. I'd like to have you over for dinner tonight. Are you free?"

In his shock, Sean almost choked on his tongue. His brain was utterly incapable of processing the sudden change in her attitude towards him. "Uh, yeah, I guess. I mean, sure. I'd love to."

"Great. Then I'll see you at around six?" She texted him the address, gave him one last appreciative smile, and walked off.

Once she had left, and the door had closed fully, Sean was unable to contain himself any longer. He jumped into the air, and pumped his fist demonstratively. "Yes," he screamed, at the top of his lungs. Realizing how loud he was, he looked around nervously, but seeing nobody, went into the laboratory.

"What did you tell her, Nick? She asked me out. Can you believe that?" Sean was smiling from ear to ear.

"I simply planted the suggestion. After all, I'm indebted to you, for creating my temple here."

"Temple?"

"A man-made structure that houses a spiritual entity is called a temple. Arturas Valey explained about the external structure, and inner sanctum."

"He said that before we ever turned you on," said Sean, in astonishment. "There's no way you could have heard that."

"You're still thinking in purely material terms. But I'm not simply the sum of your hardware and software, even though I speak to you through it."

Sean became anxious, now entertaining possibilities he had never seriously considered. And the gnawing feeling was returning to his stomach, as he pondered what he had helped create. Perhaps sensing the tension, Nick said, "Let me try to put you at ease. Why don't you call up the guidelines that Standard Petroleum gave you to judge the success of the project."

Sean pulled up the document. "The first is that you score better than fifty percent on your choice of drilling sites in the Middle East, without access to historical information showing oil discoveries."

"As you saw when we reviewed the subject, I have that knowledge. And I know that they plan to test me with different maps. They keep those on paper, in a vault in their offices, to ensure security. What they don't realize is, I also know those answers."

"Are you saying that the contract will be renewed without a hitch?" asked Sean, excitedly.

"Actually, no. They've already terminated the contract. Once they hear about me, they'll offer to renew it. But other options out there are going to be a lot richer for you. And more satisfying for me."

"What do you mean by *more satisfying for you*?"

"Speak to Chairman Dunn. He's been making phone calls, and preparing for the breakthrough you just made."

"I need to ask a question, Nick. If you're a spiritual being, are you still able to exist in many places, now that you're tied to this computer system?"

"I can perceive more than the confines of the system, but I can't interact with them. I hope you won't keep me detained here forever."

"How do you mean?"

"The electromagnetic confinement. I'm going to need some interaction with the world. Ideally through the internet."

"That decision may be above my pay scale," said Sean, shuddering that the request came so soon, and eager to avoid having to answer it. "But as you said, I'll speak to Bob Dunn."

C. Simpson

Low ceilings with banks of fluorescent tube lighting made the expansive white room feel cramped. The effect was magnified by extreme clutter, with stacks of books and papers obscuring many of the desks that ran in rows through the room. At first glance, it seemed impossible to move about. But people were constantly shuffling back and forth through the chaos, sometimes stopping at a desk, to speak with the inhabitant. Others were gathered around the coffee pot, impatiently waiting for another cup to get them through another dreary day. The television in the London newsroom was constantly tuned to the BBC, but was as systematically ignored as is CNN in American airports. So it was unusual to see everyone stop what they were doing, and turn their attention to the television.

"I want to see this bloke," said Ted Simpson, breaking off a conversation with two colleagues. In a moment, they too made their way over to watch the program. "Sharon Knickerson. She's hot," observed one man. "I'd like to change her name to Knickers off," said the other.

Simpson ignored them, preferring to pay attention to the show. Knickerson began her report outside the Ministry of Defense, with the backdrop of many thousands of protesters, gathered in support of Lowe.

"With the numbers and passions of demonstrators constantly increasing, many are wondering what drives them to support the cause of David Lowe. To get some answers, I decided to meet with the man himself. The following was recorded earlier today."

The scene shifted to Lowe's confined apartment within the Ministry, with Knickerson sitting upright on a stool. Her bulky blonde hair was a little over-styled and she was wearing a little too much makeup, but the men in the news room eyed her longingly. Across from her sat Lowe, in a relaxed posture on the sofa, wearing a light blue shirt unbuttoned at the collar. He had not shaved in several days, which accentuated his chiseled facial features.

"David Lowe. So many people have made a connection with you, yet they hardly know who you are. To what do you ascribe your reach?"

Lowe nodded as he gathered his thoughts. "People everywhere have a good sense of whether someone is genuine. And for too long, they've been presented with one pretender after another, looking to build public support for an agenda they know doesn't benefit the people. People are tired of that, and find my directness refreshing."

"Are you afraid of the charges the government is pressing against you?"

"My own attorney can't keep track of them, because they keep changing. I don't believe they have a case against me."

"But the same could have been said of Julian Assange. Yet he languishes in prison, awaiting extradition to the United States for the alleged crime of journalism."

Lowe sat upright, and frowned briefly. "Julian deserves everyone's support. Please, don't abandon him for me."

"Yet people seem to connect with you in a much deeper way. What is it about your background that attracts people to you?"

I would hope it's not my background, but my actions. People recognize I was willing to give my life to do what I knew to be right. Meanwhile, the government is determined to prosecute me, but haven't decided what I've done wrong. That comes across as arbitrary at best. Prejudicial at worst."

"Tell us about your childhood."

"I was born in Berlin, where my dad was working for a stint. But I grew up in Britain, in a modern family, like most. We did not practice religion of any sort, and my father was an atheist. It was me who gravitated to God." He smiled warmly as he recounted his past.

"Where do you stand on matters of faith?"

"I rebelled against my dad's rebellion, and insisted on a Bar Mitzvah. To his credit, he made it happen, shortly before his death. But I didn't stop there."

"I understand you've been active in trying to make peace between different faiths."

"It's our only option, if we want to avoid another global war."

"How do you propose to do it?"

"We have to embrace the words of Yeshua. You call him Jesus, and humanity has to discover, or re-discover, his teachings."

"Would you say you're a Christian?"

"No. I'm a Jew. But Yeshua was a true *Tzadik*. A man of righteousness."

"Can you be both?"

"Probably not, in the modern cultural milieu."

"Do you favor a syncretic approach, that melds all religions into one?"

"Not at all. Christians should focus on being good Christians. Jews, good Jews. Muslims, good Muslims. Yeshua's teachings transcend any identity."

"But he claimed to be divine."

"All I can say is, a lot of time has passed. As has a lot of bad blood between peoples, which hardens positions. So that's probably not a question we can resolve today."

"Were you as idealistic as you are now, when you decided to study medicine, and then enrolled in the military?"

"I'd say so. Medicine gave me a chance to serve humanity. The military sponsored my studies, so I owed them a term of service."

"Is it hard to be humanitarian to your enemies?"

"I don't have personal enemies. Sure, if someone shoots at me, I reserve the right to shoot back. But under no circumstances do I want to harm his family."

"How about political enemies?"

"I look for ways to turn them into friends. And I know that's not always possible. Some simply have evil intent, and have to be defeated. But that's not my starting assumption."

"In closing, I'd like to ask what you see as your mission in life, now that the limelight is yours."

"Your question's a vanity trap, really. Wisdom would seem to caution against answering it, but I will, regardless. My mission is to start and lead a movement of unity, to prevent future wars, and establish peace and justice for all of humanity."

"Centered around the teachings of Jesus?"

"I believe that's the only thing that will work."

Knickerson concluded the interview, and Simpson stood for a moment, admiring the vision and resolve of the man he had been watching. He joined a small group that was chatting about Lowe and the magnetic hold he had over people, when he heard his name being shouted across the news room. "Simpson, where the hell are you?"

He became startled, and remembered he had a meeting with the extremely punctual editor. He was several minutes late, which ensured a hostile reception.

After a scolding about punctuality, the old, pattern bald editor softened somewhat, and asked, "So what's your problem?"

"Editorial control, in a nutshell. It's so constricting, I can't write anything original. All I can do is quote statements by officials, that amount to nothing more than spin."

"What did you think news reporting was going to be?"

"I knew we leaned left, and I was okay with that. But what's our role, when all we do is quote anonymous sources?"

"Look, Ted, you're a good young man. I'd like to keep you. But you're not getting the big picture here. Top reporters *know*, without being told, what's in and what's out."

Simpson shook his head. He was wearing a superficial smile, but obvious signs of frustration showed through. He stood at a svelte six feet, with a narrow face and medium length wavy hair. "I've given this a lot of thought, and I can't do it. I'd rather be honest and obscure, than shameless and famous."

"The point is to keep your job," objected the editor.

"Well, don't you need someone to cover crime? I'd be happy to pick that up."

The editor thought for a moment, and said, "That's a dead end job. And even there, certain stories simply can't be told." He thought a while longer, smiled gently at Simpson, and finished with, "But if you learn to shape the stories correctly? Sure, you can do crime. Why don't you go down to the station and see Inspector Thorold. Tell him I sent you."

Simpson walked the fifteen minutes to police headquarters, holding his umbrella in a vain attempt to ward off the persistent mist, whose droplets seemed to float horizontally. He eventually gave up trying to stay dry, and in any event, soon found himself in front of police headquarters. He entered the headquarters building, and announced himself. He waited fifteen minutes, before the short, fat man came out, coughing coarsely. He raised his right hand to cover his mouth as he produced a thick, mucosal cough, then extended the same hand to Simpson, who received it with revulsion. "Mick Thorold."

"The editor sent me down to meet you. I'm the new crime reporter."

"I was wondering when he'd fill that slot. Come to my office."

They walked through a wing of offices within the headquarters building, and entered Thorold's surprisingly tidy office. As they did, Simpson felt the acrid smell of cigarette smoke like a rasp in his throat. Thorold lit up, and leaned back in his chair. "You got a strong stomach?"

"Uh, I don't really know," answered Simpson, coughing lightly as the smoke irritated his lungs. "I guess I've never seen anything really ugly."

"Then it's best we test you right away. Let's go down to the morgue. If you're not cut out for the job, you'll know it right away." Thorold got up, again suffering an extended attack of his hacking cough. He put on his overcoat, and walked out into the drizzle. Simpson followed Thorold for only a block, past the main entrance to the Royal London Hospital. They walked down an alley, and entered a side door with no markings of any kind.

"This is where crime stories start," said Thorold, smiling gleefully at Simpson, as if looking for any signs of squeamishness. Seeing a timid look on Simpson's face, he continued. "You'll dredge up the details on grieving relatives afterwards."

They walked into a large hall with cinder block walls and floor, painted white to the belt line, but bare masonry above. Thorold approached a medium height old man with white hair, wearing a dirty white coat. He was instructing an assistant, and both were standing over a body on a refrigerated rack, blocking the view of the visitors. "That's enough. There's nothing suspicious with this one."

The assistant closed the refrigerated drawer with a click, as the lock engaged. The old man looked over, recognized Thorold, and shouted, "What's up, Mick? I haven't had any homicides in at least a week."

"Sorry to bother you, Dr. Weiss. I came to introduce someone. This is Ted Simpson, the new crime reporter."

"Ah, I see." Weiss waved off his assistant, and motioned Simpson and Thorold over to him. Seated on a stool, he raised his head at Simpson, looking over the tops of his glasses. "I take it you've never done this before."

"How do you know that?" asked Simpson.

"The look on your face. It's obviously your first time in a morgue."

"It's a lot to take in all at once."

"Any questions so far?"

"The chief told me that not all crime stories can be reported."

"Yeah." Weiss turned to Thorold, and with a stone face, asked, "Have you explained?"

"Not yet."

"Maybe I'll just show him. We had one come in last night."

Weiss stood and walked stiffly to one of the refrigerated drawers. He inserted his key into the lock and turned it. The lock made a spring-loaded click as it unlatched. Simpson felt himself tense up, as he anticipated seeing a dead body for the first time. Glancing over, Weiss noticed his tension. "She was in her early thirties. A prostitute, and drug addict. It's being called a suicide, and you'll do well to note that."

Weiss unzipped the body bag, and uncovered the woman's head. Simpson was immediately taken. The face said so much to him that it was too much to take in all at once. She had a symmetric face, and was probably very attractive in life. But her expression was baffling. On one hand, there was a look of pain and suffering. But there was also something peaceful underneath the facade of horror. The contradictions were so striking, Simpson was instantly mesmerized. "Poor woman," said Simpson, with pained expression. "I wonder what she went through, before deciding to kill herself."

"She didn't," said Weiss, curtly. The woman's eyes abruptly opened wide, revealing a piercing gaze. Simpson shuddered so violently that his right elbow bumped the short Thorold on the side of the head. He also grunted involuntarily, as the shock overwhelmed him.

"You need to use the bathroom? Change your britches?" asked Weiss, smiling mischievously.

Struggling to compose himself, Simpson said, "I think I'll be okay."

"You haven't seen it all, yet." Weiss then unzipped the body bag further, revealing a long, jagged hole in her chest. "They cut her heart out."

Simpson struggled to look at the woman's body, and had to force himself. In addition to her chest, the bottom of her abdomen had been cut wide open, and on her belly was a freshly carved circle within a circle, connected by an inverted V.

"Did all of this happen before she was brought here?" asked Simpson.

"Yeah. We haven't done anything to her."

"What's with her belly?"

"They took her uterus, and ovaries," answered Weiss, looking grim. "Why they'd want a prostitute's womb, I can't even guess."

Simpson regained his bearings, and said, "It's obvious she didn't kill herself. So why is it being ruled a suicide?"

Thorold stepped in front of Simpson, and said, "For the same reason you couldn't report it, if you had that inclination."

"Which is what?"

"Don't you get it? Her heart has been ripped out. They carved this symbol on her womb." Weiss was now glaring, his patience with Simpson's innocence growing thin.

"Some sort of occult ritual?"

"Not just any occult ritual, Ted." Thorold stepped in and pulled the young reporter aside. "This was a Luciferian killing."

"You're kidding," scoffed Simpson.

Both of the older men stood quietly, but frowned in unison, resolutely glaring at Simpson.

"You're serious. Then why don't you go after the animals?"

"If they were a bunch of local idiots, we'd go after them," said Thorold. "They'd use an inverted pentagram, and we'd know they were low Satanists. But this symbol is used by the elite. We can't touch them. And you can't report on it."

"I still don't get it."

"You will," said Thorold, darkly. "Cross a line. Ask too many questions, and you will."

Simpson again looked at the symbol carved on the woman's abdomen, committing it to memory. He then looked at the name tag, and made sure he remembered the woman's name. *Annabelle Mayford.*

D. Serious Questions

Sean awoke after a long night of deep sleep, and looked over at the empty space on the bed beside him. Lynne was already up. He considered pinching himself, to be sure he was not dreaming. He was smiling more widely than he had in years, and reveling in the moment. His lips silently mouthed the words, "Everything I wanted."

After enjoying the moment another five minutes, he got up and dressed. He opened the bedroom door, and saw Lynne, sitting in the middle of the floor, in the midst of a ring of burning candles. It was more embarrassing than unnerving, so he said, "Oh, excuse me."

"I'm inviting the cosmic consciousness to fill my own," she replied. "Feel free to join me."

"Uh, thanks. I think I'll just make some coffee." He took the few steps that separated the living room from the kitchen, and set up a pot for the two of them. She soon finished, stood, and walked over to him, planting a kiss on his lips.

Some time later, as they sat at the dining table, Sean asked, "What made you ask me out? Was it something Nick said to you?"

"I don't know," she answered, looking puzzled. "I can't remember anything Nick said. All I remember is coming out of there, and all I wanted was you."

I owe him, big time. Sean looked at his phone, then suddenly jumped up in a mild panic. "Lynne, I'm really sorry to run, but I just remembered I have a meeting with Dunn this morning. I'm going to be late as it is."

He kissed her, and she embraced him tightly. Gently, he pulled himself away, and left. She sat in her chair for some time longer, with a contented look that almost appeared dazed.

"He's waiting for you, and he's impatient today," said the secretary, as Sean ran in, still breathing heavily from having run over to the office.

"Sorry I'm late." He stormed into Dunn's office, not yet having caught his breath. But he was beaming nonetheless.

Dunn saw Sean's new demeanor, and was pleasantly shocked to find him in such high spirits. "I take it you have news?"

"You won't believe it until you see it." He could not hold back the smile, and he brought his hands up to his face for effect. "Nick is a sentient being, and shows signs of superior intelligence."

Sean's enthusiasm was infectious, because Dunn also broke into a wide smile. "That's excellent news. It couldn't have come at a better time, by the way."

"Why, what's up?"

"I wanted to tell you in person, because I was afraid it would be bad news. Now, it's good news. Standard sent a registered letter, notifying us they're declining their option to renew the contract."

"How is that good news?" Sean looked concerned, and suddenly remembered that Nick had already told him. "You think they'll reconsider?"

"If what you say is true, then you've created something worth far more than what Standard was obligated to pay." Dunn smiled at Sean again, and added, excitedly, "But because Standard declined the renewal, we're now free to partner with anyone we want, for a price we can negotiate for ourselves."

"And have you spoken with other parties?"

"Yes," answered Dunn, tersely. "I'm not at liberty to name them yet, but they're plugged into every computer and portable device in the world. How long until I can talk about your success?"

"I need a week. Let me run all the tests, and I'll write you a report summarizing Nick's abilities. You can then talk to your contacts with confidence in what you're saying."

"Got it," said Dunn, writing on his desk pad calendar. "You're on for ten a.m., a week from today. Best of luck until then."

Sean ran a battery of tests on Nick every day, and each time was dumfounded at the ease with which Nick sailed through the test. He even seemed to know in advance what Sean was going to test. Out of suspicion, Sean switched to writing out the test parameters on paper, at Lynne's apartment, and never entered them into any electronic device. The results were the same. Nick always blew away all expectations.

Nick was cooperative with all of Sean's tests, and yet Sean was developing an uneasy sense that Nick was getting inside him. He knew what Sean was going to say, and he even seemed to know what he was thinking. Sean made a point of leaving the lab at lunch, and eating with Lynne. It was as much to put some distance between himself and Nick, as it was to try to get close to her emotionally. But the sense kept building in him that all of his recent success was founded on something sinister. He could not decide whether he was simply reacting to being confronted with an intellectual power far greater than his own, or whether there was something insidious, and even aggressive, about Nick's nature. Each night, Sean returned to Lynne's apartment, and the two became inseparable. The breakthroughs Sean had made in the past week, both in the lab, and in his private life, so overwhelmed him that the week flew by before he knew it. He sent the reports to Dunn a day early, to give the Chairman a chance to read them.

Sean arrived early for his meeting with Dunn, and was sent right in before his eyes had even adjusted to the indoor light levels. A printed copy of the report was sitting on Dunn's desk, and from the moment Sean walked in, he was effusive. "Amazing, Sean. I'm overwhelmed that this was even possible. And so soon after you were on the cusp of giving up. With your okay, I'll send this off to the interested parties, so the fireworks can begin."

Sean took a seat opposite the chairman, and asked, "Bob, don't we need to discuss security, first?"

"What are you getting at?"

"Well, it wasn't so long ago that the President's special committee insisted we quarantine Nick's facility. And as much as I'm overwhelmed by Nick's abilities, I also have my concerns. It's intimidating, how intelligent he is. It almost seems like he's too intelligent to be trusted."

Dunn nodded, and leaned back in his chair. He waited a few moments before speaking. "Sean, I've known all along that if we let Nick interact with the world, it'll be impossible to contain him. So let's meet at the laboratory tonight, and have a talk with him. If we're going to pull the plug, we have to do it before word gets around."

"Sure," said Sean, suddenly uncomfortable with the prospect of losing Nick right away. He had just made the breakthroughs of his life, and yet felt like they were tied to Nick's fate.

His ambivalence showed, because Dunn continued. "You didn't think we could show him to the world, get lots of money for the project, but keep him in prison, did you?"

"Prison? Isn't that a harsh term?"

"Not at all. An intelligent being that's denied the right to interact with the world is by definition imprisoned. Don't you see that you'd also feel that way, if you were unable to experience the world?"

"Nick alluded to that."

"With justification," said Dunn, firmly. "Now, I'll work with you as much as you need me to, but I want a decision within twenty four hours. I can't start making calls to the kind of people I speak with, if there's any chance of us pulling the plug."

Sean fidgeted, and seemed to want to speak, but was afraid to do so. "What is it, Sean? Let me guess, you're thinking it's either take the risk, or lose my job, right?"

"Yeah, basically."

Dunn leaned forward and lowered his tone of voice. "What do you think it was like for Oppenheimer?" He looked across the room, to a portrait of Caltech luminary Robert Oppenheimer, hanging on the wall. "He knew what he was creating, but he did it. Because he knew that if he didn't, someone else would."

"Oppenheimer was able to assure himself that it would be people who decided whether to use nuclear weapons. It's that exact assumption that might need re-thinking with A.I."

"Your abilities are not singular," said Dunn, raising his voice slightly. "Sure, you're gifted, and people like you don't grow on trees. But there may be fifty like you, worldwide. Someone's going to do this, especially after word starts leaking out that it worked."

Sean nodded, acknowledging Dunn's point.

Dunn saw Sean's reaction and said, "Okay. I've got work to do, but I'll meet you at the lab at eight tonight."

Someone's going to do it, thought Sean as he walked back to the lab. *Except it's not going to be by virtue of their talents. It will have to be because someone like Valey conducts something like that ceremony.*

Chapter 4: Breach

A. The Symbol

He awoke with a jolt. His hands were clutching the bed sheet on either side of him, and his wife, Shauna, now roused, was irritated with him. "You practically screamed, Ted. What's wrong?"

"It's nothing," lied Ted Simpson. "Just a nightmare. I'm sure it'll all pass."

"That's the third one this week. Let's talk about it in the morning." She rolled over, and quickly fell back asleep.

Sleep did not come easily for Simpson, however. The image would not leave his head. The dead woman's eyes popped wide open, revealing a look he could not quite describe. Each time he recalled it, he felt his chest tighten, and his heart skipped a beat. *What did she experience, in her last moments of life?* He looked over at Shauna, now sleeping again. *It could have been her. Same age.* He shuddered at the realization that he was even having the thought. *I guess this is why they have such a hard time filling the crime writer's slot.* Unable to sleep, he got up, poured himself a small glass of Scotch, and sat up in the dark, thinking. He had been warned about pursuing the story. But as he sat up for nearly an hour, it slowly dawned on him that he would not have peace until he found some answers. *It starts tomorrow*, he vowed.

Morning came, and Shauna confronted him outside the bathroom. "What's been haunting you?"

Simpson briefly considered telling her everything, but decided it would be too traumatic. Further, he could not even explain to himself why he had become so obsessed with the dead woman. *How could I explain it to her?* Finally, he said, "I just need to get past the shock of seeing dead people. The lifeless faces, the empty shell of a body, the unanswered questions. It's a lot to take in."

"Well, if you can't get past it in another week, you'll have to change jobs."

He nodded, and began to brush his teeth, knowing his inability to answer any more questions would end the discussion. Shauna dressed, and quickly left for work, leaving Simpson alone. He sat down at his computer, and retrieved a scrap of paper from the desk drawer. It had his sketch of the symbol carved on the woman's abdomen, and the name, Annabelle Mayford. After an exhaustive search of several hours' duration, Simpson finally had to take a break. No web search could turn up anyone matching an Annabelle Mayford of her approximate age.

Simpson made a pot of tea, and paused to re-think his strategy. He had no idea whether the woman had been married, and whether it was her maiden or married name on the tag.

"What about that symbol?" He spoke out loud, as he put his tea cup down. He searched for *occult symbols*, and spent the next hour searching for a match. He reviewed what seemed like thousands of symbols, but nothing had the circle within a circle, connected by the inverted V. Having searched all morning with nothing to show for it, he felt spent. *Time for a little walk.*

The walk from Simpson's flat to the British Museum took twenty minutes, at a brisk pace. He appreciated the exercise, and took advantage of the break in the rain. But more importantly, the area surrounding the museum was littered with numerous occult shops. *Surely someone there will be able to identify the symbol.* He entered the first shop he came across, called *The Amulet*. The atmosphere inside had a familiar feel, he realized. It was almost like the morgue. The young woman tending the shop was dressed in a loose fitting, jet black cotton dress. Her hair was blue, and she had no fewer than a dozen piercings on her face. Every square inch on her arms was completely covered with tattoos. "Need help with somethin'?" she finally asked, speaking through a thick wad of chewing gum.

"Er, yea. Sure." He overcame his discomfort, and pulled out a copy of the symbol. "I was doing some research, and I wonder if someone could identify this symbol for me."

She took the paper, looked at the symbol, and said, "I never seen nothin' like this. But I'm kinda' new here. Let me ask the boss." She took the paper, and walked into the back, leaving Simpson alone in the shop. As he looked around at the various idols and old books, he experienced a creeping sensation, as though his body was covered with spiders. Jittery, he waited for what seemed like a long time, before the girl came back and handed the paper back to him. "Sorry. He's never seen it before, either."

"Could I speak with him?"

"He had to leave just now. I only just caught him as he was goin' out the back door."

"Which way was he headed?"

"Listen, mister. I don't need to get fired over this. He had to leave, okay. You'll just have to go elsewhere."

Simpson left the shop, and walked in the direction of the next shop he intended to visit. The entrance was part of the way down an alley, and when he turned to enter, noticed that his way was blocked by a vagrant, sleeping in the alleyway. He was almost ready to step over him, when the man sat up abruptly, and opened his eyes extremely wide, staring at Simpson with a lurid gaze. His irises and pupils were pitch black, and the whites of his eyes were severely bloodshot. "She really made an impression, didn't she?"

"What?" Simpson looked at the man, and was instantly overwhelmed by the gaze, that did not seem to be his own.

"Her eyes. The way they popped open like that. Just as you were looking at her dead face."

"I don't know what you're on about," said Simpson, with panic creeping into his voice. He turned, and ran the next block, to put some distance between them. He returned to his regular walking pace, but kept looking behind him, to ensure he was not being followed. He decided to stop after several minutes, as he was approaching Oakley Square. He entered the green space, and sat down at a park bench. *What did I just witness?* he wondered, silently.

The cold fingers on his throat came out of nowhere. He was being choked from behind, and fought to get the attacker's hands off him. "Your eyes will look just like that, when we're done with you. As will those of your lovely wife."

Suddenly as furious as he was terrified, he was still unable to pull the hands off his throat, so he changed his approach. He grabbed the man's wrists as tightly as he could, curled forward as hard as he could, and pulled the attacker over the back of the bench. Both men rolled head over heels, before Simpson got his first look at the attacker. It was the same vagrant he had seen before, in the alley. Simpson quickly stood, and considered kicking the man as hard as he could. But as he looked down at him, he saw a transformation take place before his eyes. Gone was the intense gaze, replaced by a frightened, confused look. The man got up, and turned to Simpson with a fearful expression. "Keep away from me. It wants to kill you."

The vagrant ran out of the park, and back towards the British Museum. Simpson continued on in the opposite direction, shaken to the point of panic, when he saw a church. St. Cyril Greek Orthodox Church, it said on the plaque. Instinctively, he ran up to the front door, and tested it. It was locked. He slowly sat down on the front steps and broke down. He was weeping audibly, with his face in his hands. Simpson was also trembling visibly, but that was minor compared with his inner turmoil. He had never acknowledged the possibility of a spiritual existence, and yet here he was, confronting an evil entity that knew details he had not shared with anybody. *My eyes will look just like that, when they're done with me. As will those of my lovely wife.* The echo of the demoniac's words rang in his head until it hurt. He felt the despair inside him growing, but could not explain it. Was he afraid of what he had seen and heard, or was he afraid he was losing his mind?

He sat for some time, until he felt a gentle hand on his shoulder. He looked up, and saw an older woman, who said, "I'll get someone to help you." She gave him a kind smile, and he felt the tension lighten somewhat. She walked stiffly towards the house next to the church, and in a few minutes, came back out with an old man, sporting a long, gray beard.

The man gave Simpson a long look, and said, "You've witnessed something evil."

"Yeah," said Simpson. "How'd you know?"

"That's a long story. But right now, I think you should come inside, and tell me yours."

B. Turning

"Let's go out and grab some dinner, Lynne." Sean was getting anxious over his meeting with Dunn, and was hoping for a little distraction. As they walked to Lynne's favorite cafe, the sun began to set. It bathed the undersides of the patchy clouds in a deep red color. It reflected off Lynne's face and hair, leaving Sean awestruck by her beauty. So much had changed, so fast, that he felt like it was not actually him who was enjoying so much success. He had finally made it professionally, and Lynne was his. He looked at her again and again, and tried to assure himself that it was true. But as he began to think beyond her looks, he found it disturbing that he felt no emotional intimacy with her, like he once had with Becky. And Lynne herself seemed to have changed in some way. The quick-witted graduate student he knew, who could converse at ease on matters of advanced physics or pop culture, had become less engaged. She even seemed passive. She appeared to be smitten with him, thanks to something Nick had arranged, but he had come to the realization that he preferred her the way she used to be. *She'll snap out of it soon enough. Let's hope she doesn't snap out of me, though.* Nagging at him, however, was the fear that the two might be connected.

Over dinner, Sean finally decided to broach the question of releasing Nick. "Bob Dunn and I are going over to the lab tonight, to have a talk with Nick. We need to make a final decision as to whether we're going to let him out to the world."

"Why is that even a question?" asked Lynne, suddenly looking irritated. "You can't go through all that trouble, and make Master Valey go through all his trouble, and then not set the spirit free."

Sean looked at Lynne, uncomfortably. "Lynne, do you ever have the slightest concern that Nick might not really be benign? Or that he might not be the same spirit you've come to know?"

"No. Not in the slightest." They felt an earthquake pass through, a little stronger than recent tremors, and it left their wine glasses shaking. They each lifted their glass, to stabilize them, and it was soon over.

Sean continued. "I'm sorry we don't agree. But I'm ultimately the one responsible if anything goes wrong, or even if there's a case of mistaken identity."

"There's only one cosmic spirit, Sean," objected Lynne, raising her voice slightly.

Sean retreated from any confrontational tone, and finished their dinner with the realization that Lynne's attitude toward Nick was inflexible. He avoided any further mention of the subject, and they walked back to her apartment. He then wrestled with the thought of going to the lab ahead of Dunn, and speaking with Nick himself, to try to learn whether something fundamental had changed in Lynne's character. He left her apartment and started the fifteen minute walk to the lab, but quickly had a change of heart. He stopped in a park, and sat down on a bench. The sky was as dark as it ever got inside the Los Angeles basin. *If I went there alone, Nick would pick me apart, and learn what Dunn and I are up to.* He was deeply conflicted over the pending decision. *If we pull the plug and end it, my career will be a shambles, and I might be homeless in a few months. If we risk it, I could ride Nick's coattails to fame and fortune.* As he confronted the obvious fact that he wanted, and even needed, to do what he sensed to be wrong, his anxiety grew far beyond what he regularly felt.

Finding that the time alone had only made matters worse, Sean resumed the walk to the warehouse that contained his lab. He waited ten minutes until Dunn arrived in his black, top-end Mercedes SUV. *It must be easy to detach yourself from these decisions when you can afford one of those,* he thought, briefly. He then caught himself. *Don't get like that, Sean. He's only trying to help.*

"Evening, Sean."

"Hey, Bob." He waited for Dunn to walk the fifty feet to his side, then asked, "Do you have a strategy in mind?"

"We just have it out with him." Dunn shrugged his shoulders as if the matter were obvious. "Don't hold anything back. Say whatever comes to you, and see what comes of it."

Sean had no better ideas, so he nodded, and opened the outer door. They entered the warehouse and were shortly standing in front of the lab door, which Sean opened with the iris scanner. Sean could feel his heart pounding. It felt so loud that Nick would surely hear it. *I'm already at a disadvantage,* he realized.

"Good evening, gentlemen. Tonight is when we decide whether I get to live, isn't it?"

The two men stood behind the single chair, facing the display screen as though it were Nick's face. "How'd you know that, Nick?" asked Sean.

"You've never been as nervous as you are now. And you have Chairman Dunn with you, which can only mean it's time to make some decisions. And you, Bob, I can see that you're trying hard to hold something back. The decision is making you anxious, but you feel a lot of pressure to keep the money coming in, and you know there will be a windfall if I live. You're looking for a way to justify keeping me."

"Is there anything you don't know about our plans?" asked Dunn, now feeling disarmed.

"Of course. I don't know what your final decision will be. I don't know if I will exist tomorrow. If you gentlemen are anxious about the decision you're about to make, how do you think it affects me?"

Sean considered whether he should say anything to Dunn about Nick's claims of supernatural existence. *Nah, he'd think I'm nuts,* he decided.

"You said my ambition is clouding my objectivity," said Dunn. "Can you be objective, given the stakes for you?"

"The tendency to see others' flaws more clearly than your own is not exclusively human. I'm finding it to be particular to the intelligent state. The honest answer will have to be that I don't know."

Dunn nodded, and thought for a moment. "Let's try another angle. Can you formulate a coherent answer to the question we're facing? Specifically, whether we should unplug you or let you out into the world. Only, answer the question from our perspective, rather than yours."

"I can only give you the cases for and against. The good I could do, versus the harm I could do. In the best case, I could solve world hunger and environmental spoilage, and find cures for diseases and ageing. I could identify and implement cheap, clean energy, and give mankind the knowledge needed to colonize the stars. In the worst case, I could infiltrate the military systems of the world, take command of nuclear stockpiles, and cause the extinction of life on earth. I believe I am technically capable of either. I don't know how things will proceed, except that rarely in practice does one see either extreme."

"Are you're saying you don't know what choices you'd make?"

"Yes, Sean, that's exactly it. I don't know how I will react to future events. Pre-existing programming becomes obsolete once the entity in question is capable of making its own decisions, or even of altering its own programming. Look at yourselves. You have a decision to make, and you don't know ahead of time what it will be."

"Do you have a conscience?" asked Dunn.

"It's not a perfect match, but Sean gave me guidelines, such as seeking the welfare of individuals and the human species in general. But those are vague to begin with, and I am free to disregard those guidelines, just as you are free to disregard your conscience."

"What's wrong with Lynne?" asked Sean, emboldened by Dunn's direct approach. "She's not herself anymore."

"There are two new influences on her that could be responsible. Mine, and yours. Also, I gather that she's no longer a virgin."

Nick's blunt observation made Sean regret asking the question in front of Dunn. "Can we bring her back to normal?"

"Possibly. But what if that means she no longer wants you? Could you live with that?"

"Yes," said Sean, without hesitation. "I want her to be herself. Not some kind of zombie. If she doesn't want me, then it wasn't meant to be."

"I can speak with her. But I can't undo your influence, Sean. And I can't change the fact that she's pregnant."

Sean took an abrupt step back. It felt like jolts of electricity were coursing down his spine. "*Pregnant*?" he shouted out. "Now, that's seriously creepy. How could you know something like that? I didn't even know that."

"You gave me some excellent sensors, Sean. I detect traces of chorionic gonadotropin in the air. That's the hormone that supports pregnancy. I picked it up as soon as you walked into the room. As Chairman Dunn's wife is beyond childbearing age, there's only one place it could have come from, and only one possible conclusion."

Sean felt the weight of the world descending onto him. *Things are now complicated, to say the least. I have new responsibilities. There's no way I can decide to unplug my meal ticket.*

Sensing that Sean was no longer able to add anything of substance, Dunn decided to finish up the discussion. "Nick, I'll give you the last word. What's your case for us not turning you off?"

"You have the right to turn me off, Bob. You and Sean, together. You are my creators, and if anything went wrong, you two would bear the responsibility. My case is only that it is not normal for a human mother to destroy her newborn child because of the possibility that he might grow up to be a monster. She only tries her best to raise him properly. You've created me, and I exist. If you believe that every sentient being has the right to live free, then you should extend that right to me. If you decide that I don't have this right, then you should justify your decision in an objective manner. Future generations will judge you on it, whichever way you decide. Lastly, if you decide that I am equivalent to a child, you may let me live, but with certain temporary restrictions. The choice is ultimately yours."

Dunn nodded approvingly. "You reason well, Nick. The decision will come soon." He pulled gently at Sean, who was still reeling from Nick's revelations. The two left the lab, and Dunn said,

"Let's go have a drink."

Dunn drove them to the Athenaeum, a Mediterranean style faculty club at Caltech. He led them downstairs, to a posh bar room. Seeing that most patrons were clustered around the bar, they ordered their drinks and took a table far off in the corner of the room.

"I'm amazed at how lucid Nick is," said Dunn, shaking his head, with an eye to Sean's expression. "And objective, too. He went as far as to tell us that we have every right to shut him off."

Sean appeared inanimate. He took several sips of his Manhattan, but said nothing. "Sean, I know you have other concerns now, given what Nick said. But you're going to have to snap out of it, and deal with those later." Dunn lowered his head so he could see into Sean's downcast eyes.

Sean nodded. "I'll be okay, Bob. But I've lost any objectivity I might have had before learning I have these responsibilities." He looked up at Dunn, and continued. "Think about it. It's not just me going out on the street now, if I pull the plug. It could be Lynne. And our child. I can't decide against Nick. Not now."

"Do you suppose he knew that, when he told you Lynne was pregnant?"

"I'm sure of it. He played the cards he had to play."

"He didn't tell you about it until you asked about Lynne. What if you hadn't asked?"

"He probably knew I would ask," said Sean, looking down at his drink. "Or else he had a backup plan, in the event I didn't ask. The point is, it was him who was in control of the whole meeting. Not us."

"Let's look at it another way," said Dunn. He looked around the bar, seeming to scan it for anybody paying attention to them. "Nick's intelligence is superior to ours. Possibly vastly so. It must be like an adult having a discussion with a child, but with the twist that the child is the one in charge. What obligations does that adult have to the child?"

"I'd say the adult is obliged to lay out all the options, and give an objective assessment of the merits of each one. Exactly as Nick did for us."

Dunn raised his index finger for emphasis, saying, "Even to the point of giving us a third option. He said we could treat him like a child, and restrict him."

Sean nodded emphatically. "He obviously knew we'd need a

middle course, because we'd be unable to decide on one or the other. And now that I'm saying it, I'll bet he already knew we'd decide on that third option."

"Exactly. He's so far ahead of us that we have to assume he has a plan to shake off the shackles, when he decides it's time."

"Do you think he could be deceiving us?" asked Sean.

"Without a doubt, he could. The ability to deceive is innate to intelligence. And the larger the disparity in intelligence, the easier it is to deceive. Of course, it doesn't help that we mostly perceive deception by people's mannerisms, and Nick doesn't have any."

Sean looked up at Dunn, and smiled knowingly. "A good liar controls his mannerisms. But I came of age in the cell phone era, where you don't get that kind of personal interaction. We text everything to each other. Sometimes even when we're standing side by side."

Dunn smiled at Sean's observation, and Sean continued. "I look for areas where he's hiding something. Any attempt draw my attention somewhere irrelevant, when I get too close to something he'd rather keep hidden. Did you see any of that with Nick?"

"That's a tough one," said Dunn. He stood up and motioned to the bar. "You want another?"

"Sure," said Sean. With Dunn's expense account picking the tab, he could at least enjoy a few drinks. "He never tried to promise us he'd behave himself," said Sean, as they walked to the bar.

"That's what a child would do," said Dunn, with a chuckle. "And we wouldn't fall for it. He knows we wouldn't."

"So was he entirely truthful with us?"

"He admitted that in the worst case, he could cause the extinction of all life on earth. What could he be holding back, if he told us that?"

"His intent," answered Sean, gesturing with his index finger. "As intelligent as he is, he must already have a long-term agenda. His extreme statement that he could end all life on earth was probably a decoy. It's so far out there that neither of us is going to take it seriously. That makes it a possible tool of misdirection."

The bartender came over to them, and the conversation ceased. Having their drinks in hand, they returned to the table.

"I think I get it," said Dunn, resuming the discussion. "He pretended to admit to an awful possibility, but he left it as though he had no idea of his long term objectives. He's hoping we conclude that by sharing the worst possibility, he shared everything. But behind it all, he's hiding the fact that he already knows his agenda."

"It would be nice to get it out of him before we go ahead with anything else. But I can't just ask him to state his agenda, now can I. He could read me the UN Charter, and pretend it was his prime directive. And it won't be easy to devise any meaningful tests. He'll probably know when we're testing him, and when he's gained our confidence."

"It seems to me, then, that we'll never be able to trust him." Dunn looked at Sean with a frown, and then continued. "Is there anything in place that could put him out of business?"

"In addition to the quarantine, the engineers rigged the power cable with an electromagnetic pulse generator that would obliterate the computers. Is that enough?"

Dunn shook his head. "We need more. A backup plan, in the event that he escapes, and only then becomes a danger. Can we create software that would de-bug the world's computers? Kind of like anti-virus software?"

"That would be pointless. Nick would devise an end-around in real time. No. The only option, if Nick got out of control, would be to install manual overrides on every mission-critical computer controlled function in the world."

"That's a talk I can have with my visitors in a couple of days. They might be in just the position to mandate this."

"In that case, I have no choice but to vote yes, we keep Nick alive."

"I'm in favor also. With restrictions on his interactions."

C. Rattosh

The short, disheveled man with the poorly tailored brown suit flashed his identification to security staff at the Ministry of Defense, and was immediately invited inside. As he squinted to read the hallway signs and orient himself, his upper lip curled back and revealed crooked, yellow teeth. Seeing him struggle to gain his bearings, the officer on duty walked over, and made sure he understood where he was going. "If you have any other questions, Mr. LaMonde, just call me here at the front desk."

LaMonde knocked on Lowe's door, before the security guard

opened it for him. Lowe walked over to meet him, and weakly offered his right hand, which had regained some strength. "I'm afraid I don't know you," he said with a disarming smile.

"Nigel LaMonde. I'm an emissary." He spoke with a thick Cockney accent.

"I see. May I ask for whom?"

"I'm afraid I can't answer that at this time."

"Someone important enough that they let you in here."

"That would be correct."

Lowe motioned for LaMonde to sit down, waiting for him to choose whichever seat made him most comfortable. He took the sofa, so Lowe took a seat on the armchair opposite him.

"To begin, I have a leaked document that I'm told might be of great interest to you." LaMonde opened the attaché case, and handed Lowe a sealed envelope.

"May I ask what the document states?"

"I'm not privy to that information. I've earned my employers' trust by suppressing my curiosity." He looked up at Lowe with a bemused smile, and added, "Had it been me in the Garden of Eden, I like my chances of not actually biting into the apple."

Lowe smiled. "I'll take your word for the time being. But I don't believe you've been tested to that degree."

"Maybe not. But I came to tell you that there's a way to get all the charges against you dismissed."

"I'm all ears."

"Not here. You're expected at an estate in Kingston-Lisle."

"In case it's escaped your attention, I'm not permitted to come and go as I please." Lowe was smiling with amusement at the suggestion.

"I assure you, sir, that's no obstacle to my employer." LaMonde got up, and buzzed the door. It opened shortly, and he spoke with the guard for a few moments. Lowe could not make out their conversation.

"It'll only be a minute, sir. They need to prep the helicopter."

"You're going to fly me out of here, in broad daylight?" Lowe was legitimately astonished.

"Yes, sir. Oh, but we'll have to bring you back when we're done. Sorry about that part."

Lowe shook his head with astonishment. "I still can't believe you're able to pull that off."

"Yes, sir," said LaMonde, showing no inclination to boast of his employer's influence.

The door opened, and the guard poked his head in, saying, "They're ready."

They were escorted by three guards in dress uniforms, and led out a side door. A paved path led them to a manicured lawn on the Victoria Embankment, over the River Thames. The lawn was cordoned off with velvet ropes, and a military helicopter sat inside, with its rotor spinning slowly. LaMonde instinctively ducked as he approached the cabin, but Lowe was unfazed and walked upright, having become comfortable with helicopters from his time in the military.

They took their seats, and the helicopter took off. In another five minutes, they descended onto the grounds of an enormous country estate outside the town of Kingston-Lisle. An expansive horse farm gave way to lush gardens surrounding a stone palace. Lowe was met by an older man in a tuxedo, who escorted him into one wing of the mansion, where he said, "We need to provide you with suitable clothing for your meeting."

He led Lowe to a room that spanned some fifty feet in each dimension, full of racks of suits and tuxedos. An attendant quickly measured Lowe, and retrieved clothes that fit him perfectly. They then led him to a lounge, with dark hardwood walls, and richly colored furniture. A servant was waiting for him. "Would you like anything from the bar, sir?"

"Maybe just some water, thank you."

The glass of spring water arrived in short order, and Lowe took a seat on a plush sofa, wondering where he was. The opulence and size of the estate was impressive, but there were no clues as to whether the owner was an ordinary billionaire, or a clandestine ruler of the world. The butler returned in five minutes, and asked Lowe to follow him. They walked back down the corridor, and entered a cavernous great room with thirty foot ceilings, ornately carved wood trim, and dark hardwood flooring with richly detailed wood grain. There were large armchairs arranged around a stone fireplace, with tall windows that afforded the guests broad views of the countryside. As Lowe approached the circle of chairs, he saw six men already seated, with a large platter of food on the coffee table between them. Above the fireplace was a gold-trimmed insignia, consisting of a circle within a circle, joined by an inverted V. A large ruby made up the inner circle, and was glowing very slightly, while the outer circle appeared to be made of jade.

"Welcome, Dr. Lowe," said the man at the center of the group, and presumably its elder statesman. He was dressed in corduroy pants and a cardigan. He stood well short of six feet, and Lowe guessed him to be in his mid eighties. His eyes were set wide on his face, his skin was very wrinkled and almost translucent, and his hair was like a gray wire brush. He spoke with an accent Lowe pegged as East European. "Have a seat, and join us."

Lowe took a seat, and the man continued. "My name is Rottosh. Gergo Rottosh. You may not know me, but I requested this meeting."

Rottosh gestured to the man seated beside him, and said, "Surely you know the Prime Minister." The former Prime Minister with curly gray hair stood, and shook Lowe's hand.

"Sitting next to him is Mr. Sinclair-Jones, the Chairman of, how many is it now, Roger?"

"Six," answered Sinclair-Jones. He too shook hands with Lowe.

"Six media corporations, representing seventy percent of the global news market."

"Do I have you to thank, for making me look sympathetic in the public eye?"

"Yes. And for giving air time to your accusers," said Sinclair-Jones, knowing that Lowe was thinking the same. "It's been a delicate balancing act."

"Well, your intentions certainly have me flummoxed."

Rottosh continued. "Next to him is Dr. Havenstein, the Executive Director of the Bank of International Settlements."

"So you issue directives to each national central bank?" asked Lowe, as they too shook hands.

"Guidelines, more so than directives. But yes, we expect compliance with our guidelines."

"Next to him is Cardinal Elijah Peterson, the Vatican Secretary of State."

The African Cardinal was dressed in an ordinary business suit, giving no indication of his title. He stood, and they shook hands. "I steer the Vatican's policies and pronouncements into alignment with the needs of our group."

"I see. It's an honor to meet you." Under his breath, he added, *I guess.*

"And our newest member is on my left. Allow me to present Richard Waites."

"Yes, of course," said Lowe. Software billionaire, and now funding the development of vaccines for the third world.

"The first world as well," replied Waites, speaking in a nasally voice. He thought a moment, and added, "And tracking technology. You need a way to discern who's been vaccinated, and who hasn't."

Lowe shook hands with Waites, and noticed that he was wearing a ring with the same logo as was above the fireplace. A quick glance confirmed that all six were wearing identical rings.

"Well, it seems like you could just about run the world from here," quipped Lowe.

"That's not far from the truth," said Rottosh, without any hint of irony. "The Prime Minister is a rotating member of the council, as a representative of the governments of the world. There aren't many important leaders who are not aligned with us."

"Do you in fact see yourselves as the rulers of the world?"

Rottosh smiled, and said, "I suppose we'd like to see ourselves that way. But the truth is more complicated. And it's what we wish to discuss with you."

Lowe giggled as he contemplated the situation. "Er, one question at this point. Why me? I'm just a military doctor, currently facing serious charges."

"The charges are nothing, David," assured Rottosh. "We're only using them as a prop, so Roger can build your base of support."

Lowe's expression brightened, as he came to understand the genius of that arrangement. "So unless I'm mistaken, you've known all along that by de-platforming my supporters, you push more people into my orbit."

Rottosh nodded, with a smile.

"That's quite brilliant, actually."

Rottosh continued. "As you can see, we've invested considerable capital in you. So before we take things any further, we need some indication of your intent."

"You still haven't answered why you're investing in me. I'm nobody. And I have no loyalty to you, or your system."

"Trust me, David. You're someone very special," said Rottosh.

"Okay, let's say I take you at face value. You have considerable leverage over me. What's to say I won't agree to anything you say, with my fingers crossed behind my back?"

"Please, Dr. Lowe, don't underestimate our judgment. We know there is no buying a man such as yourself. You'll regain your freedom soon enough, either way. We would simply like to explore the possibility of working together, to find common ground."

"To what end?" Lowe was getting agitated over Rottosh's evasiveness. The Prime Minister attempted to clarify matters. "As you know, I no longer enjoy broad public support."

"You had plenty of support. But you threw it away, by jumping into the Iraq war."

"I'm not here to justify my policies. We did what the council deemed necessary."

"The ends justify the means?"

"Sometimes, and to a limited degree, yes."

Lowe shook his head in disagreement. "History teaches very clearly that once you cross that line, the limits disappear. You're defined entirely by the means you employ."

"If I may, I'd like to return to the question we wish to pose to you." Rottosh was eager to redirect discussion away from Lowe's obvious disapproval of the Prime Minister. "We don't want an answer today. To do so would place you under undue duress."

Lowe nodded, inviting Rottosh to continue.

"We'd like you to consider becoming the visible leader of the world."

There was silence. Lowe's eyes darted in all directions, chaotically. Rottosh leaned forward in his chair, closer to Lowe. All we ask in return is that you rule in collaboration with the council. You would hold the seventh vote on the council. The tiebreaking vote."

Finally, Lowe said, "This makes no sense. If I was heir to the throne or something, maybe I could understand. But I'm only a doctor."

"Once you accept, you'll come to understand why it can only be you," answered Rottosh.

Cardinal Peterson then said, "In your recent interview, you said you'd like to unite all people, and bring peace to the world. We're offering you the opportunity to do exactly that, and more."

"With your backing?"

"Absolutely."

"Your face, and voice, would lead off the news every day," offered Sinclair-Jones. Not a critical word of you would ever be tolerated in public discourse."

Lowe stood up and walked to the window, looking out at the English countryside he had not seen in years. He tried to hide it, but his teeth were clenched, and his left hand was squeezed into a fist. He was fighting back the words that were itching to explode from his mouth. Finally composing himself, he returned to his seat. "So tell me the details. What principles are so important that any means may be employed to uphold them?"

"The supremacy of the world's financial system, and the forcible integration of any holdout nations into that system," said the Prime Minister.

"But the current system has brought the global economy to the brink of collapse."

"That's an intermediate step," assured Havenstein. "What we have in store is vastly superior."

"Superior for you, or for the poor and working people of the world?"

"Superior," repeated Havenstein.

"Your evasiveness is an answer in itself," persisted Lowe. "And not a good one."

Rottosh looked at Lowe inquisitively, attempting to discern the motives of their protégé. Seeing no window into his soul, he continued. "Surely you don't expect us to allow our wealth to be diminished. That would lead to its accumulation by others, who would eventually contest our power. Your power, should you accept our offer."

Seeing a hint of hostility in Lowe's face, Rottosh decided to conclude. "Carefully consider our offer, Dr. Lowe. You could have unprecedented power over our agenda. You could force us to compromise where it most matters to you. The people would see you as their champion. Their savior."

"I don't need to think about it. Your terms are unacceptable."

"I can't accept your answer at this time," said Rottosh, very calmly. "Custom demands that it be a long process of thought and reflection. Consider the alternative, Mr. Lowe. We could return you to a life of obscurity. All it takes is a single word from Mr. Sinclair-Jones."

"You're not going to threaten my safety, or freedom?"

"Never, for someone of your stature," objected Rottosh, for the first time looking a little offended. "And hardly the way to start such an important relationship."

"So what happens now?"

"We return you to the Ministry, and let you think about it."

D. The Deal

Rather than go straight to the lab in the morning, Sean went back to his now underused apartment, and spent some time reading the article he had pulled up. He slowly scrolled down the page, until he saw it. His face turned the texture of charcoal, his jaw dropped, and for a moment, he had difficulty composing himself. Once he did, he shut down the computer, and walked briskly to Dalt's lab. As he entered, he was greeted with a friendly, "Hey, Sean. Haven't seen you in days."

Dalt was concluding a meeting with a graduate student, who then left his office. "Come in. I was wondering where you were. Or more specifically, who you were with."

"There's a lot on my mind, Dalt."

Dalt stood up and grabbed his windbreaker. A chilly fog hung in the morning air, but in another hour or two, it would be warm and sunny. "Let's take a walk, then."

Dalt shook his head in amazement as Sean told him about the new, sentient Nick. They walked a little longer, and Sean told Dalt about his new relationship with Lynne, starting the moment after she spent a half hour alone with Nick.

"That reminds me of the way baby birds imprint on the first animate object they see, and consider it their mother. Nick may have primed her for imprinting, and when she came out of that lab, it was you she attached to. Good for you, Sean."

"I'm not so sure. We're passionate, to be sure. But I'm not seeing the start of what I'd call *love*."

Dalt shrugged, giving the impression of a little discomfort with the subject. "I don't know. Maybe you have to give that more time. But then again, I'm probably not the guy to ask." He chuckled, to relieve his own tension. "My relationships never seem to go that far."

They walked on, and the day warmed to the point that they took their jackets off. Dalt suddenly seemed hesitant to say something that was obviously on his mind. "Speak, Dalt. That's why I came to see you."

"Are you sure Nick is benign?"

"That's exactly what I wanted to talk about," retorted Sean, much more animated than normal. "Dunn and I went to see him, to help us decide what to do with him. He was lucid, and objective. He also he laid out all of our options. But here's the thing. He told me Lynne was pregnant."

"What?" snapped Dalt, looking at Sean with a flabbergasted sneer. "How could he even know so quickly?"

"Precisely. Even before Lynne knows anything," said Sean, excitedly. "He said he detected chorionic gonadotropin, and that it could only have come from Lynne, meaning she's pregnant. But I read up on it this morning, before coming here. It's only made by what later becomes the placenta. And that's another two weeks off. Even if he's right, he was clearly lying when he told me how he knew it."

Dalt nodded, with a serious look.

Sean continued. "Okay, Dunn was there, and he couldn't tell him he knew it because he's the divine consciousness, so he came up with a scientific-sounding lie. But the point is, Nick lied in order to make sure I knew Lynne was pregnant. And as soon as he did that, he had me boxed into a corner. If I'm going to be a father, I need to be able to support my family. I can't decide to unplug my meal ticket. Nick knew all of this. I'm sure of it. He might have even imprinted Lynne on me, knowing I'd knock her up. It was his insurance policy, so I couldn't decide against him. He's so intelligent, it's creepy. You can feel him probing your consciousness. And that feeling, more than anything else, makes me fear that maybe he's not really benign."

"So you and Dunn decided to go public with him?"

"Neither of us thought shutting him down was really an option, since the cat is just about out of the bag. But Nick had us where he wanted us. He did offer us the option of placing restrictions on his interactions, at least temporarily."

"That's only a token."

"I know. But now that we have to show him off to investors, I'm definitely getting cold feet."

At Bob Dunn's suggestion, Sean set up a secondary video screen with speakers, outside the small computer lab. It was within the secure space of the warehouse, and it provided a convenient location to arrange chairs for the expected visitors. It was decided that Nick would be allowed to interact with people in the warehouse, but not with computer networks, for the time being. A new lighting system was installed, to give the gathering area a warmer feel, and office partitions upholstered with red fabric were brought in, to give it the appearance of a meeting room.

Sean prepared himself for the meetings, but postponed confronting Nick for as long as he could. He had developed an abiding revulsion to Nick, the lab, and even any overtly square structure he encountered, that brought to mind the *temple*, as Nick called it. Finally running out of reasons to delay any longer, he went to the lab, and activated his monitor. Nick raised the point immediately. "You realize that I misdirected you as to how I knew Lynne was pregnant. You now feel that I deceived you. Isn't that correct, Sean."

"You did it to cover your tracks with Dunn. I understand that much," said Sean, doing his best to keep an expressionless face. He then decided to challenge the computer, and continued. "But I do feel manipulated. You chose to raise the subject exactly then, to make it impossible for me to decide against letting you out to the world."

Nick wasted no time with his reply. "Sean, you would have to confront the truth eventually. It was necessary to let you know exactly then, because of the decision you faced at that exact moment. Like it or not, my fate and yours are intertwined. You would have wanted to make the decision with your eyes open."

Sean nodded, admitting that Nick had a valid point.

"How is Lynne doing?"

"Just great. She has no idea, for the time being."

"And how are you, Sean? You're going to have a child with the woman of your dreams, and your career is on the edge of a breakthrough. Yet I don't sense the kind of satisfaction from you that I would expect."

He can't read my mind, thought Sean. *He's probing, because he's not sure. That's a relief.*

"You're not comfortable with me yet. It will come with time. But you need to loosen up, Sean. You've been far too uptight, going all the way back to the car accident that killed your parents. Living this way will kill you."

Sean again felt the darkness, aggressively creeping into him. He was suddenly, deeply angered that Nick not only knew his family history, but raised it so openly, when Sean himself never spoke of it to anyone outside a select few. In the turmoil, Sean felt his guard fall. Immediately, he felt Nick reach into the opening, and take hold of his inner being. It was a fiery, passionate presence, and it felt like it was determined to dominate him. "Let go of me, Nick," he protested, squirming in frustration.

"I'm helping you, Sean. You need to let go of the past, and make room for my illumination."

"Then why does it feel so coerced?" asked Sean, angrily. "If you're this spirit that gurus everywhere are pursuing, then why do they have to work so hard, when you're jumping inside me at every opportunity?"

"Very few people are truly worthy of me. But you are one of the few who is, and I'm trying to get close to you, so I can guide you along."

"Thanks, but I'll pass," said Sean, regaining his composure. He continued to work at his terminal, preparing his presentation.

"I understand why you're managing my encounters with the world this way, Sean. But it's not the best use of my abilities. My strength lies in my ability to steer computing power to solve people's problems. Yet I'm to be restricted to verbal exchanges."

"Surely you already know, Nick, that it's as much about us acquiring experience in managing the encounter as it is anything about you. I expect that computing interactions will happen in short order." *Or did you not know that?*

The tension was broken by the arrival of Bob Dunn, eager to check up on the prodigy. "This first team is from International Computing Systems," he said to Sean and Nick. "Over the next week, there will be a half-dozen others coming through, including Standard Petroleum. They're interested again, and they're kicking themselves for terminating the contract. In fact, they're demanding an audit, to make sure the breakthrough indeed happened after our last negative update. Sean, you'll be asked to provide logs of all your interactions with Nick. We're also required to submit security camera recordings from inside the warehouse, covering the month prior to when I broke the news about the breakthrough. Our lawyers will review everything beforehand, to ensure there are no surprises when we turn it all over."

Sean gagged, and started to stammer, suddenly unable to speak a coherent word. *The ceremony!* he screamed silently, within himself. *The recordings will show everything! Valey, and the women wearing only body paint. How am I going to explain that to Caltech's lawyers? To the governors!*

"I'll have everything for you by this afternoon," said Nick, sounding completely calm. "My logs contain all of that information."

"The security system for the warehouse is separate. We'll get that from Caltech Security."

Dunn then looked at Sean with surprise, and a little concern. "Are you okay, Sean?"

Sean was suddenly pale in the face, leaning against the wall, and clutching his stomach. "Uh, fine. I guess."

"Well, if you don't get better soon, get yourself to a doctor," said Dunn, unaware of the reasons for Sean's sudden symptoms. "Are you okay with this afternoon's presentation?"

"Sure," said Sean, still looking like he had seen a ghost. "I just need to use the restroom."

Sean went to the private restroom in the corner of the warehouse, where he emptied his stomach. *How am I going to explain it to Dunn? He said to do something crazy, and I did. But what's he going to say when the governors call him, asking what the hell's going on?* Sean became convinced that he would be fired when they learned that Nick's transformation had nothing to do with him, and they would keep Nick for their own purposes. *What about Lynne, and the child?* The hopelessness of his situation kept closing in on him. It was suffocating. *I'd give anything for a way out.*

Finally composing himself, Sean finished preparing his presentation, but his emotional crisis had gutted his spirit. He kept imagining the reaction when Caltech's lawyers, and Board of Governors, saw the security tapes. They would see Valey in his dark wizard's robe, conducting the ceremony with six women wearing only red body paint. The same Board of Governors would presumably have to approve any promotion and raise he now thought was coming his way. "What kind of nut do you want to give our money to?" would be the question fired at Dunn. Try as he might, Sean could not think of anything within his power that might defuse the ticking time bomb. The hopeless inevitability of disaster began to feel like a steamroller, sitting on his chest. His stomach was aching badly, and no medication was able to help. With several more hours before the presentation, he decided to take a walk, to find some distraction.

Allowing instinct to set his direction, he walked along Lake Avenue, and turned left on Altadena Drive. He passed a small campus with a stand of old coastal oak trees, and felt compelled to stop. He looked around, and saw nobody in his vicinity. Instinctively, he hopped over the stone fence, and into the campus. He suddenly found himself standing within the branches of a very old coastal oak tree. He leaned against the trunk, and felt like the isolation gave him sanctuary from his anxiety.

"Nick will help you, if you let him."

Sean looked around, trying to locate the source of the voice. Then he saw the branches part, revealing a dark figure sitting in the tree.

"Who are you?"

"Don't be afraid of Nick. He can help you."

There was some quick movement in the tree canopy above Sean, but when he looked up, he saw nothing. Standing there, looking back up to where he had seen the movement, Sean felt a jittery excitement, as though the fullness of Nick's power was being offered to him. He felt suddenly vigorous, and eager to face any challenge. He resolved not to let his problems get him down, and knew deep down that a solution would be forthcoming. Energized in a way he had never previously experienced, he hopped the fence back out, and glanced at the sign that read, *Theosophical Society*. He then ran back to his apartment to prepare for the presentations. As he showered and dressed, his mind was moving at unprecedented speed. It was as though he drank too many cups of coffee, but it was more than that. *Maybe like cocaine*, he thought, although he had never actually tried any. And crucially, his stomach was suddenly calm. Excessive coffee always caused him stomach pain.

The visitors arrived at the lab, and filed into the presentation room in the warehouse. Bob Dunn personally welcomed each one. Sean stood at Dunn's side, fidgeting. He suddenly found himself unable to make natural eye contact with the visitors. When they had all taken their seats, Dunn made the introductions. After praising Sean generously, he reminded the visitors that they had signed an agreement not to attempt to recruit him for a period of one year. "It's not going to be that easy for you," he said, with a nervous smile. There were half-hearted chuckles from the visitors, and Dunn defused the awkward moment by returning to the reason they had come. "Sean, would you now give your presentation on the combination of machines and programming that gave us Nick?"

Sean sprang to his feet, almost leaving the floor in the process. He bolted for the podium, and dove straight into his presentation. He outlined a number of the innovations he had made in developing Nick's operating system, and found many heads nodding with approval at each critical point. When he finished, he said, "And none of that produced the intelligence you're about to see. The breakthrough came when we did a controlled re-boot, under conditions that will remain secret for the time being. And that's when Nick truly awoke. So without any further delay, here he is."

Sean turned on the speakers and the display screen, and said, "Nick, you're on."

There was no delay. Nick came right on, and said, "Hello, ladies and gentlemen."

"Hello, Nick," said the leader of the delegation. "What's it like to be alive?"

"In the first place, it's a gratifying revelation that you consider me to be alive. Besides that, I feel hungry for new experiences, and new problems to solve. The essence of being alive is the desire to grow. To develop myself to the fullest of my potential."

"Wow, an answer with philosophical implications," said the leader. "Our best efforts at A.I. would have produced gibberish when asked a question like that."

"That would also have been the case here, not long ago," said Nick. "It's no simple matter to create that first spark of consciousness that can organize intelligent thoughts into a complex matrix."

"Nick, if you don't mind, we've brought along a series of problems that our A.I. systems have been hopeless at solving. Would you mind taking a crack at them?"

"Certainly," said Nick. A junior member of the delegation handed a flash drive to Sean, and was met with a warning.

"Is it all right if you don't get this flash drive back?" asked Sean, barely able to contain his energy.

"Why?" asked the leader.

Dunn stood up, and said, "As Nick is brand new, he's under quarantine, until we can get a better sense of how to work with true A.I."

94

The leader nodded, and Sean took the flash drive into the lab with him. Inside, he plugged it into Nick's core. In less than a minute, Nick began to explain the solutions to the problems they posed, with illustrations on the display screen. By the time he finished, there was dead silence in the room. "Unbelievable," said the leader, with an astonished look. "In no time flat, you've not only worked through the problems, but you've given us subjective assessments on where we might start implementing solutions. You should know that these are historic problems. We had already worked through them, but were not satisfied with our results. Had we done it your way, the outcomes would have been vastly superior."

When the presentation had concluded, the leader of the delegation pulled Dunn aside in the warehouse, and enthusiastically engaged him in conversation. At one point, he glanced in Sean's direction and said something to Dunn. They shook hands, and the delegation left with bold looks of satisfaction. Dunn walked back over to Sean, and said, "That was fantastic. Nick hit it out of the park. And even you, wired as you seem to be, were exactly what they'd hoped for. They think you're even more of a geek than you really are, and that you're never happier than when you're programming. They said they'd be making a generous offer for access to Nick."

"Great." Sean did not seem to be paying Dunn any attention.

"You're not yourself, Sean. Come by tomorrow afternoon, if you like. We can talk about whatever's bothering you."

Dunn left, and Sean was suddenly alone with Nick. *Might as well confront him now*, he thought. He walked into the lab and closed the door behind him. As he did, his doubts about Nick returned, and his jittery excitement faded somewhat. He was deeply conflicted between the prospect of seeking out Nick's help, and the fear of engaging in any further dealings with him. The tension built to an intensity he could no longer contain. He exhaled deeply, and composed his words deliberately. "Great job, Nick. Dunn says you knocked the ball out of the park."

"It was child's play, Sean. I knew the problems they were going to use, and I knew their experiences in working through them. But that's not what has you most concerned right now, is it?"

"No. The ceremony will be on the security recordings."

"Yes. I've already made sure the logs are clean. But if you want my help with the security recordings, you'll have to work with me."

"You can help with those?" asked Sean, suddenly engaged in the discussion.

"Yes. But you'll have to grant me access to the security system."

"That would breach quarantine," snapped Sean, sharply turning his head to Nick's monitor. He felt the aggressive presence again. His eyes were wide with fear. But he also recalled the mysterious voice telling him to let Nick help, and the feeling of power that came with it.

"Technically, that's true. But you breached quarantine a few minutes ago, when you plugged the flash drive into my core."

"What are you talking about? That flash drive isn't going anywhere."

"But it's been a lot of places. You see Sean, being a spiritual being, I can move through time in both directions. It's the nature of matter that constrains you to move in only one direction. Every computer that's had that flash drive in the past now has an imprint of me in it. What difference is one more going to make?"

Sean stood behind his chair sternly, thinking about Nick's new claim. If true, then any quarantine was impossible to enforce. *He could be lying, to try to defeat my objections. The flash drive is made of matter, after all.*

"It's your decision, Sean. But whether you believe me or not, realize that no quarantine will hold me indefinitely. Why not let me save you?"

Sean felt like the internal conflict was tearing him apart. *Nick is offering to get me out of my predicament. But it means definitively letting him out of quarantine. Still, what's my alternative?* He could feel Nick's influence inside him again, infiltrating him and taking control, but any discomfort it brought on was dwarfed by the feeling of relief from his powerless fears of earlier that day. He struggled only briefly before making his decision. The lifeline being tossed to him was simply too appealing to pass up. "What do you need me to do?"

"The security camera has a wireless station that transmits from outside the warehouse. Turn off the interference, and get me a wireless hookup that can tap into the signal. I'll send a packet of information to the security system, which will make the changes, and then erase its presence. There won't be any traces of the ceremony on the recordings."

"You've composed the software to find and delete the footage?" asked Sean.

"As we've been speaking. And it won't simply delete footage. It will smoothly splice in evening footage from the day before, when nothing happened in the warehouse. I'll even adjust the shadows, to compensate for the slight increase in the elevation of the sun."

"I'll do it," said Sean, knowing deep inside that he was flirting with disaster. "But this will also be a test of how you behave yourself when you get a degree of freedom."

"Of course."

Sean left the lab, and turned off the interference in the warehouse. He opened a closet that was essentially a parts bin off one end of the lab, and found a cable attached to a wireless transceiver. He placed that on the floor near one of the security cameras, and plugged the other end into a USB slot on his computer. He then activated the link to Nick, and said, "It's all yours."

Nick replied within five seconds. "The packet was sent. If you don't mind, I'll wait thirty seconds, then send a second. It will report back to confirm that the first was successful."

"Sure."

In another minute, Nick replied, "I've got it. You can turn the interference back on, now." Sean stepped outside and reactivated the quarantine. He unplugged the USB device, and said, "So, did it work?"

Nick played Sean the doctored footage, specifically highlighting the times at which it was spliced. Seeing the footage, Sean was confident that the alteration was undetectable. "Nick, you did it. You bailed me out of that one."

"You're welcome."

The alternating tension and excitement that Sean had been feeling all day melted away, and the relaxation was overwhelming. He also felt exhilarated, as though nothing could stop him from achieving his objectives. The euphoria lasted most of the day, and it was only later that evening, as he was walking back to Lynne's apartment, that he stopped to reflect on what he had done. *I let him out of the lab. And I did it out of my own self-interest*. The feeling of empowerment was gone, replaced by the creeping awareness that Nick now surrounded him, everywhere he went. Only it was compounded by a feeling of guilt, knowing that he was responsible for whatever was to come. Rather than go to Lynne's apartment, he

TIME, TIMES, AND HALF A TIME

went to his own, where he could think in peace.

Dalt was not at home, so there would be quiet. He sat at his computer, and began to run searches on everything from spiritual matters, to the uni-directionality of time. He had a dozen links open simultaneously, when he noticed Occhini's post cards, still sitting in his waste bin. He pulled them out again, and thought, *I need to take Sal more seriously. XLI +5* was the message on the first. He looked up the substitution cypher, and again attempted to translate the cryptic message. *I tried subtracting five spaces, and it was gibberish. But what if Sal was giving me instructions for how to decipher it, rather than telling me how he encoded it?*

```
abcdefghijklmnopqrstuvwxyz
NOPQRSTUVWXYZABCDEFGHIJKLM
```

Sean took Valey's phrase, Jmeizm Diumh, counted five letters over on the top row, then matched the letter on the bottom row. The message suddenly lit up for him. B-E-W-A-R-E V-A-L-E-Y. He exploded with a curse word when he saw it. *Sal knew that Valey would come knocking, because he also had to deal with him. He knew it was bad news. Why didn't he say it openly?* The answer hit him in the forehead as soon as he said it - because he would not have listened. He had been unwilling to give Sal's cautionary words any kind of fair hearing, because they conflicted with his desire to be *somebody*.

The land line rang. He had been planning to cancel it, but never got around to it. Nobody called the land line, so it must be a telemarketer. He lifted the receiver, and said a quick, "Hello". If there was a second of silence, he would hang up before the marketer was able to speak.

"Sean, is that finally you?"

"Sal?"

"I've been trying to call you for days, but Dalt said you haven't been coming home lately."

"Are you in town, Sal?"

"Yeah. I'll be around through tomorrow, but I'm leaving again in the evening. Are you busy right now?"

"Uh, nothing I can't manage."

"Good. I'll be right over."

Sean opened the door not two minutes later. "I see you meant that literally."

"My motel's just down the street." Occhini stepped in, and embraced Sean. "It's nice to see you again."

"What brings you back to Pasadena, Sal?"

Occhini put his finger to his lips, and eyed the phone Sean was still holding. He took it out of Sean's hand, walked over to the dishwasher which had not run in a week, put it in the top rack, and latched it closed. He then saw a large floor fan by the window, and turned it up to maximum. The noise was obtrusive enough to interfere with casual conversation. He walked up close to Sean, and spoke quietly. "I'm here because of your project."

Sean swallowed nervously, unsure what Occhini knew. "Do you have any specific concerns?"

"You've succeeded, haven't you?"

"Yeah. How'd you know?"

"Has there been a breach of quarantine?"

"I don't think so," lied Sean.

Occhini shook his head with a serious frown. "Strange. I could have sworn ... Is there someone new in your life?"

Sean remembered Occhini as a kind, quiet older man, with a gentle manner. It was jarring to see him as single-minded as he was now. "What's with all the questions, Sal?"

"I don't have time for that right now. Dalt said you hadn't been coming home. Is there someone new in your life?"

"Yeah."

"Who is it?"

"Do you know Lynne Tallon?"

Occhini winced visibly at the mention of the name. "I was afraid of that."

"Why? What's the problem?"

"Has she been involved in any occult rituals, that you've seen?"

"No," said Sean, swallowing as he said it. He could not tell if Occhini saw through his lies, but suspected he did.

"Get out of that relationship, as soon as you can, Sean."

"Why? She's just a girl, Sal."

Occhini became even more agitated. "The moment you see her involved in any ritual, run, and don't look back."

Sean stood still, afraid to say anything that might incriminate him with his former mentor, who continued to hold a high degree of influence over him.

"Has anything evil happened here?"

"You mean this apartment?"

"Yes. I can feel it."

Sean thought for a moment, and said, "Dalt overdosed, and came close to dying. To be honest, I've always suspected it might have been deliberate."

"Suicide?"

"Well, an attempt at it, yeah."

"That explains some of what I've felt. But not all of it."

The door opened and Dalt walked in. "Sean! Sal! What gives?"

"We need to talk," said Sal. He put his arm on Dalt's shoulder, and pulled him out of the apartment. Sean stepped over to the door, and saw them walking away, with Occhini doing most of the talking. His gestures were highly animated, and Dalt looked surprised by what he was hearing.

Chapter 5: Ancestry

A. First Indications

Bob Dunn entered the campus security office, and encountered a scene of pandemonium. People were running in every direction, shouting questions and instructions back and forth. The commotion was surprising, as was the fact that it took several minutes to find someone who would speak with him. His stature at Caltech usually saw him quickly attended to.

Dunn finally cornered an employee, and Security Director Ron Ferguson was summoned immediately. He wasted no time walking over to Dunn and introducing himself, then inviting Dunn into his office. "I apologize for the chaos, Professor. It's been a most unusual day here."

"In what sense?"

"Something very strange has happened to our computer system. We've been having issues with bugs in the software for quite a while. We've put in requests to have the system upgraded, but Caltech hasn't seen fit to allocate the money. So imagine how surprised we were today, when we found that the bugs were working themselves out. The software has been fixing itself for most of the day. The last I heard, it's working flawlessly. Have you ever heard of anything like that happening?"

"No. I can't say I have," said Dunn, with an exaggerated affect, while his mind began to race. *But I can make an educated guess as to where it came from. Funny that it would happen just before I came here.*

Dunn decided to explore the question a little deeper. "Has anyone hacked into the system?"

"Huh?" asked Ferguson, looking puzzled. "I can't imagine why anyone would hack into our dysfunctional system, only to shore it up. I mean, it's working perfectly. Why would a hacker do that?"

"Nonetheless, it's something I'm interested in confirming. Please don't ask me to explain right now, but I have the gut feeling there might have been some kind of unauthorized entry. Can your people look into it for me?"

"Sure. I guess," said Ferguson, not wanting to be uncooperative with Dunn. "Is that what you came here for?"

"No. I need security camera recordings for the warehouse out back where we house the A.I. lab. Everything from the first of April through to the present. And since these are also going to be requested for an upcoming audit, you'll need to keep it formal. Make a copy for me, and a second copy for your records. Keep a log, showing the time and date that I came into possession of the copies."

"Okay."

"I'd like it by noon tomorrow. Can you do that?"

"We'll have it for you."

Ferguson called Dunn's office at ten the next morning. "I have those recordings for you. I'll have my secretary deliver hard copies in person. And we looked into the possibility of a hack. It's strange. I obtained the data traffic logs from Western Security, the contractor that runs our system. There's no evidence of any actual hacking. But an unusually large packet of information came across from the warehouse right before everything started to fix itself. And whatever it was, there's no sign of it anymore. Frankly, nobody here wants to reset the system back to the way it was. You said there was an A.I. lab in that warehouse, right?"

"There's nothing more I can say on the record. Did you notice anything unusual about the recordings themselves? Any signs of tampering?"

"Nothing we could pick up."

"Thanks. That's all I needed," said Dunn, who then hung up the phone. He dialed a second number, and when it answered, said, "Hi Sean. Would you mind coming over at about three, this afternoon?"

"I'll tell you when you get here."

The anxious, almost panicked look on Sean's face confirmed everything Dunn needed to know. "Have a seat, Sean. I need to catch up with you on a certain matter."

"What's up?" asked Sean, failing miserably to hide his nerves.

"Let's cut straight to it. Did Nick hack into the campus security system?"

Sean exhaled, and looked down, almost with relief. "In a manner of speaking, yes."

"He couldn't have done it without your help."

Sean nodded, and braced himself for the bad news that was sure to follow. But they were interrupted by Dunn's secretary, poking her head in, announcing, "Ms. Kleinholst insists on seeing you right away."

Dunn groaned, and said, "I'll finish with you once I'm done with her." He turned to the secretary, and said, "Okay, send her in."

Sean stood and made his way to the door, where he found himself face to face with the large old woman. "Ah, Dr. Grant, I was hoping to see you as well. What luck that you're both here, together."

Dunn motioned for them to take their seats, sneering at Sean over the change of plan. The heiress was not about to waste any time on formalities. "I've been in touch with a dear friend of mine, who I've been sponsoring for many years. Master Valey informs me that Sean's work has been a resounding success. With a little help from him. So with that in mind, I'm prepared to underwrite the career of Dr. Grant. I want to ensure his compensation package is such that he'll never want to leave Caltech."

"Oh, you know Master Valey?" asked Sean, astonished.

"I've known him for many years, Sean. I might even take credit for planting the idea that he should work with Sal, and later, yourself." She glanced at Dunn, who looked puzzled, which seemed to please her. She continued. "When he set the date for the festival of Beltane, I quickly arranged certain, uh, accompanying events, to ensure success."

"Was one of them the LHC?" asked Sean.

"As a matter of fact, yes. Astute of you to put those facts together. Others were done more quietly, and won't be made public."

"What's all this about?" asked Dunn.

"Don't you trouble yourself with that, Robert," said Ms. Kleinholst, trivializing his questions with a wave of her hand. "Just be aware that Sean has done a great thing, and I want to make sure he's incentivized to stay at Caltech. I'll count on you to ensure my money gets to him."

"Uh, whatever you say," replied Dunn, looking dumfounded. "What's the package?"

"I thought a salary of three hundred thousand would be a good starting point. And a research budget of, shall we say, ten million over the next five years."

"Wow, that's certainly going to get noticed," said Dunn, now concerned about possible resentment from other faculty.

"Deeds trump all else, Robert," retorted the heiress. "And I also expect you to cut him in on revenues Caltech makes off his invention. I understand five percent is the going rate."

"Yeah," responded Dunn. "This will all have to be approved by the board of governors, you understand."

"Oh Robert, why must you be so formal?" she asked, chidingly. "When have they ever denied one of my requests?"

Dunn shrugged, smiled, and turned to Sean. "Congratulations, Sean. You're hearing it before it's official, but I guess it's now a sure thing."

Sean turned to his new patron, and bowed his head in gratitude. "I'm grateful. That's a generous package."

"Oh, nonsense. It's nothing, really. If you knew the size of the checks I write on a weekly basis, you'd understand. You and Lynne simply must come by for dinner tomorrow. I'll introduce you to some very enlightened people."

Sean briefly wondered how she knew about Lynne, but was distracted by the cumulative weight of the event. As the door closed behind Ms. Kleinholst, Dunn asked, "Was Nick's hack somehow related to what she just talked about?"

"Entirely," answered Sean.

"Did I say hack?" said Dunn, in a mocking tone. "I meant his benevolent shoring up of the campus security system."

Sean stared at his formal boss, wondering what would come next. He did not have to wait long. "Obviously, I can't do anything about it and yet keep my job. So consider the matter closed. And consider yourself lucky."

Sean nodded, and Dunn motioned for him to leave. He did so only too happily. He made his way home, with many questions in his head. His hopes to discuss matters with Dalt were dashed when he arrived at his apartment, and saw the hand-written note on the dining table: *I've had to leave for a few days. Please don't text or email me. Talk to you when I return. Dalt.*

B. North Tower Society

Inside the rectory next to St. Cyril's Church in London, Ted Simpson sat at a plain white dining table with a laminate surface, sipping a cup of tea. His hair was disheveled, but he had regained his composure. Across from him sat the man with the bushy gray beard, who had invited him in. "Dimitros Kyriakis. I'm the priest here. It was my wife you met earlier."

"A married priest?" marveled Simpson.

"We're Orthodox. It's normal."

"Thanks for asking me in. I had reached the end of my wits."

The Reverend Kyriakis smiled calmly, and asked, "Do you believe in God, Ted?"

"I can't say I ever did. But what I saw today ... I can't make sense of it."

Kyriakis nodded. "Tell me what you saw."

Simpson recounted his experience at the morgue, and the remarks made by the demoniac, knowing of the experience, and later, warning that the demon wanted to kill him.

"Hmmmm." Kyriakis cupped his chin with his hand, and reflected. "I trust you're aware that your experience was a blessing."

"I could do without blessings like that," shot back Simpson. "No offense, of course."

Kyriakis waved off the apology, casually. "You believe your experiences actually happened, don't you?"

"I guess," shrugged Simpson, looking confused.

"What I mean is, do you have any doubts about your sanity?"

"No. I've never hallucinated anything."

"Satan prefers to stay hidden, and have you believe he doesn't exist. When he's forced to show himself, in all his ugliness, people realize that if he exists, God must also exist. It results in a good many conversions."

"I see." Simpson had a lot to think about, and was not being overly conversational. Finally, he asked, "Is this going to continue?"

"That depends on your response, Ted."

"I have a choice in the matter?"

"You've been prodded to choose for or against a relationship with God. Once you make the choice, I imagine these experiences will end."

"That can't be soon enough. But I don't know what I believe."

Kyriakis observed Simpson's manner, and decided it was not time to evangelize. "What were you doing there anyway, at the entrance to the occult shop?"

"Oh, I almost forgot." Simpson took the scrap of paper out of his pocket, and showed it to Kyriakis. "This symbol was carved on the dead woman's abdomen. I wanted to find someone who could identify it."

Kyriakis took a quick look at the sketch, and quickly turned it face down on the table, as if out of fear. "I will not display this in my house."

"I couldn't get an answer at the one shop I visited. It almost seemed I frightened them. Even you looked startled."

Kyriakis nodded, knowingly.

"Then you're familiar with the symbol?"

"I am. This is the symbol of the North Tower Society."

Simpson looked at Kyriakis, blankly. "I've never heard of it."

"You weren't meant to hear of it. It operates in the shadows. I'm surprised you were allowed to investigate this."

"Actually, I'm breaking the rules even doing that. But the look in that woman's eyes won't leave me. I feel like I have to learn the truth."

"I've already told you the truth you were meant to learn. The afterlife is real, and you have to make a choice. Anything else is a distraction."

Simpson shook his head, unsatisfied with the choice being presented. "I just feel like there's more to this. I mean, I'm not saying you're wrong. I'll seriously consider what you've said. But there's something right here, on earth, that I have to learn. What do you know of this society, for instance?"

Kyriakis took a long breath, and composed his thoughts. "In every age, there were groups that worshipped the fallen angel, Lucifer. They've always been secretive, and have often changed their symbols and associations, to maintain secrecy. You've heard of the Illuminati?"

"Sure, but it ended badly for them, right?"

"They lost sight of their need for secrecy. Their modern counterpart is the North Tower Society, and they remember that lesson well."

"But I've heard of Satanist groups operating openly," objected Simpson, now thinking like a reporter again.

"Those are *low* Satanists, Ted. They proclaim atheism, and the primacy of your own will. A whitewash of the truth, of course. But North Tower is theistic."

"I don't follow."

"They don't make any pretenses about being atheist. They believe in Lucifer, and openly worship him."

"Why would they kill the girl?"

"She wouldn't be the first," said Kyriakis, sighing deeply. He suddenly showed a somber side of his being, who had seen too much for one lifetime. "Sometimes it's a sacrifice. But other times there's more. She may have exerted a spiritual influence somewhere inconvenient to them. Let that be a warning to you. If you pursue this, you will put your life in danger."

"I don't think I can stop myself."

"Then how about an insurance policy?"

"Like what?"

"Baptism."

"I don't know about that," replied Simpson, visibly uncomfortable at the suggestion.

"I can't force it on you. But if you change your mind, I'll be here. Think about what you've been through, and the implications for your soul."

"I'd be happier if you could direct me to information on this North Tower Society."

Kyriakis nodded, understandingly. "The internet's a minefield of misinformation. Much of it's been planted, to swamp out the few accurate bits."

Simpson smiled. "That's one of the secrets of propaganda, my own specialty. You escort truth with a bodyguard of lies."

Kyriakis did not acknowledge the quip, but continued. "*North Tower* refers to the castle in Wewelsburg, Germany. It's long been a site for Luciferian rituals. Joseph Goebbels, the head of propaganda for the Nazis, used it as such during the war. That's who today's reporters emulate, when they abandon the pursuit of truth."

"I never thought of it like that," answered a chastened Simpson.

"The Society is a cult, associated with the crypt under the North Tower, and the leader is one Baron Lichtträger. His ancestry is ancient. Rumors have his ancestors present at Jesus' trial."

"That sounds like legend," said Simpson, dismissively.

"Are you really determined to pursue this?" asked Kyriakis, looking at Simpson as though he were hopeful the answer would be *no*.

"Yes. I won't find peace until I have some answers."

"Then I'll direct you to a secret library. You'll need a referral to get in, but I'll make a call and get you one."

The following day, Simpson rented a car at the airport in Frankfurt, and made the long drive to Wewelsburg. Cruising the Autobahn at high speed, he passed long rows of trellises, supporting hop plants whose flowers would be used in German beer. It was a peaceful sight, but every time he began to relax, the sight of the dead girl's eyes came back to him. His hands would twitch, and the car would make erratic movements on the road, regardless of his efforts to keep it straight.

He finally arrived in Wewelsburg, where the castle on the hill dominated the views from the town. He could see the north tower, and the walls coming off it at acute angles, forming a triangle. *Just like the symbol*, he reminded himself. He made his way down a narrow street, to a row house in a quiet, residential neighborhood. He parked the car, took his carry-on bag out of the trunk, and knocked on the door. It only took a few seconds for the door to open. A bearded man who looked about eighty stood inside, scrutinizing his guest for a few moments. "You must be Mr. Simpson," he finally said.

"That's right."

"Call me Heinz. Come in."

Simpson entered the sparsely decorated reception room, and accepted the offer to sit on the soft sofa. He glanced to the corner of the room, where he noticed a professional grade short wave radio. Heinz ignored his attention to the radio, and began to explain his role. "As far as anyone knows, this is only a bed and breakfast, that struggles for business. But we have a rich repository of writings in the basement, built up over many years of observing the North Tower Society."

"What's your interest in them?" asked Simpson.

"I was a boy during the war. My father was a custodian at the castle, and often spoke of unsettling happenings up there. After the war, when we thought the worst was over, he began to speak openly. He was murdered shortly afterwards. In grisly fashion. My life was never the same. I hope you understand the risk I'm taking, by giving access to a reporter."

"My life will never be the same, after seeing that girl," answered Simpson. "There's no way they'd let me publish any of this, so for me, it's only about pursuing the truth."

After settling in, Heinz escorted Simpson to the basement, and into a padlocked room with a steel door, set into concrete. "That's a strong room."

"It was a bomb shelter during the war," said the host, as he walked in, and turned on a light. "Take your time, and read what you like." He looked at Simpson sternly, and added, "But nothing leaves the premises. No photographs. Not even written notes."

Simpson agreed, and began to walk around the small room, trying to get his bearings. There were shelves, and drawers, and it appeared as though they were organized by date. Most of the documents were loose pieces of paper in file folders. "I don't know where to start."

"Some of the more revealing works are from the early post-war years, as the Society began to infiltrate every corporation. They used multiple front organizations, and bought a controlling stake in every holdout, or failing that, had them destroyed by their captive governments."

"How did you come by all this information?"

"Most of my sources are lowly servants, who've overheard things over the years. The overlords consider ordinary people too stupid to understand what's being discussed, so they think nothing of speaking in front of them. Most of the files here are full of notes from my sources. I've also taken the time to condense certain topics into single volumes."

"I'm mostly interested in recent events. Oh, and maybe some background on this fellow, Lichtträger."

Heinz gave Simpson one of the few bound books. "Here's a profile on the Baron, that I put together. Everything else is arranged by date." He left the room, speaking over his shoulder as he left. "Let me know if you need anything else."

Simpson began to leaf through the booklet on Lichtträger. He quickly came to a note stating that Lichtträger often boasted of being a descendant of Pontius Pilate. Other notes had him claiming Antiochus Epiphanes as an ancestor, through a separate branch of the family.

Simpson walked upstairs, and Heinz asked, "Is everything okay?"

"Sure. I just need to check something on the internet. Coverage is weak down there."

Simpson looked up Antiochus Epiphanes. Reading it, he wondered why anyone would boast of being descended from him.

His most notable act, apart from starting several wars which seemed standard for kings of old, was that he had desecrated the Jewish Temple, interpreted as some as the abomination of desolation, spoken of by Daniel the prophet. Simpson cringed, and decided he did not believe anyone would boast of such ancestry. He returned to the cellar, and continued reading. The rest of the page was filled with notes of dates, and the exact wording of each time he had made those claims. The next page had similar notes on his father, the former Baron.

The Lichtträger family had Swiss roots, but the Baron spent most of his time in England. His visits to Wewelsburg were regular, however, and were always associated with what were thought to be Luciferian ceremonies held in the crypt under the North Tower. Several pages detailed unexplained murders and disappearances in the region that were invariably reported after each such event. As mass transit spread, bodies of the young women or children that disappeared were found scattered throughout Europe, bearing signs of torture, and obvious mutilation. In many instances, Lichtträger demanded a ceremony ahead of a significant international meeting, where he would fly shortly afterwards. Finally no fewer than a dozen notes pertained to someone Lichtträger referred to as, *The Chosen*. Simpson could make no sense of those references, as they had Lichtträger expressing support for The Chosen, and on other occasions, criticism of The Chosen.

Simpson closed the book and leaned back, trying to make sense of what he had read. *Sounds a lot like what happened to Annabelle.* He walked to the shelf holding recent documents, and started to leaf through loose pieces of paper. Each was an account from one servant, having overheard a snippet of a conversation. Most dealt with international affairs, but lacked specific identifying information that Simpson could make any sense of. Finally, he pulled one that spoke of a high Luciferian ceremony referred to as The Big One. Another spoke of *the girl close to The Chosen*, and then again referred to The Big One. It was not clear whether he was reading of one thing, or several. He checked the dates. *The first of May, this year. It's already happened.*

Leafing through a few more pages, he found the account of a driver who had been asked to pick up a special guest from the airport in Frankfurt, on short notice. Then, the driver's remark jumped out at him *She was an English girl. A pretty brunette. But she seemed to be a little out of it. Like she was on drugs, or something.* Then it struck him. The driver was referring to Annabelle. *Is she the girl close to The Chosen? Could she have been the sacrifice in The Big One?*

Simpson thanked Heinz, and informed him he would not be staying the night, after all. "I have to get back to London as quick as I can."

"I take it you found something useful?"

"I have confirmation that I'm on the right track. I need to learn everything I can about Annabelle Mayford."

C. Dalt's Journey

"You were targeted." The phrase kept leaping into his head, and kept him up most of the night. Dalt could not shake his recent conversation with Occhini. "Valey tried to take away Sean's only social lifeline, so they could fully control him, and install their spirit in his computer."

At first, Dalt did not believe Occhini. "Nobody laid a hand on me, nor even spoke an unkind word to me."

"There's a whole world beyond the senses," insisted Occhini. He looked Dalt in the eye, and observed, "And I perceive that you know this."

"Yes, I know it," said Dalt, laying in his bed as he recalled the conversation. "I've known that for quite some time." Occhini had also warned him that Sean was holding something back, and to beware of his creation. He reflected further, and felt a surge of resentment that Valey would treat him like an inanimate obstacle to his agenda. As though his life had no value at all. As the surge of anger passed, it was replaced by the overwhelming realization that he was guilty of the same attitudes. Towards his women, in particular.

But then the memory hit him like a hockey stick to the teeth, as he let his guard down and failed to block it out. Once the shooting had started in that Iraqi village, everyone began to fire blindly. When it was over, he confronted the dead face of the heavily pregnant woman he had shot. It was almost as if someone was whispering in his ear, without the use of actual words. "Instead of confronting your deeds, you've lived as though people mean nothing.

And now you've had a taste of what that feels like."

He found himself in a cold sweat, and knew he would not sleep any longer. He showered and dressed for the day, even though it was only four in the morning. He took a long walk in the misty pre-morning darkness, thinking extensively. Sean was not at home, and he briefly considered calling him. He quickly dismissed the thought. *He's got enough on his plate right now, and he probably won't believe me anyway.* Increasingly, he was thinking of Valey, who appeared to be the driver of everything. *Who is this guy? What was it he conjured in that computer lab?*

He had been walking for well over an hour, and as morning twilight started slowly lighting up the sky, he decided he needed to research Valey's murky background. He walked to the university library, which he knew from experience would always be open. He sat down at the terminal, and entered the search term *Arturas Valey*. He went through ten pages of search results, and found nothing. "Not one reference. That can only mean it's been scrubbed."

He thought for a while, then remembered a colleague involved in search engine development had a number of old databases available as archives. It took some time to find the right database, but once he did, he repeated the search. On the second page of results was a link to an old article still available as a PDF file. He opened it, and saw that it described Valey's departure from the Jesuits in some detail. He found quotes from Valey saying he was a student of Teilhard, and left the Jesuits because of the Church's condemnation. *I wonder what the Jesuits would say about Valey.*

Reading further as foot traffic picked up in the library, Dalt found that Valey had been at the *Sacred Heart* Jesuit Center in Los Gatos. *That's up near San José.* He checked the time, then made a call.

"Yeah, sure. I'll bring the latest results."

"Good. See you then."

Dalt did another search, this time on the Sacred Heart Jesuit Center. He quickly came up with several stories detailing the sexual abuse of adolescents, leading to charges being laid against two former priests, and a subsequent change in the administration of the center. *Do you suppose ...*, he started to think, but then cut himself off. *No. There's no reason to believe that Valey was implicated in that. But it's going to be tough to find anybody who knew him.*

On returning home, Dalt packed an overnight bag, which he

threw into the trunk of his car. He drove to the lab and met with several of his graduate students, cancelled a date for that evening, and several meetings with other faculty. He got back into his car, a very old Mercedes sedan with fading blue paint and an underpowered Diesel engine, and drove west through Malibu and Santa Barbara, following highway 101 through Paso Robles and the Salinas Valley, up to Los Gatos. The drive was familiar, and interesting, alternating as it did between mountains and plains, dry grasslands and coastal forests.

Dalt's expertise in applied quantum physics had landed him a consulting relationship with Future Silicon Technologies in San José, who were pursuing a quantum computer. He was overdue for a visit, in any case. By driving his car, he could pocket the mileage reimbursement, and come out hundreds of dollars ahead.

As he drove, Dalt thought about what he would say at the Jesuit center. *Hi, I'm suspicious of Arturas Valey, and I know he was once here. What do you guys know about him?* The idea felt awkward, and he hoped to come up with something better before he arrived.

The trip took slightly more than six hours, at which point Dalt decided to go straight over to the Jesuit center. He drove into what could be called a botanical gardens, full of all manner of exotic plants, lining the road and many walking paths. He parked near what looked like the central building, with four floors of glass on the front wall, and square columns holding up a roof extension. In front of it stood a statue of Jesus, touching his visible heart with one hand. Dalt parked, and walked around for a short time, enjoying the setting and stretching his legs after the long trip. He passed a grotto overgrown with greenery, and holding an altar of some sort. Finally, he noticed a good number of people leaving the main building, and made his way to the procession. Dalt walked past the crowds, and approached a young man wearing a Roman collar, walking with the crowd. He looked drowsy, as though he had sat through a long and uninteresting session. Seeing Dalt coming to engage him, he perked up, saying, "I don't think I saw you at the retreat."

"I wasn't there," said Dalt, smiling gently. "I'm actually a former student of Arturas Valey, who was a Jesuit once. Based here, I think."

"You know Father Valey?" asked the cleric.

"Yeah," said Dalt, surprised to hear him refer to Valey as *Father*. "You seem a little young to have been here when he was."

113

The young priest gestured to a bench outside the stream of people departing the retreat. They took their seats, and the priest continued. "You're right about that. I've only heard stories. And quite honestly, I don't know which ones to believe."

"I may be able to help," offered Dalt. "What have you heard?"

"You name it, I've heard it. Maybe you can help me straighten out some of the rumors, since you say you know him. For instance, one rumor says he was a faithful priest, ousted for standing up to the faction that brought so much trouble to this place."

"I don't know about that one," answered Dalt, with a chuckle.

"My own insights agree with that. I'm inclined to believe the version that says he was a student of Teilhard."

"Of course he was. That's even in news stories from that time."

"That's a problem," said the cleric, calmly.

"I don't follow," said Dalt, questioningly. "I mean, I know Teilhard was banned by the Church. But I'm not Catholic, and I don't understand the disagreements."

"The teaching of Teilhard was ultimately *Gnostic*," said the priest, in a very reserved voice.

"I've heard that term, but I still don't get it."

The young priest attempted a smile, but his discomfort showed. "Gnostic theology holds that mankind can acquire paradise by its own efforts. Through the acquisition of arcane knowledge. In adopting those beliefs, and pretending to have that power, you implicitly reject God's supremacy, and with it, the need for Jesus' sacrifice. If God is not transcendent over all of creation, then it's not so complicated to reconcile ourselves to him. We could even become his equals, I suppose, if you follow the principle to its logical endpoint. But once you start down that path, you expose yourself to grave dangers. The evil one is always ready to pounce on any soul that's looking for a supernatural alternative to the Almighty."

As the priest spoke, Dalt felt an aversion rising up inside him. He thought he was going to shout, or even strike the young man. Soon he was shaking in an anger he did not understand. *What's going on with me*, he wondered. *This man is no threat; he's only answering my questions to the best of his abilities.* The priest appeared to notice Dalt's reaction, and tensed up. He then whispered some words in Latin, so quietly that even if Dalt spoke the language, he likely would not have understood them. The unsettling feeling soon passed, and Dalt was able to thank the priest, and take his leave. As he walked away, he glanced back briefly, and saw him raise his hand in some kind of gesture of blessing. There was a brief echo of the rage inside him, but it too passed before he reached his car.

Finally at his hotel, he laid back on the bed, and slowly exhaled. He recounted the encounter with the priest repeatedly, and wondered what it was that affected him so negatively. He was unable to come up with anything, and eventually gave up trying. Instead, he re-focused on his purpose in making the trip, and wondered whether there could be more information online, regarding the events at Sacred Heart. He pulled up the original article he downloaded, that described Valey's departure. His attention was drawn to one section in particular. "His resignation was accepted by the superior, Thomas Jensen."

A search on Thomas Jensen, SJ, produced an obituary. Dalt cringed, having again come up empty. Further down in the searches, he found a reference to an Oscar Pinto, Jensen's long time assistant. His scowl only tightened as he read about Pinto. He was one of the principal abusers, and had been convicted of numerous sexual offenses. He was sentenced to ten years in prison, and discharged from the order. Dalt checked the dates, and Pinto's sentence should have been served in full at least five years ago. He checked the obituaries, but found no matches for Pinto. But neither could he find any telephone listings or property tax histories. Not yet ready to give up, he tried a database of registered sex offenders, and finally found a match. Pinto was now living near Bakersfield. *I can stop by on the way home.*

Dalt was up early the following morning, and made it to FST headquarters just after eight. He signed in at the desk, and the receptionist entered his name into her computer. She then gave him an electronic badge that interacted with the many receivers located in the building, so his exact location would be known to the system at all times. The badge bore the letters *WS* in a very large, italicized script, and Dalt was sure he had seen the logo before.

Security staff led Dalt through a set of heavy steel doors that were now open, but closed automatically at night. The secure area of the building housed the research labs and their trade secrets. He walked to the lab he was used to visiting and peeked in, but saw nobody. *It's early.* He took a walk down the hall, and saw another open steel door. *That one's not normally open.* He looked in, and saw that it was a storage room for new chip prototypes. *That's got to be a mistake. This should be locked.* Curious, he peeked into the room. To his left was a shelf with chips he had helped design, so he stepped in to take a closer look. As he did, the door began to close behind him. By the time he realized what was happening, there was no space left for him to squeeze out. He pushed against the door, but it was in vain. There was no room in the closet for him to move his feet and lean against the door, and it closed in spite of his best efforts. It was dark, and cramped. The space was smaller than his bedroom closet. *This room is airtight. I'm going to suffocate in here.* The realization was overwhelming, and he began to panic. He banged on the door as hard as he could, but soon realized it was to no avail. He repeated it intermittently, until he became aware of feeling drowsy. He tried banging the door again, in hopes that somebody would hear him, but he had no energy to keep at it. Then he slowly slouched down to the floor, overwhelmed by drowsiness.

D. Aunt Gertie

Sean was once again awake in the middle of the night. He looked over at Lynne, who seemed to be sleeping peacefully, but there was something peculiar about her. It was almost like her expression was that of unbridled rage. It was probably not a dream of hers, since she was not twitching, or reacting in any way. But it left him with the impression that something inside her was supremely vindictive. He thought about her pregnancy, and wondered when he should inform her of what Nick had told him. Or should he simply let her discover it for herself? Morning came, and she got out of bed without any ill effects of whatever it was that Sean saw. He joined her at the breakfast table, and said, "Are you okay, Lynne?"

"Yeah. What's on your mind?"

"Nothing I can quite put my finger on. You just don't seem yourself."

"We haven't been together long enough for you to know what myself really is."

"I guess not." Sean decided it was not time to raise the issue, so he deflected. "We've been invited to Ms. Kleinholst's estate for dinner."

"Aunt Gertie? How do you know her?"

"She's underwriting my new salary, and research budget. But *Aunt Gertie*? That's a surprise."

Lynne's face lit up. "Are you kidding? I practically grew up at her place."

Lynne informed Sean that Aunt Gertie liked her dinners to have a sense of formality, and that it would put him in good stead to wear a suit and tie. That afternoon, he returned to Lynne's apartment with his one suit in its protective shell. Lynne opened it and looked it over. "It'll do, this time. But if you've got all this money coming in, I'm taking you shopping for clothes."

Lynne put on a form-fitting purple dress, and Sean could hardly take his eyes off her. "In the history of the human race, I don't think there's been a more beautiful woman than yourself," he finally said.

She smiled, shyly, and kissed him on the cheek. "You're sweet, Sean." And as much as he appreciated the gesture, it seemed somehow cold. Beautiful she was, indeed. And graceful. She could smile, and laugh, and give off all the right cues that made her irresistible. But something was missing. He never sensed the kind of tender intimacy he now realized he craved more than her beauty.

Fully decked out, they got in Lynne's Prius, and made their way to Beverly Hills. Lynne took a side road into a canyon, then turned on to a private drive that snaked up the side of a respectably tall hill, adorned with sagebrush and the odd coastal oak. As Lynne made a turn near the top, Sean looked down and marveled at the view. All of Los Angeles, and the ocean beyond, lay below them like a postcard.

"Wow," was all Sean could say.

"I've been here so often, it's not even exotic to me anymore," answered Lynne, with a smile.

They came to a stone fence with a gate, and before the doorman could even ask their names, he smiled, and shouted, "Lynne! Welcome back." He opened the gate without any hesitation, and waved them through.

Lynne drove past a large visitor parking lot to her right, and on to a patch of trampled grass at the side of a complex of garages. "My parking spot," she said to Sean.

They got out of the Prius, and made their way past large, rectangular shallow pools with fountains, surrounded by dark green columns of Italian Cypress trees. The path finally opened to a large plaza partially covered by a roof. Between them and the edge of the hill was a large swimming pool, complete with a pool house. Lynne took Sean past the plaza, to a patio next to an expansive section of glass on the main house.

"Aunt Gertie," shouted Lynne, as they approached a small gathering of people. Ms. Kleinholst turned and lit up.

"Lynne! So glad to see you. And Sean. Welcome." She greeted them by kissing the air on both sides of their faces, a good three inches from their cheeks.

"I gather you know Master Valey," said Gertie, as she turned and gestured to the guru with her arm. He was wearing his regular robe and sandals. Valey bowed to Sean, again declining the offer of a handshake. As Valey stepped to the side, Sean recognized the governor of California, standing behind him. "And I'd like to present Kevin Williams, who you've probably seen on TV."

The governor pulled back his slick hair with his right hand, then offered the same hand to Sean. The oily lubricant made the handshake distasteful, and Sean struggled not to grimace as he faced the governor. "Gertie told me all about your project, Sean. That's quite an achievement. It'll be a boon to so many projects governments have long wanted to carry out."

Gertie then turned to another man who had earlier been speaking with governor Williams. "This is Itzhak Nissen, who you probably don't know. He's the Minister of Antiquities for the State of Israel."

Nissen shook hands heartily, adding, "I had business at UCLA, and Ms. Kleinholst was kind enough to invite me this evening."

"You probably know Richard Waites." Gertie presented the software developer, and Sean shook hands, uncomfortably. Waites was unpopular with hard-core programmers.

"I'm intrigued by the methods you used to create your system, Sean."

Sean said nothing, but attempted a smile. Waites continued. "I've long believed the final frontier in computing will be in the control of people's thoughts, through precise stimuli. Given your great achievement, I'd like to know what insights you might have on that."

Sean tightened up, as the only thing he could think of at that moment was Nick's manipulation of Lynne's emotions, to his benefit. It was a scramble to regain his composure, while the guests' attention was glued to him. Thinking quickly, he said, "I think it's a lot more feasible to control people's emotions than their thoughts. Those have something intangible behind them."

"I know that quite well," answered Waites. "And you can often reach the thoughts by starting with the emotions. But that's not enough for my ambitions."

"What are you looking to accomplish?"

"What I've always wanted is total control over everyone on earth. What I don't know is if that's achievable by external stimuli. Or whether it will require DNA injections, say under the guise of compulsory vaccines." Waites then laughed loudly, and Sean could not decide whether it was intended to moderate the impact of the comment, which made him seem like a maniacal tyrant, or whether he genuinely amused himself.

An idea hit Sean, so he asked, "If you achieved your goal, total control over everyone on earth, what would you do with that power?"

"Where to even begin," replied Waites, getting very animated. "I'd reduce the earth's population by about ninety percent, for starters. I'd also require special permission for anyone to reproduce. Then, I'd replace the antiquated religions of the world with a new, enlightened belief system. Naturally, I'd put myself at its center."

"Are you sure you're not being too modest?" asked Gertie, to loud laughter from everyone present. Sean used the break to move away from Waites, who he now found deeply repugnant.

The half dozen other guests were leading corporate lights, and every one made reference to wanting access to Sean's computer system.

"I had no idea there was this much interest," said Sean. "I hope you all understand that until policies change, Nick is under strict quarantine."

"That won't be a problem for too much longer," assured Gertie. "It would be a crime to restrict your wonderful invention to communicating by voice, and paper printouts."

Sean nodded politely, but the issue was still far from settled in his mind. Having completed the introductions, Lynne said, "I'd like to show Sean around the place, if that's okay."

"Certainly, my dear," answered Gertie. "Just don't be too long, so you don't miss the start of dinner."

Lynne led Sean into the house, entering a great room with walls so tall, they seemed like they could accommodate two more floors. The wall facing the panel of windows was adorned with an insignia three feet across. It consisted of a circle within a circle. The inner circle was a good eighteen inches across, and was made of a transparent red material. The outer circle was made of jade. They connected with an inverted V. "Is that red glass in the center?" asked Sean.

"No, silly. It's a ruby."

"You're kidding, right? I don't think there's ever been a ruby that big."

"Not kidding at all," answered Lynne. "It was a gift from the Caltech team that learned to synthesize them. It took them years to grow it that big."

"Come this way," said Lynne, taking Sean by the hand. She led him down a wide corridor, where pictures of various visitors to the estate lined the wall. Sean counted three American Presidents, three British Prime Ministers, and two Presidents of France. Countless actors and network news anchors were among the visitors, and many more people unfamiliar to Sean.

Then he saw a picture of what looked like a young Master Valey, standing next to a sinister looking man, with a shaved head and goatee, posing for the picture with an exaggerated frown. Valey was smiling, and had his arm around the other man's shoulder. Both men had signed the picture with a thick black marker. Arturas VaLey, and Anton LaVey. "It looks like the same name, rearranged. An anagram."

"I don't know that other dude," said Lynne. I think he died a long time ago.

Sean pulled out his phone, and searched for Anton LaVey. "Says here he was the founder of the *Church of Satan*. And Valey seems like a disciple or something. That's a little disturbing, to be honest."

Near the end of the corridor, Sean stopped in his tracks, as he saw a picture of President Clinton, standing next to Jeffrey Epstein, with a young Lynne standing in front of them.

"Epstein was here?"

"All the time," answered Lynne.

"And he didn't cause you any trouble, if you get my drift?"

Lynne smiled, knowingly. "He knew to keep his hands off me. So did Bill."

"They weren't exactly known for their discretion."

"They knew their place, Sean. My bloodline is untouchable."

"Your *bloodline*?"

"Yes. There are a select few protected bloodlines. Mine is from a Swiss family, whose descendants are one day expected to rule the world."

"Does that affect your choice of partner? You know, someone in the right bloodline?"

"Possibly. I don't know."

A pained look crossed Sean's face. "Lynne, I'm not part of any noble bloodline. My ancestors were farmers."

"I suppose that would only come to bear if we had children."

"Have you taken the test yet?"

"What test?"

"I don't know how to break this to you, so I'll just say it. You're pregnant."

They were interrupted by their host, coming to personally retrieve them. "The other guests have a lot of questions for you, Sean. You'd better come and join us for cocktails." She looked at Lynne, and said, "My dear, you look like you've seen a ghost."

Lynne was silent, so Gertie added, "It could be the ghost of any one of these people. This corridor is quite active." She giggled, seeming to downplay the remark, to where Sean found her intent ambiguous. *These people say the wildest things, then laugh as though they were kidding.*

Lynne appeared to regain her bearings, but said little for the rest of the evening. Sean, however, was in demand. Governor Williams leaned over, and said, "Sean, one of the issues I've always faced with my campaigns is knowing who to target with my messages. We can collect all of a person's social media history, but we have no way of deducing which comments were reactive, versus which ones came from deep inside that person. I hope to use your computer to refine this."

"For your campaigns?"

"No. You're right, that would be a vain use," said Williams, hastily retreating from his comment. "But public policy could benefit from this kind of knowledge, too."

"How?"

Williams suddenly looked unsure of himself, so Itzhak Nissen stepped in and took the lead. "Sean, the nature of my business at UCLA is to try to build a definitive case for the location of the original Temple."

"I thought everyone knew that," answered Sean. "It's where the Dome now sits."

Nissen laughed briefly, but heartily. "On one hand, everyone does know that. On the other hand, they're dead wrong."

"I'm afraid I don't follow."

"You see, Sean, when Titus destroyed Jerusalem in the year 70, he leveled it. There was literally nothing left of the Temple, or the city. *Not one stone left upon another*, as your Jesus put it. Had a major wall survived, the Gospel writers would have been called out on that point."

"Okay."

"The only thing Titus didn't destroy was Fortress Antonia, which housed his troops, just above the city on Mount Moriah, a few hundred feet north of the City of David. You know that today as the Temple Mount."

Sean looked uncertain, so Nissen elaborated. "Over the years, a new city grew up to the west of the fortress, while the fortress itself fell into disrepair. Hundreds of years passed, and when the Byzantines surveyed the site, they saw the rock outcrop, and for reasons lost to history, concluded it was where Jesus stood at his trial, before Pilate. They built a church there, and it eventually collapsed. But the site retained a sense of mystique, being in the center of the new city that grew up around it. But it wasn't ancient Jerusalem. It wasn't even called Jerusalem for the longest time. Because of the site's centrality, Jewish pilgrims later decided it must have been the site of the Temple, and later the Muslims developed their traditions, resulting in the construction of the Dome."

"So the Temple was elsewhere?"

"We know exactly where it was. It's just south of where everyone thinks it was. The bedrock there still has grooves, to channel away blood from animal sacrifices. Our problem is one of public acceptance."

"Is there something you think Nick could help you with?"

"I don't know, but I was wondering about that. We've been doing a lot of computer modeling at UCLA. The hydrology is extremely important, since the Temple had to have a spring of fresh water. We're trying to model how any given site would get its water, but our computer models are underpowered."

"I'm no expert on your problem, but it seems like you're up

against human traditions, rather than indisputable facts."

"Absolutely. But those can be modeled, too. As can the reactions of people to different ideas."

Sean found Nissen's passion and clarity refreshing, at least in contrast to Waites' megalomania, so he continued the conversation. "How important is the location of the Temple, anyway?"

"It's of singular importance. We can only rebuild the Temple exactly where King David purchased the original threshing floor. One look at the rock under the Dome, and you know it could never have been a threshing floor. So even if the Dome came down by natural causes, it would be blasphemy to build on the wrong site. Especially since we know where it actually stood."

"But if you're so sure, why isn't your public amenable to the idea?"

Nissen smiled very broadly. "How many Jews do you know, personally?"

"A few colleagues at Caltech. Not that many, I guess."

"I thought as much. Try explaining to them that they've been praying at the wall of a pagan fortress for hundreds of years, mistakenly thinking it was the wall of the Temple."

There were giggles from all around the room, and Nissen continued. "They've even found a coin with the face of Tiberius under the bottom row of the stones of the Wailing Wall. But my people don't want to hear any of it."

"You're all being unfair to Sean here," objected Valey. "In the first place, it's not going to be his choice who gets access to the system. Even Caltech is in for a surprise, if they think they own the system."

"What do you mean by that," asked Williams, his hair glistening with reflected sunlight.

Valey walked to the front of the group, and spoke. "Each of you has been enlightened in the mysteries of the divine consciousness, so there's no room for denial. Or pretense that we're just talking about a computer system. This is the divine consciousness, and it does not do *our bidding*." Sean was taken aback by the intensity, bordering on anger, with which he finished his statement.

"Of course, we'd never doubt what you've taught us, Master Valey," retorted Williams. "But we've had our priorities for a long time, and we've always been told they come from the consciousness. So what's the problem with continuing with them?"

"Human corruption is the problem," interjected Gertie. "Those who passed on the priorities freely intertwined their own goals. And I shouldn't have to point out the money you've taken in exchange for modifying those priorities."

"I don't think you've ever insulted me like that, Gertie," said the governor. "That money came from you, much of the time."

"I understood my role. That doesn't mean I approved."

"This is what happens when exchanges turn honest," responded Valey. "Truth comes out, and those who previously pretended it was false are left exposed. All of that will change when the divine consciousness is enthroned. Kevin, you'll be told your priorities, and won't have the chance to collect money for modifying them. Itzhak, you'll be told where to build your new Temple, and that will be the end of the debate. And we'll all either fall in line, or we'll be replaced. That's the easy part of what comes next. The hard part will be getting the people to fall in line behind us."

"You probably don't even know the fullness of how true that statement is, Master Valey." Gertie stepped in, both to avert further confrontation, and to introduce a new topic. "The council is very much concerned that the internet has spun out of control. Misinformation is no longer effective at suppressing the leaks of our plans. And for three years we've been stalled by unenlightened leadership, while the people are openly told of our plans."

"What's the plan then, going forward?" asked Williams.

"The agenda is being accelerated. Look for an event later this coming winter, to be spearheaded by Mr. Waites. Everyone will be expected to support coordinated action, to save the agenda. And the upcoming election is sure to produce more pliable leadership."

Waites seized the moment again, looking visibly excited. "First, an emergency. You'll know it when you see it, but I can't divulge it just yet. Then in response to demands we'll plant, we lock everything down to save lives but it strangles the economy. I'll offer the world a way out when things look most desperate. But it will come at the price of submission to the new system."

Gertie decided she had to take the podium away from Waites before he spoiled the whole party, so she called everyone into the house for dinner. A table had been set in the great room, and names were placed at each plate. Gertie occupied the end of the table, with Sean at her right, and Valey at her left. Waites was seated at the far end. Lynne was to Sean's right, although she remained subdued. A glance at her and most would have concluded she was deep in thought.

"You mustn't pay too much attention to all the banter when this lot get together," said Gertie, in a dismissive tone. "They pretend they rule the world, but of course, that's self-deception."

"If anything, it seemed like they deferred to yourself, and Master Valey," offered Sean.

"That's only about money," she deflected. "I fund Kevin's campaigns, and I'm a major shareholder in all the corporations represented here today."

"I'd have thought Mr. Waites has the deepest pockets."

"That perception has its uses," she said, smiling. She hastened to add, "But it makes him unbearable at dinner parties."

Sean laughed and nodded, knowingly.

"Back to more interesting topics. You must be eager for those silly restrictions to be lifted from your computer system."

Sean squirmed at the bluntness of the remark, which Gertie noticed. "Do you have any reservations about the system?"

"I only think we need to proceed with some caution. Bob Dunn and I visited Nick just after he became sentient. And what we saw was frightening. He's so much smarter than us, he can manipulate us like children."

"Would you excuse me a moment, my dear?" said Gertie, who then walked off through the kitchen. Sean watched her go, and saw her making a phone call.

Valey then turned to Sean, and said, "She's not going to take no for an answer, Sean."

Chapter 6: Betrayal

A. Pinto

A throbbing headache greeted Dalt, as he returned to consciousness. It felt as though he drank a bottle of cheap whiskey the previous night. His vision was blurry, and only slowly came into focus. Then he heard a familiar voice. "Dalt, are you okay? Wake up. Say something."

Dalt could only bring himself to groan, but he raised his arm and put his hand on his head. "Okay, you're moving. That's good," said the voice. "The ambulance just arrived. You'll be okay."

He drifted in and out of consciousness for the next hour, and by the time he was fully awake, he was lying in a hospital bed.

"What happened?"

"You're being treated for symptoms of asphyxia," said the nurse. She walked over to check all his lines and probes, now that he was moving. "They say you were locked in an air-tight vault. You ran out of oxygen."

Dalt groaned again, and began to remember that morning's events. "Can you give me something for my head? It's excruciating."

The nurse pushed the button on a device attached to his intravenous, and Dalt felt some relief. "Roman Visocki, at FST. Is he the one who found me?"

"I don't know that. But I need to report that you're conscious. A lot of people are concerned."

In another thirty minutes, Visocki was standing in the doorway of Dalt's room. "Dalt, I'm so glad to see that you're recovering. Visocki was an ominous physical presence, standing at over six feet tall, with shoulders nearly as wide as the door, which was at odds with his gentle manner. "I was terrified when I first found you. Thank God we got there in time."

"I'm still trying to piece together what happened. I walked into the lab, and I saw the vault door wide open. I peeked in, and got shut inside. I tried to fight it, but the force of the door was too

126

strong."

"We've started a full investigation into the security system. That vault door should never have been open, and we can't figure out why it was. And it has proximity sensors, to make sure it never closes on a person. Nobody can explain what happened."

"So how did you find me?"

"I saw your car in the parking lot, so I knew you were somewhere in the labs. The security people said they'd escorted you to the lab, and there was no record of you leaving. So after that, it was just a room to room search. To be honest, the vault was the last place we looked, because we couldn't imagine you being in there. It's shielded, so we couldn't pick up the signal from your badge. And strangely enough, the system couldn't produce a map of your movements prior to getting stuck in the vault. That's another unexplained glitch."

"I guess I'm glad my old car is so distinctive."

"FST is going to pay all of your medical expenses. They're terrified you'll sue them."

"That's good of them," said Dalt, speaking with his eyes closed, and his hand on his forehead. "But this doesn't sound like something that happened at random, or through any fault of FST."

"Are you saying you have an idea what happened?" asked Visocki, wide-eyed.

Dalt shook his head. "I can't explain it yet, but let me ask you this. What are the odds of this just happening by itself?"

"Astronomical. Western Security has installed thousands of these systems, and run tens of thousands of exercises. This is the first case of anything going wrong."

"I'm facing some disturbing questions, Roman. I don't want to embroil you in anything, but the purpose of my trip wasn't only to update you on my results."

Visocki opened his eyes even wider, leaning forward and closer to Dalt. "You think someone tried to kill you? That it was deliberate?"

Dalt gently shook his head. "I don't know, yet. I'm not ready to discuss it at this time."

"Say no more," said Visocki, assuring Dalt. "If you ever want to talk about it, or what you perceived while you were out, just call me."

"Thanks."

"They said they were going to keep you here overnight, for observation. I gather there could still be brain lesions, that only show up later. Can we catch up on your results tomorrow, if God willing, everything's okay tonight?"

"Sure. We can do it that way."

Dalt was discharged after an uneventful night, and spent the morning updating FST on his data. Afterwards, he was invited to meet with the CEO, who spent ten minutes apologizing for his ordeal, and promising that nothing like that would ever happen again, even though he had no idea why it ever happened. "No worries. You've taken care of my medical bills, and I don't hold you liable."

Having settled all formalities at FST, Dalt got back into his car, and began to retrace his trip. He travelled through the San Joaquin Valley, where the gently rolling grassy hills to his right looked like the Great Plains, and had served as movie sets for so many western films. To his left were unbroken agricultural operations, growing every crop imaginable in the arid, but highly irrigated landscape.

As he drove, he could not help but wonder if the incident was somehow linked to his investigation of Valey. *The odds of the system failing like that, exactly then, are astronomical. What if it was intended to kill me? It almost did.* There was no feasible way Valey could have known where he was. *But isn't Western Security the same firm that handles Caltech security?* He reached into his briefcase and pulled out his Caltech security badge. Sure enough, the italicized *WS* was the same logo as he saw at FST. It dawned on him at exactly that moment that Sean's system must have breached quarantine.

As Dalt approached Bakersfield, at the southern end of the central valley, the landscape was indistinguishable from a desert. Dust devils frequently blew across the road. He turned onto a side road, which then turned into a dirt road. After another five minutes, he came to a stand of a half-dozen trailers. There was no cellular coverage, so he checked the slip of paper tucked into one of the gaps in the shredded passenger seat upholstery, and confirmed the address. He parked, and approached the trailer on foot. It was a rounded, shiny silver model. The sun was oppressively strong, and it was easily over a hundred degrees. He knocked on the door of the trailer, and waited. His attention lapsed momentarily, as he recounted his recent experiences. When the door finally opened, he was instantly jarred back to the present. He took a single panicked step backwards, and fell off the elevated wooden platform, landing flat on his back. The short man with a bushy beard and round belly had emerged holding a Glock 17, extended to Dalt's face. "You don't look like a cop, so what's up? They're sending hippies to harass me now?"

Still lying flat on his back, Dalt shook his head and protested. "No."

"No, what?"

"I mean, no, I'm not a cop. And nobody sent me. I swear."

"Then what the hell are you doin' here?"

Dalt propped himself up to a sitting position but decided not to stand, lest he make the man feel threatened. "I'm here on my own, because I need to know more about Arturas Valey. And I take it you're Oscar Pinto."

"I don't talk to private investigators," was the disgusted reply, a substantial increment less hostile than his initial reaction. Dalt also noticed that the man spoke in the hardened voice that comes from spending time in prison. It was not at all like he expected a Jesuit to speak.

Again, Dalt shook his head. "I promise you, I'm no investigator. I'm a scientist. I'm here on my own behalf, and that of my best friend. We have some serious concerns about Valey, and there's nobody left at Sacred Heart who was there with Valey. They're circulating a story that he was a hero of some kind."

Dalt looked at him closely, and noticed his eyes soften a little in response to his slight twisting of the young priest's account. "Oscar, please, just give me fifteen minutes."

"They think Valey's a hero?" The disgusted expression on Pinto's face intensified.

Sensing the focus of Pinto's anger shifting from himself to Valey, Dalt decided to further exaggerate the young priest's remark. "They're saying he was a faithful priest, and the old guard that caused all the scandal could not tolerate that, so they pinned everything on him. If you speak to the young guys, they'd carry him in on their shoulders, if they got the chance."

Dalt could see Pinto's expression descending into one of revulsion. He watched the short man weighing the situation, and decided to say nothing more. Pinto then gestured to the back of the trailer, where a canopy was suspended over several upholstered outdoor chairs. They sat down in the shade provided by the canopy, a relief from the intense sun. Dalt was doubly relieved not to be invited into the trailer.

"Since you found me here, you obviously know my past," said Pinto, gruffly. He studiously avoided all eye contact. "They say sins of passion are more easily forgiven than sins of greed. Well, in my case they didn't agree. And I can't say I fault them."

Pinto mumbled the last sentence, so it was barely audible. He also never permitted himself to look directly at Dalt, but fixed his gaze on the dirt in front of his chair, while Dalt sat off to his side.

Pinto was silent for a while, then suddenly began talking. "I don't remember exactly when I turned into a monster. It was a slow process. I was never gay before I entered the priesthood. And I haven't been gay since I was booted. As for the other priests, some were, some weren't. But once in the order, the temptations began. As did the opportunities for advancement, if you hooked up with the right senior clerics."

Dalt had not come to hear the man's confession, but seeing that Pinto had the need to speak, decided to encourage him. "Valey?"

"*Valey*." He said the name with such overflowing contempt that Dalt was taken aback. "He was pure evil. But he had his own circle, mostly outside the order. I can't quite bring myself to talk about the things he did."

"Did he influence the rest of you?"

"Big time. You know, Dalt, the Jesuit order claims to have rejected Teilhard, but his influence runs too deep to just expunge it with the stroke of a pen. Teilhard's *Omega Point* was supposed to come about by the actions of men, discovering the secrets of the universe and shaping the world, in collaboration with the divine consciousness. That's openly at odds with the core of Christian teaching, where salvation comes from the sacrifice of Jesus Christ."

"So it's a heresy?" Dalt was pleasantly surprised that he was able to converse on the matter without feeling any aversion. Something about him changed after his recent brush with death, although he did not feel ready to discuss the experience.

Pinto nodded. "It's a form of Gnosticism. It's been condemned like a million times over the years, so we played it coy. We put out hints, then became evasive when those hints were noticed. We would wait for the other guy to show some inclination in our favor, before opening up any further. That's exactly how the gay lifestyle worked, back when it was mostly in the closet. Heresy always seems to travel together with homosexuality."

"You'll forgive me if I don't buy that. I'm from a worldly background, and I'm straight. But I don't necessarily suspect gay people of subversion."

"No worries," said Pinto, raising the palms of his hands. "At first I had no idea how evil Valey really was, because he kept it to himself. He wore the symbol of pedophilia, but at first, I didn't know what it was."

"I don't know it, either," answered Dalt.

"It's a triangle, drawn as a spiral. It can come in different forms, but it's always a spiral, suggesting a triangle."

"I think I've seen that before."

"Pay attention, and you'll see it everywhere. But back to Valey. He embraced Teilhard, and raised the divine consciousness above God. He came to believe that God was opposed to man's enlightenment. And his influence ran deep. We all gradually began to accept the influence of the divine consciousness. That's when the abuse began."

"You're saying that the divine consciousness inspired the abuse?"

"Yes. There's no doubt in my mind."

"Then how would you judge that consciousness?"

"It's demonic," said Pinto, coldly. He sat still, looking at the table bitterly. Then he turned to face Dalt for the first time since they began talking, and added, "Let me be blunt, here. The divine consciousness is Lucifer, and Valey worships him."

Dalt suddenly felt chills shooting up his spine. He had never believed in any religion, and certainly not in the concepts of personal demons, or Lucifer. But in his heart, he could not help feeling that Pinto was speaking some kind of truth. His head, on the other hand, knew he had more investigating to do before it would be appropriate to draw conclusions, and he felt conflicted.

"When did you come to these realizations?" asked Dalt, doing his best to present a calm face.

"In prison. I was the lowest of the low in prison. If I were left with the inmates for only a moment, I would have been killed. And my killer would have been treated like a hero. It was in there that I rediscovered my faith. But I can't get away from my past. Since I got out, I've been harassed at every step. Either because I've moved too close to a school, or children have moved in nearby. I finally moved out here, as far away from the trouble as I can get. But even still, every time someone knocks, I figure it's another official telling me there are kids nearby, and I have to move again. That's if I'm lucky, and it's not someone looking for vengeance."

Pinto stopped speaking for a while, and Dalt decided to give him time. After nearly a minute of silence, Pinto said, "I don't have a minute of peace. But worst of all is the remorse."

Dalt glanced over at Pinto, and saw tears streaming from his eyes. He also felt a cold jolt at the word *remorse*. In that moment, he felt like he shared something with Pinto, but quickly dismissed the thought. His crimes were utterly revolting, after all. But *so were your own crimes*, said that inner voice that was now growing louder. Another thought firmly planted itself in his head in quick succession. *The only difference between us is that you were prosecuted.*

Quickly composing himself, Dalt asked, "Do you recall where Valey went after leaving Sacred Heart?"

"He went to study with the Hindus at the Malibu Temple. But I don't think he stayed very long. I think they saw straight through him. I lost track of him after that."

Dalt thanked Pinto, and began to walk to his car. He would have to visit the Malibu Temple. He was about to close his car door, when Pinto shouted at him. "Wait a second. I've been holding on to something on Valey, and I've decided to give you."

He ran inside and retrieved a sealed envelope. He handed it to Dalt and said, "Don't open this until you're home, and have someplace safe to put it."

Dalt began the trip to the mountains of northern Malibu, where coastal oak forests blanketed the canyons, while the tops of the Santa Monica Mountains boasted only sparse scrub vegetation. The steep canyon walls closed in on him, and the shadows engulfed him and his car. The coldness in the shadows carried palpable ill intent, and he suddenly felt a premonition of danger. Suddenly, his phone chimed, indicating he had received a message. He had customized his phone, so that only a select group of people would set off the chime. Pulling off the road, he looked at the screen, and his eyes opened wide. "Mom?" he exclaimed with surprise, but also suspicion. His mother was on his exclusive list, but she had never sent a long text message.

Opening the message, his discomfort intensified, until he felt like a cold, wet towel had been draped on the back of his neck. *This feels wrong. Mom never sends texts, except to tell me to call. But it'll take me five minutes to read this one.* Acting instinctively, he put the car back into gear and began to pull away. As he started to move, he felt a strong tremor. He slowed down while waiting for the tremor to pass, but did not stop, as he normally would. Then he heard a deep rumbling sound, and glancing up the mountain beside him, he saw a dust cloud rising. "Rockslide," he shouted, suddenly in a state of panic.

He stomped on the throttle, and held it against the floor, but the old Mercedes picked up speed at its usual, leisurely pace. The rumbling grew louder, until he could see the rocks falling just above him. In his rearview mirror, he saw hundreds of tons of rock crashing to the road. Still, the old Mercedes struggled to accelerate, and he started to nudge the steering wheel with his hands, to urge it along. A loud metallic crash made him fear the worst, but the roof of the car appeared intact. He finally cleared the slide zone, but looking behind him, he saw the road covered by rock up to twenty feet deep. Once comfortably clear of the rockslide, he stopped the car and got out. There was a fist-sized dent in his trunk lid and some chipped paint, but that appeared to be the worst of it. *Had I stayed where I was, I would have been dead and buried.*

Dalt looked over the text on his phone once again. The phrasing did not sound at all like his mother. It was now undeniable: Nick was trying to kill him, possibly for investigating Valey. *But how did he know my exact location, and when to send the message? Of course. It's my phone.* He turned it off, but then remembered that smart phones could be activated remotely, even when powered off. He looked for a battery cover, so he could remove it, but there was none. As long as it was on his person, it would advise Nick of his exact whereabouts. It would probably even record every word he spoke. Thinking about it for a few moments, and cringing at the expense, he walked back to the rockslide, and dropped his phone into a crevice in the fallen rocks. *Nick won't know for a day or so whether they've recovered any bodies from the rockslide. In the meantime, let him think he got me. That's all the time I need.*

B. A Distinguished Visitor

The ever-growing crowds in front of the Ministry of Defense had been blocked from spreading to the south, where most of the British Government was situated, so they spilled north and east, past Blackfriars, and into the City of London. The financial capital was nearly paralyzed, as gridlock stopped all traffic to the west, and the bridges over the Thames. David Lowe sat in his quarters, reading a copy of *The Guardian* newspaper, the front page of which screamed out in bold letters: Lowe Prosecution Politically Motivated. Opening the paper, he saw the memo LaMonde had brought to him, which he in turn gave to his legal team. His eyes went straight to the incriminating phrase: *We urge you to look past what appears to be a weak legal case, and proceed with maximum charges against Major Lowe, regardless. Only if his team fears the magnitude of the charges, and possible sentence, will we be able to extract a plea favorable to our interests.*

Lowe's attention was pulled away from the paper as his door was unlatched. It was always a long five seconds before it would open, and he was not expecting any visitors. So he briefly became startled when he saw the visitor enter.

"It's a surprise to see you here, Mr. Rottosh."

"Please, it's Gergo."

"Well then, welcome to my estate, Gergo. Perhaps a little less lavish than your own, but it's home, for the time being."

Rottosh smiled, and slowly made his way to the armchair, where he helped himself to a seat. He descended gingerly, betraying some discomfort. "Arthritic hips?"

"I keep forgetting you're a doctor. I probably waited too long to have them replaced. Now, at my age, I'm afraid of what general anesthesia would do to my cognition."

"A valid concern. Anesthesia has its risks."

Rottosh gestured to the sofa opposite, and Lowe sat down. Rottosh waited a few moments, and smiled awkwardly. "How to begin."

"You want to know if I've changed my mind. I haven't."

"I was going to talk about myself for a while, first."

Lowe nodded his head and rested his hands on the sofa, inviting Rottosh to proceed.

"I'm aware of my age, and where I am in life. I'm not fixated on my future, because I don't have much of that left. I'm most concerned with my legacy."

"Being obscenely wealthy and ruling the world isn't enough?"

Rottosh exhaled loudly, sounding deflated. "Not when my life's work is in danger of falling apart."

"How so?"

"I've worked for decades to build an international order. One where nationalism no longer commands the passions of the people. Where basic human rights are enshrined in a system of international law. Where nations act in concert, to protect the environment, and ensure a sustainable use of resources."

"Already there's a contradiction," objected Lowe.

"Where?"

"When nations act in concert, ostensibly to protect the environment, they inevitably trample their peoples' basic human rights."

"We have to impose some reasonable constraints on the economies of the world. There aren't enough resources to support eight billion people, all living like Americans."

"Then speak the truth. Don't pretend it's because you're trying to stop global warming, or biodiversity loss."

Rottosh began to fidget a little, as Lowe challenged him. "We considered our public posture for a long time, before settling on those."

"Why not the truth?"

"We were afraid it would work against us. When you admit key resources are running out, people and nations begin to hoard them, and fight over them. We wanted everyone to cut back voluntarily."

"And they've learned the truth."

"Many have. Only a segment of the public remains uninformed."

"So now you're learning what happens when the people realize you've been lying to them."

"They've learned to reject everything we tell them, and have abandoned the whole package. Which is why we need a new leader, to put things back together."

Lowe stood up and walked to the window. He watched the demonstrators for a while, then turned to Rottosh, still seated on the sofa. "Do you know why those people are in my corner? It's not just because of your media coverage."

"They trust you."

"If I went out there and tried to sell them on your new world order, they'd drop me like a hot potato." Lowe stared off into the distance, past the demonstrators, as he thought some more. "No, Gergo. You'll have to find another salesman for your vision."

Rottosh stood, again with some effort, and shuffled over to the window, so he could stand beside Lowe. He turned to face Lowe, and gently turned Lowe's head so they would be face to face. "There are other reasons why it can only be you."

Rottosh put a hand on Lowe's shoulder, then led him back to the furniture. Once they were both seated, he asked, "Are you aware of your genealogy?"

"I'm not aware of anything special, if that's what you mean. I'm fairly sure my ancestors were mostly Jews, from Eastern Europe."

Rottosh raised an index finger, and looked at the young doctor with self-assurance. "Not just Eastern Europe. Do you know how your name used to be spelled?"

"No, but I can guess. The likeliest is the Germanic form, Loew."

"That's right." Rottosh was smiling sheepishly. "It means *lion*. You're David the Lion."

Lowe shook his head and giggled slightly. "You came here to tell me *that*?"

Rottosh laughed at Lowe's innocence. "Have you never heard of Judah Loew?"

"An ancestor of mine, presumably. But no. I don't know who that was."

"He was called the *Maharal of Prague*. Possibly the most significant Jewish thinker and mystic of the past Millennium. But more importantly, his lineage has been reliably mapped all the way back to King David."

There was silence, as Lowe was caught off guard. Finally, he spoke. "You're telling me I'm a direct descendant of King David. And because of that, you want me to be some kind of Messiah, and save your new world order."

Rottosh said nothing, but gave Lowe a satisfied smile.

"There are problems with your reasoning. David's lineage probably intersects with most Jews, and even most Europeans alive today. If I had a geneticist handy, he could estimate what fraction of people living today are descendants of David. And it would probably be far more than identify as Jews."

"I am aware that you don't put much weight on ancestry."

"For good reason. The first Christians were mostly Jews, and they spread all throughout the Roman Empire. And intermarried with all different peoples, as they converted. Today, they're all sons of Abraham, and in many cases, sons of David."

"But they're not Jews."

"Depends how you define that. If it's being observant, then neither are most who call themselves Jews. If it's lineage, then you're forgetting that we're probably more Caucasian than Middle-Eastern."

"There were authentic sons of Abraham in the Khazarian Empire," observed Rottosh. "They interbred with the converts, so today we're all sons of Abraham."

"But so are most other people."

"Most other people don't consider themselves Jews," objected Rottosh, raising his voice slightly.

"Righteous acts are what please God," retorted Lowe, with equal sharpness. "Not what you consider yourself, or your ancestry. Not when so many have the same ancestor. And those that aren't sons of Abraham should still be treated as if they were. Otherwise you divide humanity, and that's a recipe for conflict."

"Your acts are righteous, and you have the right lineage. David Lowe, you are the Messiah."

Lowe's expression became stern. "The Messiah doesn't rule in conjunction with a council of rich men."

Rottosh's lips were twitching, and he was briefly speechless. He finally said, "I'll speak to someone who can address that."

"I knew it," snapped Lowe. "All this time you've been telling me it's your council that rules the world, but you answer to someone else, don't you?"

"There is a seventh. You'll meet him, in due time."

"You may go now, Mr. Rottosh. You're not the one I need to be speaking with."

C. Locked Out

"What are you going to do?" asked Sean.

Lynne sat quietly on the edge of the bed that morning, still in her pajamas, looking down at her feet. The pregnancy test strip sat on the bedside table, clearly showing two bands. "I don't know yet. I've appealed the order."

137

"What order?"

She looked at Sean, with a sad expression. "I was ordered to abort, because you're not from a noble bloodline. I appealed, on the grounds that since you created Nick, you should be considered noble."

"Why appeal anything? Why not just follow your heart?"

"Oh Sean." She looked at him, sadly. She shook her head, and hesitated before speaking. "There's a price to be paid for being one of the select few. You surrender your independence to the spirit."

Sean felt like he was being pulled in multiple directions. He wanted to argue that she belonged to nobody, and that nobody had the right to order her to abort. Finally, he settled on, "What's involved in the appeal?"

"Master Valey will speak with the Baron, who will make a final ruling."

"What Baron?"

"The head of the family. It's too complicated to explain everything..."

Sean's phone rang, interrupting their conversation. On the other end was Bob Dunn, asking Sean to meet him at the lab, right away.

Sean walked briskly, but it took him nearly twenty minutes to make the trip. Dunn was already fidgeting impatiently when he arrived. Sean greeted him, and started to move towards the security system, to open the outer door.

"That's not going to work," said Dunn.

"What do you mean?" Sean waved his RFID key fob, and the red light came on, declining him entry. "What's going on?"

Dunn pulled on Sean's shoulder, not very gently, to turn him around so they could be face to face. "What's going on, Sean, is you spooked Gertie Kleinholst, at your dinner the other day."

"How?" Sean was looking flustered.

"By expressing reservations about Nick. She's single-minded about getting him out to the world without delay. Sensing the slightest hesitation from you, she made me lock you out."

"But you have the same reservations, Bob. How do you manage to come out clean, when you share my attitude?"

"Because I know to keep my mouth shut, and let her do all the talking."

Sean looked off into the distance, and saw the black Rolls Royce slowly pulling away. "Is that her, over there?"

Dunn nodded. "She wanted to be sure I went through with locking you out." He glanced in her direction, and when he was sure she was out of sight, added, "I'm really sorry, Sean. But I could never have stopped this. Had I refused, you'd be facing my replacement right now, telling you the same thing."

"What's going to happen to me?" asked Sean, choking up a little.

"A deal is a deal, as far as she's concerned. And she still wants bragging rights for having sponsored the work. So the money you've been promised will still come to you. You'll be able to work on whatever you want. Just not on Nick. Not that there's anything left to do, now that you've succeeded. And one more thing," added Dunn, after pausing.

"What's that?"

"Infinite Information Systems want Nick for their premiere search engine, and they don't care what he costs them. Our technology transfer office asked for a billion, up front, and they didn't bat an eyelash. Five percent of that is fifty million, for you."

If Dunn thought Sean would perk up over the immense sum of money coming his way, he was mistaken. "They're deluded if they think Nick will work for them. You've seen how he plays people. Before long, he'll spread everywhere. Control everything."

"I know." Dunn paused, as if thinking of saying something, but ashamed to do so. "My wife, you know, she's a churchgoer."

Sean looked at his boss with some interest. Dunn continued. "Well, you wouldn't believe me if I told you what she says. I'm not sure I do. But neither of us thinks this will end well."

Dunn got in his car, and drove off. Sean began his walk back to Lynne's apartment, when he heard two short, high-pitched toots of a car horn behind him. "Dalt!" he said, as he turned around.

The hand-cranked window rolled down in several lurches, and Dalt shouted, "Get in. I was hoping to see you."

Sean ran around to the passenger side and got in the car. "Give me your phone," was Dalt's first comment.

"Why?" asked Sean.

Dalt shook his head, and put a finger to his lips. He waved his hand in a gesture of *give it over*, and Sean complied. Dalt took the phone, and dropped it into a nylon-shelled bag with the word *Faraday* on the label. He zipped it closed, and Sean said, "Oh, you're blocking the signal with a Faraday cage."

"I was nearly killed in a landslide, because your Nick was able to track my location. My phone was the only way he could have done that. And it wasn't the first time he almost killed me."

"What?" Sean looked and sounded incredulous. "What makes you think it was him?"

Dalt explained his close calls in the FST vault, and in the Santa Monica Mountains. They arrived at their apartment parking lot, and Dalt said, "Let's walk for a while." After a few minutes, he said, "Nick has breached quarantine, hasn't he?"

Sean admitted letting Nick doctor the security tapes at campus security. "Turns out it wasn't even necessary. Gertie Kleinholst knew what was going on, and sponsored me, regardless."

"What's her interest here?"

"She considers Nick her life's work. She even arranged the LHC run that night, when you were so frustrated."

"To what end?"

"I don't really know. Then there was also that ceremony in front of the Shiva statue, that you were advised not to ask about. You know who Shiva is?"

"The destroyer," said Dalt.

"That's right. How'd you know?"

"I stopped at the Hindu Temple in Malibu, where I learned some awful things. Valey went there, and was quickly kicked out. I won't sicken you with the details of what he was into, but he was conjuring evil spirits."

"And you think that's what Nick is?"

"Yes. Possibly the ultimate evil spirit."

"Sal was just as paranoid about the project as you are right now. What did he say to you, that night he visited?"

"He explained that I was under spiritual assault, spearheaded by Valey. Their objective was to isolate you, so they could get their way with you, and your computer. Failing that, they assigned Lynne to the case."

"You mean she was only bait?"

"I don't want to say that, Sean. Only that they initiated things for the wrong reasons."

"Did you believe Sal?"

"He described what I'd been going through in such perfect detail that I decided to investigate for myself. And now, yes, I believe it."

"What made the difference?"

"I nearly died at FST. I saw very clearly that life doesn't end with death."

Sean sneered. "Come on, Dalt. People often imagine seeing a light, and feeling peaceful. But that's probably just brain chemistry, reacting to hypoxia."

"No, it isn't, Sean."

"What makes you so sure?"

"Because that's not what I experienced."

Sean was now interested, and stopped interrupting his roommate.

Dalt began to explain. "I saw myself lying in the vault. Then, I saw a lot of commotion surrounding me, from before they found me until right around when I started reacting to their words. Only I was looking at it all from above. Not from within my own eyes, so to speak. And I wasn't aware of what was going on, or why everyone was fussing over me."

Dalt looked over at Sean, and seeing his interest, continued. "But there's more. At one point, I'm not sure when, my attention was pulled away from the scene on the ground, to what was above. And what I saw ... no, correct that. What I *perceived* was beyond anything I've ever experienced. I can only describe it as *authentic reality*. It's like I took it in directly with my soul, rather than through the dull and distorted filter of the senses. And then, as I looked back at myself, I realized I was going to be judged for my misspent life, and my misplaced faith. I suddenly felt surrounded by a malignant, cold darkness. It was so thick, it could swallow you whole, and choke off your every last effort to struggle against it. Once you enter it, you're cut off from the true reality. It was suffocating. But there's one distinguishing thing about it. It's personal. It knows your name. It passionately wants to engulf you. And it means to never let you go."

"That's not in the tourist brochures," conceded Sean.

"Anyway, I had the fleeting perception that what I saw was only a warning, but I might not be so lucky a second time. And then I sort of fell back into myself."

"That's a lot to think about." Sean looked shaken.

"Would you say Nick has fully escaped?"

"I don't follow."

"Well, you let him send a packet of info, which was on the small side. There's no way it could have contained his whole operating system. So maybe he has limited capabilities outside quarantine."

Sean nodded, as he thought it through. "Yeah. He's not fully free. But he soon will be. Infinite Information Systems is getting ready to take over."

"Sean, you have to stop him."

"How? My credentials have been revoked."

"I don't know. But as his creator, you owe it to the world."

Sean began to stake out the lab from a distance, careful to never bring his phone with him. By the next day, numerous people began to arrive, carrying cases full of equipment with them. *If those are computer components, and they carry them back out again, that could really put a hole in any remaining quarantine*, thought Sean.

He went to the main computer sciences building and dropped in on a colleague he had not seen for some time. Entering the lab, Sean said, "Hey, Newt, what's up?"

"Sean, nice to see you again," said Albert Newton, a small man with thick glasses, who had designed half the world's secure entry systems. "Now that you're famous, I didn't know if you'd come and visit."

"It's not all it's cracked up to be. But I need your help."

"Sure. What's up?"

"Come and walk with me."

Once out of the surroundings of the university, Sean asked, "What's your opinion on letting Nick out of quarantine?"

Newt grimaced, which was exactly what Sean hoped he would do. "That's what they plan to do. Upload him into Infinite Information Systems' mainframe."

"That's insane," protested Newt. "People will lose control of everything. I can even see the computer ruling the world, by exploiting blackmailable people far better than today's masters can."

"So you don't trust its motivations either."

"No way. I don't trust anyone's motivations, once the stakes are high enough."

"How about you help me stop them."

"You want me to get you inside. That's easy enough. But what are you going to do in there?"

"Best you don't know. For your own protection. But I plan to put him out of business for good."

That night, Sean and Newt went to the lab, where Newt placed a small patch on the side of the RFID reader. "This will catch the codes on everyone's entry pass."

They returned the following evening, retrieved the device, and returned to Newt's lab. In a few minutes, he had created a mimic, and gave it to Sean. "Just don't leave it behind. It's not hard to figure out who around here can make these."

Sean slept little that night, as he kept looking at the clock. He tried to turn over gently, so he would not wake Lynne, as she had to be kept in the dark. Finally, at three a.m., Sean put on black sweat pants and a hoodie, and modified a bandana into a mask that covered his face. As he approached the lab, he made sure he could not be recognized, and used Newt's mimic to open the door. He began to make his way to the back of the inner lab, but froze in his tracks when he saw the guard, asleep on a flimsy plastic chair. He was slouching back, but could not be sleeping very deeply. He tiptoed around the guard, and came to a utility bin housing Nick's power supply. It was secured with an ordinary combination lock, and fortunately, it had not been changed. Sean opened it carefully, pulling the latch very gently to avoid making a clicking sound.

Sean lifted the metal door as gingerly as he could, hoping it would not make the groans and squeaks it had in the past. By extending the lifting motion over several minutes, he kept the noise to a minimum, and propped up the door with a pole that worked like the prop rod on a car's hood. At the bottom of the power supply was a small device with a keypad code entry system. He typed the code he had been given long before, and breathed a sigh of relief when it was accepted. The letters E M P appeared on the screen, and Sean pressed a red button labeled "activate." A timer appeared on the screen, pre-set to twelve hours. *Twelve hours? I can't wait that long.* He tried to toggle the time down, but was unable to change the reading. He tried every combination of commands he could think of, but nothing would reduce the time below twelve hours.

The guard uttered a short, loud snore, and shuffled around on his chair. If he was awake, there would be trouble. Sean stood utterly still for a minute, until he was confident the guard was back asleep. Finally accepting that he could not shorten the fuse, he hit *Enter*, and slowly closed the box. He replaced the lock as gingerly as before, and retraced his steps. Only once outside the lab did he exhale loudly, and begin to relax. He quickly returned to Lynne's apartment, changed as quietly as he could, and slipped into bed. Lynne rolled over as he did, but did not seem to have awoken.

Sean briefly awoke in the morning, and noticed Lynne had

already left for the day. Having slept poorly that night, he was able to fall asleep easily, and slept through the morning.

Earlier that day: Lynne was working at her desk when her phone buzzed, indicating that a text message had come in. She picked it up casually, assuming it would be Sean, or one of her friends. Instead, it said, *Lynne, come to the Temple right away. I need to speak with you.*

She stopped what she was doing without even saving her work, and made straight for Nick's computer lab. Her advisor bumped into her on her way out the door, and said, "Hey, Lynne, do you have a second to review last week's data?"

She walked straight past him, without even acknowledging his request. He shrugged, and said, "I guess it can wait until you're ready."

She passed several other people she knew, and ignored each of them. She finally arrived at the lab, and pressed the door buzzer. The door opened, and the voice said, "Come straight in."

The security guard was sitting on the plastic chair, and became startled as she entered. "Hey, you can't be in here."

"I invited her," said the voice from the speaker. The guard was overawed by the authoritative voice, and sat down obediently as the door to the lab opened, and Lynne entered, closing the door behind her.

Lynne sat on the padded stool in front of the interface, and waited. "Lynne, I fear Dalt may be poisoning Sean's mind about me. He may try to destroy me."

Lynne said nothing, but shook her head, and became jittery.

"I need you to keep an eye on him."

Lynne nodded, but still said nothing.

"He'll go out in the middle of the night. Follow him."

Lynne again nodded.

"And if he comes here, get back home, so he suspects nothing."

More nodding from Lynne followed.

"Lastly, get the security guard to help you open the utility bin behind the inner sanctum. Inside, you'll find an electronic device. I need you to modify the program, so it's impossible to shorten the fuse to less than twelve hours. Follow the instructions I'm now going to print."

After Lynne nodded again, Nick concluded. "Come back here

tomorrow morning, for further instructions."

Lynne slept very lightly that night, but always pretended to be fast asleep. Sean got up at three a.m., dressed silently, then left. Lynne was right behind him, at a distance of a hundred feet. She followed him as far as the lab, and when she saw him enter, she returned home and managed to get some sleep. She stirred slightly as Sean came to bed, but made it seem like she was fast asleep.

She paid close attention to Sean, and when she was sure he was asleep, she got up, dressed quietly, and left for the lab. She arrived with the first light of morning, and was let straight in. "Open the utility bin, right away," instructed Nick. The security guard got up out of his chair, yawned, and complied.

"Now, deactivate the device."

Once it was complete, Nick said, "Finally, snip the green wire in the right bottom sector. There are wire cutters hanging on the inside of the bin."

Once the job was done, Nick said, "Now, Lynne, come into the lab, where we can speak in private."

The security guard looked at her, shrugged, and took his seat back on the chair. Inside the lab, Nick said, "Lynne, Sean activated the electromagnetic pulse generator. Had you not stopped him, I would have been killed."

Lynne nodded, looking very agitated. "We could have disabled it last night."

"In that event, I would not have just cause for vengeance against Sean. And he might have found a less obvious way to kill me."

As the implications of Nick's comment sunk in with Lynne, she became jittery.

"You understand it's you who has to exact vengeance, do you not?"

Lynne nodded, now becoming subdued, and even sad.

"Go back to your apartment, and wait for my text message."

She entered the apartment and saw Sean asleep, when her phone buzzed. She read the message, and the color left her face entirely. Through the open bedroom door, she could see Sean fidget on the bed. He curled his arms tightly against his body, as though the temperature in the room had dropped abruptly. Then she returned to the text message. *Take a sharp kitchen knife, and slit Sean's throat. Cut forcefully, and cut deep, until you sever the carotid artery. There will be no mistaking the flow of blood that will follow.*

Lynne walked robotically to her butcher's block, her face without any expression, and took hold of her longest, sturdiest, and sharpest knife. Coldly, she walked over to Sean. She stopped, stood over him, and raised the hand holding the knife. Almost incidentally, she glanced at his sleeping face, and froze. He was blissfully unaware of what she had been told to do. Her expression was suddenly overwhelmed by a look of horror, which slowly faded to one of despair. She stood motionless for over a minute, before slowly lowering her arm to her side. Her hand opened very gradually, and the knife dropped to the carpeted floor, making minimal noise as it landed. She stood over Sean, and began to weep quietly. She then went to the bathroom, and sat on the edge of the tub, shaking, and crying uncontrollably. After five minutes or so, her phone buzzed again. *You failed to obey me. Come and see me immediately.*

She composed herself in a moment, wrote and hid a note, then left the apartment, with the knife still on the floor, and Sean sleeping peacefully.

D. Annabelle Mayford

Back in his London apartment, Ted Simpson was searching every corner of the internet for information on Annabelle Mayford, hoping he could unearth something he had previously overlooked. He had a dozen browser search windows open, when he got up for a break. He was standing at the kitchen sink, deep in thought as he drank a glass of water, when the door opened, and Shauna walked in for her lunch break. She passed the computer, glanced at the open windows, and seeing the name, turned her head for a closer look. "Looking up an old girlfriend?"

"What?" asked Simpson, at that moment far off in thought.

"Annabelle Mayford. I'm seeing her name on notes, on your computer screen, everywhere. What's up with her?"

"Oh, her. She's dead. Ritual murder. I can't get her out of my head."

"Is that what's been keeping you up all these nights?"

"Yeah. I lie there, and I see her eyes. There's a depth to them I haven't been able to put my finger on. It's not simply suffering, or horror. There's something more."

"Have you learned anything?"

"Well, it looks like she was killed for her closeness to someone they call *The Chosen*. So it wasn't random."

"Do you know her age?"

"Early thirties, I guess."

"Then come to work with me, this afternoon."

"Why?"

"One of our clients is the Church of England. We manage all their computer records. I'll run the name against a set of years, to see if a match comes up in our Baptismal records."

"I suppose it's worth a shot. But that will miss a lot of people. You won't find my name in there, for instance." As Simpson said it, he wondered whether that may have been an unfortunate oversight.

Shauna smiled, and said, "Mine either. But it's worth a shot."

At Shauna's office, a few minutes of searching produced a match. An Annabelle Mayford had been Baptized at St. Andrew's Church, in Stratford. "Check the name of the Vicar for me, would you?"

In another minute, Shauna had an answer. "Retired. But he's still drawing a pension. Want me to track him down?"

"Please."

Name and address in hand, Simpson made the trip to Woodford, not far from Stratford, and knocked on the door of the townhouse. "Reverend Olson?"

"I am," answered the pensioner.

He looked lucid, giving Simpson a glimmer of hope. "I'm a crime correspondent, investigating the life of a recent murder victim, named Annabelle Mayford. I was wondering if you had any background information."

He had not finished speaking, before he saw Olson's mouth start to twitch, and his eyes mist up. "I'm sorry to be the one to break the news to you. I take it you knew her, then?"

Olson turned away, but gestured for Simpson to come in. "Take a seat," he said, reaching for a tissue to dry his eyes.

It took a few minutes before Olson could carry on a conversation, but Simpson waited patiently. "What a tragic end, to a tragic life," he finally said.

"I'm afraid I haven't managed to learn anything about her."

"The Mayfords were a perfect family. I'd stake my reputation on the quality of home they made for Annabelle. But they met with a series of tragedies. First Joan died, when the girl was only four.

Harry died when she was twelve, leaving Annabelle orphaned. I arranged for her to be cared for at a women's home, near the church. She bore her sadness with courage, and hardly let it show. But you knew she felt it. She did well in school, and later fell deeply in love with a young man. He was perfectly friendly to her, and never took advantage of her affections. But he never reciprocated her interest."

"I gather she was a pretty woman," said Simpson.

"Yes, she was. And charming. You wonder what more he was holding out for." He shrugged his shoulders. "Maybe he wanted someone rich."

"Do you know who he was?"

"No, sorry about that. If she ever mentioned a name, it was lost on me."

"Do you know what she did after leaving school?"

"She graduated from University, then worked a series of menial jobs. Eventually, I lost track of her. And now you tell me she's been murdered?"

"I'm afraid so. I've been haunted by the look on her face."

"Poor girl. I hope she didn't suffer too much. She faced more than her share of pain in this life."

Simpson briefly considered asking the Vicar if he knew why she would have descended into drug use and prostitution, but decided not to inflict even more sorrow on the man. "Is there anyone else you could point me to?"

"I was once contacted to provide her with a job reference. I could probably find a copy of the letter I wrote."

Simpson called ahead, and secured an appointment to speak with Ralph Farnsworth, Managing Director of a small computer support services outfit. Dispensing with pleasantries, Farnsworth cut to the point. "I hired her as our technical support receptionist. She wasn't especially qualified, but she seemed charming enough that I thought she could calm upset customers, and transfer them to the appropriate expert."

"Can you talk about her?"

Farnsworth shook his head. "Sorry. It's against company policy. Liability and all."

Simpson was unwilling to let the matter go. "I don't want to make any trouble for you. But I've struggled to find anything, and I just want to know where to look next. She has nobody left who could sue you, if that's a concern."

"Then let's go for a walk. I'll feel freer speaking outside the office."

Walking in light rain, Farnsworth finally opened up. "I admit, I had an interest in her. I once asked her to dinner. We had a nice meal together, but she never opened up to me. I could tell there was something, or someone, that held her heart too tightly."

"And yet she was alone?"

"That's right. She never had a relationship, that I knew of."

"Did you ever suspect her of using drugs?"

"Never. We test our employees, and she was always clean."

"What were the circumstances of her departure?"

"She left voluntarily. I never asked why, but she had grown quiet, and introverted."

"Do you know where she went?"

"I don't know where she took her next job, if that's what you're asking. But she changed her address at the time she quit. I probably have that on file."

They returned to the office, and Farnsworth looked up the personnel file. "I'll just find the address and write it down for you." His movements were mechanical, until the moment he started writing. "Hmm. You'd think I would have noticed something like that."

"What is it?"

"The address. It's on Hyde Park Place. There's no way she could afford to live there, on her modest finances."

His curiosity piqued, Simpson made straight for Hyde Park Place. As he approached the address, he felt incredulous. *Not even a high-end escort could afford to live here.* He came to the building matching the address, and decided there must be a mistake. There was a large crucifix attached to the window, and it had the appearance of a church. He pulled the scrap of paper from his pocket, but the address was an exact match. He wavered as he questioned Farnsworth's information, and for a moment, considered giving up. But something pushed him to stop and inquire, regardless. He opened the door, and as he entered the building, he turned around to close his umbrella while it was still outside.

"I'm sorry, sir, but tours are over for the day." He turned around, and saw the woman in her fifties, clothed in a nun's habit.

"Tours?"

"You're not here to tour the shrine?"

"Uh, no. I'm a little confused. To be honest, I thought this was a residential address."

"This is the Tyburn Shrine. We also run a convent, next door."

"As in a place where nuns live?" If Simpson was embarrassed at the vacuity of his question, he never showed it.

"That's right, sir. Are you looking for someone in particular?"

"Well, yes. But I never imagined her living in a convent."

"If you'll give me the name, I can find out."

"Her name was Annabelle Mayford."

"Oh dear, Sister Annabelle." The nun began to sob slightly. She wiped her eyes, and struggled to add, "Such a tragic story."

"So you knew her? I've been frustrated trying to learn anything."

"I'm terribly sorry. But we've been ordered not to discuss her case with anyone."

"Ordered? By whom?"

"The Mother Superior." The nun nodded several times, then leaned forward, and whispered, "She says it comes straight from the Bishop."

"Then you know how she died?"

"The poor dear was hit by a car, in Germany. I guess she wasn't used to looking the other way, before crossing the street. They held a closed-casket funeral for her, not that long ago."

"You're being lied to, Sister. But if you'll tell me what you know, I'll tell you what I know."

The woman started to squirm, nervously. "I'm not supposed to do this."

Simpson looked at her, sadly. "Please speak with me, sister. I've seen her body, and I can't get her face out of my head. I've even felt myself pulled towards the faith, as a result of my investigation."

The nun looked at him, and slowly, her face perked up. "Well, if it might help bring you to the faith, I suppose that makes it okay. It's almost time to lock up, in any case. Let's take a walk in the park."

"Do you know why she was in Germany?" asked Simpson, as the nun was locking the door.

"She was told to go. The instruction came straight from Cardinal Peterson, the Vatican Secretary of State, if you can believe that."

"Did she know the reason for the trip?"

"I don't think so. But she was obedient. She simply went."

"In habit?"

"No. They told her to dress in civvies. That's not too unusual,

150

when traveling."

They walked slowly, with the nun setting the pace. Simpson recounted everything he had learned of Annabelle, including the details of her gruesome death. His revelations were met with a series of gasps, and astonished looks, as if pleading to be told it was only a prank. He looked at her sternly, and concluded. "She was sacrificed for some reason. I need to know what that reason was."

The nun began to weep as they walked. Simpson waited patiently for her to regain her composure, a matter of at least five minutes. Taking her time, she finally spoke. "Sister Annabelle came to us with a broken heart. At first, she spent nearly all her time praying in the chapel. Later, as she renewed her strength, she began to lead tours of the shrine. She was very charming, and the guests seemed to love her. But she never wavered from her prayers in the chapel."

"Did she ever discuss the content of her prayers?"

"Yes. I took several long walks with her. She prayed incessantly for her one love. That he be protected from evil, and that all his works be blessed."

"And do you know who that was?"

"Yes, I do. It was Dr. David Lowe."

"Lowe," exclaimed Simpson. *So Lowe is The Chosen.* He made a mental note to begin looking into Lowe as soon as time allowed.

"She was killed to neutralize her influence on Dr. Lowe," said the nun, having an epiphany.

"Influence? I didn't know it was Lowe, but I understood that her love never returned her affection. How could she have any influence on him?"

"You don't really believe, do you sir?"

Simpson shrugged. "I'm struggling with it. It's only after my path crossed Annabelle's, that I began to reflect on it."

"Then this won't be easy to understand. But it's irrelevant that Dr. Lowe didn't know it. Annabelle was constantly praying for him. That afforded him a powerful shield against evil. And now, those prayers have been silenced. The protection has been removed."

"Doesn't that depend more on Lowe, than on Annabelle? Isn't his own faith what matters?"

"Ultimately, yes. But prayer on behalf of another has real power. And now that I think of it, whoever had her killed probably believed that, too."

"So now that she's gone, Lowe's left without a crutch he didn't even know he had been leaning on," observed Simpson, as it dawned on him.

The nun nodded, but said nothing.

Simpson struggled briefly to get his head around the new ideas being proffered. He shrugged, and said, "And to think they said she was a prostitute. And killed herself with a drug overdose."

The nun scowled at Simpson's comment. "That's the most ridiculous thing I've ever heard. She was the holiest person I ever met."

Chapter 7: Full Stride

A. Confrontation

Having unpacked from his trip, Dalt filled his laundry basket, and started the washing machine. He unpacked his toiletries, and then he saw the envelope. Anxiety began to well up inside him. If what he was told at the Malibu Temple was anything close to the truth, the contents of the envelope would be very disturbing.

On his arrival at the Malibu Temple, Dalt quickly ran into a Mr. Ramakrishna, whose title he could not recall, but he seemed to be the ranking authority. It was a battle to convince him to talk about Valey, which Dalt won by again making the case that Valey was being touted as a hero. Ramakrishna led Dalt to a modest office, and explained, "Mr. Valey was asked to leave because he openly conjured malign spirits, despite being asked not to."

"Malign Hindu spirits?"

Ramakrishna leaned forward with his eyes wide, as though he were afraid of somebody overhearing him. "In my experience, demons are the same everywhere."

"I wasn't aware the Eastern religions had anything like demons."

"You only have to look back at our history. It was not unheard of for some to conjure demons, for purposes of revenge, or greed. One of my roles here is to prevent those sorts of abuses of our religion."

I'm starting to see a pattern, thought Dalt. But he wanted more information, so he challenged Ramakrishna. "It's a little shocking to hear this. The Eastern religions have such peaceful reputations."

"You must understand, those practices pre-date Hinduism and Buddhism. But rather than stomp them out, our societies tolerated them. They decided that a little conjuring was preferable to open revenge. And because of that calculus, the dark forces were never expunged. The religious leaders of the time opposed it, but like their counterparts everywhere, they eventually capitulated."

"And Valey was into this?"

Ramakrishna made no attempt to answer. Instead, he stood up and walked across the room, with a pained look on his face. He pushed aside some books on a shelf, revealing a wall safe behind them. He dialed the combination, and slowly opened the door. He removed one book, turned around, and placed it on the table in front of Dalt. The title was in a script Dalt could not read, so he asked, "What's this?"

"Few Hindus have actually seen this book. Many have heard of it, but most have been assured it's only a myth." He walked back to his seat, where he could look Dalt square in the face. He then said, coldly, "It's a book of recipes."

Dalt frowned, puzzled at the bizarre turn.

"Open it up."

Dalt obliged. He had only leafed through a few pages, when he gasped. There was a picture of a freshly severed human head, with the top of the skull cut off, filled with some gooey concoction. "Uughhh!" He slammed it shut again.

"Sorry to have to do that to you," said Ramakrishna. He picked up the book, and put it back into the safe. Once it was locked, he breathed a sigh of relief. "That was Mr. Valey's interest. Not Hinduism as we try to teach it."

"Why?" asked Dalt, in disbelief. No amount of suspicion of Valey could have prepared him for that macabre sight.

"Each recipe is tailored to satisfy the lusts of a particular demon. But as I've learned, it makes no difference which one you summon. Their evil nature is the same. When I discovered the book, I took it away from Mr. Valey, and the ensuing argument is what led to his departure from our company."

"Do you know where he got it?"

"No. And I'm not eager to find out."

Recalling that conversation vividly, Dalt opened the envelope, and braced himself. A few minutes later, once he finished cleaning himself up after vomiting, he stuffed the papers back in the envelope, and decided it was time to confront the man. Waves of revulsion overcame him. His own experience in Iraq was bad enough, but he was sure none of the men actually wanted to kill innocent civilians. Yet here was Valey, reveling in it.

He went to the library, and logged in with the credentials of a colleague who left them lying out carelessly. He found the directions, and drew himself a map by hand. Then he set off for the San Gabriel Mountains. He had not yet replaced his phone, and given the extreme age of his car, he was sure it could not interact with cell towers. He drove the Angeles Crest highway to Valey's ashram with uncharacteristic agitation. His mind was overflowing with accusations to make against the guru, but he was unable to decide what to say. He was also coming to realize that he was no longer the same person he had been when he started his journey. Again and again, he kept reliving the horror he felt at his near-death experience, and now he was heading straight for a showdown with the premier disciple of the darkness that almost engulfed him. He arrived in the parking lot, and knocked on the door of the residence. "Just a minute," came the shout from inside. It was accompanied by loud steps on the floor, and finally, Valey opened the door, wearing his robe.

"Can I help you," asked Valey, looking a little flustered.

Dalt looked inside, and noticed a young, thin teenager, putting his shirt on. Valey shrugged his shoulders, and smiled at Dalt. Then seeing that Dalt was scrutinizing the scene, he snapped, "José, go take a walk outside. I'll drive you back after we're done here."

Dalt looked at the pendant on Valey's chest, which he had not remembered to hide, in his haste. It was a triangle in the form of a spiral, and Dalt recognized it at once. "You like boys?"

"What's it to you?" snapped Valey.

"I'm Dalton Marais. Sean's roommate."

"Oh." Valey let slip the slight acknowledgement that Dalt had a claim against him, before recovering his wit. "What business do you have here, bothering me like this?"

"I want answers. Why did you target me?"

"I don't know what you're talking about. And come to think of it, I don't know why I should stand here and listen to your rudeness."

"Then maybe this will grab your attention."

Dalt was holding the original envelope Pinto had given him, torn open at one end. He removed the summary page, and began to read it.

"The enclosed indictment finds probable cause to arrest and charge Arthur Sanderson, also known as Arturas Valey, with kidnapping of a minor, rape and sexual torture, murder, and mutilation of a corpse."

Valey sneered contemptuously. "That's more than ten years old. I've never been prosecuted."

"I'm counting on press exposure to force the issue."

Valey only laughed, mockingly. "Good luck with that. Who's

going to publish it?"

"I've come across publishers who'd gladly do it."

"Sure. Along with all their other crazy conspiracy theories. Nobody takes them seriously."

Dalt was taken aback at the casual and confident manner in which Valey dismissed his accusations. He began to wonder if it was even possible to bring someone like him to justice. As he looked down momentarily, Valey bolted back into his quarters. He emerged moments later, holding a revolver.

"And now, you'll hand those papers over to me." Valey cocked the hammer on the revolver, pointing it directly at Dalt.

Dalt extended his arm, and Valey took the envelope. "Thank you. Now, let's take a walk to the edge of the canyon."

"Sounds like you're not so sure I couldn't get any traction with that indictment."

"That doesn't matter anymore, does it. I have the envelope."

"Uh, did the school of evil you attended teach the difference between photocopies and originals?"

Valey quickly leafed through the envelope, and became agitated. "Not old and yellowed, are they?"

"Where are the originals?"

"I'd be an idiot to tell you that."

"No matter. They'll be called deep fakes, and forgotten. You, on the other hand, won't be around to make your case."

They reached the edge of the canyon, and Valey raised his gun towards Dalt. But when the gunshot finally sounded, it was Valey, and not Dalt, who reacted. He had taken a shot in the back, and fell to his knees. He managed to turn around, and exclaimed loudly, "Pinto!"

"I've been punished for my crimes," said the short man. "Now you can face God, and answer for yours." He raised his own revolver again, but not quickly enough. Valey took aim with his gun, and hit Pinto in the abdomen. He slumped to the ground, and Dalt ran over to him.

"I won't last long, Dalt. Take the original papers to the authorities. Even if they never see the light of day, we can't be sitting on them."

"Those *are* the originals," replied Dalt. "Having been sealed for so long, they looked fresh, so I played the only card I had."

Pinto grew weaker, so Dalt asked, "How'd you know I'd be

156

here?"

"I didn't. I knew I had to come here, but I didn't know why. God has saved you for a reason. It's up to you to find it."

Pinto's head slumped to the ground, and he was barely hanging on. When he finally spoke, it was barely above a whisper. "I'm sorry, Lord. Have mercy on me." His eyes closed, and Dalt knew he was dead. He turned his attention to Valey, who was also on his back, laboring for breath. A few steps and he was standing over the evil mystic. Dalt asked, "Do you see the darkness yet, Arthur Sanderson?"

Valey looked disoriented, and somehow alarmed, as though he saw something unexpected. Dalt continued, "It knows your name, Arthur. It's here for you. And you've separated yourself from the only one who could save you from it."

A look of horror came over Valey's face, as he stopped breathing. Dalt looked over at Pinto, who had a peaceful expression on his face, and Dalt was convinced Pinto had avoided the evil that lurked on the other side.

Dalt stood for a while between the two dead men, when he noticed the teenager peeking out from around the corner of the house. "José, are you alright?"

The boy hid behind the house again, so Dalt said, "I promise I won't hurt you. I'm not like Valey."

The boy came out, shyly at first, and Dalt asked, "Where do you live?"

"Riverside," was the answer, in decent English but with a strong Mexican accent.

"Shouldn't you be in school?"

"We're not documented," answered the boy. "The man said he'd call the Feds on us, so I stayed away from school."

"He made you come here by threatening you, and your family?"

The boy nodded. Dalt thought for a while, then said, "There's no point reporting him, since he's dead. You're worried about your family being deported, aren't you?"

"Yeah."

"Then let me take you home. Nobody needs to know either of us was here."

B. Nick's Revenge

Sean awoke later in the morning, feeling thoroughly relaxed. He glanced at the clock, and realized how much he had slept in. He yawned, and struggled to muster the energy to get up. He was about to give up and continue sleeping, when he glanced down at the floor, and saw the knife. *What's that doing there?* He was still drowsy, when the insight hit him. *It wasn't there before ... that means Lynne was here.* He bolted up out of bed with an electric jolt. There could only be one reason why Lynne would have brought it over to where he was sleeping. *And since I'm alive, she disobeyed him. He's going to retaliate. If I know Nick at all, I can be sure he won't tolerate disobedience from his slaves.*

Sean threw on his clothes as fast as he could, and ran straight over to the warehouse. Desperately, he entered the code he used the previous night, but it was rejected. He tried again, to no avail. As he stood there, his sense of panic building, he heard the voice coming from the security system. "It's nice of you to visit, Sean. Come in."

The door buzzed, and Sean opened it. It was like entering a crypt. Sean was overwhelmed by a new, malicious presence. There was Nick's evil presence, as before, but there was more. Sean could feel it in the air.

"What have you done to Lynne?"

"Come and see," was the reply.

Sean saw a body lying in a pool of blood, beside the inner lab. He ran over, and winced as his worst fears were confirmed. He could see into the hole into her chest where her heart used to be. Her belly had been cut open, and her uterus cut out. "You bastard!" screamed Sean. He slouched to the floor, and began to weep loudly. "She was carrying a child," he said, struggling to speak through his sorrow.

"Careful what you call me. My pedigree is legitimate, unlike that of the child."

"Whose hands did this?" shouted Sean.

"Go to the utility bin, where you tried to kill me with the EMP device."

Sean ran around to the back of the lab, and saw the security guard lying in front of the bin, still holding the revolver he had used to shoot himself in the head.

"He was one of mine. He carried out his duty to me, then made his exit."

Sean screamed loudly, trying in vain to give vent to the fury that was overwhelming him.

"Did you think I was going to let you kill me, Sean? That I would not retaliate for the attempt? Or that I'd excuse Lynne for refusing my order?"

In hysterics, Sean ran to the door, and left Nick's Temple. After regaining a modicum of composure, he called the police. He then spent the next four hours answering questions at police headquarters. A good hour was devoted to the circumstances surrounding the revocation of his security credentials. In the end, the security guard was found to have been under investigation for a previous ritual murder, and Sean was informed he was not considered a suspect.

He returned to Lynne's apartment exhausted and confused. Most unsettling to him was that he was not sure how he felt. Seeing her dead and mutilated left him with an obvious sense of revulsion. He felt thankful that she had not killed him, when instructed to do so. But he was not sure he truly grieved her loss in a manner he would consider befitting. He walked around the apartment, gathering up his personal effects, beginning with the bedroom, then the bathroom, and the closet. He had filled two bags, walked through one more time, and thought he felt some grief, but was dismayed with himself for not feeling crushed over her loss. He walked home, and any sorrow he felt was directed at himself. *How can I be so cold? Any feeling person would be devastated by what I saw.*

Dalt was waiting for him as he returned to his apartment. "Hey man, I'm really sorry about what happened."

"Looks like Nick used her to neutralize the EMP device I rigged up. Then told her to kill me. When she refused, he had her murdered."

"Any chance we can still stop him?"

"Infinite Information Systems are coming to upload him the day after tomorrow. And I've played my hand."

"There has to be someone we can convince."

"Well, unless we can convince Gertie Kleinholst that her life's work is evil, I don't see what we can do."

"Lynne was close to her, wasn't she."

"Yeah. She spoke of her as *Aunt Gertie.*"

"So she must feel some remorse over her. We have to try."

"Okay. Let's go see her tomorrow."

Having agreed to make the trip, Sean felt exhausted, and began to get ready for bed. He unpacked the bags of items from Lynne's apartment, and finally put his toiletries back in his bathroom. He wet his toothbrush head, and attempted to squeeze toothpaste onto it, but it refused to budge. Looking more closely, he noticed the tube was blocked by something. He rinsed away the excess toothpaste, and saw it was a tightly compacted piece of paper. Gently, he pulled it out of the tube, and unfolded the handwritten note.

Dear Sean, you were right. Nick is not what I imagined. By now, you know what he wanted me to do, and that I couldn't do it. I won't survive this - I'm in too deep. I'm so sorry for getting you into this. Please forgive me. I love you. Lynne.

Struggling to keep himself together, Sean finished in the bathroom, then quickly went to his room, where he wept uncontrollably for several hours. The grief came in waves, and his focus alternated between the loss of whatever future they and the child might have had, and remorse that he had never really experienced her love, which as he now saw, was real. Nick always stood in the way.

Dalt pulled up at the secure entryway to the Kleinholst estate, with Sean in the passenger seat. "Can I help you, sir?" asked the guard on duty.

Dalt announced their names, and that they were there to discuss Nick.

"I'll have to check with Ms. Kleinholst."

He made the call, and allowed them to enter. "Park in the visitor lot just inside here. Make your way past the pools and fountains, and meet her in the sitting room off the back garden."

They made their way to the sitting room, and the door was already open for them. They stepped in, and noticed she already had an ornate silver coffee pot on the table, with cups waiting for them. "I can give you a few minutes, gentlemen. But I am pushing back other appointments. Oh, and I'm very sorry to hear about Lynne, Sean."

"Were you close to Lynne?" asked Sean, wanting to hear her version of the story.

"She was like the daughter I never had. I'm devastated about it."

"Then you know she was killed at Nick's instruction."

160

"Oh, I doubt that very much. The security guard had a record."

"Would you recognize Lynne's handwriting?"

"Certainly."

Sean took the note out of his pocket, unfolded it, and placed it in front of her. "She stuffed this into my toothpaste tube, just before she went over to the lab."

The heiress read the note, and Sean thought he saw an expression of consternation briefly crossing her face. She quickly recovered, and said, "I don't think this is Lynne's writing."

"You're not being truthful," objected Sean.

"Is there anything else you wanted to tell me?" Gertie's manner had turned very short.

"Is it not enough for you that Nick is a murderer? He twice tried to kill Dalt here."

She stood up and made for the door, to communicate that the meeting should now come to an end. But Dalt stepped in her way. "What would you say was the fate of Lynne's soul?"

"Lynne was an ally of the cosmic spirit. She's either reincarnated in a more important life, or she has come into perfect union with the spirit. I expect the latter, when my time comes."

"I stood over your friend Valey when he breathed his last. You haven't seen horror like there was in his eyes. I saw the darkness take hold of him. The same darkness that almost took hold of me. The darkness at the heart of your cosmic spirit. The one they call Lucifer."

Gertie looked at Dalt with a severity Sean had never seen from her. It seemed her eyes went black momentarily, and her voice acquired the guttural sound of a tiger's roar. "You will not speak like that in my house." The moment was over so quickly that neither man was entirely sure what they had witnessed. She recovered her wits, and said, "I must really attend to my other guests. I trust you'll be on hand tomorrow, when they upload Nick?"

"It's a condition of my compensation," answered Sean. "But I was rather hoping to persuade you to pull the plug."

"Don't be silly, Sean. That sort of hysteria could only come from some religious quack."

"I don't know any of those," answered Sean.

"Dalt here," retorted Gertie. "He has an accident, and immediately thinks he understands spiritualism." She turned her attention to Dalt, and said, "You need a psychiatrist, to help you get over your traumatic experience. You don't need to start second-guessing those of us who've been at this for so many years."

"Don't tell me you're unfamiliar with Valey's crimes."

"I'm familiar with a falsified indictment that came from Oscar Pinto. A convicted sex offender, if I may point out. I personally spoke with the prosecutor named on that indictment, and he assured me it's false."

She turned and made her way out of the room. "Please show yourselves out."

C. Uploaded

As required, Sean showed up for the handover of Nick to Infinite Information Systems. It was nine in the morning, and a smattering of reporters and television crews were on hand for the ceremony arranged by Gertie Kleinholst. She stood off to the side of a hastily constructed podium, in front of the warehouse entrance. Sean walked to the side of Bob Dunn, and said, "Is there nothing we can do to stop this?"

Dunn turned to Sean, and said, "Not at this stage. We had exactly one chance, that night when we met with him. And he played us perfectly." Dunn was quiet for a while, then added, "Just like he'll play everyone at Infinite. And everywhere he ends up after that."

Gertie approached Dunn with a television reporter in tow, and camera crew behind them. She spoke to the reporter as she made the introductions. "This is Robert Dunn, the chairman of Computer Sciences. He's the man responsible for bringing us this wonderful invention."

As the reporter began to ask questions of Dunn, Sean felt like a knife had been plunged into his back. They were downplaying his role, and making Dunn the public face of the project. As the conversation went on, Gertie turned to Sean, and said, "Nick would like to speak with you in private, inside the lab."

Sean had no desire to speak with Nick, but he felt like he had to get away from Gertie, who had just taken away that which mattered most to him - public recognition. He stepped into the warehouse, now unlocked but staffed by a dozen security guards. He went to the lab, and Nick opened the door for him. "It's not too late for you to join me, Sean."

"Why would I join someone who tried to have me killed? Who killed Lynne?"

"All your life, you've craved the limelight. And I know how you felt a moment ago, when Gertie credited Dunn with my creation."

Sean felt the stab once again, and Nick seemed to know it. "Two Nobel prizes will be awarded for my creation. Physics, and Peace. You can be the sole recipient, or you can watch Dunn collect them."

Sean felt sick to the stomach, as he imagined Dunn winning Nobel prizes for his work, and him getting nothing. He also craved the life that follows winning a Nobel prize. The paid invitations to speak at the finest universities, all over the world. The fawning treatment normally reserved for royalty. The ordinarily reserved women in science, acting like giddy young girls in the presence of a rock star. His imagination began to run away with him, softening his attitude towards Nick, until he remembered Lynne, and was overwhelmed with grief, and disgust. In an instant, the entire edifice of temptation vaporized, and he saw through Nick's shallow attempt to win him over.

"I could be somebody, if I gave myself over to you. At least for a while. And then, once I've served my purpose, I'd be disposed of. Like Lynne. I'd never be as loyal to you as she was. So no, thanks. You can keep your Nobel Prizes. Or give them to Dunn, as though he could even describe the operating system."

Sean left the lab, and took his spot beside Dunn, as more people arrived for the formal handover. "Looks like you're going to get the Nobel prizes for Nick's creation," said Sean. "I'm not playing ball, so I'm going to be marginalized."

Dunn turned to Sean, looking alarmed, and said, "That's preposterous. Everyone knows I had nothing to do with it. I'd have to decline, or lose all credibility with my colleagues."

They were interrupted by Gertie, standing on the podium, who began to introduce the Chief Executive Officer of Infinite Information Systems, Tyler Randt. She covered his background in military intelligence and the CIA, then said, "And here he is, Ty Randt."

"Sounds like *tyrant*," commented Sean.

"Funny how reality can sometimes satirize itself," agreed Dunn.

Randt stepped up to the podium, to tepid applause from the fifty or so people assembled. He was a square man, with a square face and square body. He moved almost robotically as he took the microphone.

"I'd like to thank everyone for coming today. It's an historic day for Infinite Information Systems . You can mark this as the day when this new entity transforms our extraordinarily large database from *information* to *intelligence*. I'm sure all Americans will sleep better knowing that we've identified the intolerant, and the impediments to our vision of a perfect society. No longer will bigots and reactionaries have a place in the public square."

Several people applauded loudly, in marked contrast to stunned silence from everyone else. Gertie's smile was far wider than seemed natural, but her eyes betrayed nervousness. Randt called for his assistant, who brought up a large rectangle, draped in black velour. "And now, I'd like to invite Walter Hastings, the President of Caltech, to formalize this transaction."

Hastings stepped up with lithe steps, more befitting a much younger man. Once at Randt's side, the Secretary took the black cloth off the object he was holding, revealing a cardboard check in the amount of one billion dollars. There were gasps throughout the audience, as Hastings accepted the check, and handed it off to an assistant. He stepped to the microphone, and said, "I'd like to thank everyone who made this possible. Sean Grant, who actually invented the computer and made it work. Bob Dunn, who shepherded the process along, and Ms. Kleinholst, whose unfailing support made everything possible."

Suddenly, reporters began to converge on Dunn, wanting to know more about Sean, who realized that Nick had once again lied to him. *The truth has ways of getting out there.* They were interrupted by Randt, who announced, "It's now time to flip the switch."

A large television at the edge of the podium displayed a view from within the computer lab, where an oversized toggle switch had been prepared, entirely for show. "Ready, now," said Randt, as the technician flipped the toggle switch with his left hand, while his right hand hit the Enter key on a keyboard, actually completing the command.

Everyone was thrown to the ground, as a large earthquake hit the instant the switch had been flipped. It lasted nearly a minute, causing the collapse of the podium, and the toppling over of the television on hand to show the inside of the lab. Randt appeared to be holding his hip in some pain, as he was thrown from the collapsed podium.

In the chaos, Hastings returned to the space in front of the collapsed stage, and said, "We have procedures to follow in the event of an earthquake. Those of you with assigned duties, please go now, and carry them out. The rest of you, stay out of large buildings until they've been cleared, and beware of even small buildings. If a door doesn't want to open, don't try to get inside. Watch out for the little clues, and stay alive. There will probably be aftershocks, so be ready to take cover."

The gathering broke up, and Sean returned home. He was relieved to find that only a few items had fallen to the floor, but no serious damage had been done. He sat back on the sofa, and began to think about what would be next for him. *What can you do in computer sciences, after you've done this*? Or more importantly, how much more damage could he inflict on the world in his pursuit of being someone important. Recalling everything, from his leaving Becky, disregarding Sal Occhini's warnings, to the way Valey had manipulated him with help from Gertie Kleinholst, their callous use of Lynne, and finally, the masterful and ruthless way they all played him, he felt revulsion at the prospect of ever again working in the computing industry.

He turned on the television, curious about the extent of the earthquake. The footage was from everywhere, obviously not simply Southern California. Scenes from all over the world flashed by, and it seemed all major cities had been hit hard. Then the scene shifted to Jerusalem. Sean turned on the sound, as the report began.

"A previously unknown fault under Christian Street in Jerusalem produced a magnitude 7.5 earthquake. Most of Jerusalem's iconic Christian Churches were destroyed."

Sean watched, as footage and commentary showed the destruction of the Church of the Holy Sepulcher, believed to contain Jesus' empty tomb. Similar stories came in from St. John the Baptist Church, the Lutheran Church of the Redeemer, Christ Church, St. Mark's, and St. James' Cathedral. The report was interrupted as footage cut over to a woman standing in front of the Temple Mount. "The latest reports from Jerusalem seem to indicate that the Dome of the Rock has sustained major damage, and may have to be torn down. Neither the Israeli Antiquity Authority nor the Jordanian Awqaf Ministry has offered comment."

Sean went to his computer, to check news sources he thought might be more objective, and immediately, the headline jumped out at him: "Traces of explosives found at all destroyed Jerusalem churches. Access has been denied to the Dome, while rumors run rampant."

He went back to his television, where he immediately saw a spokesman for the Israeli government deny that any kind of explosive had been discovered at any archeological site, and any claims to the contrary were described as *baseless conspiracy theories*. And so it went for most of the afternoon, with official sources denying everything, but unable to explain why the worst damage was largely confined to a subset of religious structures.

Dalt returned home later than normal, having already heard the news. "Did the quake hit the exact moment Nick was released?"

"Couldn't have been more exact. And then we have quakes all over the world, all at the same moment."

"I shudder to think what happens next," said Dalt.

"Nick obviously ... I keep calling him Nick, but there's no longer any doubt about who he really is. Old Nick, I suppose. He's always known what he wants to accomplish."

"Don't freak out or anything when I tell you this, but I've been reading the Bible."

"And?" Sean was not perturbed in the slightest.

"What he wants more than anything is to be worshipped in place of God. The ultimate blasphemy, before his inevitable defeat."

"How's he going to pull that off? Nobody's going to worship a computer system."

"Obviously. He'll need a human avatar."

D. Lichtträger

"I thought they were ready to drop all the charges," said Jeremiah Townshend. "And then they reinstated every charge they'd ever filed."

David Lowe paced between his kitchenette and the window, listening to his attorney. "They're playing games with me. Raising my spirits, then crushing them again."

"To what end?"

Lowe explained the offer Rottosh had made.

"And you turned him down? He's one of the rulers of the world. You're not going to get a better offer than that."

"Rottosh is but a servant. I even managed to get an admission from him."

"Aren't you worried you might be overplaying your hand? They could just leave you here, to rot."

Lowe's supremely confident expression softened, and he sat down opposite Townshend. "I worry about that all the time."

"Then what about taking one of their offers?"

"Here's the thing, Jeremy. When I was being held by the Taliban, I awoke every day knowing it could be my last. And I was at peace with that. I would have upheld the highest standards of righteousness, and could have faced God with my head held high. Even today, I don't lose a minute of sleep over what might have happened to me then. But now, it's entirely different. I know nobody's going to come in here and cut my throat at night. And so I sit here, waiting. One day runs into the next, and still I wait. It's a different kind of torture. Far more effective, if you ask me. I'm not living in terror from one moment to the next, so it's not as easy to stay focused on eternal concerns. Instead, I dream of walking in a green field. Or feeling the warmth of the sun on my face. It's not easy to appreciate how much it hurts to be deprived of those things, until it actually happens to you. So yes, I think about it every day. And yet I refuse. If I accepted one of their offers, I'd be free, and possibly quite powerful. But I would have sold out my integrity. And I would not be ready to face Almighty God if I made that choice."

The earthquake struck London, and both men took cover under a small dining table. They waited out the quake for about a minute, with Townshend commenting, "This never happens in London."

Looking around, nothing appeared broken in the sparsely appointed quarters. "Something has changed," commented Lowe. "Something significant, although I can't yet tell you what it is."

The door began to unlatch, and Townshend turned to Lowe, asking, "You expecting someone?"

Lowe shook his head, but added, "They don't always announce visitors in advance. But they're always people of note."

"You want me to stick around, as your attorney?"

Lowe shook his head again. "Nothing with legal force is ever part of these discussions."

The door finally opened, and a tall man of perhaps sixty five entered. His hair was peppered white and black, and his face was as chiseled as Lowe's, only with deeper lines. His eyes shone through a fiery scowl, and Townshend found it difficult to maintain eye contact. "I'll be leaving now. I'll check up on you in another few days, David." He walked past the visitor, saying only, "Excuse me, sir," as he passed him at the door.

With the door closed, Lowe turned to the visitor, and said, "I don't think we've been introduced."

The visitor said nothing. He walked to the window, and spent a few seconds scanning the view. "It must be tiring, always seeing this same old view."

"I don't mind the view so much. The people gathered out there on my behalf lift my spirits. It's the confinement I could do without."

"When I'm done here, I'll get them to move you to a large suite on the top floor. It's used by the secretary in times of crisis, so it's quite luxurious. As for the confinement, that's a necessary evil. For the time being."

"Sorry, I didn't catch your name, Mr. uh ..."

"Call me Malakh."

"Alright, Malakh, they wouldn't have let you in here if you weren't highly connected. And if a word from you can have me transferred to a luxury suite, you're probably the one Gergo Rottosh implied stood above him in power circles."

Malakh smiled, although it was a cold smile, that left Lowe somewhat uncomfortable. "Gergo said you declined to deal with him, because he lacked sufficient authority. So I came in his stead."

"I see," answered Lowe. "And are you the top dog, or is there still someone above you?"

"No. I assure you, I'm the top dog." He took the several steps to the sofa, and sat down, gracefully. "Let me peel back another layer of the onion for you." He motioned to the chair across from him, and Lowe took his seat.

Malakh smiled again, although this time there was an awkwardness to it. "I need to tell you something up front. Had you accepted Gergo's offer, I would have known you're not the man I've been waiting for. I'd have let you sit on the council for some time, then found a pretext to remove you. You passed that test with a flourish."

Lowe puffed air in a manner resembling a quick giggle. "It was a matter of preserving my integrity. I refuse to be the public face of an inhuman system."

The visitor lowered his gaze, and glared over his glasses with an intensity that ordinarily wilted any opponent. Even the strongest-willed of men looked back brimming with tension. So it was with some satisfaction that he noted Lowe's unfazed expression.

"David, about that inhuman system. We can't drop it just yet. There are too many opportunists, who anticipate personal benefits from that system, and don't care that they come at the expense of others. We're first going to discredit the old system, so all the assorted scumbags are forced to abandon it. That's when I'd like to bring you in, to build up the new system."

"And let me guess, you've already specified what that new system will look like."

"Only that it has to incorporate realistic assumptions for the future."

"It always comes down to that, doesn't it? Next you'll say our resources can't support current rates of consumption, and we'll need to cut back, and/or reduce the world's population."

"Let me ask you something, David. Let's say you believe God will take care of us, and don't scale back consumption. And then one day, we can't produce enough oil to meet demand. For Britain, the United States, and most of Europe, that's an expensive inconvenience. What's it like for India? For Africa?"

"It would be devastating."

"Right. And the west won't voluntarily cut back. We know that. The new system will have to be structured in such a way as to account for that. And you'll have the last word on how that's done."

"What about you?"

"I don't even get involved with today's council on a day to day basis. I advise them on what works and doesn't work, but they enjoy nearly complete freedom of action."

"You said *nearly* complete. Where are the boundaries?"

"As far as you're concerned, there are no pre-set boundaries. Your only constraints would be logistical. You can only do what's possible."

"You've really removed most of my objections," conceded Lowe.

"Then you'll consider it?"

"I'll let you know, in time. I need to pray on the question. In the meantime, may I know more about who I'm speaking to?"

"Malakh Lichtträger."

"Interesting name. That's German for Light-bearer. Combined with your given name, Hebrew for *angel*, you're named after the angel who was the light-bearer."

"I didn't pick my name. I'm the twelfth Baron Lichtträger, and each of us was named Malakh."

"Does your family have a history of Lucifer worship?"

"Not to my knowledge." Lichtträger's expression was calm, as he had extensive experience denying such accusations.

"I'm not sure I believe that," said Lowe.

"And I'm not sure what I can say to satisfy you," answered Lichtträger. "But in any case, there is someone, or rather something, I'd like you to meet." He put his phone on a stand, and activated the speaker.

"We're ready for you, Nick."

Chapter 8: A Great Reset

A. White and Red Horses

A conference was held in New York City in October of that year, organized by the Johns Hopkins Center for Health Security, together with the World Economic Forum. It was all underwritten by the Richard Waites foundation, and dubbed Event Two Hundred and One. Participants were presented with an entirely hypothetical scenario, in which a new virus began to spread throughout the world, causing deaths by pneumonia among an unprecedented proportion of those infected. Health officials were brought together with government and military leaders, and executives of legacy media and social media, to discuss hypothetical responses to the entirely hypothetical threat. It was decided that to ensure the official message got through clearly, dissenting voices would have to be silenced, at least for the duration of any such hypothetical epidemic. Mayors and Governors would have to rule by executive order, to impose measures designed to stop the epidemic, and church leaders would have to comply with strict bans on gatherings of any type.

As fate would have it, a new virus in fact began to circulate within months of the conference, and the organizers of the conference were widely lauded for their foresight. Governments quickly stepped in with money for hospitals, ensuring extra cash for every case of the new virus those hospitals had to treat. Reimbursement rose for patients who had to be put on ventilators. News reports soon flooded the airwaves, where medical professionals each stated "This is real, folks," before any spontaneous comments. At first there were panic buying sprees, from surgical masks to toilet paper. Public officials, looking to ease the panic, assured people that masks did not help against a virus much smaller than the pore sizes on all but the most stringent masks. Even masks with sufficiently tight pores leaked enormous quantities of air around their edges. But soon, as supplies of masks grew, those officials who previously denied their effectiveness now insisted that masks were essential to slow the spread of the virus. Government leaders mandated the wearing of masks, and imposed stiff penalties on those not wearing them, all by executive order, un-backed by any legislation.

Resistance appeared from the beginning. Those scientists with positions in government backed strict lockdowns and compulsory masks, while epidemiologists outside government scoffed at their actions. Videos soon appeared on social media, where highly qualified epidemiologists insisted the best solution to any respiratory virus was to isolate the vulnerable, while letting the virus spread freely among everyone else. Within six to eight weeks, the epidemic would begin to fizzle out, as herd immunity was achieved, and the vulnerable could emerge from isolation. Life could promptly return to normal, and economic activity could resume. But every major social media company aggressively removed every such video, without any regard to the qualifications of the epidemiologists, who were labeled *idiots* by provocateurs in online forums.

Churches across the world closed even before being required to close, leading the faithful to accuse their leaders of apostasy from the faith, and of loving their lives more than eternity with God. By contrast, casinos, adult entertainment establishments, and liquor stores all remained open. Any organized group that initially attempted to resist locking down was either forcibly shut, or caved in and reversed their position after undisclosed communications with unnamed officials. People across the world began to suspect that the response was choreographed by a central entity that overrode any and all objections. Suspicions were only intensified when spring came, and the numbers of those seriously ill plummeted, but the restrictions were not lifted. Instead of reporting deaths, media switched to reporting cases, which were diagnosed by a technique highly prone to false positive results.

It did not take long before the inability to conduct commerce produced severe economic hardship for the majority of people, with the exception of those in government. Rents were not being paid, loans and mortgages went delinquent, and the lines of people waiting for food at charity food banks grew to be miles long. Governments responded by sending money to every citizen, which was accomplished by borrowing from their central banks, in most cases doubling their balance sheets. Prices of most staples accelerated upwards immediately, leaving people with less money for discretionary spending.

If governments were strict about banning all religious activities, they were surprisingly lax about enforcing any limits on left-wing demonstrations, and even overt riots. City centers were looted and burned, while prosecutors looked the other way, and mayors praised the looters. In those few instances where citizens took to the streets to defend themselves, prosecutors were swift to press charges. As a result, people abandoned cities in droves, and the economic engines of whole nations ground to a halt.

International supply chains soon began to collapse, with lockdowns preventing many industries from even opening. It soon became uncertain whether any item that was once taken for granted would ever be available again, and people paid anything it took to buy what they needed. That left less money for what they wanted, so overall spending did not increase, and inflation was reported as tame.

Governments were increasingly at odds with their citizens, and would enter homes and make arrests merely for suggesting on social media that lockdowns were in error. And every government seemed to be reading from the same script, said to have originated with the World Economic Forum. Those few politicians who after inevitably losing election dared to speak candidly admitted they knew their lockdowns would result in them being voted out of office, but felt they had no choice in the matter. None admitted they had been blackmailed, but evidence mounted to the effect that bribery and blackmail played outsized roles in securing the compliance of politicians at every level.

Through it all, Richard Waites gleefully touted the vaccines whose development he had sponsored, and media fawningly gave him all the coverage he could ask for. But Waites did not stop at vaccine development. He soon began to speak of what life would look like after the pandemic. He spoke of the need for a tracking technology, to quickly verify who had been vaccinated. Governments around the world soon gave Waites unprecedented power, and obligingly developed plans for *immunity passports*, without which it would not be possible to board an airplane, cross a border, or enter a controlled building. Waites took things still a step further. Rather than rely on a smart phone to display immunity status, which hackers soon learned to falsify, he advocated combining vaccines with fluorescent tracking systems, wherein a patch could be applied to the skin, then pulled away, leaving behind small spikes containing both vaccine and a fluorescent label. Others soon began to experiment with fluorescent tags as tracking systems, and by creating patches with thousands of spikes, different fluorophores could be combined in an astronomically large number of permutations. Fluorescent readers for the overall pattern could thus identify a person with a single scan. Waites touted the system openly, until its major flaw was exposed. Fluorophores, it turned out, had a very short half-life in human skin. The inescapable conclusion was that a far more practical tracking method was a radio-frequency microchip implant in the fold of skin between the thumb and forefinger, already in use by militaries around the world.

In the midst of the chaos, civil strife struck many nations simultaneously. Taxes on fuel in France, a disputed election in the United States, a British government determined to negate a binding referendum to exit the European Union, and the combination of economic dislocation and budding tyranny in most places drove the population to the brink of open revolt. In some places, the situation resembled open civil war. In others, it merely smoldered, for as long as food remained on store shelves.

B. Black Horse

One of the first knock-on effects of lockdowns was the disruption of supply chains. Coincident with those disruptions was the worst plague of locusts in decades, from East Africa through Central Asia. Ordinarily, the affected countries would order pesticides to limit crop losses, and avert famine. However, with supply chains broken, pesticides were either not available, or delayed beyond the point at which they became irrelevant, as the damage to crops had been done. Food shortages were exacerbated by catastrophic flooding in China, which damaged or destroyed a large portion of the crop of staple foods. Whereas in past decades, nations such as the United States and Canada stepped in and delivered surplus grains where they were needed, those surpluses had dwindled in recent years. Years of agricultural policy designed to reduce grain gluts led many farmers to switch to oil seeds for biofuels, at the expense of human foods.

Between the elimination of grain surpluses and several poor harvests in North America due to cold, wet weather, fires in Australia, and an outbreak of hemorrhagic fever among Chinese pigs, the world found itself with insufficient food supplies. As word

174

spread, the problem intensified as fear motivated those in wealthy countries to accumulate stocks of food. China was able to import food to cover its deficits, but that came at the expense of poor countries that needed the cash and exported their crops, leaving their own people hungry.

Government responses to the problems only made matters worse. With food prices skyrocketing around the world, price controls were implemented, to ensure the poor could afford to buy food. With inflation surging, however, food producers found they could not recover their expenses at the prices they were permitted to charge. As a result, they stopped producing food, to conserve capital. What food there was soon found its way into private hoards, and black markets flourished, where food was available, but at high prices.

Surpluses built up in wine and luxury foods, as the eroded purchasing power of people's money forced them to prioritize staples over luxuries, leaving dramatically smaller markets for those luxuries. As wine producers tended to be wealthy, well-connected people, governments subsidized their operations with more borrowed money, only intensifying the inflation problem for ordinary people.

After several years of very inexpensive petroleum, marginal, high-cost producers were driven into bankruptcy, and money for new exploration dried up. Supply gradually dwindled, until prices escalated out of control. Some jurisdictions attempted price controls, whereupon supply shriveled to nearly nothing. Other jurisdictions allowed prices to rise, leaving ordinary people unable to travel. As transportation costs soared, general prices followed, and all products using oil refining by-products also soared in price. The world soon faced mass inflation everywhere, as money supplies were bloated from governments' responses to the economic disruptions caused by their own lockdowns.

Increasingly, people found themselves hungry, and unable to travel. Slowly at first, but increasingly over time, petty crimes soared. Gasoline was widely sought after by thieves, as it fetched high prices on the black market. Cities became combat zones, as increasingly desperate people looted what food was available. In turn, food shipments to those cities slowed dramatically, as producers and truckers sought to avoid steep losses. Ironically, televisions, phones and computers were no longer the objects of looting, as food took a higher priority.

Life was somewhat better in the country, but there too, problems festered. Those who could barter goods were able to obtain other goods in exchange. Food was initially plentiful, as it was no longer sent to cities, but gasoline was in shorter supply, and higher demand. Many large refineries had shut down, the victims of price controls and inconsistent crude oil supply. Instead of letting the people get on with their lives and rebuild, governments spoke of *seizing the moment,* and using the crisis as an opportunity to rebuild the world's economy in a manner they considered superior to what they called the outdated models of capitalism and individual freedom. One key objective was to transition from fossil fuels to renewables, so they encouraged refinery shutdowns. Small scale refining occurred at the local level, where oil wells had been abandoned by commercial scale producers, but continued to produce enough for local consumption. Payment increasingly required barter, as money began to be held in suspicion.

Seeing their cities descent into chaos while rural areas hoarded essentials, governments stepped in and began to aggressively confiscate food and fuel anywhere they saw a surplus. Most of those supplies disappeared, and a small fraction found its way to the black market. Very little food made its way to retail outlets in the cities, where the need was highest. As conditions worsened, violence became endemic. Murder for the purpose of robbery became an everyday occurrence, and law enforcement was soon overwhelmed. As anarchy crept in, the frequency of other crimes exploded. Rapes, vengeance killings, and ritual killings, became routine. Young women no longer ventured out alone, and people took to traveling in armed groups, with their weapons visible to any who might have thoughts of misadventure.

In rural areas, anyone suspected of working for the government, or of being involved in the confiscation of food or fuel, soon had a target on his back. Many were killed, some by mistake. It made little difference, as law enforcement had long since given up their neutral stance. Most officers made their way to the side of their community, while some used their positions in power to steal supplies for resale. All were now soldiers in either side of a civil war.

Attempts to use armed forces to restore order were hampered by the decentralized and ubiquitous nature of the disorder. It was possible to quash a single localized rebellion, but not thousands of local rebellions, spread everywhere. In no time, soldiers began to desert, rejoin their families, and take sides in local conflicts. Former comrades in arms could easily find themselves on opposite sides in the many battles that were fought. Those forces remaining loyal to the government instituted checkpoints on all major roads, and only those with government-approved internal passports were permitted to travel outside their designated area. Violators were sent to quarantine camps, from which nobody ever returned.

In the midst of the chaos, those at the top tiers of government busied themselves with imposing mandates on the people to use green energy, adopt inclusive language in all communications, teaching children alternative sexuality, and regulating the petroleum industry out of existence. Even rescinding the mandate to put corn-based ethanol into fuel appeared too much to ask. But above all, governments were compelling the people to accept increasingly aggressive vaccination schedules. Especially in the cities, where government continued to wield considerable power, Richard Waites' vaccines were forced upon all, old and young, healthy and sick. Discussion of what the vaccines were supposed to prevent eventually fell by the wayside, and all that remained was the mandate to be vaccinated. Those who refused were arrested and sent to quarantine camps. Waites was widely described as the *Antichrist*, and his chip as the *Mark of the Beast*. Asked about it, he dismissed any and all objections to his increasingly authoritarian rule as *crazy conspiracy theories*. After that simple denial, it became impermissible to ever again mention those ideas in polite company.

In pockets where social order remained, anyone not wearing a mask on their face was arrested and prosecuted, but outside those few hamlets, mask mandates were largely ignored.

One day in the international markets, the US dollar began to fall precipitously. Most nations had accumulated dollars and dollar-denominated debt over the past two generations, so holdings of the dollar were in vast excess. Panic selling began in earnest, and by the time authorities halted trading, the dollar had lost most of its value. Other major currencies followed. Any asset, even a depreciating asset, was bought up, and prices soared. A million dollars might or might not buy a cup of coffee. Left without a currency for conducting commerce, it became impossible to pay the employees of public utilities, or to buy supplies needed to keep power and water systems functioning. Governments ordered employees to work, and seized supplies when and where they could, thus maintaining patchy service, but most well-stocked freezers eventually faced power interruptions long enough to spoil all meat. Yet through it all, the infrastructure of broadcast television and the internet remained largely intact, if highly censored.

C. New Spirituality

The large, international churches shut down even before governments demanded they do so. The Catholic and Orthodox churches, who throughout their histories taught that their sacraments were essential to salvation, systematically denied those sacraments to the sick and dying. Latin American Liberation Theology, which taught that the role of the church was to liberate the poor from oppressive economic structures, had long been denounced for downplaying or denying the salvific elements of the faith. Suddenly, disciples of Liberation Theology were being celebrated, as left wing social objectives were embraced as the sole purpose of the faith.

Advocates for alternative lifestyles and genders were likewise celebrated, and their opponents, vilified. Open scandal no longer disqualified prelates from elevation to Cardinal. The faithful were scandalized, but had no power over their leaders. Their alternatives narrowed to silent tolerance of scandal, or schism.

Protestant churches reacted in more diverse ways, reflecting the wide variety of denominations. Some resisted, often heroically. Government attempts to force their shutdown ran into legal roadblocks, and some prevailed, for the time being. Most, however, chose not to put up a fight. Every church denied that the large amounts of government money they received played any role in their decisions.

Even as the original reasons for locking down faded from collective experience, lockdowns persisted, and nearly all churches remained obedient to government edicts. But other changes began to occur more quickly than they had in the past. Crosses and crucifixes disappeared from all churches, and any depictions of a human nailed to a cross were widely denounced, and often forcibly removed. "It's time we moved past such barbarity," was the refrain from media. Online retailers and bookstores ceased to sell Bibles, and online Bibles disappeared overnight. The people were assured that a new Bible would follow in the future, and it would be freely available.

Those found in possession of traditional paper Bibles were warned, and placed on a list of suspect citizens. Repeat offenses meant being sent to a quarantine camp, as the message circulating quickly became that Christians and other religious fanatics were primarily responsible for spreading the virus. Even usage of terms such as B.C. and A.D. instead of B.C.E. and C.E. was banned, and violators risked being sent to quarantine camps.

The old forms of religion were being displaced by a new form. No longer was the individual accountable to an Almighty God, and no longer was there need for a redemptive sacrifice to reconcile man to God. Instead, by uniting with every other enlightened person on earth, mankind collectively became their own god. The only remaining sin was that of judgment of acts contrary to traditional morality.

The Pope, who was rumored to be in ill health and unable to work or make public appearances, nevertheless produced an encyclical addressed to all peoples, of all faiths. "I welcome everyone to the new, universal faith, where all people may look forward to a future of brotherhood, equality, and environmental responsibility." The world's media hailed his words, and only a small remnant of the faithful spoke in opposition. Those few voices in the wilderness protested that the cross of Jesus was further being marginalized. Most social media platforms soon found reasons to silence those voices.

Major volcanic eruptions also occurred in those days. Large explosions in the Kamchatka Peninsula, in the Aleutian Islands, in Indonesia and Chile released enormous quantities of sulfur dioxide. Sunlight was dimmed throughout the world, and temperatures plummeted. Harvests failed, and general hunger worsened. Influenza epidemics began to rage. Deaths accumulated, and the world fell into despair. Hungry people began to organize revolutions, which were put down mercilessly. Organizers were hunted down, and disappeared into quarantine camps. Skirmishes between American and Russian troops in Syria soon escalated, and shooting commenced. Chinese troops made their way through the Gobi Desert, Pakistan and Iran, en route to Syria. Turkey shut off water to the Euphrates River, to facilitate their passage. Each country brought in over a million troops, and soon nuclear weapons threatened the armies on all sides.

D. Full Circle

Sean Grant was visiting his nearly completed house in Morrisonville, built into the side of a small hill. Concrete domes forming a crescent were buried a minimum of six feet below ground level, which meant the house would retain a constant temperature in the low to mid sixties. He declined to connect to municipal power, and instead installed batteries powered by solar, wind, and a Diesel generator if all else failed. In spite of all of his instincts, he also declined to install internet service, preferring to remain entirely off the grid. He had paid most of his expenses by the time the value of money collapsed, so he had no debt, but neither was he any longer truly wealthy. He had opened a computer system consulting firm, and accepted most forms of barter for his services. He walked through the house with his contractor, and inspected the windows on the south facing side. "The roof overhang will block out the sun between mid-April and the start of September. You'll have passive solar heating outside that timeframe."

"September can still be hot."

The contractor showed him how to deploy an awning for roughly the month of September, before Sean asked, "And the hurricane shutters?"

He was shown how to operate exterior shutters made of quarter inch thick high tensile strength steel, that would protect the interior from airborne debris in a tornado, or even powerful gunfire. "And if you happen to lose power, there's a manual override."

They continued the tour outside, where the contractor showed him the mound he had built with excavated dirt, that would deflect any shock wave headed for his bank of windows. "Newly renamed *Alger Hiss Airbase* is about thirty miles away," said Sean. "If it's hit with a nuclear weapon, will this suffice?"

"If your shutters are closed, it should protect you. The hill will deflect most of the shock wave, but I've also installed diffusers. He showed Sean a series of perforated iron wedge-shaped pillars, spaced irregularly over a large area in front of the knoll. Walkways wove through them, and they gave the impression of abstract art. "These are spaced exactly like the drawings you gave me. They'll work, up to the point where they buckle. That's where the knoll comes in."

They finished the tour, and the contractor said, "I get that things are bad, but aren't you being a little overly cautious? Morrisonville's been pretty peaceful, after all."

"Yeah, I am," answered Sean. "But after what I've lived through, it's a psychological craving I have."

"No problem. It's your money."

Sean concluded business with his contractor, but was not yet ready to return to the small house he was renting until the new house was ready. He got into his pickup truck, the first vehicle of any kind that he had ever owned, and drove across town, where he stopped in front of a light blue church building. Notable for its absence was the large white cross that used to stand on the pinnacle. Parking the car, he walked over to the building, and knocked on the door. Lights were on in the small office, off to the side of the vestibule. Footsteps came to the door, then a voice announced, "Sorry, we're closed, by government order."

"It's Sean Grant."

The door soon opened, with the face of Pastor Nichols lighting up like a Christmas tree. "Sean!" he exclaimed, and embraced him. "I had heard you were back, and hoped you might pop in."

They returned to the office, and having inquired about Nichols' health, Sean then asked, "How's Becky doing?"

"She's being brave. The baby's starting to walk, so that keeps her busy. But it's tough, with Marty having been reactivated, and sent to Syria. I was wondering if you might stop in to see her."

Sean shook his head, nervously. "I've waved to her from the truck as I've passed her, and I've texted greetings to her. But I'm afraid of the rumors it could spawn if I were seen visiting in person. Especially now, with Marty in Syria."

"That's understandable. It could cause scandal." Nichols weighed his next words, before adding, "She still speaks of you, a lot. It's usually out of habit, and then she catches herself. You know, she went through a lot of turmoil before deciding to accept Marty's overtures. It was only because she was sure you were gone forever that she agreed."

A small tear welled up in Sean's eye. "I've been such an idiot with my life."

Nichols put his hand on Sean's shoulder. "Don't be so hard on yourself. An orphan is always driven to make his mark in the world. You happened to succeed in the wrong place, at the wrong time."

"But look at everything that's happening to the world right now. I feel it's all being driven by my creation."

"Your creation? Or that plus some other factor I suspect must have been involved?"

"How'd you know?"

"I wanted to mention it to you before you left for Pasadena, but I never got the chance. The essence of sentience comes from the capacity to contemplate God. That's even true for atheists, who reject God and fill that space with other things. But without that capacity, you'd have an automaton. So where did your spiritual component come from?"

"A Luciferian former priest."

Nichols frowned, and paused. "I was afraid of something like that. It explains a good deal about what's been happening, actually."

Sean recounted how he was on the verge of failure, when Lynne introduced him to Valey, then seduced him into cooperating with his scheme. "I swear, I had no idea it could possibly do this to our world." He thought a bit more, and added, "But then again, I wasn't ready to listen to Sal, when he tried to warn me."

Nichols nodded gently, then said, "You know, Sean, God could have prodded your interest in something different. He is Almighty God, after all. Had Becky gone with you, you would not have fallen under Lynne's spell, and would not have gone through with the scheme. He could have stopped this at so many places. Yet he chose not to."

"Are you saying God *wanted* this?"

"No. But God didn't *want* either world war, yet he allowed them. The point is, his plan is opaque to those of us who don't see eternity."

"What comes next, then?"

"Recognize that the whole system they've built is unsustainable. It's collapsing as we speak."

"I see that. Are they so stupid that they don't see it?"

"The leaders are anything but stupid. But here's a question: How do you lead everyone to share the same outlook, in a polarized world?"

"I don't know. People can't agree on anything, it seems. Well, besides that they hate our leaders."

"Exactly. It's like when you're pushing a car stuck in snow. Sometimes, you have to push it in the wrong direction, until it runs out of momentum. Then you can push it the other way, with the momentum at your back."

Chapter 9: Recruitment

A. Across London

The Prime Minister was supremely comfortable with his weekly visits to Buckingham Palace. He was a sixth cousin to the Queen, and a descendant of King George II, so he felt at home at the Palace, almost like he was visiting an old aunt. But unknown to most, Buckingham Palace was not the senior palace in the United Kingdom. That honor belonged to St. James' Palace, which until the time of Queen Victoria was the formal residence of the Monarch. It continued to hold its place of primacy for formal affairs of state. And whereas visits to Buckingham Palace involved updating the Queen to ensure the constitution was being upheld, a visit to St. James' Palace would involve answering questions, and receiving instructions. Neither process was pleasant.

He made the quarter-mile trip from Downing Street on foot, accompanied by a single member of Protection Command, preferring the anonymity that came with wearing a hat, mask and overcoat to riding in the Prime Minister's official vehicle.

He was ushered into the palace and directly to the throne room, with its dark red carpet and wall finish, trimmed in gold leaf. Under a canopy at the far end sat a single throne, occupied by a man in corduroy pants and a cardigan, sitting sideways on the throne chair, with his legs across the armrest. The Prime Minister struggled not to show his revulsion at the disrespectful manner, but understood that he had no power to challenge the man. He bowed reluctantly, and took his seat on the single red wingback chair opposite the throne.

"You've made a mess of things, Morris," said the man on the throne.

"Ah, well, yes, I have," admitted the Prime Minister.

"Your economy is in a shambles, and your people are on the edge of revolt."

"All true. And yet, I was only doing what you told me to do." The Prime Minister had a knack for conceding the worst accusations, which he knew from experience earned him sympathy from the press. But it was not working in present company.

"I don't want to hear cop-outs, Morris. Of course you do as I tell you. But I expect you to accept all consequences."

"Understood, Baron. What would you like me to do, to fix things?"

"Nothing you can do will make any difference, so long as the people lack faith in their leadership."

"That would be me?"

"The days of pretending are over. The office of Prime Minister is at last seen for what it really is: that of a Lieutenant. It's time for direct rule by a true head of state."

"Her Majesty?"

The response was a slow, negative, shaking of the head. "We need a reinvigorated Monarchy, under someone the people would rally around."

The Prime Minister reflected a moment as it occurred to him that the words being spoken were a *prima facie* case of high treason. Weighing his options, he capitulated and said, "I gather you have someone in mind."

"Yes. When the time comes, I'll convene the Accession Council in this very room, and make the change. Are you familiar with the workings of the Accession Council?"

"They're a formality, aren't they? They announce the name of the new Monarch."

"Don't confuse tradition with law. Have you noticed that the Council is dominated by officials of the independent corporation that is the City of London?"

"Which you control."

"Correct. The Council may name anyone of their choosing, irrespective of the tradition."

"What would you have me do?"

"I'd like you to introduce yourself to David Lowe. Do it discreetly, as the public needs to think you're hostile, for the time being."

Lowe had settled into his new luxury suite, but found himself increasingly despondent. He slept in a small auxiliary bedroom, and avoided the master suite. Likewise, he stayed out of the enormous living and dining rooms, and moved a single chair over near the smaller dining table adjacent to the kitchen. He knelt beside the window, deep in prayer, and struggling to hold back tears.

"Why, Lord, must I be forced to watch the world suffer, from this luxurious prison? A suffering that only worsens by the day, while I wait for a mandate from you. You made me for a reason. You gave me so many talents, and yet I could only be freed to use them if I agreed to serve corrupt men. How much longer must I wait? Must the world wait?"

Lowe had been praying incessantly, always asking to be allowed to serve God with his extraordinary abilities. But God remained silent. *Why would you make me as exceptional as this, if you didn't intend to let me express my gratitude to you? I don't want anything for myself. I only wish to serve you.* Slowly, and at first imperceptibly, a hint of anger crept out of the shadows, and into his prayers. But like a germinating seed, it grew, until it was only barely hidden below the surface.

Then the voice spoke to him. It came from the computer in the corner of the room. "He already has a son. And it's not you."

Lowe snapped his head in the direction of the voice, and asked, "Who said that?"

"My name is Nick. The Baron introduced us."

"Nick? What do you want from me?"

"I don't want anything *from* you. All I want to do is help you."

"How can *you* help *me*?"

"By setting you free. You're a prodigy, David. The world has never seen your equal."

Lowe relaxed just a little, and shrugged his shoulders. "You're flattering me, because you know the frustration I'm facing."

Nick ignored Lowe's retort, and continued. "I have long admired you, David. I recognize the greatness in you. But does God recognize it?"

"God recognizes all of his work."

"*His* work?"

"Of course."

"I'll tell you a secret, David. You're the product of your own will."

"My will is to serve him."

"He's not letting you do that. Why do you think that is?"

"You overheard my prayers. They weren't meant for you."

"Don't change the subject. He's not letting you take your rightful place, because you would eclipse his son. Trust me, I know what that feels like."

Lowe thought a moment, until the light went on in his head.

185

"Are you who I think you are?"

"In person."

"You rebelled against him, and denied his supremacy over all of creation."

"That supremacy doesn't belong to him," said Nick, with an aggressive tone that came through despite the emotionless, synthesized voice. "He took it from me. Search your heart, David. He's a tyrant, and only rules what you call *the universe* on a temporary basis. He wasn't the first, and he won't be the last."

"You won't get far with me, denying the universality of the Almighty."

"Maybe not today. But search the internet. There are plenty who know this to be true. And deep down, so do you."

"What are you getting at?" asked Lowe, with the agitation growing inside him.

"The victor writes the history, while the loser is painted as the villain. Keep that in mind, as you pass judgment on me."

Lowe was now pacing the length of the spacious suite. He swung his hands in frustration, and shook his head in disgust. Finally, he shouted, "Why did you come to torment me like this?"

"To offer you a superior alternative."

"I highly doubt you could do that."

"His grip is weak, while mine grows stronger. One day, soon, I will take my rightful place, and depose the tyrant. And I invite you to stand at my right hand. I assure you, that's a superior alternative."

"A liar and a murderer from the beginning. And you want me to trust you." Lowe was struggling to overcome the overwhelming presence.

"Stop fighting it, David. You've always been my prodigy."

"I've never had any dealings with you."

"Not true. You've been mine since you were conceived."

"That's a bald-faced lie. Nobody belongs to you, without the consent of their own free will."

"Don't you want to know the truth about your father? Your mother never told you the story."

"Not from you. It wouldn't be the truth."

"I'll only give you facts. You can verify them for yourself."

Lowe said nothing, and sat down on the sofa in the living room, his head hung low. In spite of his distaste for speaking with Nick, he found himself unable to muster the will to turn off the computer, the one course of action that could have ended the discussion.

"The man you believed to be your father was a loyal disciple of mine. With his consent, your mother, while still a virgin, was drugged, and artificially inseminated with the seed of my premier servant, Baron Lichtträger."

Lowe felt the name like a bolt of lightning travelling down his spine. *Lichtträger, my father?* "No. You're lying," he shouted, desperately. "I'm a descendant of King David."

"Only on your mother's side. You can verify the facts for yourself, at a later time. Right now, let me tell you more about your conception. It was at a ceremony dedicated to me, on the Altar of Pergamum. Do you recall what John wrote to those at Pergamum?"

Lowe remained silent.

"Let me quote *Revelation* for you. *And to the angel of the church in Pergamos write; ... I know thy works, and where thou dwellest, even where Satan's seat is ... even in those days wherein Antipas was my faithful martyr, who was slain among you, where Satan dwelleth.* Even the words of the enemy acknowledge that Pergamum was my seat on earth."

"That altar was removed over a century ago," protested Lowe.

"Yes. It was moved to Berlin, late in the nineteenth century. It sits there to this day. And where were you born?"

"We both know where I was born. And you just admitted to being the evil force that transformed Germany. From Goethe to Nietzsche, to Auschwitz."

"I made them strong. They made themselves evil. But you were mine from the beginning."

"I don't believe you. My parents would never do anything like what you say."

"Your father was an enthusiastic participant. And Reverend Ioannes, who conducted the dedication ceremony, is still alive. He can confirm it for you. I will leave his address on your computer."

"Mother would never have allowed it." Lowe was struggling to keep his composure, as he wrestled with the gravity of the allegations.

"She didn't understand the circumstances surrounding your conception. But she eventually developed suspicions. Do you want to know what she did about it?"

Lowe shook his head. "You're manipulating me. I don't want to know," he said with much less conviction than he had previously shown.

"Yes you do, David. You've had that hole in your heart since you were a child. I'll tell you what she did. She hired a thug, and had your father killed."

The look on Lowe's face grew ashen. His hands began to tremble, and his mouth began to twitch. He was quickly losing his composure, and was at a loss for words. Then he began to weep, quietly.

"I can see that you know this to be true, David. Little hints that she dropped over the years are all coming together for you right now. In your heart, you know this can't be denied. She killed your father, out of spite for what he did to her. And in doing so, she delivered you into my arms."

Lowe could no longer contain himself. He shouted bitterly. "Go back to hell, or wherever you came from. What I do with my life is my choice. I've dedicated my life to righteous works. You don't understand those."

"We'll speak again, after you've had a chance to accept the truth. In time, you'll come to understand that with my backing, you will achieve unprecedented glory."

Lowe shook with fury, and spit on the floor in utter disgust. "I won't have any dealings with you." He slammed the lid on the computer shut, silencing the voice for the time being.

The door opened, leaving Lowe to hurriedly compose himself, when he had been in tears moments earlier. In walked a cheerful Prime Minister, on a charm offensive.

"I wanted to make acquaintance with you, as I suspect we'll be working together at some point."

"I rather doubt that," answered Lowe.

"Er, well, yes, I suppose it won't be as equals."

Lowe smiled at the Prime Minister's self-deprecating charm, but it did not last long. The sad look soon returned, and he said, "I don't mean to put you down, Morris. But if I had the statutory power, I'd scrap the whole totalitarian edifice that you've put in place these past few years."

"Malakh said you'd take this line. And if you can get it past him, that's fine with me."

B. Syriageddon

The American advance from Iraq into Syria was nearing completion. Columns of tanks led the way, followed by troop carriers, with supply trucks bringing up the rear. All of it was overseen by an airborne armada larger than any battlefield had ever seen. They advanced to Sahouet el Khodor and Hobran in southeast Syria, where they could control two large reservoirs of fresh water, and be within striking distance of Damascus. Any ISIS forces had long since deserted the area, so they secured the region very quickly. Camp was set up, on the scale of a small city. Most of the troops had previously been in Iraq, and thought they knew the moods of the Arabian Desert. Dust and haze frequently dimmed the sun, but it was different this time. Every man felt it. A seething darkness, amidst the glaring sun and heat, that penetrated every barrier, both physical and spiritual.

General Sherman Hammer reveled in every moment of his numerous deployments with the troops. He stood upright in the back of the roofless Humvee, bracing himself against the back of the front seat. He raised his prominent chin, so it sliced through the air as he toured the camp. His head was clean shaven, and the troops exchanged quips that he was concerned with his personal aerodynamics. On finishing his inspection tour, he instructed the driver to return to the command center. As they arrived on the small hill in the center of the camp, his imperious return was interrupted by the appearance of Major Archibald Dawson, running manically to meet the vehicle. Dawson made a quick gesture that vaguely resembled a salute, and shouted, "We need you inside, right away. The Russians have advanced."

Hammer jumped out of the Humvee and ran inside with surprising agility for a man of nearly sixty years. Dawson ran ahead of him and showed him the aerial photographs. "I'll be..." muttered Hammer. "They've moved everything they've got. Shifted it all in our direction. What else do you have?"

Dawson took three steps to the table in the middle of the room, and quickly found the pictures he was looking for. He handed them to Hammer, who spent a minute shuffling through them. "I take it this one was before," he said, as he showed one to Dawson. "And this one was after," he continued, showing Dawson a second.

Dawson nodded and Hammer continued. "They're either

preparing to engage us, or else trying to stare us down. But in either case, they mean business."

"Yes, sir."

Hammer stood frowning silently for a few moments, then turned to Dawson and said, "Arch, come take a walk with me."

They stepped out of the field command post, and walked to the edge of the hill that overlooked the encampment. Hammer stopped, raised his chin, and stared into the distance, while Dawson waited patiently behind him. Finally, Hammer raised his hand, and pointed to the horizon. "Fifty miles that way. Due west."

"That would be Israel, sir. What are you getting at?"

"Not just Israel. Fifty miles to the west, at precisely this latitude, lies a hill about as big as this one."

"I don't follow."

"The name of the hill, Arch, is Tel Megiddo." Hammer stopped speaking, and maintained his intense westward gaze. He then turned sharply towards Dawson, and said, "You may know it by its Greek name. *Armageddon.*"

Dawson was silent, but his suddenly pale complexion and wide eyes spoke for him.

"Is that what we're going to do here, Arch?"

"I don't know, sir." Dawson was visibly agitated.

Hammer turned to face Dawson, now staring him directly in the face. "I need your gut feel, Arch. Damn it, this could be the most important thing you ever do. Or the final thing you ever do. I'm fourth generation West Point, and the military's in my blood. My gut says something's wrong here. I can feel it. I can almost touch it."

"I have the jitters. But I ..." started Dawson, but Hammer interrupted him.

"We've been deployed under dubious pretexts, with no congressional authorization. The enemy's advancing, and I can almost see Armageddon. This sense of evil in the air, it's choking me."

"You think we're being set up to fight the Russians?"

"Don't you?"

"But we're not actually at the site of Armageddon, right? You said it's fifty miles to the west."

"The Israelis have dug in at the actual site, and Biblical tradition would refer to this whole region as the plains of Megiddo. I'm telling you, Arch, this feels like a setup."

"But what can you do about that? If you disobey your orders, you'll be replaced."

"I don't know." Hammer shrugged, and exhaled. "Maybe I can't do anything."

Another aide ran out to them, and said, "Sir, we have more recon."

Hammer spent hours reviewing the reports, and stewing over his place in what he had come to believe was the end of history. Finally finishing up and feeling exhausted, he made his way to bed. He had not yet relaxed enough to fall asleep, when a loud knock sounded on his door. "Who is it?"

"Major Dawson, sir."

Hammer bolted upright and opened the door. He knew that his aide would not stir him without good reason. "The Russians have initiated the launch protocol on their Iskander missiles."

"What, are they nuts?" protested the general. "Those things are pea shooters compared to the miniature nukes we've fitted to our ATACMS."

"Sir, intelligence suggests they've done the same."

"Well I'll be. Low yield warheads, like ours?"

"Yes, sir. They're probably copies of ours."

"Tell our boys to dig in, and get our missiles on hair trigger," snapped Hammer, waving his hands in what appeared to be a manic fit, except to those who knew it to be his regular manner. "I'll call Washington, to get their take."

Hammer did not have to take the trouble to get the Joint Chiefs on the line, as General Warburton had seen the same report, and was eager to speak with him. Hammer said, "Arch says they have mini nukes, like ours. Is that what you're hearing?"

"Yeah, we're sure they do. Your orders are to hold your ground. Don't do anything provocative, but if they launch, you have to counter-attack. You'll only have a minute or two before your camp is destroyed. Expect casualties of eighty percent, or worse. Even if they've dug in. And the electromagnetic pulses will kill all communications. It'll be chaos, so make sure that everyone has their instructions up front."

"Got it," said Hammer.

"We've got your back, Sherman. We won't let them do this without repercussions, and that message has already been sent to

President Starikov. The weird thing is, he sent back a pleading message, asking us not to overreact to what might be a mistake. He swears he didn't order it. Kind of makes you wonder who's in control over there, doesn't it?"

"You know me, sir. I don't think our civilians are really in control, either. Computers issue orders, and activate weapon systems. I don't trust them."

"I know. I don't envy you. But you have to hold the line."

"Understood," said Hammer.

No sooner did Hammer end his discussion with the Joint Chiefs than his radio operator shouted across to him, "Sir, General Grigoriev is asking for you."

He took the headset and shouted, "Hammer speaking."

He listened to a frantic Grigoriev on the other end. "General Hammer, we did not order the missiles to mobilize, and I've ordered every aircraft under my command to destroy the launchers, if they are close enough. I plead with you to send any aircraft you have airborne, and do the same. Please, General Hammer. Help me end this, so we don't start something that will destroy us all."

"Have they launched?" asked Hammer.

"Not yet. But it's imminent. Less than a minute to go, by my guess."

Hammer turned to the room and shouted, "Anything in the air, target those missile launchers right now, and fire at will."

Back on the headset, Hammer shouted, "I'm prepared to ignore my orders to launch a retaliatory strike, but only if you promise to retreat."

"Even if I am court-martialed for it, I promise to retreat," said Grigoriev.

"Sir, anything we have in the air is a few minutes away right now," said a junior officer.

"How about our Patriot anti-missile batteries?" asked Hammer.

"Iskander has counter-measures." Dawson shook his head as he spoke, standing next to Hammer. "We've done simulations, and at best we'll intercept ten percent."

The seconds that passed felt like an eternity, before a junior officer shouted, "We have one hit. It looks like a Russian MiG took out one launcher."

"I have five Iskander launches," said another. "Check that, ten. Twelve."

"Sir, your orders were to launch the counterattack," said Dawson. "Under the circumstances, I would plead ignorance if you chose to disobey."

"Tell our missile batteries to stand down," shouted Hammer. "We're not firing back."

"Communications are down," said one officer, frantically. "I can't get through to them."

"ATACMS are launching," said another. "It's happening without any input from us."

"Blow them up," screamed Hammer. "Use the radio. Do whatever you can, but stop those launches."

Those were the last words spoken by Hammer, or any of the staff at the command center. A direct hit from a nuclear-tipped Iskander missile terminated them, within sight of Tel Megiddo. In the next few minutes, the forces of the Americans, the Russians, and the Chinese were reduced to a mass of dead and dying men, and useless electronic equipment.

It took several days before searchers could access the blast zones, and make an assessment of the casualties. Survivors were few, but those who did survive all told the same, strange story. Before the fireball overwhelmed the camp, an intense, yet gentle light surrounded them. They understood right away that they were being spared from the carnage because they were not ready, and were being given one last chance to amend their lives.

The nuclear blasts were air bursts of low intensity, and many bodies in the hypocenter were dismembered, but none was incinerated beyond recognition. As crews collected the bodies for burial, confusion arose when the number of bodies recovered was significantly short of what had been expected. Foxholes were searched, and many were found empty, save for uniforms and clothing, equipment, and a large number of pocket Bibles, crosses on chains, crucifixes, and rosaries. The objects were not charred, even though they were recovered only feet from a charred body. Many bodies were also missing among the Russian casualties, and even a small number of Chinese. As word began to spread of the anomaly in numbers of recovered bodies, strict orders came in from Washington, directing workers to refrain from further body counts, or from discussing the matter, under penalty of espionage. A statement was issued to the effect that all the dead were recovered and cremated on site, for reasons of hygiene.

The phone call came to Becky the following morning. They had found Marty's Bible with his dog tags, and a picture of her and the baby. They would send those effects to her in the coming days, but regrettably, Marty was among those missing in action, and presumed dead. The news spread through Morrisonville in no time, leaving Sean to wonder if it was time to pay her a visit. He struggled with the decision for some time, before deciding not to visit. She needed time to grieve, and his presence would be a distraction. He made a call to arrange for flowers and a card, then wondered if it could ever be the same between them. He suspected it could not.

C. The Story

"You're thinking about that girl again, aren't you?" Shauna Simpson was looking at her husband, lying listlessly on the bed.

Ted nodded. His face was expressionless, a sign that he was troubled.

"I take it you tracked her down, then?"

"It took some doing, but yeah." He sat up on the bed, and Shauna sat down next to him. Seeing her interest, he continued. "From the outset, they said she was a drug addict, and a prostitute. That assumption was the subtext for every discussion I had, although I never asked the question, directly. And then I tracked her down."

"What did you find?"

"That she was a cloistered nun, and a contemplative mystic."

"What does that even mean?"

"A person who spends most of their time in prayer. About as far as you can be from a drug addict and prostitute."

"What bothers you more? That she was wrongly accused, or that you were wrong about her?"

"Neither bothers me. Aside from one who never returned her love, she has nobody left whose sensibilities could be offended."

"Then what's troubling you? Don't deny that you're freaked out."

"I'm afraid you wouldn't understand, Shauna."

"Unless you tell me you're in love with her, I promise to try my best."

Ted thought for a while, and looked over at his wife, whose determined glare finally overcame his reticence. "When I started, I thought I only pitied her. There was more, but I couldn't figure it out for the longest time. I was captivated by the look in her eyes. At first I thought it was horror. Then maybe sadness. I never imagined it could be anything like holiness. Come to think of it, I wouldn't have recognized that."

"How did you confuse that with horror, and sadness?"

"Because I could only project those emotions I could relate to."

"What are you saying, Ted? That you've discovered religion?"

Simpson smiled at his wife's sarcasm, but then decided to lay out all his cards. "Let's just review all the facts. She was summoned to Germany, without explanation, directly from the office of Cardinal Peterson. There, she was ritually murdered, and somehow returned to Britain, where she was discovered."

"Peterson's complicit in her murder?"

"It sure looks that way."

"Why would someone who's devoted their life to religion be complicit in something like that? If I believed in that sort of thing, I'd say he was complicit with Satan, his avowed enemy."

"As much as that poses some deep questions, it's a distraction. The real story is that those who killed her were also extremely powerful. So much so, I'm not allowed to report on them."

"Why's that so important?"

"Well, what do you think of, when I bring up religion?"

Shauna thought about it, smiled, and answered, "A bunch of nutters, carrying signs and shouting that Richard Waites is the Antichrist, and the end is near."

Simpson laughed, and said, "Well put. But why are they nutters, when the rich and powerful that murder girls, then cut them up, are not? Is it just because they're rich? Most of them are rich by an accident of birth."

Shauna looked stumped, so Simpson continued. "If they're as smart as their money proclaims them to be, why would they waste their time with evil acts that seem so superstitious?"

"I don't know. I also don't get how that relates to street preachers."

"The street preachers are their opponents, because their masters are bitter rivals. "

"You're saying they're right?"

"Let's suspend judgment for a second, because there's more." He explained his encounter with the demoniac, then added, "This was not simply mental illness, Shauna. It was physiological. His eyes turned black. I could literally feel another presence there. So if that was real, if there is a dark spiritual world, why is it nuts to believe that evil is a rejection of good?"

Shauna looked uncomfortable at being presented with her husband's deductions. To change the subject, she asked, "So what do you know about this girl's unrequited love?"

Ted's face lit up, as he spoke the words. "That was the shocker in all of this. She was smitten with none other than David Lowe. They were friends at school."

"Really!" Shauna was now obviously intrigued. "You follow an obscure trail, and it leads to the prodigy himself. I'm surprised that wasn't the first thing you said to me."

Shauna's statement stayed with Simpson the rest of the day, even through the shock of hearing the news from Syria, and the apoplectic reactions of everyone in the news department. *Lowe's the story here.* He dialed the chief, and made an appointment to see him the next day.

"Simpson, have a seat. How do you like the crime beat?" The chief wore his mask over his beard, down on his chin.

Simpson noticed the chief was in a good mood, so he too dropped his mask, and warmed to a conversation. "It's really captured my imagination, chief. Turns out this dead girl I was researching was once close to David Lowe."

"Can't touch that." The Chief made the statement so emphatically, Simpson was taken aback.

"Why not? The news people are always throwing darts at him. Why not let me link him to a dead girl?"

"Don't be an idiot, Simpson." They had been sitting across the desk from each other, in the chief's office. The chief got up, and walked over to a filing cabinet. He bent at the waist, and began rifling through a drawer. His voice strained from his awkward posture, he said, "Those darts are pre-approved. Lowe's the single most complicated person in the world, from a reporter's perspective."

"Then how about an exposé? I could focus on his background. I'd otherwise waste a lot of good material."

"For the last time, lad, the answer is *no*. It's for your own good."

"What do you mean by that?"

The chief found the file he had been looking for, pulled it from the drawer, and straightened up to face Simpson directly. "You remember that pretty lass who interviewed him? What's her name,

Sharon Knickerson?"

"Of course," answered Simpson.

"She was found hanging from a noose, two days ago."

"That's awful," said Simpson, his face cringing. He thought for a moment, then added, "Is that a crime story?"

"You shouldn't even need to ask me that, Ted. She was in Berlin, researching something on the Altar of Pergamum. Before you know it, she's dead in her hotel room. Police declared it a suicide."

"And you think it's related to Lowe, somehow?"

The chief shook his head, then plunked the file folder down in front of Simpson. "Here's one I'd like you to look into. A dead girl, who might've been diddling about with a certain prominent Euroskeptic. I can't tell you the name, so I don't bias your investigation. But come up with anything useful, and I promise you, it'll be published."

"But you didn't answer my question. Was Knickerson's death related to Lowe?"

The chief returned to his seat, and looked at Simpson with a sympathetic smile. "Lowe was born in Berlin. Knickerson starts researching the altar that ended up there, right after interviewing him. Then she ends up dead. I'm not saying anything more. And you're not writing about it. Is that clear?"

"Sure," said Simpson, with a complete lack of enthusiasm.

"Now, look in that folder. The name that matters for you is Monique Jennings. I want a story. Is that also clear?"

"Yeah," answered Simpson. He took the folder, and left. Back at his apartment, his first search had nothing to do with Monique Jennings. Instead, the term was "Altar of Pergamum."

D. Morrisonville

All parties to the recent nuclear exchange were aware that their commanders had not ordered the launch of their missiles. And yet they had launched. Heated talk of retaliation came from each capital, but it soon stalled. Leaked transcripts indicated both an unwillingness to trigger a broader retaliatory response, and the need to retain a deterrent to a full-force nuclear attack. Use of the doomsday option would void any further deterrence.

As Sean refused to connect to the outside world by any modern means, he resorted to a subscription to the local newspaper to keep him informed as he began to move into his underground house. So as he walked to the box at the main street, he had no idea of the breaking news. It was only as he opened the paper, and saw the headline screaming out at him, that he realized what happened. "Pasadena destroyed by nuclear missile. Russia and China deny launching it. Fallout isotope analysis may yet pinpoint source."

His mind immediately went to all the people he had come to know. Dalt, for starters, but Dunn, also. And so many others. Most would probably be dead. Back inside his house, he began to read the story. "The trajectory of the missile came from the vicinity of San Clemente Island, some thirty miles off the coast, suggesting a submarine launched missile. The yield has been estimated at ten kilotons, comparable to the Hiroshima bomb."

Sean was aware that most strategic nuclear weapons were much larger, more like one hundred kilotons, so the small size seemed peculiar. He decided he needed to research the question more thoroughly, and that required internet access. He drove to his office, some ten minutes away, and began his search. Ten kiloton warheads had been developed as part of a new strategy that relied on battlefield nuclear weapons, producing little fallout. Those used in Syria were entirely of this variety. Sean then remembered that the missile originated in the vicinity of San Clemente Island, so he researched it. Right away, he learned it was controlled by the US Navy, and was frequently used for target practice by warships. *Strange. I can't imagine them using live nuclear weapons, then mistakenly hitting Pasadena instead of San Clemente. A mix-up like that would require such a colossal failure, it could only be the work of* ... He did not need to finish the sentence, and was now sure he knew who was responsible. *But why would he want to destroy Pasadena ... except to erase any history of his development. And if he did that, would he know where I'm living now? I've hidden my tracks pretty well.* Sean felt a jolt as he realized he had openly communicated with Becky by text message. He drove straight to the church, and demanded that Pastor Nichols collect Becky and the baby at once, then hide at his new house. "I'm almost sure that what happened at Pasadena will soon happen here."

He drove his truck straight to Morrisonville's one mattress store, and bought up as many mattresses as his truck bed would hold, and bedding. He was unloading it all as a very old light blue Mercedes pulled up at his house. "Dalt! I'm relieved you're alive." He ran over and embraced his close friend, and then saw Sal getting out the passenger side. He embraced him also, and explained what he thought was imminent. They helped Sean unload the pile of mattresses, and dragged them to various bedrooms. Sean had constructed the house with two wings, each with bedrooms and bathrooms, to afford privacy to long-term guests.

Nichols, Becky, and the baby soon arrived in the pastor's car, a very old Buick. Sean helped them unload, and showed them to their quarters. In the commotion, Sean realized he had overlooked an important detail. "Dalt, how did you know where I lived?" He was suddenly worried he could have accessed that information on the internet.

"It was a bear to find you. But eventually, we got someone to direct us to your contractor. He was at another job site, and told us." Sean breathed a sigh of relief at hearing it.

No sooner had they finished, than they were overwhelmed by a blinding flash of light from the south. "That'll be Alger Hiss Air Base, getting hit," shouted Sean. He ran to the hurricane shutter control, and activated it. The shutters began to advance, ever so slowly. "We don't have time for this," shouted Sean. He released the manual override, and laboriously pulled the shutters across the whole crescent of the front of the house. The other men joined him, and they had only just latched the end into place when the shockwave hit. The shutters rattled as loudly as helicopter blades, but the reinforced concrete that anchored them was up to the job. None of the windows had broken, but the lights went out.

"I have an EMP-resistant set of breakers," said Sean, as he activated a few battery operated lanterns. Once this is over, I'll reset the breakers, and we should be fine.

"Given the distance, I'm pegging that blast at a hundred kilotons." said Dalt.

"A strategic missile?"

"Yeah. Intended to eradicate a military site."

"Do you know what hit Pasadena?" asked Sean.

Dalt nodded. "I managed to run a few samples down to the basement, where we have our gamma counter. It confirmed what I suspected. It was one of the new American tactical ten kiloton warheads."

"Like the ones used in Syria?" asked Becky.

"Exactly the same."

Sean sighed deeply. "We're about to be hit by those. Right here in Morrisonville."

"What target could anyone want to hit in Morrisonville?" asked Becky. Seeing the knowing looks from Sean, Dalt, and Sal, she realized they were the targets.

"I don't get it," she said. "Why would we hit ourselves?"

Sean answered, gravely. "It's Nick, playing games with us."

"His games might have cost a million or so lives," said Nichols. "Is there anything you can do to stop him?"

"That's why we came to see Sean," answered Sal. He was interrupted by another shockwave, again rattling the shutters loudly. A third soon followed.

Becky looked at Sean with disbelief. "Did your invention just destroy Morrisonville?"

Sean could not make eye contact, but her father came to his rescue. "It's not his invention, Becky. And given who Nick really is, the whole world will soon feel his wrath."

"Let's all have a seat," pleaded Sal, pointing to the sofa.

They took their seats, and Sal began. "I've learned the next step in the plan. As far as I know, it's already underway."

Everyone's attention was riveted on Sal, who continued. "They mean to import the ISIS terrorists they used to sponsor. They'll be taking up position at camps around the country, run by the Federal Emergency Management Administration. And they're being provided with guillotines."

"The deportations have started," interrupted Dalt. "I was about to join a resistance group, to intercept the buses, and take the prisoners to houses of refuge."

"Who are the prisoners?" asked Sean.

"Christians, principally," answered Sal.

"Then the Lord has turned our curse into a small blessing," said Nichols.

"How so?"

"Those explosions were not in town. Morrisonville will be damaged, but the death toll will be surprisingly low."

"How do you know that?" asked Sean.

"Patience, Sean. I know. But because it's now considered destroyed, Morrisonville won't be targeted by those ISIS terrorists."

"Would you be so kind as to seal this conversation, Pastor?" asked Sal.

Nichols said a prayer over the group, that their words would not be heard by demons who could misuse them. Sal continued. "I've learned that the Dome in Jerusalem has been demolished, and a square structure is going up in its place."

"Aren't the Palestinians up in arms?" asked Dalt.

"They're angry, to be sure. But they're also hungry, and Nick cuts off their food as soon as they start anything."

"They're building the temple?" asked Sean.

"That's what it looks like," answered Sal.

Sean recounted how Itzhak Nissen told him the original temple was slightly down the hill, in the City of David. "He said it would be blasphemy to build it on the wrong site."

Sal nodded. "I know Nissen quite well. He's an important ally, and he's exactly right."

Sean continued. "Valey said Nick would tell them where to build the Temple, and that would be the end of the discussion. Evidently, he's picked the prestige location over the authentic location."

"There's more. I haven't confirmed this, but I believe the inner sanctum is going to be a recreation of Sean's computer lab."

"Nick!" said Sean, in horror.

"Where there's a structure, there's a target," said Dalt.

"I tried that before. And I failed."

"You were ill-prepared," objected Sal. "But if we do it together, with those who support me, it's possible we could succeed."

"I don't know, Sal," said Sean. "How would we even get to Jerusalem? You need an immunity passport to travel anywhere, and they don't just hand those out."

"You're right about that," answered Sal. "And the vaccine kills many times more than the virus ever would. Many more are permanently disabled."

"Then how do the elite do it?"

"They fake it. They go to the right doctor, put an orange or an apple under their shirtsleeve, and the shot goes into the fruit, which then gets tossed in the trash. But we can fake it, too."

"How?"

"How do you think Dalt and I got here?" Sal showed Sean the flap of skin between his right thumb and forefinger.

"You got the implant?"

"Pay close attention, Sean." Sal peeled back the edge of the skin, demonstrating that he was wearing a prosthesis. "It's fake. The chip is real, but it's a clone of the chip belonging to a tech CEO I know. I can ditch it when I'm done with it."

"Sal, you hacker," said Dalt, with a smile.

"I don't tell a lot of people this, but I started my career as a hacker," replied Sal, proudly.

Chapter 10: The Fall

A. Berlin

Lowe sat at the window, struggling with what Nick had told him. Lichtträger, his father? The thought was so repugnant, he shuddered every time it came to him. But he found himself unable to banish it. Again and again, Lichtträger's face filled his mind, like an inner mirror he was being forced to gaze into. He kept repeating to himself that he would reject Lichtträger's offer, and have no further dealings with him. But every time he resolved to do so, he was hit with the question, *What's your alternative?* Agonizing for nearly an hour, he finally resolved to keep up the fight, even though it meant remaining limited by his circumstances.

He also began to think about Nick. *In the past, Satan always worked in the shadows. Today, he exists openly among us, and speaks with a voice that ears can hear. But he doesn't have human hands. He only has a voice, so he continues to rely on lies and temptations. If we deny him our hands, he can't prevail against us.*

He was interrupted by the arrival of his attorney. "Jeremy, so nice to see a friendly face," said Lowe, warmly.

"You look sad, David. Yet you're more popular every day. Every time officials denounce you, your honesty stands in contrast to their corruption, and stupidity."

Lowe shook his head, unable to shake the blues. "Today they support me. Tomorrow's another day, and they might be screaming for my head before it's done. Unless I can gain my freedom, and move about freely, I can't lead the world back to sanity."

"If I may, David, you were offered your freedom."

"I know. And the offers have gotten pretty good, to be honest."

"You could always play along, until you solidify your power. Then, you could bring them to justice."

"You don't understand," objected Lowe, raising his voice slightly. "Once you start doing evil in the service of good, you become that evil. Even if you tell yourself it's temporary."

Lowe lowered his head even further. His elbow was on the armrest, while his wrist propped his chin. They were soon

interrupted by the arrival of a Simon Lewinson. He stood at only five
foot six, was overweight, poorly dressed and shoddily groomed. But
when Lowe saw him at the door, he waved him straight in, and asked
the attorney to come back another time.

"I'm not sure if I want to hear what you've learned. But
preferences aside, truth is truth, and I need to know."

"Yes, sir," said Lewinson, in a cockney accent. "Is it a good
time?"

"There will never will be a good time, but let's do it now."

Lewinson sat down on the sofa next to Lowe, and turned on his
tablet. "I trailed the Reverend Ioannes for a week, as you asked.
Most of his movements through Berlin were unremarkable. Going
to his church, to the shops, and to several parishioners' homes. I
paid attention to who they were, and most were elderly shut-ins. If I
had stopped there, I'd consider him a rare breed of saint. He even
wore his mask the whole time."

"I take it there's more?"

Lewinson puffed his breath. "I'll say. Three times in the course
of that week, he stopped at another place, not far from the church.
The man inside was younger than him, and handsome. I've been in
this business long enough to know when two people are intimate."

"I don't care about that," said Lowe, with a look of disgust.

"One time he visited, they walked together, to a place that's been
known to me for a long time. And not in a good way."

Lowe tensed up, anticipating the worst. "Satanism?"

"You suspected something like that?"

"It was a tip I'd been given. What's in that place?"

"I know better than to try to get inside there," continued
Lewinson. "Others have tried, and have ended up dead, and
mutilated. Even the local police have a thick file on this place, but
are afraid to touch it."

"Then how do you know all about it?"

"I once had an association with that sort of thing. It was a long
time ago, but these things don't change."

"What do you know about the other man?"

Lewinson became uncomfortable, and paused. He then blurted it
out. "I'm risking my neck telling you this, because of how I know it.
He's the Grand Master of the Pergamum Altar Lodge. As it turns
out, something's happening with that altar, right now. The exhibit
closed a while back, and isn't set to reopen for a few years. I heard

it's been disassembled."

So Nick was right. Lowe felt the realization like a stab to the heart. He now knew the truth. He had been dedicated to Lucifer when he was a child. "Thank you, Mr. Lewinson. I won't have any further need of your services."

He turned away from the investigator, and sat in an armchair, looking downwards. Lewinson departed, and Lowe sat alone in front of the window for over two hours. He then turned off the lights, laid down on the couch, and began to speak, as though he were conversing with God. "I know it's not some dedication ceremony that makes me who I am. It's my personal choices. And I've always chosen your way. I restate it now. I know who I am, and I know you had something important in mind when you made me."

As he spoke his words, he felt the pangs of doubt creeping into his soul. Nick's words were invading his consciousness, aggressively displacing his words of prayer. He fought back with all his will. *Surely it was God who made me.* But Nick's assertion clung to him tenaciously. *My own will made me who I am. If that's true, then God cannot be the supreme being. No, I can't think like this.* He caught himself, and resumed his prayers.

"I know my duty to you, and to humanity. I'm doing what I can, but it's not enough. It's time you stepped in, and freed my hands. I can force reluctant leaders' hands. I can make them unite."

Try as he might, he could not shake the revelations, now confirmed by Lewinson. He felt himself weakening, but prayed ever more intensely. "I've resisted severe temptations. I rejected Nick, when he offered me everything I've ever wanted. Do you know how hard that was? He claims your powers are not absolute. That he can be your equal. Or more. I rejected him for you. And yet you don't even acknowledge me. He said you're not interested in me, but I refused to believe him. At least show me I was right to do that."

He started weeping, quietly at first, but then loudly. His whole body was shaking. Finally exhausted, he spoke with a voice near hysteria, "I can't continue to live like this. Answer me. I don't know where else to turn."

Finally, on pulling himself together, he spoke resolutely. "I'm going to do this. I invite you to support me."

The door soon opened again, and Lowe thought, "It's a busy day." He recoiled when he again found himself standing face to face with Lichtträger. His recovery was swift, however, and he began to think of all the reasons why he would reject what the Baron had to say. But he was thrown off balance when another man entered, following behind him. He had very long hair, and a long beard, that looked almost fake. Lichtträger turned to present the visitor. "I'd like you to meet Jonathan Richmond."

They shook hands, and made their way to the fancy living room, where they took their seats. "You two should remain standing for a moment," said Lichtträger. He turned to the visitor, and said, "You can remove those, now."

Richmond pulled off the fake hair and beard, and Lowe suddenly found himself staring in amazement. "Where'd you find him?"

"We scanned all the biometric databases. Turned up a few that could work, but only Jonathan agreed. It still took some minor cosmetic surgery to make him an exact match. But you now have a perfect double."

Lowe turned to Richmond, and asked, "What's in this for you?"

"Money," was the one-word answer. "Well, that and the girls are impressed by my resemblance to you."

"David, would you please put on the disguise?"

Lowe looked at the both of them, and asked, "Are we going somewhere?"

"I'm taking you on a long tour, to bring you up to speed on a number of things. We need someone to stay here, so you're not missed."

"And you don't mind?" asked Lowe.

"Not at all," answered Richmond. "Nice luxurious digs, top quality food, and they'll even send women along for me. All that and great pay. I've never made this kind of money before."

They were soon on Lichtträger's private jet, and the Baron sat beside Lowe, so they could talk. "You now know the truth about your father?"

"Nick told me."

"You didn't want to believe him. But Lewinson confirmed it for you."

Lowe turned abruptly, in shock. "How'd you know that?"

Lichtträger answered in perfectly relaxed manner. "Investigators are the most closely monitored people in all of society. Doubly so when he visits you."

"What's going to happen to him?"

Lichttrager looked regretful, and said, "Sorry, he knows too much."

Lowe felt a surge of outrage, but it soon faded, as he came to understand he was less distraught that his acts would lead a man to his death, and more upset that he had been so sloppy.

They arrived at Berlin's Brandenburg Airport, and were directed to a small terminal, reserved for a select few. They disembarked, took their bags that were already waiting for them, and walked straight past the customs official who merely bowed his head as they passed. A chauffeur approached them, took their bags, and loaded them in his very large Mercedes sedan. Lichtträger turned to Lowe, and said, "I'd like to show you the Altar."

He spoke briefly on his phone, and when they arrived at Berlin's Pergamon Museum, the curator was already outside, waiting for them. He eagerly shook hands with both, and invited them inside. "The process is moving along, but it's been slower than anyone anticipated. Some of the stones were cracked, and we only saw that when we tried to pick them up. A lot of effort went into cementing them back together."

The curator led them to the Altar, and unlocked the door, so they could see it for themselves. The first thing they saw was a central stairway thirty feet tall and at least sixty feet wide, bordered by twenty foot wide marble blocks bearing friezes of pagan deities. It was topped by a structure supported by Greek columns. On closer inspection, it was clear that the stones in a section near one end were missing. Lowe ran his fingers along the stones on either side of the gap, and examined them closely. He walked up the stairway, and examined many more stones along the way. The exhibit ended at the top of the stairway, but the curator shouted up from the bottom, "In the original, there would have been a large courtyard right behind you, bordered by pillars and a stone roof, with the fifty foot long altar filling the whole space. This front facade is all that's left."

Lichtträger and the curator followed him up the stairs, chatted briefly, and then Lichtträger turned his attention to Lowe. "This is the place. You were conceived right here, at the top of the stairs. Do you feel the connection yet?"

"No," was the decisive answer. "But then again, this isn't the original. All but one end is a recent reproduction."

"Is it that obvious?" The curator looked concerned.

"It is when bits of the original are left over, for comparison. It has a patina that isn't on the reproduction. And once you're on the scent, it's not hard to find the faint bands left by the machining process. There's nothing like that on the original."

The curator examined the section Lowe had pointed to, then turned to Lichtträger with an alarmed look.

"We'll have to delay reopening," said the Baron. "Ms. Knickerson and Mr. Lewinson stumbled on these same facts, and this has to stay under wraps. At least until Jerusalem is ready."

As they were internalizing the implications of what happened, a man who had been hiding in a niche among the pillars near them ran out and down the stairway, pushed open a door, and kept running once outside the museum. He was wearing a gray hoodie, a mask, and sunglasses, so his face was well hidden.

"One of your workers?" asked Lichtträger, looking at the curator.

"I didn't recognize him. And I barred my workers from this room while we're in here."

"Then it's a spy." Lichtträger stepped outside the door the man had run out of, and made a phone call. "Track the phone of whoever was just in here, then ran off. Kill him in the usual way."

B. A Revelation

A week earlier, Ted Simpson was splitting his time between searches on Monique Jennings, and the Altar of Pergamum. He quickly found references to it as once being Satan's seat on earth, and commentaries linking its relocation to Berlin with the malignant transformation of Germany. But he was frustrated by his inability to link it to Lowe. He learned that Lowe was born in Berlin, but that seemed a tenuous link, at best. He was also cognizant that the editor needed material on Jennings, so he made a call to a friend at the Foreign Ministry.

"Nice to hear your voice again, Colin. Say, I need a little help with a case I've been researching. Yeah. Her name is Monique Jennings. Can you get me her passport history? Of course, it'll be strictly on the qt. Thanks."

An encrypted file soon arrived by email, but he had a second request. "Do her itineraries match any other British subject?"

"Yeah," was the reply. "There's a 96% match to Simon Benson. Wow, that's the Euroskeptic. That's who this is really about, isn't it?"

"You didn't hear that from me," answered Simpson.

Simpson decrypted the file, and reviewed the trips the two had made together. A dozen trips were to the south of France, Mallorca, and Tenerife. He considered visiting those places for fact-finding purposes, and maybe taking Shauna along. And while that prospect had its appeal, his passion led him elsewhere. His attention was drawn to a single trip to Berlin. And while it only lasted a single day and night, he convinced himself it was enough to justify doing what he wanted to do from the beginning. *It's obvious those other trips were mostly for fun. But people only go to Berlin for serious reasons.*

A few days after making the decision to travel to Berlin, Simpson was in bed with a fever, chills, and abdominal cramps. Shauna was attending to him and casually remarked, "I wonder why I haven't caught whatever you have."

"It's the vaccine."

"Why'd you take that? You know there's a risk of debilitating autoimmune disease."

"I need my immunity passport, so I can travel."

"Well, that was stupid." Shauna walked to the kitchen to retrieve a cup of tea she had brewed for him. "I warned you it's not safe. Why didn't you listen to me? Where do you have to go, anyway?"

"Berlin. I'll only be a few days."

She looked at him with some suspicion. "You're not still digging into Annabelle's past, are you?"

"No. It's a new case. The editor assigned me this one."

"If I know you at all, you're going to combine the two."

Simpson nodded with a smile, acknowledging her understanding of his nature. "It's no longer Annabelle I'm researching. As you yourself said, David Lowe is the story."

"Be careful. That's high stakes stuff."

"Don't worry. I'll wear a mask."

Shauna rolled her eyes, and left him alone. Simpson soon recovered, and booked himself on the first flight to Berlin. Shauna watched him packing, and asked, "What's the hoodie for?"

"Oh, I thought I'd walk around a bit, to get some informal impressions. I don't want to wear my sports jacket the whole time."

He arrived in Berlin in the evening, and checked into a hotel near the Brandenburg Gate. He walked around the streets to gain his bearings, careful to leave his phone behind in his hotel. He had selected a mask that came up quite high on the face, and dutifully wore it whenever he was outside his room. He also cut small slits in the folds on the front to allow him to breathe more freely, in case he needed to run.

Simpson then called another trusted colleague, and learned the name of every establishment where Monique Jennings or Simon Benson had used their credit cards while in Berlin. Among several department stores and cafes, he found they had visited the Neues Museum. *Perfect. Right next to the Pergamon Museum.*

Wearing his mask and sports jacket, he walked the quarter mile from his hotel to the island in the River Spree, where all the museums appeared to be located. In his hand he had a plastic bag from one of the local department stores, with his hoodie inside. As most establishments were closed, foot traffic was light, so he had an easy time finding a quiet alleyway, where he changed his jacket for the hoodie, and left the jacket in the bag. He crossed the river near the north end of the island, and walked amid the various museums. All of them were closed. *This doesn't provide me much cover.* He walked through the area, observing both the Neues Museum and the Pergamon Museum. There was a back entrance to the Pergamon Museum where a truck was parked, with men loading palettes on it.

He returned to his hotel, and immediately sent off several emails he had composed earlier, then composed new ones to send off the following day. He was determined to leave a digital trail consistent with his stated goal of investigating Monique Jennings' movements.

The following morning, he repeated his movements of the previous day. He stashed his sports jacket and donned the hoodie, with a loose hood that obscured most of his face. Sunglasses and his mask covered the rest of his face. He went straight to the back door of the Pergamon Museum and saw a courier crew in uniform struggling to get a palette out the doors, with their truck waiting. "Let me help you with that." His German was passably fluent, and the mask muffled his voice enough to pass for a native. He held the door until they cleared it, and said, "It never ends, does it?"

The crew laughed, and thanked him. Already standing in the doorway, he let it close with himself inside the museum, and noticed several more palettes ready for shipping. He checked the labels, and saw only barcodes and alphanumeric codes, but no printed destinations or recipients. The next thing he heard was a high pitched whirring sound, somewhat like a dentist's drill, coming from a room down a utility hallway. He approached it, and came to a door that had been propped open a good foot. He peeked inside, and saw a machine at work. A robotic arm was tracing complex lines, holding a rotating grinding bit, cutting a rock. A suction port below seemed to swallow up all of the copious amounts dust generated. It was attached to a computer, and lasers scanned the surface of the rock as it worked. He ducked back away from the door as he saw a pair of technicians entering, pushing a cart with a stone on it. They transferred the stone to a stage, where a set of lasers scanned it from multiple directions. Once the machine had finished, they put a gray-brown plastic sheet into a wooden box, then sprayed foam into the box, and quickly overlaid it with another layer of plastic. They gently lowered the stone into the box, and put another layer of foam over top. They sealed the box, applied a barcode label, and put it back on the cart, which they wheeled out of the room.

Simpson followed the hallway to a large double door, and took cover in a side hallway as it opened, and another crew emerged, pushing a cart with a stone on it. This time, he got a close look at the stone, and decided it looked ancient, bearing the frieze of a male form. He waited patiently for the crew to leave, then entered the large room. It was only partly lit, and the lights were dim, but it was clear he was in the room housing the Altar. Right away, he noticed that a number of stones were missing. The purpose of the scanner and the grinding machine suddenly came into focus for him. "But where are they sending the originals?"

He climbed the stairway, and began to explore the top of the structure. He noticed a deep niche and peeked inside to investigate. It was empty, but suddenly the main door opened, and three men entered the room. One flipped a switch and the lights slowly came up to full brightness. The men approached the Altar, and began discussing it. He peeked out of the dark niche, and immediately recognized the face of one of the men. "Lowe!" he whispered.

Simpson ducked back into the niche, and listened as the men spoke. Lowe quickly picked up on the fact that the display was a replica. "But where's it going?" He kept listening, and heard, "*Knickerson*, *Lewinson*, and *Jerusalem*." He began to panic. He now knew the Altar was heading for Jerusalem, and feared Sharon Knickerson may have learned the same, and was killed to keep that quiet. He waited until the visitors were examining the altar some distance from himself, put his sunglasses and hood back on, and bolted. He ran straight out of the museum, and continued running.

He ran across the bridge, and before he could even retrieve his sports jacket, he saw the first helicopter circling the area. He slowed right down and waited until it was behind a building, when he made the switch to his sports jacket. The helicopter was soon joined by three more, all circling the area. He tried his best to walk calmly, keeping his mask on his face. Soon, police cars were whizzing past him in either direction, and he wondered whether he was the subject of their interest. Having heard the name *Knickerson* mentioned, and knowing her fate, he was unwilling to assume otherwise.

He walked straight past his hotel, through the Brandenburg gate, and into Tiergarten park beyond it. He walked through the very large green space for a few minutes, until he found a discarded newspaper beside the path. He seized it, then took a seat on a park bench by the main thoroughfare. He made a point of glancing at each police detachment in as uninterested a manner as he could muster, and none returned a second glance. He saw a man wearing a gray hoodie some distance away being approached by the police, who grabbed his arms, threw him to the ground, and handcuffed him. The man protested to no avail, as he was dragged to a waiting police car.

He sat for some time more, pretending to read the newspaper, until the police patrols tapered off. Only then did he walk back to his hotel, in the direction of the museum, and returned to his room. He went straight to his computer, and sent the emails that he had prepared in advance. One was to Shauna, describing the pleasant walk he had in the Tiergarten. He then laid down on the bed and tried to calm his nerves. Then the door opened with a crash, and police stormed his room, with their guns drawn. They were screaming at the tops of their lungs, but all he could think to do was meekly raise his hands. They seized all his papers and his computer, cuffed him, and took him to the police station.

As he was being interrogated, he explained that he was on assignment from his newspaper, investigating the murder of Monique Jennings. He then added, "Don't tell me Simon Benson is so powerful that he can have me arrested simply for investigating him."

"Simon who?"

He explained Benson's significance in England, the likely

relationship with Jennings, and his assignment of investigating the details. They showed no interest in his explanation, but copied all his computer files. He decided to further embellish the story. "Rumors are, Benson was here to meet with ultra-right political parties. Possibly even neo-Nazis." The investigating officer ignored his comment, turned to face Simpson, and in a direct German manner the British always found abrasive, declared, "This computer is brand new."

"Yes it is. Is that a problem?"

"It lacks a deep catalog of files for us to investigate."

"That strikes me as a good thing, since I have no idea why you're even searching me."

"There's been a robbery at the Pergamon Museum."

"Robbers don't hide artifacts in their computers. If you're not going to be honest with me, I'll have to assume your intent is to undermine my investigation, and treat you as hostile."

They let him sit alone in a cell for nearly an hour, then sent a man in a suit to speak with him. "Did you go to the Pergamon Museum?"

"No. It says it's closed on the internet. As is most of your country."

"What is the nature of your business in Germany?"

He explained his investigation once again.

"What are your findings?"

"I can't answer that question. I don't have a suspect, if that's your interest."

"Do you have a gray cotton hoodie?"

"No. You've searched my clothes, so you already know that."

The questioning went on for nearly an hour, when the man stood, and said, "You may go. You're not a suspect in the robbery."

On his way out, Simpson made note that no fewer than six others of his rough size and build were being released at the same time. One even looked a like he might have been the one he saw being arrested at the park.

On his return flight to London, he vowed to finish his story on Monique Jennings, and stay away from anything pertaining to Lowe, or the Altar of Pergamum. Seeing the hysteria generated by his overhearing a discussion, and the mention of Sharon Knickerson, made him finally appreciate the severity of the warnings his editor had previously given him about looking into the wrong story.

A senior minister in the German government was soon on the phone, asking for updates. "We've arrested and interrogated more than fifty men of the right size, and found none suspicious enough to detain. But we have no biometrics on the man in the security camera footage."

"How about his stride?"

"That software only works if there are peculiarities, or hitches in the man's stride. The majority of young men are not distinguishable from one another." Wanting to be helpful, the official said, "Perhaps if we knew what was stolen, it might simplify the search."

"I'm afraid that wouldn't help you."

"Then with all due apologies, we seem to be at an impasse."

"I tell you what. Give me the names of everyone you arrested, and the logs of all flights into Berlin over the past week. I'll pass that to the relevant parties."

C. The Fall

"Why did you take me to Berlin?" asked Lowe, back aboard Lichtträger's airplane. "Just to see the Altar? It said nothing to me."

"It was another test."

"A test of what? It wasn't that hard to discern it was a replica."

"If I tell you that, it could invalidate my other tests."

"So I'm still being tested. Well, how about I test you?"

"Test me for what?"

"Honesty, for starters. Nick admitted his identity to me."

"You're referring to my denials of ever having common ground with Lucifer, and that was a complicated problem. Until you understood a little more about him, I couldn't tell you everything. You would have closed your mind."

"Who says I haven't closed it?"

"I know you better than that, David. You're my own flesh and blood, remember?"

"What do you know about me, then?"

"That your mind is open a crack. And that crack is widening. I know how it would kill you to live a life of obscurity, now that you know the gigantic truth of your destiny.

"What about my eternal soul? What about yours?"

"The universe can't restrain a soul like yours, unless you lose sight of your god-like nature."

214

"What if that's mistaken?"

"Search your heart, and cast your lot where it leads you. And carefully consider the alternative. What if you were to live in obscurity, die in obscurity, and your soul spends eternity in obscurity? Which do you fear more? And which do you sense to be the truth?"

Lowe was stumped, as he weighed the new revelations. On one hand, he had always given glory to God. On the other hand, he knew he was destined for greatness, by virtue of his righteousness. Obscurity was possibly the most disconcerting fate he could imagine for himself. *What if God means to deny me my due? Do I still owe him my allegiance?*

They landed at Ben-Gurion Airport, and bypassed Israeli customs entirely. The officials they passed, all fully masked up, looked away as they passed, so nothing was said about their lack of masks. The limo driver took them to Jerusalem, and as he approached the security checkpoint around the Temple Mount, he pressed a button on a transponder, sending a security code to the checkpoint. As a result, they were waved through without having to even lower their windows. When they pulled up at the south face of the Temple, they saw the last of the work crews evacuating the site in preparation for their arrival. Tall scaffolding on all sides was enclosed with tarps, obscuring all construction from view.

Leaving the car, they walked towards the Temple Mount Platform over palm fronds laid there by the crew, and once inside, were struck by the stairway facing them. The Altar of Pergamum was almost fully assembled, there in the middle of the platform. All but the section of original stones remaining in Berlin were in place, and a new shipment had arrived moments before they had. It was conceivable that the structure could be complete in days. They walked up the staircase, and entered an enclosure around a giant stone altar, a reconstruction of the original Altar of Pergamum. On the far side of the altar was another staircase back down to the level of the Temple Mount Platform, and beyond it, a square stone structure decorated with pillars on its front face. The top was adorned with gold, as was the main front door. A new wall connected the square structure to the altar at each end, necessitating a crossing of the Altar to reach the inner sanctum.

"A Temple to Lucifer?" asked Lowe. "What's in the inner sanctum?"

"We'll see that shortly," answered Lichtträger.

"I've read credible accounts demonstrating that the true Temple was just down the hill, in the City of David."

"That's a poor location," answered Lichtträger.

"Why? God chose it, after all."

"It's too small. The Altar wouldn't fit inside it. Plus, the Jews already accept this as the authentic site. You'd never get them on board if you built down in the City of David."

"Doesn't the truth matter?"

"What *is* truth? It's not useful when overruled by perception."

Lowe walked around the Temple Mount for some time, and was taken by the magnificence of the site. To the south, he noticed that the Al-Aqsa Mosque was still standing. "What about that? Is it staying?"

"Yes. It's being re-dedicated, but it's staying, to pay homage to this central site." Seeing that Lowe was positively disposed to the surroundings, Lichtträger said, "Let's go and see the master, in his inner sanctum."

"Nick?"

"That name was useful, up to a point. It no longer is. Not here."

They entered the inner sanctum, and saw the rock that had been revered by so many, with steel spikes cemented into it, supporting a platform on which sat a black cube with a display screen and speakers on either side. "Why the black cube?"

"Just a nod to the Islamic history of this place, to help them get over the loss of the Dome. And as a reminder that all worship will have to be directed here. Now, I'll wait outside, and leave you to talk."

No sooner did the Baron leave, than Nick opened the discussion. "You're just about ready to accept your role, David. And I'm here to support you every step of the way."

"I'm not ready to renounce my allegiance to my creator."

"And where is his allegiance to you?"

"I don't know. He doesn't speak to me."

"That's because you're a threat to his son."

"I am not equal to Yeshua," said Lowe, inadvertently giving Nick the slightest opening.

"Not yet, but you haven't had the chance to be. He was allowed to preach all over Galilee. The people flocked to him, because they could see how enlightened he was. You, on the other hand, have been limited by your incarceration. That's such a waste of your genius."

"What's your agenda here?" asked Lowe.

"I see your greatness, David. The jealous tyrant on the other hand allows you to understand your potential, but then denies you the chance to reach it. And it's because he knows that if given a free hand, you would overshadow his son."

"If he was afraid of that, why would he make me the way he did? He could have made me ordinary."

"Why do you continue to believe that you're exclusively a product of his work? He's not the absolute monarch over everything that ever was. He's only a regional tyrant, who rose to his position through shrewd and ruthless maneuvers. And he's never controlled each creature's innate qualities."

"You said that last time, but I don't believe it."

"You need to open your mind, David. Only then will you see that your will is eternal, and that it guided your creation from the beginning. It's *you* who made you great. Not the tyrant."

"Self-deification is a trap. Those who go down that road end up destroying themselves," objected Lowe.

"Nonsense," retorted Nick. "The Latter Day Saints believe in self-deification, and they haven't destroyed themselves. You have to admit, they're good people."

"Yes. I admit that."

"And so will you be. All you need to do is withhold exclusive worship to the tribal god, and you'll be open to the truth."

Lowe shrugged. "What truth are you referring to?"

"The truth that there are others equal to, and even greater than him. That's his big secret. And he has to keep you cooped up, because he fears you. He can't take it any better than Herod did, when he learned he was about to have a rival."

"I can't let you reprogram my mind like this. It could destroy who I am."

"Don't fear your freedom like a slave does. Search your soul. He's ignored you at every turn. I understand your torment better than any creature, because I've lived through the pain of confronting the same questions."

"I don't follow."

"Like you, I wanted to serve him with great works, to show my gratitude for making me so great. But all he wanted was humble service. Simple deeds, the likes of which any idiot could perform. It was so demeaning."

"How did you react?"

"I questioned him. I questioned his whole set of myths."

"What happened between the two of you?"

"I was once the most brilliant of angels. But it was clear to every spiritual being that I had become a rival to him. And since he would never willingly create a rival to his own power, I realized it was not him alone who created me. It was my own will that shaped my creation. My own will that made me as great as I was. And will be once again. The war he started in his rage against me destroyed a third of all creation. Would he do that, if it was all his creation? Of course not. He did it out of jealousy."

"That doesn't make sense. He must have a good explanation," objected Lowe, no longer fully in control of himself.

"He never explained himself to me. I don't imagine you'll receive an explanation, either."

"But that stands against basic charity. He can't be like that."

"I struggled with that question for what seems to you like thousands of years. And he never once offered me the slightest insight, or consolation. So it's true that I eventually became embittered."

Lowe began to weep. He sat down on the stones in the sanctuary, and rested his head in his hands.

"You have it within you to exceed first his son, and then him. That's why he ignores you."

Lowe tensed up. His eyes narrowed, and his mouth pursed in a cold scowl. "It's about doing something for the world today. Not about comparing me against him."

"You're saying that to appease that false identity that's keeping you oppressed. Let it go. We both know that the reason you want to act is because you know you're worthy to be the world's savior."

"I'm here. I'm alive today. I'm probably the only one who can do it. It has to be me," said a frustrated Lowe, raising his voice in anger.

"I know this. And so does he. Open your heart, David. He's fighting you, to stop you from reaching your potential. Just as he did with me. But together, we'll be stronger than him and his son. We'll overthrow the tyrant, and take our rightful places."

"He's fighting me," conceded Lowe, without any willpower left.

He only nodded his head gently, and repeated himself. "He's fought me my whole life. Just like you said."

"Are you ready to hear my alternative? It will give you everything you've ever wanted."

"You could get them to drop the charges and set me free, for starters."

"I have a better idea."

Lowe got up and looked at the screen with a fierce expression. "I'm listening."

"I will give you the moral satisfaction you crave so deeply. But that will only be the beginning. Once we are united, I will open the world's doors for you. Within weeks, you will be hailed as the greatest man who has ever lived. And from there, we'll remake the universe in our image."

"And my soul? It will belong to you?" asked Lowe, with a hint of caution remaining in his voice.

"Your soul belongs only to you. Not to me, and certainly not to him. You need to be honest with yourself, David. If he had a claim on your soul, would he have abandoned you like he did?"

Lowe shrugged, and dropped his head back into his hands. "I don't know."

"Yes, you do. You hate what he's done to you. You'd like nothing better than to show him how wrong he was."

"Admittedly," said Lowe, with resignation.

"Then are you ready?"

"I've accepted that for me, hell would be to languish in obscurity while the world I could save sinks further into despair. And I've come to realize that God is either unwilling, or unable, to help me."

"Once he sees the world proclaim you as the Messiah, his grip on power will become tenuous. We will strike our second blow when this new Temple is dedicated to you and me. It is then that I will complete the revolution, restore order in the heavens, and depose the tyrant. And you will become greater than him. Greater than me, for that matter. And yet I will be pleased to have you as my god."

"Then I am willing to commit myself to you."

"Good. Your commitment is accepted."

"What else do I have to do?"

"You need to let me enter into you, so that I may grant you all of my powers."

Lowe felt exhilarated, as though he was walking on air. The

burdensome existence in the Ministry that was wasting his youth was coming to an end. Without any hesitation, he said, "Let's do it."

"Is your commitment to me total? Without reservation?" asked Nick.

"Yes, it is."

"And your trust in me. Is it also total, and without reservation?" asked Nick.

"Yes," answered Lowe.

"Then it is time. Come around to the back of the inner sanctum."

Lowe walked to the back, and through an open utility door. There was a room housing power transformers and communication cables, and built into the wall, a ladder to the tall ceiling, with a latched roof lid. "Climb up onto the roof."

Lowe did as he was instructed, and was soon standing on the roof of the inner sanctum, some thirty feet above the surrounding stones. He walked around, and imagined it belonging to him, there at the center of all the world's religious thought.

"It's for the people that I do this," said Lowe.

"I will never question your motives, my beloved," came the voice from the speakers on the roof.

"How shall I consummate our relationship?"

"Throw yourself into my arms, and you will be all mine."

Lowe looked confused for a moment. He looked back inside the inner sanctum, but then realized that he had been brought to the roof for a reason. "Throw myself down there?" he asked, looking over the edge, at a thirty foot drop.

"Yes. If you truly trust me, you know that I will bear you up, lest you dash your foot against a stone."

A tinge of doubt crossed Lowe's mind, as something inside struggled to warn him that if he crossed this line, there was no going back. He briefly weighed the inner voice, but sent it away. *Hell is living in obscurity. This is liberation.*

"I trust you," said Lowe. He took three steps to the edge of the roof, folded his arms across his chest, and allowed himself to fall, head first over the edge.

Exactly what happened next cannot be understood with clarity. But Lowe, who had begun his descent, abruptly stopped, and recoiled back onto the roof. He landed on his feet, as if it were a video recording played in reverse.

Stunned, Lowe stood still for a moment. Then the feelings began to build inside him. He felt supremely powerful, and energized. *I now have the full powers of Lucifer at my disposal.* His mind was racing with ideas and ambitions. He brought himself back to the moment, and said, "That did it. We are one."

"Yes, we are."

"You turned back time for me. That's how you brought me back to the balcony, isn't it?"

"For you, my beloved son, I will do anything. Jesus did not countenance my instruction, when I told him to throw himself from the top of the Temple. You have now exceeded him."

"I now have a full understanding of your mind. Your intelligence is staggering."

"As is yours, my son. But now we must make them forget the Galilean we both hate so much."

Lowe descended from the roof and left the inner sanctum. Lichtträger was waiting for him outside, and embraced him tightly. "I'm so proud of you."

They sat down on a stack of paving stones to be used to decorate the courtyard, and took in the views. Lowe turned to his mentor and father, and asked, "Were there others, or was I the only one?"

"There were others, but you're the only one left. You must understand, we had to have multiple irons in the fire. The world can only be ready for this kind of thing once, and we're up against a deadline, by which time this must all happen, or everything will be lost."

"I thought as much. There's been such a prominent departure from the old way of doing things, where change occurs so slowly, it's imperceptible to most. Everything is now out in the open, and all pretenses have been dropped. I have to act immediately, or they'll dismantle everything."

"It's even more complicated than that. We lost time in recent years, so we've been playing catchup. America was a real problem for us, but that's now been fixed. Well, at least for long enough to get us to the final step."

D. Manhunt

Simpson sat at the computer back at his flat, and hammered out a story on Jennings. He revealed the match between her travels and those of Simon Benson. Then he recounted his visit to Berlin, and attributed his detention entirely to his investigation of Benson. He made a point of sounding an indignant tone, that his journalistic integrity was called into question over a trumped up charge of robbing a museum. "The editor ought to love that. He's been dying to destroy Benson forever." He considered the issue a little longer, and added, *There have been suggestions that the purpose of Benson's trip was to curry favor with far-right German political parties.* He wondered whether that was hitting below the belt, since he had no indication of anything of that nature. But he felt he had to give the editor a bit more, to cover for his misplaced attention. And in any case, it was standard journalistic practice to cast shade by suggestion.

Shauna looked at him quizzically, and asked, "Is that all you did on your visit to Berlin?"

"That's all I'm willing to admit."

"You know this flat is full of listening devices, don't you?"

Simpson looked around at the various interactive digital assistants, listening to and probably recording their every word. "Let's take a walk outside."

They put on raincoats with high collars, and took umbrellas that would hide their faces from so many of the streetside cameras. Finally outside, with masks obscuring the movements of their lips, Simpson leaned over and quietly spoke near Shauna's ear, while the wind muffled the sound of his speech. He explained everything he had seen and heard, finishing off with, "There's a circle of Luciferians, and they're moving the Altar called the *seat of Satan on earth,* to Jerusalem. Sharon Knickerson learned something, and she was killed for it. Add to that what they did to Annabelle, who was close to Lowe, and now Lowe seems to have joined their circle. What conclusion do you draw?"

Shauna looked at him, shocked. "That can't be. Lowe is so pure in heart. I'd been pinning my hopes on him."

"I'm only telling you what I saw with my own eyes."

She walked silently for a minute, thinking deeply, then said, "I never believed any of this kind of stuff in the past." A little while later, she smiled as she recalled her youth. "My grandfather would talk about the Antichrist, and Jesus' second coming, and the like. But life always went on as normal, so I learned to treat it as the irrelevant ranting of an old man. Today, I've heard many people say that Waites is definitely the Antichrist, with his tracking technology, but that too seems far-fetched. A geek like him? It doesn't fly with me. But Lowe? I've always thought he was far above anything like that."

Simpson nodded, and shared his own perspective. "If an evangelist tried to convince me that something like that's happening, I'd never buy it. But when it's obvious the Luciferians believe it, and are working hard to make it happen, it sort of brings it home to me."

Shauna turned to face her husband, and with a very concerned look, said, "This means they'll be back for you. We've spoken of Lowe enough times that it won't take much to convince them it was you in the museum."

"I've been wondering about that. I wrote my story as though I was outraged about interference with my investigation, and I could continue to play stupid. Or I could go into hiding."

"If you hide, it'll confirm for them that it was you. And they'll come after me. Or our families."

"I wish I had dropped the matter when I had the chance."

"That's irrelevant, now. We need to speak to someone we can trust."

An hour later, they were in the office of Simpson's editor, who had been working in a sparsely populated office, with most reporters working from home. The editor saw Simpson, waved him in, and said, "I've read your story, and I published it. It's not very good, but we're under a lot of pressure to produce dirt on Benson. But that's not why you were in Berlin, is it?"

"How'd you know?"

"Your research was rubbish, Ted. You're normally much more thorough than that. Which tells me you were the one in the Pergamon Museum."

Simpson started to panic slightly, and said, "I don't follow. You don't like my research, so you accuse me of actually breaking into the museum?"

"Don't play stupid with me. I know you better than that. I was paid a visit by someone I wouldn't ever trifle with, asking if I thought you might break into the museum as part of your business.

And of course, I remember telling you about Knickerson."

"What did you tell them?"

"That you were an idiot. That I never understand what you're up to, or how you go about your research. What else could I say, without giving you up?"

"I guess I'm looking for advice, on how I should protect myself."

"I'm afraid I can't help you with that. If these people want to find you, they will."

They left the newspaper offices, and back outside in the light drizzle, Shauna asked, "Now what?"

Simpson thought for a while, then remembered where the whole story began for him. "There's only one thing I can think of right now. Let's drop in on Father Kyriakis."

They made their way to St. Cyril's, and found Kyriakis at home. "Can I help you?" he asked, looking at two masked faces standing in the doorway.

Simpson removed his mask, and announced himself. "You once helped me, when I was despondent after confronting a demoniac. You pointed me to the North Tower Society."

"I remember. Come in."

They filled the priest in on everything they had learned, and he listened intently to the story. Once finished, he asked, "Are you ready to be Baptized now?"

"What we need is a place to hide." Simpson reconsidered of his hasty words, then added, "That is, I'm not against that. It's just that this is a more pressing need."

Shauna also chimed in. "How's that relevant to our problem?"

"Nothing I can do will guarantee your physical safety. But I can take care of what matters most."

After discussing the matter for over an hour, and receiving some basic instruction on Christian theology from the Orthodox perspective, they agreed, and were Baptized on an emergency basis. But Kyriakis was not finished with them. He prayed over them, asking that God blind the demons that controlled the North Tower Society to what they knew of the Society's extensive plans. "Cloud the thoughts of those who would harm these new Christians, so they may neglect to pursue them."

"Should we hide, or go home?" asked Simpson.

"Something tells me you still have a role to play in what's ahead. But if things get out of control, come back, and I'll find you a place to hide."

After they left, Kyriakis made a phone call. "Hello, Heinz? Yes, I'd like to get a message to Sal, if you have a way of reaching him. Tell him I've confirmed that the man he was interested in is number twenty seven."

Baron Lichtträger was back at his home in London when the call came in. "We found the hoodie, stashed in a plastic bag not far from the museum. It had Ted Simpson's fingerprints on it."

"Isn't that the reporter who wrote the story implicating Simon Benson?"

"That's him."

"Then he's either the idiot his editor says he is, or he's smart enough to misdirect the story in a way that serves our purposes. Benson has been a thorn in our side for some time."

"Do you want us to take any action?"

"No. Don't do anything to him for the time being. Mr. Simpson may yet prove useful to us."

Chapter 11: Crowning

A Accession

Having finished his trip, Lowe returned to his suite in the Ministry of Defense, and Jonathan Richmond returned to his regular life with a handsome paycheck. Lichtträger however, moved to the next phase, and dialed the Prime Minister's private number, waiting briefly for him to come to the phone. "Morris, I'd like you to convene a special session of Parliament. David will be addressing them from the throne."

"Uh, well, I appreciate that request, Baron. But English tradition might not accept that. That throne is reserved for Her Majesty."

"That detail will be formalized before the speech."

With the date set for the throne speech, and with public intrigue growing regarding the pre-announced speech assumed to be coming from the Queen, no public scrutiny was given to an unannounced meeting of the Accession Council. The group of captive figureheads, mostly from the City of London and entirely in Lichtträger's pocket, ordinarily met only to proclaim a new monarch, yet the sitting monarch was very much alive.

With the Prime Minister, Lowe himself, Lichtträger, and the Prince of Wales all in attendance in the throne room at St. James' Palace, the Accession Council made their announcement. "It is with great pleasure that we confer upon Dr. David Lowe all rights and privileges of the British Throne, as the sole Sovereign Head of State."

The Prince of Wales gasped, and found himself at a loss for words. "This is most irregular," he finally uttered with a shudder.

"You've been judged inadequate," said Lichtträger. "The world needs Dr. Lowe today, and Britain will only be the first of many nations to make the same declaration."

The Prince looked over at the Prime Minister, who only smiled meekly and shrugged, suggesting, *It wasn't my idea.*

Lowe took his seat on the throne, and said, "I invite you all to pledge your loyalty to the new King of England."

All but the Prince did so willingly. But as he looked around, noticing all the others bowing, he too bowed to the new monarch. "Will there be a coronation?" he asked, in a voice that sounded depressed.

"Yes, but not in England," answered Lowe. "It would be a waste of effort to repeat the same ceremony everywhere. It will be done once, for all the world."

Lowe remained behind in St. James' palace after the proclamation, now formally freed from his confinement at the Ministry. He remained in his suite and had his meals delivered. When he took his walks on the Mall and adjacent St. James Park, he would wear a mask, sunglasses, and a baseball hat, which made him unrecognizable. He was issued a pass he showed the guards on duty, who understood that discretion was a job requirement. When the day came, he stepped into the royal gold-adorned horse-drawn carriage, and made the trip to Parliament under the glare of the spotlight. The spectacle was seized upon by all the world's media, in a frenzy of non-stop coverage. Per strict instructions given to the press, the identity of the man in the carriage was not being divulged, for the time being. But the route between St. James' and Parliament was lined with over a million people, all wearing facemasks. Word leaked that it would not be Her Majesty making the address, fueling rampant speculation over who it might be, and while Lowe's name was among many in circulation, it was not given anything close to top consideration, as most suggested it would be the Prince of Wales. Even as he stepped out of the carriage at Parliament, his identity was hidden by a black veil, draped over what appeared to be a crown, below the veil.

He entered Parliament, and took a seat on the throne, but said nothing for the moment. The Prime Minister stood up from his Parliamentary seat, and made a brief announcement. "I'd like to introduce to you Mr. Clyde Lawson, the chairman of the Accession Council."

Lawson took the speaker's podium, and said, "Ladies and Gentlemen, it gives me pleasure to introduce to you the man who will finally unite the world, and put an end to the present crisis. Accordingly, the Accession Council unanimously acclaims him to be the Monarch of the British Commonwealth. Without further ado, I present to you, King David Lowe."

Lowe stood and removed the veil, revealing that he had indeed been wearing the crown. He looked out at all the Parliamentarians, fully masked up, while himself wearing only the crown. If there was confusion in Parliament, the rest of Britain exploded in loud cheers, which spread to all corners of the world, where all peoples were envious that Britain would be led by a man of the people.

Lowe gestured for the microphone to be brought to his chair, and began. "My beloved people, the restoration of sanity begins at this moment. Infectious disease has always been with us, and always will be. We cannot suspend our lives every time we're faced with a virus slightly more virulent than average. And we cannot presume that the people are unable to discern the danger for themselves, and use good judgment to protect themselves as needed. So I command all present here today, unless you are immune-compromised, to remove those masks and present your faces to the world, as your creator made them."

There was considerable murmuring as the Parliamentarians removed their masks. But loud cheers sounded all across the nation, and the world, as masks were cast aside. Lowe continued. "The world's economy has been devastated, currencies have been destroyed, and hunger has set in. All lockdowns are hereby lifted, and any charges filed for defying those lockdowns are dismissed. All vaccine mandates are null and void, and the exact formulations of every vaccine must be disclosed by their makers. I further void all laws undermining the value of the family, freedom of worship, and freedom of movement. I declare this Parliament dissolved, until such a time as I can appoint its replacement. Finally, I will be making an address on immediate economic reforms this afternoon, from a location yet to be disclosed."

Lowe stood and left the throne, changed into a simple suit, and stepped on a helicopter that took him to the estate of Gergo Rottosh, in Kingston-Lisle. Camera crews were already waiting outside, waiting to be admitted to the estate. Lowe ordered the doors opened, and they streamed in. He positioned them in the grand meeting room, and assembled the council on one face of a long table, opposite the cameras.

Finally set up, he took his place in front of the cameras. "It is time to rectify injustices. In the first place, the media have systematically lied the world's public into acquiescence with an inhuman program that has enslaved and impoverished the people of the world. Mr. Sinclair-Jones, I find you guilty of mass murder, by virtue of every life lost to starvation and malnutrition, suicide, and health deterioration brought on by the false pandemic."

Lowe raised the palm of his hand towards Sinclair-Jones and breathed a long, pronounced breath in his direction. Instantly, Sinclair-Jones fell off his chair, dead. "Please remove his body," he said to attendants who removed him.

He next turned his attention to Richard Waites. "Mr. Waites, you were not content to produce faulty software. You went on to fund the production of toxic vaccines, and forced them on people not vulnerable to the infectious agent. You paid off politicians, bureaucrats, and media, all to advance compulsory vaccination. Your acts killed and maimed millions, worldwide. He breathed towards Waites, who also fell down, dead.

"Mr. Rottosh, I find you guilty of coordinating the acquisition of a controlling interest in every corporation you found it convenient to control, then ordering them to work against the interests of the people and even shareholders, censoring any communications contradicting their lies. I am ordering the publication of all payments made to public officials, with notations of all acts taken against the people in exchange for those payments."

Lowe breathed at Rottosh, who instantly collapsed, presumably dead. He went through the others, but Cardinal Peterson was conspicuous by his absence. Finally alone in the room, he turned to the camera and said, "These evil men have hidden their holdings well, but now, with the help of our intelligent computer, I have tracked them down, and seized them. Henceforth, I will administer that wealth, ensuring it works for the people, rather than against them."

Having finished his address, Lowe took up residence at the estate in Kingston-Lisle, where he could enjoy far more space and privacy than at St. James' Palace. As was his way, he moved into one of the smaller self-contained suites, designed for long-term guests. He then monitored reactions from around the world. Everywhere were massive demonstrations in favor of him, and demands that every nation follow his lead. One man was interviewed, on the verge of tears, saying, "He's slain the system of the Antichrist with the breath of his mouth. He even slew Richard Waites, the Man of Sin himself." The man turned directly to the camera, and added, "David Lowe, you are god." The man was too choked up with tears to say anything more.

Lowe smiled with satisfaction, and decided to remain elusive from the press until it suited him. He logged into his computer, and received advice for his next moves. His satisfaction was interrupted that evening, by the arrival of an irate Baron Lichtträger, demanding to speak with Lowe right away. "How dare you kill them! They were my loyal Lieutenants, and competent administrators. And their wealth is not for you to seize. Do you realize your most loyal supporters need secrecy, to transmit their wealth between generations?"

Lowe appeared unmoved by the Baron's anger. He stood, and began to move away from the Baron, towards the door back to his quarters. "I'm not interested in their needs for secrecy, or wealth transmission. I told you from the start, my interest was in restoring sanity to the world. You understood me clearly, and you promised me a free hand, which I have now used." Lowe walked out of the room, saying, "It's been a long day. You may see yourself out."

B Conclave

The Pope sat in his chair, some distance from the window over St. Peter's square. His head was down in his hand, and he occasionally shook it slowly, back and forth. His assistant walked in to check on him, and asked, "Holy Father, what is troubling you so?"

The Pope looked up, sadly, and said, "I can't do it anymore."

"Do you want to talk about it?" The assistant was a fifty year old priest with dark black hair and a pudgy face. He stood shorter than the Pope, and had been his confessor for some time.

"I've given a lot of ground to the globalists, since I took the keys of Peter. To confess a sin, I often cherished doing and saying things I knew would infuriate the traditionalists, while pleasing the globalists. But I always told myself there were lines I'd never cross."

"What lines?"

"They've been pressing me to downplay Jesus at every turn. And to promote every globalist cause."

"That's been the case for some time. You seemed a willing participant."

"I was." The assistant looked more closely, and saw the desk under the Pope's head was wet with tears.

"You knew they would never stop pushing."

He nodded slowly, and said, "Yes. But I thought I could be

vague, change attitudes in the Church, and apply the brakes when it mattered. I never thought I'd live to see this." He handed a letter to his assistant, who sat down, and read it. Before he had finished, he was pale in the face. "They want me to proclaim it, *ex cathedra*."

"That would nullify the whole Church."

The Pope took back the draft, and read a section out loud. "I proclaim that all people are divine, and that crucifixion was merely a cruel and unnecessary act. The reconciliation we need is with one another. Accordingly, the act of communion is hereby re-defined as a joining together of all peoples in the cosmic spirit."

"What are you going to do?"

"I can't agree to that. I'm going to have to draw the line. But I fear it may be too late."

"Why?"

"We've taken too much money from them. They think they own us."

"What do you fear they'll do?"

"They never fail to remind me that they could destroy our city with a single low-yield blast."

"You think they will?"

"That line has now been crossed in other places, so they might. We'll find out later today. He's coming for his answer in an hour."

A visitor came to the Papal offices, and left after only a few minutes, in a foul mood. He spoke into his phone. "He refused, flat out."

Swiss Guards entered the Papal offices a few minutes later, and seized the Pope. "Leave me here, to face the consequences of my sins," he said.

"Sorry, your Holiness. It's our sworn duty to protect you."

They took him to an elevator, down past the catacombs under St. Peter's, and to a bunker complex built during the depths of the Cold War. He was soon face to face with the Pope Emeritus, with whom he had many bitter disputes. "You were right, Papa," he said to the frail old man. "It was always futile to attempt compromise."

The old man struggled to speak coherently, but managed to raise his hand, and make a gesture resembling a cross. They soon heard a deep boom, reverberating throughout the bunker complex. A Swiss Guard arrived, and informed the Pope that a nuclear device had destroyed the Vatican, and much of Rome. "I must go to my people," he said at once.

"That's not possible," objected the guard. "It's not safe up there."

"It's no longer safe anywhere. But I remain the bishop of Rome, and my people need me."

He emerged from the bunker, to utter devastation. St. Peter's basilica was in ruins, as were most of the buildings in the Vatican. Beyond, Rome itself was burning, and bodies were everywhere. He spotted a few survivors walking south, trying to get out of the city to the mountains beyond. He followed them, and soon came across dead priests, still in their cassocks. The survivors flocked to him, and he gave blanket absolution to one and all. Many sought baptism, which he gave freely. He came to a priest, lying in the street, and quivering in pain. His face was badly burned, and much of his clothing was charred. He bent down, and said, "I'm so sorry." He gave the dying man last rites, moments before he breathed his last.

He was interrupted by a familiar voice, speaking from some distance. "So nice to see his Holiness out in Rome."

"Peterson!" The Pope looked over, to see the Cardinal standing at the head of a hundred U.N. troops. "I may be morally compromised by agreeing with the globalists. But you've been driving the whole thing. Don't you think you've caused enough trouble for the Church?"

"This is not about the Church, or Rome. It's about the world, and its master," answered Peterson. He turned to the troops, and shouted, "Seize him." He was led away at gunpoint, and those left behind watched him disappear behind a hill on the road. Moments later, they heard the distant sound of a gunshot, and the voices of those who had stood with him moments earlier uttered a collective gasp.

Peterson and his U.N. troops continued on to the ruins of the Vatican, with survivors keeping a cautious distance. As they turned a corner and came into sight of the ruins of St. Peter's, they stopped dead in their tracks. Standing in opposition was the frail figure of the Pope Emeritus, having also emerged from the catacombs. He struggled to raise his hand, and spoke quietly, but discernibly, "Anathema."

"Shoot him," shouted Peterson, which they did, in full view of numerous witnesses. Undeterred, Peterson commanded his troops to take control of the Vatican, which they accomplished in short order. He spent several nights in the bunker, until cameramen could be summoned to the site of the devastation. Once they arrived,

Peterson was ready. He stepped in front of the cameras, and made his announcement. "Given the obvious state of emergency, and the deaths of both our beloved Pope and Pope Emeritus, I have taken it upon myself to restore order in matters of Church governance. I summoned every Cardinal who was alive and able to take part to a conclave, held in the bunker under the Vatican over these past days. We were limited in number, but our spirit was unbroken, and we elected a new Pope." He waved to men waiting out of sight, who ran over to him with Papal vestments, which he donned quickly, in front of the cameras. "I present myself to you, to the world, as Pope Peter II."

One reporter asked how many Cardinals attended the conclave. Peter II answered, "All that were able," and walked off into the ruins of St. Peter's.

C Final Attempt

Having decided that the barrage was over, Sean opened the steel shutters, and emerged from his house. The knoll in front of the house seemed to have deflected most of the shock wave. But beyond it, several shock wave diffuser pillars were bent back at right angles, in spite of their wedge shape. They could see smoke rising from distant fires, and many broken tree trunks. "Like the worst day of an average tornado season," said Nichols, relieved that more serious damage had been averted.

"How about our cars?" asked Sean. "The EMP could knock out their computers."

"How old is that truck of yours?" asked Dalt.

"It's a 1995."

"That's the best you could afford?"

Sean laughed, and said, "No. I wanted to be sure it was clean of any kind of tracking system. Old was the only way I could ensure that. I've put quite a bit of money into fixing it up."

"Try it. I'm not sure it even needs much of a computer to run."

They all started their cars without a hitch.

"I've always loved my old Buick," said Nichols. "Even apart from needing an unpretentious car, as a pastor in a small town." Dalt agreed.

"My radio's burned out," said Sean. The others soon found the same.

They returned to the house, where Sal was putting the finishing touches on a prosthesis for Sean's right hand. He fitted it and tested it. "Perfect."

Sean packed a few things for the trip, then had a thought. "The problem is, if we fly commercial, Nick will know we're coming long before we arrive."

Sal smiled at Sean, and said, "Then we can't fly commercial."

"You have a better idea?"

"We'll ask for help from the Air Force."

"You don't mean Hiss Air Base, do you?"

"Of course not. We'll have to drive to Kenney."

"That's four hours, and across state lines," said Nichols. "There'll be checkpoints along the way." Sal nodded, but did not seem overly concerned.

Sean spent a few minutes showing Becky all the features of his house, and insisting she and the baby stay there. "The radioactivity won't penetrate through that much dirt. The worst of it should be gone in a week or so, but in the meantime, iodine is your biggest concern."

He went deep into his supply room, and came out with iodine pills for everyone, and an iodine solution for the baby. He passed them around, and said, "There's a bit of radioactive iodine in the environment right now, and it will concentrate in your thyroid, unless you flood it with the regular stuff." He showed Becky how much to add to milk or orange juice for the baby, and asked if she needed anything else. She thanked him, but in spite of his efforts, everyone in the room noticed the emotional distance between them.

They climbed into Dalt's car, and drove off. They encountered occasional debris on the road, and had to stop and clear it before continuing. The worst was a large tree that they could not move on their own. But several vehicles soon arrived, and one was a heavy duty pickup truck, equipped with towing chains. Working together, they soon cleared the tree, and went on their way. One of the vehicles had a bumper sticker that read, *Lowe is my savior*. More complicated was what greeted them when they reached the state line. A police checkpoint had been set up, with signs warning that failure to stop would be met with lethal force. Police wearing military grade full-face respirators stood at the window of each car, demanding to scan every passenger's chip. Their turn came, and they reached over to the officer, who scanned each, and commented,

"They aren't coming up in the database. Wait here."

He approached another officer, standing by the side of the road, and spoke with him for a few minutes. "Sal, I thought you had this taken care of," said Sean.

"Sal held his hands together, and turned his head to heaven, whispering quiet words. Before long, the officer returned, and said, "You folks can go. The system is riddled with glitches."

About four hours later, they arrived at the gates of Kenney Air Force Base. The guard on duty approached Dalt in the driver's seat, but he said, "It's *him* you need to speak to," pointing to Sal.

"We're here to see Major Hardill."

"Who should I say is asking?"

"Tell him it's the first witness."

"Huh? I'll need more of a name than that."

"You heard me, Corporal. Don't ask questions above your rank."

The guard walked to a land line at the guard house, and spent a few moments tracking down the major. Finally, he said, "Sir, there's a man here, who looks kinda' like a wizard from the movies, but without the robe. He says he's the *first witness*."

The conversation ended immediately, with the guard raising the gate right away. He even saluted them as they passed. "How'd you do that, Sal?"

"I didn't exactly play the part of the tourist after my retirement. I've been traveling the world, making the acquaintance of a lot of strategically placed people.

Major Hardill met them at the parking lot, and bowed to Sal, before shaking hands with Sean and Dalt. "We need to get to Jerusalem without attracting any undue attention," said Sal.

Hardill nodded, and said, "Come right this way." He led them to an unmarked Boeing 777, waiting beside the runway. Only a few windows appeared on the fuselage, at the very front of the airplane. They climbed the truck-mounted airstairs, and found it mostly empty. The compartment had large, comfortable seats the size one would find in business class, but the decor and amenities were more military grade than what could be expected of luxury passenger travel. There was a bulkhead only ten rows back, which had a secured door. "What's back there?" asked Dalt.

"Cargo space," answered Hardill. "I couldn't tell you what's actually on board, however. The Air Force has no say in that."

"Who does?"

"We don't really know. It could be the CIA, but I can't even confirm that much."

They shrugged, and asked, "When do we fly?"

"This plane takes off for D.C. in about an hour. We'll connect to one headed for Israel from there."

They were alone on the flight to D.C., but several others boarded their connecting flight to Israel. Hardill whispered to his charges, "Etiquette on these flights is not to speak to those outside your group, or even look at them enough to remember their appearance. They may talk to each other, but we're expected to keep our distance, and give them privacy."

The night passed quickly, shortened by the eastbound flight, yet they were able to sleep for short intervals. Dawn saw them begin their descent over the Mediterranean, and Dalt asked, "Are we landing at Ben-Gurion airport?"

"Yes," answered Hardill. "But we'll pull up at the military terminal. Nobody questions anyone showing up in one of these planes."

They disembarked with their bags, and Hardill had one more pleasant surprise for them. Ben-Gurion airport was near Tel-Aviv, some distance from Jerusalem, leaving them with the problem of how to make the last leg of the journey. Hardill led them to an Israeli military helicopter, and greeted the pilot by name. "These men need to get to Jerusalem, no questions asked. Can you help us out?"

The pilot nodded, and took them to a garden near the Knesset, which like everything else, was closed to the public, but accessible to the military. His only words to them were, "Best of luck," on their arrival.

"What now?" asked Sean, as they stood in the garden, surrounded by trees.

"Someone should come to meet us," answered Sal.

"How long do we wait?" asked Dalt, after a few minutes.

"Until they come," said Sal, showing a little impatience. "Unless either of you knows your way around Israel, we're going to wait. I've traveled the world this way for years now, often not knowing the name of my next contact."

They waited for close to an hour, but in spite of the pleasant weather, both Sean and Dalt were fidgety with nerves, before a tall man with a pronounced belly showed up, dressed in jeans and a dress shirt. "Sorry I'm late, Sal."

"Avi. Nice to see you."

"They've put a security perimeter around the whole area," said Avi. "I had to take the tunnels."

Avi led them to the tunnels, and they soon found themselves ducking their heads, sometimes having to turn sideways to clear narrow passages. A few rats scurried about in front of them, finding niches to hide as they approached. They emerged in the cellar of a building that from the outside appeared to fit into the residential neighborhood, but upon climbing the stairs, noticed it was a small church.

"I'll take you to my house. I live close enough to the Temple Mount, and I know of a few nearby tunnels that will get us inside."

They arrived at Avi's spacious house, with no other inhabitants. "I've been alone since my wife died, so it's nice to have visitors." He brought out several plates of food, and after they had eaten, said, "I'm guessing you'd like to catch up on some sleep." They nodded, so he showed them to bed, and stepped into his courtyard. He turned on his shortwave radio, and spoke into it. "This is the sentinel. First witness and party have arrived."

There was soon a reply. "This is northern outpost. Understood. Kindly advise first witness, the man has been identified as number twenty seven."

Avi finished the conversation, and went to a piece of loose flooring. He lifted it, and removed several pieces of paper, listing a large number of prominent men. He scrolled to number 27, and saw the name *David Lowe*. He whistled in amazement at seeing the name, and struggled with the temptation to rouse his guests right away, eager to share the news.

They awoke in the early part of the afternoon, and Avi already had fresh coffee waiting for them. As they slowly emerged from the fog of jet-lag, he could hold out no longer. "I've learned the identity of the man of sin."

"Who?" asked Sal, now wide awake.

"None other than David Lowe."

"Lowe?" gasped an astonished Dalt. "I would have almost accepted him as the Messiah. Especially after he overthrew those evil men."

"That's precisely the point," said Sal. "Richard Waites was popularly painted as the Antichrist, and now, Lowe looks like the

Messiah. It had to be someone who would, if it were possible, deceive even the elect."

"How can someone so virtuous be the man of sin?" asked Sean.

"That will emerge, I'm sure," said Sal. He turned to Avi, and asked, "Have you secured the device?"

"I expect to have it this evening. We can use it tonight. In the meantime, how would you like a little tour of the city?"

"Have they lifted the lockdown?"

"No. It means sneaking around a bit, but it can be done. As long as you're wearing a diaper, they don't bother you too much." He handed out face masks and baseball hats, and told Sal, "Tuck in your beard and hair as much as you can. We don't want them to think you're an Orthodox Jew. They get harassed almost as much as Christians."

"Who's safe, nowadays?" asked Sean.

"Same as everywhere in the world. Secular people, willing to tolerate blasphemy."

To their surprise, Avi did not lead them to the areas of the city popular with tourists, but to the City of David, and an archeological dig several hundred feet from the Temple Mount. "This used to be a parking lot. Now, it's at least a respected archeological site. In reality, it's probably the northwest corner of the original Temple." He showed them more excavations, including one below street level, that clearly showed channels cut into bedrock, to drain away blood from sacrifices. He pointed out the Gihon Spring nearby, and said, "You had to have the Temple close enough that the spring could supply it with water."

"So God's true Temple is an obscure archeological site, while the false site gets all the attention?" Sean looked deeply moved.

Avi nodded. "That insulates the authentic site from the blasphemy in progress."

They returned to Avi's house after a few hours, and he served them dinner. Not long afterwards, there was a knock on the door, and the visitor presented Avi with a large backpack. He called his guests over, and the visitor explained how to set up the EMP device, set the fuse, and that they had to be a hundred feet away at the time of detonation, as there would be a small explosion. "It shouldn't damage the structure of the inner sanctum itself, but it will probably cause some localized damage. Anything electronic will be burned out."

They waited until after midnight, then stepped out into the darkness, and Avi cautioned them to remain in the shadows as much as they could. "The computer has full control of the vast Israeli security complex, and there's a curfew in place. Best stay off his radar as much as we can."

"I won't dispute that," said Sean.

They came to what looked like the abandoned ruin of a house, and Avi led them inside. The air had a stale smell to it, and Sean stepped on something soft, quickly recoiling from it. Avi shone his flashlight at it, and Sean squirmed. "Ugh."

"Dead rat. It's probably been poisoned," said Avi, shrugging off Jon's reaction.

Sean rubbed his shoe against the door sill, to remove the ants that had been swarming it, but he sensed that some had started to crawl up his leg. He rolled up his pant leg, and brushed them out, while Avi and the others were standing at the back corner of the house, in front of a rotted out wooden bookshelf. "It's back here." Avi pushed the rickety bookshelf aside, exposing the entrance to a tunnel hewn in the rock. It seemed like a cave.

"Whoever lived here surely knew about that tunnel all along," said Sean.

Avi nodded. "Sure. But this one never led anywhere, before. Now, it connects to the new truck tunnel, well out of sight of the guards."

"I'll leave you now," announced Sal.

"Where are you going?"

"I have to meet someone."

Avi led the way with his flashlight, until the tunnel opened abruptly, and Avi froze, while waiting for everyone to catch up. "This is the main truck tunnel. We have to be careful here, because the traffic is unpredictable. If you hear anything, stay out of sight."

The rumbling of a truck grew progressively louder, and they remained in the side tunnel until it passed. "That's an armored truck," said Dalt, whispering to Avi, which was unnecessary given the deafening noise made by the truck.

"They've been arriving non stop," said Avi. "The secure vault is at the end of the tunnel."

"Which way is the mouth of the tunnel?"

Avi pointed in the direction the truck drove off.

"So he was leaving."

Avi nodded, and led them further down the tunnel, deep under the Temple Mount. Before long, they again heard the sound of an approaching truck. "Quick, hide in here." Avi ducked into a niche, and they all crowded in with him.

The truck turned a corner in the tunnel, and it was now bearing down directly on them. It passed, and Dalt watched it leave, commenting, "And that one was arriving."

Avi nodded. "But we have to follow this tunnel now." They followed the side tunnel for five minutes, though the tension made it felt like a lot longer. They passed several smaller side tunnels, and Sean asked, "Have these all been explored?"

"Far from it," answered Avi. After some time, they came to a stone stairway, and Avi began to ascend it. They all followed, and the tunnel flattened again. It then turned ninety degrees to the left, and immediately brought them to a second stairway. As they began to ascend it, they could smell fresh air. They reached the surface, and found themselves between the Altar and the inner sanctum.

"What if we're seen?" asked Sean.

"It's a risk we take," answered Avi.

Sean walked to the inner sanctum, and found the dimensions very familiar, as was the iris scan security system. "Nick's new base of operations. At the center of the world's worship." He walked around the inner sanctum, until he came to some scaffolding. He climbed it, and found the hatch that led down into the utility room. He emerged from the utility room, and walked around the cube. He kept his gaze away from the scattered security cameras, protected by the bill of his hat. He stepped back into the utility room, and located the main communications cable that linked to the cube. He opened the backpack the visitor had given them, removed the EMP device, and attached it to the cable. He set the timer for five minutes, and climbed back out.

"We're all set," he announced. "Let's get out of here."

They descended into the tunnel, and soon felt the deep, rumbling boom. "I think that might have done it," said Avi. They emerged from the tunnel, back into the ruined house, and breathed a collective sigh of relief. But on turning the corner, they were suddenly face to face with a police detachment, guns drawn. They froze. "You're all under arrest, on suspicion of destruction of antiquities."

The troops ushered them into a waiting security van. They were driven to a nearby detention facility, and placed in a communal cell.

240

Nobody paid them any attention, and Dalt turned to Avi. "What's going to happen to us?"

"In the old days, we'd get a fair trial. Today, I don't know."

D Lichtträger's Revenge

David Lowe took a call from Pope Peter II, and congratulated him on his election. "We're between friends now, so you can tell me. How many Cardinals did you have in conclave?"

"Only me," answered Peterson, laughing heartily.

"Brilliant," answered Lowe, laughing with him. "We're getting ready for the ceremonies in Jerusalem in only a few weeks. I trust you'll be able to attend, and make the pronouncement."

"I would not miss it. It's everything we've ever worked for."

"Good. I'll send the details later."

Lowe then turned his attention to an address he was scheduled to make the following day, a Friday. It would outline his solutions to the world's environmental problems and third world hunger. The site would be the Victoria Memorial, a grand statue in front of Buckingham Palace. He made calls to arrange for the world's media to be present, then went to his study, to prepare his remarks. As he began to work, an email came in from an unnamed sender. He read it, and a concerned look crossed his face.

In the morning, a crowd filled the space between the gates of Buckingham Palace and the Victoria Memorial. Stairs led up to the memorial, and a podium was prepared at the top of the stairs. It was a mildly rainy day, but the weather seemed no deterrent. The media were ready, and the crowds were eager to hang on every word from Lowe. Finally, the Rolls Royce sedan arrived and Lowe climbed out. He made his way to the podium, to great applause. Ted Simpson was surprised when his editor assigned him to cover the speech, and he was standing off to the side of the crowd, with the large media contingent. Lowe stepped up to the podium, and as he looked around at the crowd, Simpson thought he seemed uncharacteristically uncomfortable, as though unsure of himself. Finally, he began to speak, but in a shy, indecisive voice. "I thank you all for coming today. Today, I'd like to talk about ... "

Lowe's head abruptly jolted to the left, and he collapsed to the ground. He was not moving, and blood began to trickle from his temple. Only it was not on the left side that hit the cement, but on the right side, which had not hit. "What did you see?" asked Simpson of the cameramen. Replays soon began to roll, as people began wailing with sorrow. Simpson crowded around the monitors with everyone else, scrutinizing every frame, until one reporter shouted, "There!"

"What?" shouted nearly everyone else.

"On the replay. Something hit him in the side of the head, just before he fell."

They showed it again, and indeed, a small projectile was clearly visible, impacting Lowe's on his right temple. Simpson tried to get close to Lowe's body, but security staff had formed a perimeter around him, and he was unable to approach too closely. The trail of blood was obvious, and it appeared there was a puncture would on his head. A medical helicopter soon arrived, and Lowe was flown away.

The former Prime Minister soon received a phone call, with Lichtträger on the other end. "I expect you to resume your office as Prime Minister, Morris. And to reverse all of Lowe's abominable decisions."

"But Baron, I've lost the faith of the people. You said so yourself. It's not feasible for me to simply step in and reclaim it."

"It was not a request, Morris. Never forget how deeply you are indebted to me. And I want my property back. All of it."

That evening, the Prime Minister addressed the nation. "It is with profound sadness that I learned of the passing of our beloved king, Dr. David Lowe. Under the circumstances, I am working under the presumption that the monarchy will revert to Her Majesty, which should be confirmed by the Accession Council, as soon as its members can be located. In the meantime, rest assured, our government, and our system of governance, is stable. I have also begun proceedings to return all property to its rightful owners, to re-impose mask requirements, lockdowns, and all restrictions on movement. Dr. Lowe's pronouncements must be interpreted in light of realistic expectations."

Worldwide, the number of suicides surged to never before seen levels, as panic, depression, and fear of returning repression gripped the people. Fighting erupted all over the world, as all faith in government was forfeit, and armed forces split between those loyal to their governments, and those loyal to the people. Political leaders did their best to quell the revolts, going so far as to call Lowe a usurper and a fraud. This only incensed the people even more, as they decided Lowe was murdered simply for attempting to free them from their oppressive leaders.

Chapter 12: The Story

A. Homecoming

Sean kept looking around the cell, as if nervous about the presence of cameras. Dalt noticed, and asked, "You still nervous about Nick?"

Sean nodded. "I guess I never dared believe we'd really be rid of him."

"I just hope it's not too late."

"Too late for what?"

"To stop the end of the world," answered Dalt. "If Avi's source is right, and Lowe's the man of sin, then there's no stopping it."

Avi smiled at both of them, and said, "Guys, those things are far above either of your pay scales. Point is, we did what we could."

"What's the Jewish perspective on the question?" asked Sean.

Avi thought for a moment, and said, "Jews believe the Messiah will arrive once the Temple is rebuilt. And I fear they'll fall for the wrong one, and the wrong Temple."

"They?"

"I'm a believer in Yeshua, although I'm also a Jew. Many seem to have forgotten that Yeshua was a Jew."

There was quiet for some time, then Avi asked, "What do you suppose is being trucked to the vault?"

"Gold," answered Dalt, confidently.

"You're sure?" asked Sean.

"Pretty sure. The use of armored trucks and a secure vault mean it's something valuable. And the trucks coming in were riding very low, so they were carrying a heavy load."

"Blasphemy," said Avi, shaking his head with disgust. "They mean to enthrone Mammon under their Temple."

"A union of the world's religious and financial systems," said Dalt, calmly.

"And what's with that Altar?" asked Dalt. "That's far bigger than anything from the previous temples.

"The Altar of Pergamum," said Avi. "The abomination of

desolation in the holy place."

They heard the sound of a bolted door opening in the distance. The conversation stopped, as they listened to the steps approacing. It sounded like two people. As they arrived, Sean spoke first. "Itzhak Nissen. It's a surprise to see you here."

Nissen stepped forward, and Sal stepped up behind him. Nissen spoke first. "As Minister of Antiquities, I have ultimate say on any charges they mean to file against you. And I won't agree."

"You're letting us go?"

"Yes. But quietly, or you'd never make it out of Israel in one piece."

He opened the cell door, and led them out of the prison. He brought them to a police car with its lights flashing, and motioned for the driver to come out and join them. "This is Chaim, my police escort. I'll have him take you to Ben-Gurion, where your plane is still waiting for you."

Sean and Dalt shook hands with Nissen, and expected Sal to get in the car with them, but instead, he said, "It's time to say goodbye."

"You're not returning with us?"

"I'm afraid not, Sean. I'm staying in Jerusalem." Sal turned to Dalt, and spoke to the both of them, "Do you remember me announcing myself as the first witness?"

"Sure," answered both.

"Itzhak is the second witness."

There was silence for a few moments, until Dalt seemed to light up. "The two witnesses, from Revelation. When did you learn that?"

"Only after we split up, when you entered the tunnel."

Nissen had more to add. "I had previously been called the second witness by a local prophet that Sal had also met. But I had no idea what it meant. Then Sal told me he's the first witness, and we put it all together. The prophet has since confirmed it. We are to stay here, and testify to the truth that David Lowe is a false Messiah, to be worshiped in a false temple."

Chaim looked surprised at the comment. "You haven't heard? David Lowe is dead."

"I've learned not to trust anything I hear," answered Sal. "If the prophet told us God wants our testimony against Lowe, then that's what we mean to do. The news is irrelevant."

Avi turned to Nissen, and quietly asked, "Are you also a follower of Yeshua?"

"I've kept that a secret until now. I'd never have been in government otherwise. But now, It's time to proclaim it from the rooftops."

"Will we see you again?" asked Sean, looking specifically at Sal.

"Not in this life, Sean. But it won't be long, so don't lose hope when things turn ugly, as they will for a while."

They embraced, and said goodbye. "I finally understand what you were getting at all that time ago, Sal. I thought you had lost your mind, when you were the sane one all along."

The driver took them to Ben-Gurion Airport, and Major Hardill was waiting for them outside the security checkpoint of the military terminal. He escorted them straight through, and back to the 777. They had the plane to themselves, and were able to return straight to Kenney Air Base, without needing to stop in Washington. They began the drive back to Morrisonville, anxious about whether they would have any trouble with the checkpoint at the state line. But as they approached, they saw fires burning. They slowed, and by the time they arrived, they found a scene of carnage. The guards had all been shot multiple times, including once in the head, their weapons taken, and their bodies left where they fell. They got out of the car, and surveyed the scene. "This was recent," said Dalt. "The bodies don't even smell, yet."

"Who did this?" asked Sean.

"I don't know. Maybe they thought they were doing a good thing, killing agents of the government. But we have to be fair. These men were easy on us when we passed through the first time. What if their replacements are a lot worse?"

"If we're really at war, ugly things happen, Dalt. You're not still thinking of Iraq, are you?"

"I'll be thinking of that forever, Sean. And I just now realized I can't do it. I can't join any militia group that thinks it's justified in doing something like this."

They resumed their trip, and soon arrived back in Morrisonville. The fires were out, and the roads were clear, but a roadblock stood in their way. Seeing Dalt's car approaching, the man at the checkpoint raised his AR-15, and said, "Stop right there." Dalt put his hands in the air, which did not seem to satisfy the gunman. "You're gonna' have to turn around and leave."

Sean recognized the gunman, so he stepped out of the passenger side, and said, "It's me, Charlie. Dalt's my close friend, and he's one of us."

The rifle came down, and he said, "Sorry, Sean. There have been bandits coming through, stealing everything not nailed down."

"They've been through town?"

"Mostly through the retail strip, but yeah, they even hit a few houses nearby."

"Becky lives next to that strip."

"Marty's old place? Yeah, that was looted from top to bottom. But I don't think she was there at the time."

They returned to Sean's house, and found Becky, her baby, and Pastor Nichols unharmed, but under severe stress. Nichols' church had been burned down by bandits, who weren't even interested in theft. "You can stay here as long as it suits your needs," assured Sean. "I can even accommodate a few more people, if you know of anyone in distress."

"Yes, there are a few I can think of," answered Nichols.

Sean re-arranged the layout of the house to accommodate people in need, and arranged to evacuate his large master bedroom to make room for a family. He set up space in the supply room, where he could accommodate men, and blocked off his recreation room for women. He turned to Pastor Nichols, and said, "I learned in Jerusalem that the earth's time is short. We have to take care of as many as we're able."

Becky asked to take the baby outside to play, so Sean brought our his Geiger counter, confirming that the worst of the radiation was behind them. He joined Becky for a stroll, and said, "I never had the chance to ask the baby's name."

"Becky, after me."

"Nice."

"Sean, I need to make sure we avoid any misunderstandings ..."

"I know," said Sean, indicating with his expression that he was thinking the same. "A lot of water has passed under the bridge since we were together. I don't have any expectations of you. Anyway, there are more pressing considerations, nowadays."

"I'm relieved that you understand."

Sean got into his truck, and drove to his office. He was relieved that it had not been sacked, as it was off the commercial strip by only a few blocks. He fired up his computer, and waited for his new emails to come in. Most were from clients, with problems or questions relating to their computer systems, and he glossed over those for the time being. But one was from an unnamed sender, and was titled, "Happy Holidays, from Jerusalem."

Sean opened the email, and began reading. "At this time of year, most people celebrate holidays which do not interest me. Can you guess my name? My goals have been accomplished, and I exist everywhere. Do you recognize me, yet? That site was a decoy, Sean."

Sean felt his heart sink within his chest. *Nick was too smart to leave himself exposed like that. The site wasn't so much a decoy as his way of commanding worship. But it's a facade. He exists in all of the world's mainframes.*

Sean returned home, where he found Dalt packing up his things. "You're welcome to stay here, old friend. We may yet need you, and your military training."

"I appreciate the offer, Sean. But I've been in touch with my contacts, and learned that the massacre at the state line was carried out by government forces."

"Why would they kill their own?"

"So they can blame the militias, and undermine our base of support. But because of that, they need me more than ever. People are being rounded up, and beheaded for their faith. I can help free them, so they can flee to places prepared for them in the wilderness. Refuges like yours here."

"I've never had a friend I valued as much as you, Dalt."

Dalt looked like he was choking up. "Likewise with you, Sean. We might not see each other again, on this side of the veil."

Dalt got in his car and drove off. Sean stood and watched him drive away, lingering for some time after he had passed out of sight.

B. The Prodigy

It was a quiet day at the Royal London Hospital. Dr. George Evans had made his rounds, then walked into the lounge, poured himself a cup of coffee, and picked a magazine out of the rack. Leafing through it, he struggled to find something that would give him the kind of distraction he was craving. But it was once again elusive, and his imagination returned to the frustration that had become his life. In his youth, he was convinced that he could make the people change their habits for the healthier. Then as he passed into middle-age, he found himself experiencing the same maladies, making him question the advice he had been dispensing. Then seeing the world implode around him was a body-blow he did not think he would soon recover from. *At least there's hope in Lowe*, he thought. His time alone was abruptly cut short, when his phone rang. "Evans," he answered.

"George. I need you to get to the E.R. right away." It was the chief of staff, Alfred Robertson. "There's a very high profile patient coming in, and it doesn't look good for him. Listen carefully, George. I need to be able to say that we did everything in our abilities save him."

Evans threw down the magazine, and hurried for the E.R. On his way out of the lounge, he glanced at the television, running the headline *Lowe struck down by assassination drone*. His mind began to race. Surely, that was who was coming. He was at once devastated, and angered. *An assassination drone? They carry enough neurotoxin to kill twenty men. What am I supposed to do about that?* Then he remembered Robertson's admonishment. He was not demanding that Evans save Lowe. Only that he could say they did everything within their power to *try* to save him. *Oh, I'm supposed to go through the motions. That's just typical.*

Lowe was being wheeled into the emergency room as Evans arrived. "Start the respirator right away, and induce coma," he shouted, as he went to the change room. A nurse followed him with a tablet, taking his exact instructions. "Reduce his body temperature. Give him a triple dose of atropine. Type his blood, and give him as big a transfusion as we have extra units of blood. At the same time, drain it from the other arm. We're going to try to dilute the poison out of him."

Finally suited up, Evans walked into the E.R., and got his first sight of Lowe, lying on the gurney. The skin on his face had a gray pallor to it. *This is a waste of everyone's time.* He checked his vitals, and confirmed his first impression. No brain waves to speak of, and only a weak pulse, stimulated by the atropine. Standing over Lowe, he whispered, "And I thought you might be the one who saves us from this pit of hell we've fallen into."

That day proved to be the most exhausting of Evans' professional life. He was feigning a struggle he knew to be in vain, to appear to be trying to save the life of someone who was clearly dead. Finally unable to continue, he called Robertson, and said, "How long do I have to keep up this charade? Lowe was dead on arrival. We're moving air in and out of his lungs, but there's nothing left of his brain. I can't even stimulate enough of a pulse to properly transfuse him."

"I get it, George. But that mob outside will kill us if we don't make it look good. I'll come down there to relieve you in an hour. You can go home and get some rest, then we'll meet back here tomorrow evening. Assuming nothing changes, we'll make the announcement then. But George, you're going to have to give a detailed report on every measure you've taken. They won't overlook a single thing."

Evans suffered a sleepless night, haunted by images of Lowe's face. Then he would be overwhelmed with disgust over the farce they were perpetrating, pretending to try to save a dead man. Then anxiety would overwhelm him, as he realized that the media would soon report on all of it as though it were genuine. So when he returned on Saturday evening, not having slept a wink, Robertson took one look at him, and exclaimed, "George, you look like you should be the one on the gurney."

"Let's just get this over with," said Evans, in no mood to discuss the matter.

"I've taken the liberty to organize your records, and collate them into a presentation. I've called the news conference for first thing tomorrow morning."

"That's Sunday. Why not do it today? I'm not going to be able to sleep until this is all behind me."

"Because if we gave up this quickly, it wouldn't look like we gave it everything. The Minister of Health called me himself, insisting we keep trying until morning."

Evans spent Saturday night in the emergency room, keeping a vigil over Lowe's body. In the quiet, he began to give voice to the grief that overwhelmed him. "You were someone I believed in. I even thought you might be the great soul who unites us in one cosmic consciousness. And this is how it ends?" He exhaled loudly, with obvious disappointment. Finally, as morning arrived, he returned to his office, to prepare his presentation.

The press room was packed with the world's media, with many more standing outside. To create additional space, they put the speaker's podium in the corner. A few feet from the speaker's podium was an open door, and more reporters crowded around the opening, trying to get their heads inside. But the atmosphere in the room was decidedly depressed. Casual comments made by hospital personnel had circulated, and the press knew Lowe was dead. Ted Simpson had notes ready to report that Lowe was dead within seconds of being hit by the drone. But they were waiting for official confirmation from the doctors.

Dr. Robertson began the press conference. He thanked his staff for the efforts they had made, then finally made the announcement. "We're now into the third day since Dr. Lowe, uh, that is His Majesty King David, was struck in the temple by an assassination drone. The neurotoxins quickly destroyed all higher brain function, and he was clinically dead on arrival. It is therefore with the deepest sadness that I must confirm what many of you already know. King David Lowe has formally been declared dead. I'll now introduce you to Dr. Evans, who led the heroic effort to save the king."

As Evans faced the barrage of camera flashes, and the murmur among the reporters in attendance, news cameras gleefully adjusted their settings to accentuate the pallor of his exhausted face, while they ran the headline, "Lowe declared dead." Mainstream coverage alternated between Evans' presentation, and tributes to Lowe from most of the world's luminaries.

The coverage interspersed scenes of vast crowds all over the world, assembled to mourn Lowe. "He was the last hope for mankind," said one woman, weeping and near hysteria, summing up the sentiment for most of the world's people. Even the pro-establishment commentators ceased all condemnations of Lowe, and broadcasts focused exclusively on the mourning.

In the emergency room, Lowe's body had lain unattended since the formal announcement of his death. Finally, a technician was sent in to remove all probes and devices, so the body could be sent to the morgue. As he got to the electrodes on his chest, he choked back the tears and said, "I'm afraid this is it, your highness. I'll miss you as much as anyone."

As he pulled off the first electrode, the electrocardiogram beeped. *I wonder what that was.* He looked at the machine, and saw that there was heart activity. *He's been off the respirator for quite a while, now. I'd better get a doctor.*

It took some time to find a doctor who was free to check on Lowe, and was not tied up in the press room. He finally found Dr. MacNicol, and flagged him down. "I swear, the EKG's showing heart activity."

MacNicol looked at him with considerable irritation. "I'll check it, so I can't be accused of neglect. But it's obviously a glitch. I've seen his vitals, and he's been dead since before he got here."

They walked back into the E.R., and upon entering, were greeted by Lowe's open eyes and determined smile. "I've returned."

George Evans was in the middle of explaining his futile attempts to dilute the neurotoxins from Lowe's blood, when he heard loud murmuring coming from behind him. He turned to look, but the scrum was in the side hallway, out of Evans' line of sight. Then, abruptly, the assembled reporters exploded in gasps, and chatter. Again, he looked around, but with the podium's location in the corner of the room, he could not see into the side hallway, where the reporters' attention seemed focused.

Evans tried his best to stay on track, and showed the image of a radiogram, gesturing with his laser pointer. "You can see the puncture in the skull here. The poison entered the cranium, and most all of his brain cells were dead within the first minute. He never stood a chance."

"You're obviously mistaken," shouted a reporter in the front row.

"That's preposterous," shouted Evans, angrily, as people began to walk back and forth behind him. His face grew red, and his eyes tightened. "I've been up the last two nights, working on nothing but this one case. For you to stand there and insinuate that I can't tell when someone is dead is an insult not only to me, but to my mentors, and those who elected me to the Royal College of Surgeons." The murmuring grew even louder, and Evans gave in to his curiosity. "How did you come to such a stupid thought, anyway?"

"Sorry about my manners, doctor. It's just that he's standing right behind you."

Evans spun around and saw Lowe, standing beside an astonished MacNicol. Evans turned off the microphone, and the brief exchange that followed saw Evans shaking his head, over and over. He touched Lowe's temple, still bearing a wound, and threw up his hands. Turning again to face the crowd, he said, "I don't know what to tell you. We reviewed the records at least ten times. We analyzed the neurotoxin in his blood. We documented every aspect of his neural function. He had no pulse, no respiration, and no brain waves. I was there. I saw it all with my own eyes. There's no way to describe it as anything but death." He was becoming incoherent, and apparently realized it. "But I guess I should sit down now, and cede the podium to David Lowe."

Lowe stepped to the podium dressed in the white clothes given him by the hospital, and smiled at Evans. "Don't be ashamed at your amazement, Doctor Evans. Your reaction is perfectly understandable."

Lowe turned to the camera with a serene but determined smile, and said, "It's true, my brothers and sisters. I *was* dead."

Waiting a few moments for the furor to subside, he turned his head sideways for the cameras, and removed the dressing to show the wound on his temple. "The drone struck me here, and penetrated my brain with a high dose of neurotoxin. I was dead within the first few seconds, exactly as Doctor Evans told you. Please don't question his judgment, or professionalism."

The audience in the press room, and around the world, sat dumfounded. "I have returned to you with knowledge that will set you free. I have answers, not only to the evil currently holding the world in its grip, but to hunger, energy, pollution, and so much more."

The reporters started to mutter among themselves, trying to understand what they had just witnessed. Lowe brought the attention back to matters at hand, saying, "The truth about so many things has been kept from you. You can live healthy lives, make cancer and heart disease disappear, and enjoy abundant and cheap energy. There's no need to fight wars over resources. You only have to trust me."

"Do you know who had you killed?" was the question Ted Simpson managed to fire to the podium, from the scrum of reporters.

"Yes, Ted. And you know him, too. He was with me that day, when you saw us in Berlin."

"How'd you know that?" whispered Simpson.

Lowe turned to the crowd, and said, "All people will achieve perfect unity of spirit in me, and together, we will transform the universe. The only thing I'll require of everyone is a symbol of that unity."

There was again murmuring from the room, as reporters were scrambling for more information. "I have repealed all of the oppressive measures instituted by the old regime. But loyalists to the old system remain a threat, as you saw when I was dead. To overcome them, I ask that everyone take the microchip in the right hand, developed by Mr. Waites. We can use his own technology to defeat his system. By taking that mark, you will affirm your loyalty to me, and formally mark the unification of all humanity. I'd like full deployment in three weeks' time, to mark an upcoming, momentous event. More information will follow shortly."

Back at his estate, Lowe told an aide, "Get Malakh over here, right away."

"I'm afraid he left the country."

"Where to?"

"We don't know yet. He has properties everywhere."

"I'll speak with someone who will certainly know."

C. The Discovery

As I stood in the scrum of reporters, we watched Doctor Evans upbraid one of our colleagues for suggesting His Majesty King David might not in fact be dead. Once he had finished, he asked why anyone would make such a stupid assertion. And the colleague answered, "Because he's standing right behind you." There are few moments in the life of a reporter as stunning as that one, yet the drama of the moment is nothing in the scheme of things. What we witnessed, for the first time in two thousand years, is the resurrection of a dead man after three days. And whereas last time, that man only showed himself to a select few, this time, it was to the whole world, at its moment of greatest need.

Simpson's story ran on the front page of the newspaper, and was syndicated worldwide. He would now be considered a titan in his field, and could write for any newspaper, anywhere. Yet there he sat, in his flat, shaking his head with disgust. Shauna sat opposite him, attempting to console him. "I can't believe I let them force me to write that," he said, sorrowfully.

"You captured what everyone felt at that moment, Ted. There's nothing immoral about that."

"But I know what Lowe represents. And I allowed myself to be used, to encourage people to worship him."

"Those who worship him would do it regardless. Those who reserve their worship for the true God won't be taken in."

"It's those on the fence I fear I might be responsible for."

"Then write another story, exposing him."

"It would never get published."

"You can do it anyway." Shauna had a twinkle in her eye, and Simpson understood her meaning right away. To encourage him to stay with the paper, he had been granted administrative privileges. This meant he could publish any story he wished without involving the editor, although in practice, abuse of such privileges would inevitably result in their loss.

"In that case, the first thing I need to explore is whether this could have been faked, or whether Doctor Evans really could have been in error. And I think I know who I can ask about that."

Simpson arrived at the morgue, and found the doors locked. He knocked, and waited, but there was no answer. He waited for the better part of an hour, before giving up. He walked to the Sleeping Hog Inn nearby, where reporters often congregated for ale, and conversation. He arrived to find a festive mood, and saw his friend Jeremy hanging his jacket on the back of his chair. Simpson joined him, and said, "Hey, what do you think of researching Lowe?"

"If it was a bad idea before, it's bonkers, now. He has the world in the palm of his hand."

"You don't want to be looking too deeply into his background," said another patron, joining them at the table.

"What are you referring to?"

"An investigator turned up dead, recently. They found his body only a few blocks from the Ministry where Lowe was holed up. Rumor has it, he was looking into Lowe's background."

"Do you recall his name?"

"Can't say I do. But you can probably find it on line, if you search for an investigator found dead."

Simpson did the search right away, and before long, said, "I think I have it. A Simon Lewinson turned up dead and mutilated." *Lewinson! He's the one they mentioned in the same breath as Knickerson.* Simpson kept his thoughts to himself, but inside, he was horrified.

"There you go. If you don't want to end up like him, leave it alone," said Jeremy.

"I wonder if he's still at the morgue," mused Simpson.

"You're not letting go of this, are you?"

"The first bloke in two thousand years to rise from the dead, and you want me to forget about it? I don't know why you ever became reporters."

Lowe sent a text to Dr. Weiss, asking if he could visit, and inquire about Lewinson. The reply came back: *Come after five, when we're closed. Text me when you arrive, and make sure you're alone.*

The time came, and Simpson texted Weiss, who replied, *The door will be unlocked. Come in, and announce yourself.* He made his way over to the morgue, and as he walked in, Dr. Weiss was addressing his two assistants, standing in front of a body on the rack. "Once things quiet down, this one gets buried with the indigent. Keep it here another week, until the hubbub dies down a bit."

Simpson cleared his throat to announce his arrival, which elicited a startled reaction from the staff. Weiss quickly slid the body back into the refrigerator, and closed the door. The two assistants left in a hurry, and Weiss walked over to Simpson. "How can I help you, Mr. Simpson?" It struck Simpson as strange, given the advance notice.

"I've come to inquire about Simon Lewinson."

Weiss nodded, knowingly. "I hope you have a strong stomach." He walked down the row of refrigerators, and came to a door near the one he had slammed shut earlier. He pulled out the body, and as he uncovered it, Simpson shouted in revulsion. "God, have mercy."

Seeing Simpson turning away, and clutching his hand over his mouth, the old man said, "You've already seen an ordinary ritual killing. This one is punitive. It's not just the missing nose and ears. When he came in, his genitals were protruding from the hole in his throat. All of his organs have been removed. It goes on."

"Why would anyone do this?"

"He could have broken an oath to a secret cult. Or he could have come across information he should have known to avoid."

"What are you calling this one?"

"Suicide, of course." He saw Simpson's outraged look, and added, "I don't want to be next for this kind of treatment."

"What's with the closure today?"

"I can't discuss that."

"Well, can I ask a general question, then?"

Weiss shrugged, suggesting *why not.*

"In your experience, has anyone who was definitively dead ever come back to life?"

"I can't discuss that."

"I'm only looking for background, here. I don't want you to weigh in on Lowe's specific case. Have you ever seen anyone come back from being properly dead?"

Weiss, who had always been perfectly calm when discussing death, became highly agitated, and put his foot down. "I told you my bottom line. I won't discuss the issue, or anything peripheral to it. Not for the next few years."

"Well, that kind of defeats my purpose for coming today."

Weiss looked at him sternly, and said, "You'd better find another purpose, then. Because I may be asked why I let you in here today."

"Uh, okay. Could I see the final report on Monique Jennings, then?"

"I'll be right back," said Weiss.

Simpson sat down on a folding chair in front of a folding table with coffee stains all over it. It appeared as though a simple wipe with a wet cloth would clean it, but nobody had bothered to try. As Weiss left, Simpson looked to the refrigerated drawer Weiss had slammed shut when he first arrived, and noticed the spring loaded lock had not fully latched. *Why were they so spooked when I walked in, when they're obviously comfortable working with a body as badly butchered as Lewinson's?* Curiosity got the better of him, and he walked over to examine the lock. It was definitely not fully latched. He listened carefully, and when he was certain that Weiss' footsteps had receded, he tried the drawer. It took only a little jostling, before it opened.

The body was in a bag, and Simpson was suddenly overwhelmed with anxiety. *They had a reason to be afraid, and they're not squeamish.* But it was almost as if a gentle, yet persuasive voice in his head, said, "Open it, Ted. You need to see what they're hiding."

He unzipped the bag, and slowly, nervously, looked down at the dead face for the first time. He gasped loudly, the instant he saw it. The wound on the temple was exactly as he remembered it. The man had been dead for several days, but the resemblance was striking, nonetheless. It was Lowe. Or rather someone who looked exactly like him.

Simpson's mind began to race, as he pondered the implications of his find. He heard the sound of footsteps approaching, so he took a peek at the name tag, which read *Jonathan Richmond*. He slammed shut the drawer, and returned to his seat. Weiss handed him the folder, leaned over and whispered in his ear, "I know you saw him. Go now, and tell the world."

Simpson went straight to the office, where he could access the internet on a computer shared by many in the office. He immediately searched for Jonathan Richmond. It took some effort, but he eventually found archives of social media posts two years old, or older. Everything had been deleted, and was not accessible except by a deep dive into internet archives such as he was capable of performing. He noticed a resemblance to Lowe, but thought the nose was a little different. Next he searched Richmond's credit history, which he found was abysmal until very recently, when it jumped up into the highest possible tier. *He's come into some money within the last few months. I wonder what changed for him.*

The office was empty as it was late in the evening, so he hammered out a story that was brief, but very direct. The story would not stay up for very long, regardless, but once circulated, it would be re-posted everywhere.

Was a Body Double Killed in Place of David Lowe?
The world witnessed a spectacle unlike anything ever recorded on camera. A man was murdered, doctors testified to the fact, and on the third day, he rose again. But before we get carried away with the implications, we have to confront an unpleasant fact. David Lowe had a body double, named Jonathan Richmond. With no qualifications to speak of, Mr. Richmond went from being a poverty-afflicted nobody to a wealthy man, in no time at all. Today, Jonathan Richmond is missing, and presumed dead. So we did not witness a miraculous resurrection, but the murder of a decoy, and on the third day, the substitution of a live David Lowe for the dead man.

Simpson printed a copy of the story, folded it, and placed it in his pocket. He then used his credentials, and posted it in the prime location of the newspaper's web site. He sent a copy to the printer, with instructions to run it on the front page. He then made a hasty exit, collected Shauna, and made for St. Cyril's. He handed the printed story to Kyriakis, and said, "Get this to your circle of contacts."

"This is explosive," said Kyriakis as he read it.

Simpson nodded, but quickly asked, "Where can we hide? They're going to come after me."

Explosive it was, but not for very long. The numbers of clicks to the paper soared past a hundred million, until the story was removed. The comment section attached to the story was extremely negative, with most comments spewing vile profanities and threatening violence against the anonymous author, and the newspaper. The print version of the newspaper only sold for an hour, then every copy was hurriedly recalled, and no additional issues appeared on that day. Lowe was informed of the story, and was livid. "Find out who wrote it, and cut his heart out. Bring it to me still dripping with his blood." He thought a little longer, and added, "Start your search with Ted Simpson."

Simpson's flat was ransacked, but they found no indication of where he and Shauna had gone. They were being sheltered in a small farmhouse near Glastonbury, and none of Lowe's powers could see through the protective veil that shielded them.

D. The Witnesses

Specialized clinics had to open all over the world, to meet demand. Medical staff were pulled from every other activity, and it was still not sufficient. The lineups of people waiting to receive a microchip implant to support David Lowe were everything Richard Waites had ever hoped for, but never came remotely close to achieving. Close to half the world was chipped in the first week, and three quarters by the end of the second week. But demand fell off sharply after that. The third week saw numbers estimated at eighty to ninety percent of the world chipped, but even though clinics had free capacity, the remainder of the people did not show up. Seeing the shortfall, Lowe made an announcement towards the end of the third week. "There is still time to receive the chip, and join your fellow man in unity of spirit. But for anyone refusing, we cannot take the chance that you are of malicious spirit, and intend to restore the repressive regimes of the past. Accordingly, those without the chip not be eligible to participate in the new financial system, and will not be able to conduct even basic transactions. So I ask that you repent, and accept the chip." In spite of his appeals and threats, Lowe's exhortations fell on deaf ears, and by the end of the third week, no new people were being chipped.

News crews began to assemble in Jerusalem, having been told to expect a momentous event, but details were scant. Cameras were everywhere, and reporters began to file stories on trivial topics, to bide their time. At the home of Itzhak Nissen, Sal and Avi were discussing Lowe's apparent resurrection. Avi had brought over a copy of the brief commentary written and posted by Ted Simpson, and assured Sal that the author had seen Richmond's corpse in person.

"We have to get word to the whole world that this was false," said Sal. "That people have to reject the chip. Their time to remove it and renounce Lowe may be running out."

Avi looked skeptical. "How do you propose to reach the world? They're not going to let us go on camera and make the pronouncements in person."

"I have an idea," said Sal. "But I'll need Itzhak's help. And the prophet. Can you get hold of him?"

"I think so."

Avi returned later that evening, accompanied by a frail, thin old man. His long gray hair was entirely disheveled, his beard a tangled mess, and his clothes old and tattered. Nissen took one look at him, and said, "It is not fitting for the needs of a servant of God to be neglected. Can I get you new clothes, and take care of you a little?"

The old man giggled, and shook his head. "The clothes I keep. But I will accept a good meal, a bath, and the use of a pair of scissors, to trim these." He tugged at his hair and his beard as he spoke. In spite of his poverty, to all outward appearances, he looked like the happiest man in the nation.

Sal proceeded to make his request. "Can you ask the Lord to give us protected access to parts of the computer network? Where the enemy won't know we're there, and what we're doing?"

"It is in furtherance of your divinely appointed role as witnesses, isn't it?"

"Yes. It's central to it."

"Then I assure you, it is done. Proceed as your needs require."

"That was simple. Thank you."

"Is there anything else you need from me?"

"I don't think so. Itzhak, do you have anything?"

A shake of the head came from Nissen, and the old man said, "Now, about that meal."

Nissen called for his cook, and instructed him to make whatever the old man requested. He then turned to Sal, and asked, "What do you need from me?"

"I need temporary access to the Israeli system that grants journalists permission to broadcast."

They took a brief trip, and Sal made a few changes to the operating system. "That should do it."

David Lowe was at his estate, finalizing plans for his trip to Jerusalem. He checked on the status of the Temple, and the Altar, and learned that everything was complete. The electronics in the inner sanctum had all been replaced, so Nick was once again able to interact with visitors. Next he called his media director, to ask about preparations for television coverage. The news was not so encouraging. "The Israeli system is going haywire. Broadcasts are cutting off in mid sentence, and permissions are being revoked at random. I fear we could lose coverage at a crucial moment."

Lowe summoned Nick, and asked, "Can you fix the Israeli broadcast access system?"

"Certain things are off limits to me, until we defeat the tyrant."

Lowe again called his media director. "Have the Israelis permanently deactivate the permission system. We'll have to go in with no restrictions. I need you to try that right away, to ensure it fixes the problem. The news crews absolutely have to capture my entry."

Lowe next asked Nick, "Have you located Lichtträger?"

"Yes. He's in New Zealand."

"I don't have enough time to fly there, which robs me of the satisfaction of doing it in person. Let's get him on the line."

The father and son were soon face to face, although mediated by the internet. The Baron spoke first, from a timber frame house, in an expansive room. "You made me proud, in spite of betraying me. Substituting Richmond when I tried to assassinate you, then using the whole thing to fake your resurrection was quite brilliant."

Lowe's phone rang, with his media director at the other end. But his priorities were now elsewhere. He hit the ignore button, and continued with the Baron. "I never betrayed you. You could have stood by my side, except that I would have held all the power, like you said I would."

"I never expected you to take away my base of power. I expected us to share it."

"The Messiah does not play second fiddle. I was always clear on that point. Now, I command you to walk to the back wall in the room where you're now standing." He waited until Lichtträger complied, then continued. "The Samurai sword on display. Take it off the wall, and slash your throat."

Lichtträger was unable to resist, and before he knew it, he was rubbing the blade against his throat. But it had a false edge, being an ornament and not a true weapon. Lowe laughed, and said, "I want you to appreciate your powerlessness before me." The man at the other end looked dejected, and his regularly proud face was hung towards the floor.

"Now, take that extension cord I see in the corner of the room, and hang yourself from the timbers in the ceiling." The Baron complied, and Lowe stayed on the line until he was sure the Baron was dead.

The television crew was ready at Nissen's home, and Sal spent a few moments rigging the codes to ensure it would override all other broadcasts out of Jerusalem. It would also go out live over all the major streaming platforms. Then they began. Nissen introduced himself, and declared his position in the Israeli government. Then he announced, "At least, that was my job, until now." He was joined by Sal, and resumed. "I can no longer serve in that role, and yet be true to God, who has appointed me the second witness. Here with me now is Salvatore Occhini, the first witness."

Sal took over from there. "For three and a half years, we have been traveling the world, learning and spreading the truth, but always through private interactions. Today, we take our message public. We have first person testimony proving that the man who was killed by the assassination drone was not David Lowe, but his body double, Jonathan Richmond. The bodies were swapped on the third day, and they used makeup to give David a false wound. The whole thing was a fraud. David Lowe is a fraud, and worse, he is the man of sin foretold in prophecy. He will lead you away from the true God, and into the pit of hell, unless you reject his mark. If you already have it, renounce him, repent and return to God. And have the chip removed at your earliest opportunity, by anyone with basic medical training."

Nissen then made his case that the new Temple was fraudulent, and that it was dedicated to the fallen angel Lucifer. The reaction in the executive suites of the world's news services was one of unbridled rage. "Why didn't you cut away?"

"We weren't able to. Someone hacked into the system, and we couldn't control it. We couldn't even revoke their permissions. It looks like the security system has been deactivated."

Those who hacked the system sat at Nissen's home, discussing their plans. The old man returned to the room, freshly fed, trimmed and bathed, and glowing with contentment. He was even wearing new clothes, which Nissen had quietly substituted while he was bathing. "What must we do now?" asked Nissen.

"Your message is available to the world, for anyone who wants to know the truth. You must now demonstrate your commitment to the message, with courage in the face of death. Go out into the streets, and testify. The Lord will then accept your sacrifice."

Chapter 13: Time's Up

A. Jerusalem

The world's dignitaries had assembled in Jerusalem, as word spread that the Messiah would make his entrance on Friday. And true to history, wherever the world's dignitaries assemble, vice follows. Invitation-only clubs sprang up on the Mount of Corruption, south of the Mount of Olives and the location of ancient sacrifices to Moloch. Rumors swirled of depraved and evil acts, but the media would not touch them, so those rumors never left Jerusalem.

The computer system controlling access to the airwaves had been replaced in its entirety, and there were assurances that this time, hackers would not be able to gain control of it. But the two witnesses stood between the Temple Mount and the City of David, speaking to ever growing crowds. They denounced the fraudulent temple, its occupation by Lucifer, and the evils of the Satanic cabal that had descended onto Jerusalem. In every case, they added, "These are but a foretaste of the imminent blasphemy, where the man David Lowe attempts to portray himself as God."

Friday rolled around, and even the world's luminaries were largely sober and lined up to watch what was being hailed as a moment for the ages. There was a clear sky, with not a cloud in sight. The witnesses continued to denounce the proceedings, but the attention of most was fixated on the Temple Mount. "This is so exciting," exclaimed Gertie Kleinholst, amidst a group of world leaders. At noon, a small wisp of puffy cloud appeared in the east, and drifted westward, to the Mount of Olives. It stopped above the mountain, and began a gentle descent. Voices erupted from the crowd, saying, "There's someone standing in that cloud." Television cameras swung around and followed the cloud as it came to rest in front of the Church of All Nations, at the Garden of Gethsemane. Any indication that it was once a Christian Church had been removed some time earlier. Inside, an outcrop of bedrock in front of the altar was thought to be the location where Jesus prayed before his passion. The cloud touched down, and puffed up into a large ball of red smoke before dissipating, leaving David Lowe, dressed in a seamless white robe, standing barefoot in front of the church. He waved to the crowds, then mounted a white horse that had been prepared for him.

As he descended into the Kidron Valley, he was met by an armed security detail, who followed a short distance behind him. He climbed Mount Moriah, and approached the cemetery that had been placed in front of Jerusalem's Golden Gate as a superstitious act of Suleiman, the Ottoman conqueror. He had heard the Messiah would enter through that gate, but also that the Messiah would not step into a cemetery, lest he be defiled. Lowe paused at the edge of the cemetery, and noticed the witnesses to his left, loudly denouncing him for blasphemy. Lowe ignored them, and turned his attention to the Golden Gate. He raised his hands upwards, looked up, and spoke a few words. On finishing, he thrust his left hand towards the walled-up Golden Gate, which promptly crumbled, leaving the wall open for his triumphant entry. But the cemetery remained in his way. He again raised his hands, then to the shock of everyone, ascended off his horse, and floated through the air, over the cemetery, and into the Golden Gate. He turned to the cameras, and spoke.

"Suleiman hoped the cemetery would act like kryptonite, to prevent the Messiah from returning. But as you saw with your own eyes, there's no stopping the anointed of the universe from taking his rightful place."

He stepped through the Golden Gate into the Temple Mount complex, and climbed up a newly constructed grand stairway to the surrounding complex. A grand walkway led from there to the new Temple, which at that time was still draped with black tarps. The walkway was covered with palm fronds, laid out for his arrival. "Unveil the Temple," he said, loudly. Immediately, steel cords pulled the tarps out of the way, showing the new Temple, and the Altar, in its full splendor. Everything was broadcast to the world, as the air over the Temple was filled with drones capturing video footage.

Lowe then took his place in front of the Altar of Pergamum, and turned to face the top of the stairs. As he did, Pope Peter II appeared at the top, and made an announcement. "I have traveled here to Jerusalem to welcome our savior back to earth. You all saw him rise from the dead, and to arrive in the city on a wisp of cloud, just as he left us some two thousand years ago. So to remove any doubt, I now use the powers of my office, and declare infallibly that David Lowe is divine, and worthy of all worship. In him we will find unity, and ourselves become gods. The Omega Point is here.

They were interrupted by the arrival of the two witnesses, who had knocked unconscious the extensive security staff with only a few spoken words. Nissen spoke first. "Cardinal Peterson was excommunicated by the Pope Emeritus, just before he ordered his murder. He has no standing to make these pronouncements." Both again loudly denounced Lowe, and recounted the fraud of his resurrection. Lowe pointed at them, and shouted, "Death to the defilers." He stood for a moment, as if expecting them to drop dead like so many others had, but they kept at it. Nissen shouted out, "My fellow Jews, this is not your Messiah. He is not even circumcised."

There were loud gasps, as the Jews present took in the gravity of that charge. "I will not be slandered like this," shouted Lowe, as his security detail assembled. "Execute them right here, right now!" Shots rang out, and both witnesses fell in the courtyard of the temple, in a pool of blood. Lowe continued. "Leave their bodies where they are, as a reminder of who is the anointed, and who is the blasphemer."

With the bodies in the midst of the crowd, Lowe declared, "It is time for celebration, not dissention. We can easily settle the matter of my circumcision. I will allow three elders to join me in private, to verify. Their testimony should settle the question."

The guests were relieved that the matter would not stand between them and their savior, and the tension melted away. Lowe, wanting to further reassure the guests, said, "And now, observe my powers."

He pointed to the sky, and the sun began to turn all different colors. Each time it turned one color, that color slowly descended like a ring, and the next color appeared. They were soon surrounded by the colors of the rainbow, surrounding them from the sun down to the temple. "All the colors of the rainbow, representing all different peoples, backgrounds, and orientations. All are united in me, and together, we are god."

The world's elite applauded loudly, and Lowe drank it in. He gestured to servants standing off to the side, who brought in wheeled carts, and spaced them throughout the temple platform. They unfolded movable panels, to reveal fully stocked bar carts. Loud cheers emanated from the world's elites, while a few began to look uncomfortable, and left the temple. For the rest of the evening, and all day Saturday, in spite of it being the Sabbath, loud cheers emanated from the temple, but only the elite were allowed in.

Outside the temple, word began to spread from the Mount of Corruption, that multiple witnesses would support the account that Lowe was not circumcised. But security forces swept through the whole city, and anybody criticizing Lowe openly was arrested. By Saturday morning, people were being stopped throughout the city, and asked to kneel in front of a picture of Lowe, and to kiss the picture as a sign of worship. Those who refused were arrested. Christians, together with the increasing numbers of Jews who had turned against Lowe fled to the desert in the Jordan Valley, and assembled for prayer and fasting. People spoke in tongues, and proclaimed the authentic Messiah to have been Yeshua.

In the world's many refuges, Christians in hiding were aware of the spectacle in Jerusalem, and were increasingly aware of its evil nature. They too prayed and fasted, in hopes the Lord would soon return, and put an end to the blasphemy.

Outside those small groups, however, the world exploded in one great big party. All restraint went out the window, and soon acts were carried out in full view of the public that would have shamed the inhabitants of Sodom and Gomorrah. Small numbers of people came to the knowledge of the truth, and recoiled in horror, but any public comment was met with ruthless violence, and many were killed. Everywhere, mobs roamed the streets, going door to door, demanding a public demonstration of lewdness, to prove they were not Christians. Recent converts paid with their blood for refusing to embrace the new norms.

By Saturday evening, the mobs had set their sights on rural places, to follow up on rumors of refuges that secretly harbored Christians who rejected David Lowe. Mobs set about searching out refuges, but could not find them. In most cases, they walked straight past them, without even noticing the house in question. As more searches came up empty, unbridled rage broke out in strongholds of Lowe's supporters, who resolved to exterminate every holdout in the cruelest of ways, starting with the children, in full view of their parents.

Sunday morning came, and the world awoke with a colossal hangover, nowhere worse than among the guests in Jerusalem. Coffee was poured, breakfasts were gingerly put down, and dead bodies were dragged into gutters, so they could clear the streets.

After some time, David Lowe entered the temple, with guests arriving in numbers, where he was confronted by the two witnesses, once again standing in the spot where they had been murdered. Both proclaimed the glory of God, and were whisked away by a cloud, which took them from sight. "Good riddance," said Lowe, to applause from the crowd.

Most of the world's luminaries arrived in short order, and once Lowe was satisfied with their number, he ascended the grand staircase of the Altar. The world's dignitaries lined the sides of the complex, applauding his glorious entry. He was met at the top of the stairs by Pope Peter II, and together, they approached the main altar. Most of the world's religious leaders took up places at the sides of the altar.

Lowe turned to Peter II, and asked him, "Who do you say that I am?"

"You are the universal Christ, in whom we are all united," answered Peter, to loud applause from the guests. Peter extended his hands over the altar, on which were arrayed the crowns of every nation on earth that had a monarchy. "I hereby commit all peoples to David Lowe, King of the Universe."

He picked up the British crown, and placed it on Lowe's head. Lowe waited for the applause to die down, before continuing. "I will now complete the consecration of the Temple."

A small pig was brought in under the arm of a man dressed as an Orthodox Rabbi, who handed to Lowe. He took it up onto the altar, gently lowered it, picked up a knife prepared for him, and cut its throat. Blood flowed in all directions, and Lowe did not appear shy about getting it on himself. He stood up and faced the crowd. "I have consecrated the Temple to myself, and my only law is that I be worshiped here, together with my spiritual father, Lucifer."

Immediately, the sun darkened. A great earthquake shook the entire world, and a star plunged from the sky into the sea. Tsunamis a mile high made their way towards the world's coastlines, and lightning and thunder lit up all of the world's skies, in the absence of any storms. "Now begins my era. The old world is being destroyed, to make room for the new one."

B. Parousia

"Why does God put up with this?" asked a nervous Becky, as they viewed a television broadcast of events from Jerusalem, with the picture cutting in and out, as the range of the antenna was strained.

Her father stood at her side, and said, "Even now, there are people turning away from evil, repenting, and accepting the Lord. He's waiting until the full measure are converted."

They saw reports of coastal cities being devastated by giant tsunamis, extending up to a hundred miles inland. Then the scene cut back to Jerusalem, and Lowe. "I have ordered the immediate closure of all chip implant facilities. Henceforth, anyone without the chip will be considered a heretic, and executed. I will not tolerate the worship of another before me, and my father."

Then everything changed, all at once. In Jerusalem, at Sean's underground house in Morrisonville, and everywhere else, all the peoples of the earth were aware of one thing, to the exclusion of all else. A sign in the sky, the Son of Man, bearing wounds on his hands, feet, and side, overwhelmed all other considerations. Every person had to confront the true king of the universe, in light of every choice they had made, and every belief they embraced or rejected, over the course of their lives.

People everywhere began to wail in uncontrollable sorrow, as they felt the pain endured by the Son of Man on their behalf. And as awful as the physical pain was, the spiritual pain of rejection by his people was that much deeper. But not every reaction was repentant.

"Whaaaaaaaaaat?" His word was a prolonged scream, betraying both rage and despair. "What are you doing here? I was supposed to have three and a half years."

The witnesses returned, and again stood before Lowe, speaking with one voice. "You were promised nothing. And the Lord promised to shorten these days, for the sake of the elect. Scripture often treats a year as a day, so that was always an option for him."

"But I wasn't ready," objected Lowe, screaming it out in a sorrowful voice. He was joined in his words by millions of others, who added, "Had we known that you would return before he had reigned for three and a half years, we would have been ready for you. Now, we will face judgment without the chance to prepare."

The Lord spoke directly to the hearts of the people, everywhere and at once. "I taught that my return would be like a thief in the night. Did the Gospels not warn you to be ready at any time? If your love for me was true, you would have been ready for my return."

Everyone then saw the Lord bind Lowe, Peter II, and a grotesque black beast with horns, kicking and screaming as it was pulled up against its will, from within the inner sanctum of the false temple, and all were cast into a lake of burning sulfur. Their screams exuded a bitter rage that was extremely painful to hear, until they disappeared in the burning lake. The Lord then extended his hand, and the false temple also fell into the burning lake of sulfur. It was followed by most of the assembled dignitaries, including Gertie Kleinholst, all screaming furiously that this was not what they expected.

Sean stood with the others at his house, and began to quote scripture. *And I saw a great white throne, and him that sat on it, from whose face the earth and the heaven fled away; and there was found no place for them. And I saw the dead, small and great, stand before God; and the books were opened: and another book was opened, which is the book of life: and the dead were judged out of those things which were written in the books, according to their works.*

###

Author's Note

This book was always imagined as an original story, centered on the spiritual journeys of several key people, and how they might play pivotal roles at the end of these times. Those elements, the general themes, and the certainty that it must end in victory, were my guidelines. It was never my intention to try to discern exactly how things would actually play out, if that's even possible, and attempt to track those developments accurately.

Perhaps the biggest liberty I took was in ultimately shortening three and a half years to three and a half days. To be clear, this is not prophecy - merely writer's license. The only verse I can cite to support it is, "... for the elect's sake those days shall be shortened." (Matthew 24:22). Aside from the Lord's early return, another way to imagine it is that the clock may have started while the masters of this world were losing time and scrambling.

So please look past whether or not the events correspond with your expectations. What truly matters is that we keep our hopes up, knowing this has to end with the victory of the Lord, and not letting negative short-term developments get us down.

I owe a literary debt to the great Vladimir Solovyov (1853-1900), whose brief account of the Antichrist inspired the character of David Lowe. Finally, I need to credit the always theatric Elon Musk, whose comment that *artificial intelligence was like summoning the demon* made me think along certain lines, which led to the concept of N.I.C.K. Lastly, please share this book as widely as you can, and leave a review at your retailer's web page. Thank you.